More Praise for

Famous Writers
I Have Known

"James Magnuson's new novel is an anything-goes mash-up featuring, among other hilarious elements, a legendary fistfight between two titanic authors on *The Dick Cavett Show*, a prank call to Günter Grass, a novel called *Eat Your Wheaties*, and a whole flock of 'circling buzzards,' including one who has translated *The Divine Comedy*. It's funny, it's poignant, it's scarily on-target when it comes to writing programs and dreams of literary immortality—and, best of all, it's out of its mind." —Steve Harrigan

"Jim Magnuson has done something remarkable—written a page-turner about the life of a writer. In his insights into the particular Famous Writer considered here, Magnuson's peerless eye has not missed a single telling detail. His comedy is huge but it's also sly: just under the surface of this Portrait of the Almost-Artist as a Cranky Old Man lies a moving meditation on the quest for immortality that drives us all, the mad cry from *Othello*: 'Reputation! Reputation! Reputation!' " —Anthony Giardina

"Wildly entertaining and insightful, Magnuson's book is an unsparing look into the fragile, orphaned hearts of writers and con men alike. Its pitch-perfect narrator, Frankie Abandonato, is a hilarious, lovable American anti-hero for the twenty-first century." —Cristina Garcia, author of *King of Cuba*

Famous Writers
I Have Known

Also by James Magnuson

The Hounds of Winter

Windfall

Ghost Dancing

Money Mountain

Open Season

The Rundown

Without Barbarians

Famous Writers I Have Known

A Novel

James
Magnuson

W. W. NORTON & COMPANY

NEW YORK   LONDON

F
Magnuson,
James

Copyright © 2014 by James Magnuson

For information about permission to reproduce selections from
this book, write to Permissions, W. W. Norton & Company, Inc.,
500 Fifth Avenue, New York, NY 10110

For information about special discounts for bulk purchases,
please contact W. W. Norton Special Sales at specialsales@
wwnorton.com or 800-233-4830

Manufacturing by RR Donnelley, Harrisonburg
Book design by Daniel Lagin
Production manager: Devon Zahn

Library of Congress Cataloging-in-Publication Data

Magnuson, James.
Famous writers I have known : a novel / James Magnuson. —
First edition.
pages cm
ISBN 978-0-393-24088-7
1. Authors—Fiction. 2. Impostors and imposture—Fiction.
3. Satire. I. Title.
PS3563.A352F36 2014
813'.54—dc23

                          2013036677

W. W. Norton & Company, Inc.
500 Fifth Avenue, New York, N.Y. 10110
www.wwnorton.com

W. W. Norton & Company Ltd.
Castle House, 75/76 Wells Street, London W1T 3QT

1 2 3 4 5 6 7 8 9 0

To the memory of Wendy Weil

Famous Writers
I Have Known

Prologue

MacArthur Federal Prison
December 12, 2002

Sometimes writing a sentence can be harder than serving one. At least that's what our instructor, Dr. Pajerski, claims. She teaches at the local community college and meets with our writers' group here at the minimum-security facility a couple times a month. She is on the far side of fifty, with graying hair that comes down to the middle of her back, and favors Indian prints. She has published several stories in quarterlies. I suspect that she wishes our souls were a little more whacked than they are.

Not that we're a bunch of saints. We have our share of celebrity prisoners in the group—me, of course, as well as a former Secretary of the Treasury who's found religion during his time here, and Brooks Nickerson, the high-flying mutual fund manager convicted of skimming millions from his clients. The others are pretty much your run-of-the-mill check kiters and drug offenders, though there's a couple of them you wouldn't want to run into in a dark alley.

Every session three members of the group bring in work to be critiqued. Most of it's dreck, frankly. The ex–Secretary of the Treasury is writing a novel about Christ's thirty days in the wilderness with Satan, and Mr. Mutual Fund is halfway through a thriller about Swiss bank accounts. Nobody would dream of getting into Iowa with this crap, but Dr. Pajerski always finds a way to say something good about everything. She goes to the blackboard to lead us through an explanation of Freytag's triangle, the classic theory of dramatic action. The Secretary of the Treasury, suck-up that he is, takes notes furiously. About half the chuckleheads in the room are nursing erotic fantasies about her, but he's got it bad.

We sit on tiny chairs donated by some long-defunct elementary school and through the thin walls we can hear the clanging of weights in the gym next door. I'm aware that my presence in the class has made it awkward for Dr. Pajerski from time to time. I told her at the start that she shouldn't treat me differently than anyone else, but how could she not be aware that I've nurtured some of the most brilliant young talents in the country in my time, a far cry from these bush league scribblers?

None of that matters now. Despite all of my fame, the reality is, I've still got a lot to learn, and I am amazed at what a struggle it is. I type away nine or ten hours a day. For the others in the group, writing is pretty much a hobby, a pleasant way to pass the time, but for me, it's a matter of honor. You've probably already read a lot of those slanderous articles about me. But there are always two sides to every story, right? There are those in high places who would pay good money to keep my mouth shut about all this, but it's too late for that. No doubt some of you will pick up this book for its gossip value, to see me take cheap shots at a couple of the biggest names in the literary world. You won't be disappointed, but I can assure you, my friends, I'm after bigger game than that. For starters, I'm going to have to take you back about five years, to 1997 and one sizzling August day in the Big Apple.

Chapter One

I sat in a pizza joint on Eighth Avenue, fingering the doctored lotto ticket. It was a piece of art, a real Leonardo da Vinci, but it wasn't going to do me a lot of good if the mark didn't show with his money. It had been twenty minutes and it was starting to look as if I'd been blown off. Which was not a big surprise, given the way Barry had screwed up the works.

The place smelled of burnt crust and oregano. It was the middle of the afternoon and business was dragging. A bag lady had all her loose change out on one of the tables, moving her grimy dimes around like she was planning D-day. Up front a couple of teenage girls shook garlic on their slices, flirting with the big Rasta man behind the counter while they waited for their cheese to cool.

I sipped at my Sprite and straightened my Golden Gopher tie in the mirror on the far wall. With my Ronald Reagan haircut and my clunky L.L.Bean shoes I couldn't have looked like more of a rube. Which was the point. My name for the day was Harold. It was my first time in New York. I was here for the Outdoor World Expo to sell some of the handcrafted canoes that me and my Chippewa compadres had made back in Minnesota. Of all the stories I'd made up about myself in my life, I was sort of proud of this one.

A cab had been parked at the curb on the far side of the street for the past five minutes. I figured it had to be Barry, but I just ignored him. If I was waiting, he could wait. A little carbon monoxide might sober him up a bit.

I shoved the lottery ticket back in my shirt pocket and picked up the *Daily News*. Giuliani was cracking down on the squeegee men and some guy named Bobby Bonilla was playing third for the Mets. There was a big photo of the president wailing away on his saxophone, backing up Bruce Springsteen in Madison Square Garden. I'd been away for a while. After spending the better part of the nineties in the slammer for various escapades, New York felt like a whole other world.

Just as I was turning to the article on Demi Moore and her big comeback, a tap on my shoulder nearly made me jump out of my chair. The mark stood over me, grinning, his gym bag swinging at his side.

"Hey, Joey," I said, "how you doin'?"

He slid his bag under the table and took the seat opposite me, looking all sly and happy. I should give Barry some credit. When it came to picking a mooch, he had quite the eye. The guy was perfect. The suit must have set him back at least a grand and he was flashing more big rings than Donald Trump. He was weight-lifter muscly, but not tall. Think Tony Danza and knock seventy points off the IQ.

"Sorry to keep you waiting," he said. "There was a big line at the bank."

"They didn't give you any trouble?"

"No, no trouble." Up front the girls had disappeared. The Rasta man scraped out the ovens with a long brush while reggae music played on the radio. "So, Harold, you still got the ticket?"

I tapped my shirt pocket. "Right here."

"You mind if I have another look?"

"No problemo."

I handed it to him and he ran his thumbs across the smooth surface, brooding. I didn't like it that he seemed to be thinking so much.

"Can I see the paper?"

"Sure."

I shoved the *Daily News* across the table and he flipped it over. The winning numbers were printed across the top of the back page, above the photo of Derek Jeter sliding under the tag at home. Joey lined the ticket up under the numbers in the paper, just to be sure.

"Still look all right?" I said.

"Still does," he said. "And the best thing about it, it still says one-point-two million."

I've pulled off a lot of scams in my life, but what I've always loved about this one was how simple it was. You go out in the morning, buy a paper, and look up the winning numbers for the day. Then you go into your local luncheonette, buy a lottery ticket, requesting the same numbers.

Legally, those numbers are no longer valid, since they were issued after the public announcement, but if you've got a steady hand and know what you're doing, it shouldn't take you more than twenty minutes to alter the date so that no one without an X-ray machine and a team of FBI-trained sniffer dogs would be able to tell the difference.

"So where'd you buy this?" he said.

"At the newsstand. In the hotel."

He turned the ticket over and started reading the fine print. It took him a while. Like I said before, the guy was probably a taco short of a combination plate. Or was he getting cold feet? Light flashed off one of the taxi windows on the far side of the street. My stomach churned. The last thing I needed now was Barry doing something stupid.

"When you checked the paper and saw what you had . . . you must have about had a heart attack."

"Oh, my goodness," I said. "I was shaking all over."

"So what did you do?"

"What did I do? I didn't know what to do. I went back up to my room. Started throwing pillows around, jumping up and down . . . it was embarrassing. You've got to understand, I've never won anything, ever, even as a little kid, and this . . . this was a life-changer. I was trying to think, who can I call? But then I realized, I couldn't call anybody. Because I couldn't cash it."

"Well, you could cash it," Joey said.

I was silent for a second. The bag lady waddled out into the sunshine. The calzones in the glass cases looked like dozing collies. "I could cash it if I wanted to give it all to my wife and her divorce lawyer."

"I know, Harold, you told me all that, but you've got to be exaggerating. They wouldn't get all of it."

I rubbed at the grease spot on my Golden Gopher tie. "But I don't want them to get any of it. The woman sleeps with our choir director for two years, she's getting the house, the cabin on the lake, half the canoe business . . ."

Joey hunched over the table, idly scratching at the numbers on the ticket. I couldn't believe it. What a son of a bitch. I grabbed the ticket away from him and waved it in his face.

"I would rather tear it up right now and walk away than let her have one cent of it, you know what I'm saying?"

Joey put a hand up to calm me. "Hey, it's okay. I was just asking."

I slipped the ticket back in my pocket. Up front, Rasta Man peered at us through his dreadlocks, jabbing at a mound of dough and then pounding it flat.

"I'm sorry," I said. "I know how crazy all this must sound to you. I don't want to get in trouble. I don't want you to get in trouble. It's just that when I saw you and your friend at the bar in the hotel . . ."

"That idiot? He's no friend of mine. I just met the guy."

"Whatever. But you seemed like upstanding, respectable people. Maybe it's too goofy of me to think I could ask a couple of total strangers to solve all my problems, but what do I know about the way the world works? I make canoes for a living. For a month, every time I came home and my wife was on the phone, she'd hang up real quick. I just figured she must have been planning my surprise birthday party . . ."

I started to cry. It's not something I can pull off all the time, but when I get worked up, I can be convincing—the trembling chin, the moist eyes, a real tear trickling down my cheek.

"Shit," Joey said. He reached across to put a hand on my arm. "You know what I say? I say screw the bitch! You hear me, Harold? I say screw her!" He took a glance over his shoulder to be sure no one was watching. Rasta Man swung to the music, spinning the pizza dough as if it was a limp Frisbee.

Joey reached into his jacket and pulled out a thick envelope. He offered it to me under the table. I groped for a moment, found his knee, then his hand, then the envelope. It had a nice heft to it. I kept it low and out of sight, checking the contents. It was all hundred-dollar bills, so crisp and new they looked like play money.

"You don't need to count it," he said. "It's all there. Ten thousand dollars. Just what you asked for, right? I'm trusting you with it, Harold." I wiped away a tear with a knuckle. "The deal is this. You give me the ticket and you wait right here. I saw a pay phone back about a block or so. I'm going to go call these lottery guys, okay? And when I come back, we're going to get you all set up. We split the money fifty-fifty, just like we agreed. I'll show you how to open up an account your wife's never going to find in a million years. How does that sound?"

"It sounds good," I said.

He put his palm out. I laid the ticket in it. Jimmy Cliff was belting "The Harder They Come" over the radio. Joey slid from his chair and retrieved his gym bag. "And then maybe we'll go out and buy you a couple of decent ties," he said.

He gave a thumbs-up to Rasta Man on his way out. I sat for a moment, draining my Sprite, and then pushed to my feet. As I leaned over to shove a buck tip under the napkin dispenser, I spied a flash of something on Joey's chair. A bunch of quarters and dimes glistened in the bucket seat, spill from his trousers, I figured. There was something else too—a key with a blocky red top and a number etched in the plastic.

It was a locker key and probably useless to anyone who didn't know where the locker was, but what can I say? I'm a collector. It's a weakness of mine. I scooped up the coins and the key and shoveled them into my pocket.

I walked to the door of the pizzeria and peered out, making sure the coast was clear. As far as the eye could see, there was nothing but women pawing through open bins of clothing.

The cab on the far side of the street edged into traffic and then did a screeching U-ey in front of a city bus. The back door swung open as the taxi skittered to the curb. Head down, I hustled across the sidewalk and hopped in.

I slammed the door shut behind me. Barry hung to one of the straps, looking eager as a puppy.

"So how'd it go?"

"Just fine," I said. "No thanks to you."

"What do you mean by that?" Barry was a big man and was scrunched up against the window so he could extend his bad leg.

"I'll give you three guesses," I said. The turbaned driver stared at us in the mirror. "Ninety-fifth and Broadway!" I hollered at him.

I'd first met Barry at the Children's Center on 104th Street in New York when we were twelve. My foster parents had managed to get themselves tossed into jail for welfare fraud and Barry was a runaway the cops had picked up in Port Authority.

In our dormitory, Barry inspired awe. He was red-haired, nearly a foot taller than anyone else, and gave killer Indian rope burns to anyone who tried to buck him. He was the closest thing to a professional criminal any of the rest of us had ever known.

I, on the other hand, was a study in pathos, your basic drowned rat. I was the kind of kid Jesus Christ Himself would have been tempted to pick on. Every day we marched across to Central Park where our counselor, a sullen 260-pound tackle on the Jets taxi squad, would make us run pass patterns. His greatest pleasure in life was seeing if he could drill me in the back of the head with a ninety-mile-an-hour spiral.

My only defense was that I was a world-class liar. If I didn't have my homework done, I had a story. If I was supposed to go down to Metropolitan Hospital with my dorky social worker to get a battery of shots, I had a story. When the other kids in the dorm ragged me about why no one ever came to see me on visiting days, I made up this tale about how my father was flying secret missions over Russia, but when he came back he was going to take me to live in a big house we owned on the beach on Long Island with its own go-kart track, indoor basketball court, and heated swimming pool. At night, I told them, we let Doberman pinschers out to roam the grounds, dogs that had their vocal cords cut so in case any robbers tried to break in there would be no warning bark before the dogs attacked. Barry ruled the roost in that dormitory, but he was impressed with my powers of invention.

We flew up Eleventh Avenue, hitting every pothole in sight. Neither of us had said a word for ten blocks.

"This the way you're going to be all day?" Barry said.

"You blame me?"

"You think you might be getting a little histrionic here, Frankie?"

That was the way he talked. Barry was big on self-improvement. He had one of those calendars where you learn a new word every day. He was always trying to work them into conversation, words like *purported* and *sesquicentennial*.

"Histrionic? What do you mean by *histrionic*? Rule number one, you're never supposed to drink with the mark. Two, what was this quizzing me about what part of Minnesota was I from?"

"I was just playing with you, man."

"Hell if you were! You were trying to show me up! It was just your little way of letting me know just how beneath you it all was. All that bullshit about how you had some cousin in Cloquet, and did I know where Cloquet was . . . I don't know bupkus about Minnesota!" I tugged at the knot of my Golden Gopher tie. "And then, just to top it all off, you go and spill scotch on the man's shoes."

"I know. It wasn't the smoothest."

"The smoothest? It was a disaster! I know you think we're supposed to be big time, way too good for these penny-ante operations, but goddamn it, I'm trying to put some cash in our pockets."

"I take your point," he said. A dozen cabs wove back and forth in front of us like a school of dolphins. "So you got the money?"

"Yeah. I got the money."

"You mind me taking a look at it?"

I pulled the envelope out of my back pocket and handed it to him. He held the envelope between his knees, counting the Franklins. "So what's this?"

"What's what?"

He tugged a crumpled slip of paper from the wad of bills. I took it from him and smoothed it on the tattered armrest. It was the bank's withdrawal slip and above the scrawled signature was the neatly printed name and address: Joseph Cannetti, Jr., 318 Elm Street, Fort Lee, New Jersey.

"Oh, shit," I said.

"What?"

"Take a look."

We traded, withdrawal slip for envelope of cash, and he stared at the wrinkled paper for several seconds. "Well, goddamn," he said.

"Exactly."

"Maybe it's another Cannetti," he said.

"Some other Cannetti? Some other Joseph Cannetti *Junior*? In Fort Lee, New Jersey?"

He had no answer. I shoved the envelope of bills back into my pocket. Outside the window of the cab I could see a Korean grocer misting his lettuce.

The Cannettis were the second biggest mob family in New Jersey— the biggest until they ran afoul of a crusading attorney general. The father, Big Joey, was rumored to have been the one who buried Jimmy Hoffa somewhere out in the wetlands. I didn't know a whole lot about him, other than that he had three sons, one who was supposed to be a genius, one who was supposed to be vicious, and one who was supposed to be the world's biggest fuckup.

"How could you not recognize him?" I said. "Jesus Christ."

"How was I supposed to recognize him?" Barry said. "It's not like they put out a yearbook with all the mobsters' pictures in it."

"You're the one who's supposed to size these people up! That's your job!" I caught the taxi driver shooting us a look in the rearview mirror. "You trying to tell me you were drinking with the guy for an hour and you had no clue?"

"Twenty minutes!" Barry said. "I was drinking with the guy for twenty minutes!" I waved a hand at him, disgusted. "So what do we do?"

"I don't know."

"You think we should try to give it back?"

"How are we going to give it back?"

"I'm going to have to think about that," he said.

"You do that," I said. "You think about it."

The cab shimmied its way up Broadway. If I'd been in a foul mood before, it was positively nasty now. This was serious shit. If this Cannetti wasn't smart enough to figure out who'd ripped him off, he had uncles and brothers and nephews who were.

The taxi dropped us off at our hotel on Ninety-fifth Street. Back in our room, we divided the money. I tossed the Golden Gopher tie and changed into regular shoes and my wrinkled old blazer. It was still midafternoon, so we went out for a coffee and took a walk in Riverside Park. We were still plenty pissed at one another. I kept walking him on his crummy knee, just to punish him a little, while we tried to sort things out. It felt as if the temperature was still rising, the sky yellow as a bruise, but there were still a good number of people out—runners and mothers with strollers, a Dominican family having a cookout, a black kid trying to dribble a worn basketball behind his back.

I finally relented and we found a bench where Barry could rest his bad leg. He was limping worse than ever. He started lecturing me about how we needed to upgrade our act. The way it was now, we were throwbacks, dinosaurs. The world had changed and we needed to change with it or we were doomed, like the dodo bird.

He'd been boning up. There was a new scam where you send out a flood of emails, claiming to be a Nigerian prince whose hundred million dollars' worth of assets have been tied up by the corrupt military government. What you say you're looking for is an upstanding American who would allow this fortune to be transferred into his U.S. account. In exchange for this favor, the upstanding American would be promised a substantial cut. Once you had the sucker's bank account number and a few other key bits of information, you could totally clean the guy out.

"If you think I'm going to pose as a Nigerian prince, you're crazy."

"Did I say you were going to have to pose as anybody? That's the beauty of it. It's all done on the computer. It's totally risk-free."

"I'm not wearing any goddamned robes."

"Who said anything about robes? Jesus Christ, Frankie!" He shifted his bum leg to a more comfortable position.

I stared out at a tugboat churning up the Hudson. I knew what I needed to do. The only question was whether or not I had the guts to do it. Con men are not a sentimental lot. We steal from widows, retired school crossing guards, medical missionaries, no problem. But ditching your partner after forty years was a major deal.

Barry was the one who'd brought me into the business. We'd had our triumphs. We'd been raking in a quarter of a million a year on the Lake Havasu Estates deal until the state of Arizona closed us down. We would have made ten times that if the Indian casino license had come through, even though me passing myself off as a Mohegan chief had been a killer from the start.

But ever since he'd come back from upstate, Barry had gotten kind of random on me. He didn't have the old sharpness, the old confidence. And in our business, when a confidence man loses his confidence, he might as well shove himself off on an iceberg and wait for the polar bears to come eat out his liver.

We ate dinner that night at a Cuban restaurant on 104th and when we got back to the hotel Barry rumbled around in the bathroom for a while, downing his vitamin supplements, gargling, brushing his teeth, singing "Danny Boy." I turned on the TV and flopped down on the bed, hoping to catch some of the late scores. What I got was a somber young newsgirl standing in front of an Italian restaurant with all the usual crime scene trappings behind her—the yellow tape, the police cars, the flashing lights.

"Hey, Barry," I shouted. "I think you need to take a look at this." Barry poked his head around the bathroom door, toothpaste still foaming from his mouth. I punched up the sound.

The girl looked like she was just out of college, and one of those thirty-grand-a-year colleges at that. Her voice shook as she spoke. "At approximately ten-fifteen this evening, Joseph Cannetti Junior was gunned down as he left Arturo's Clam House with a group of friends. Several onlookers reported seeing two men fleeing in a late-model black El Dorado, but thus far no one has come forward with a description of the possible assailants. Mr. Cannetti is the youngest son of Big Joey Cannetti, who for many years was the head of New Jersey's most powerful crime family."

The camera cut to the anchorman in the studio. "Tell me, Dina, have the police mentioned any possible motive for the shooting?"

On one half of the divided screen, the newsgirl pressed her finger to her ear, making sure she heard the question. A trio of teenage boys crowded around behind her, waving to the camera. "Not as yet, Robert, but when I spoke to one of the waiters, he said he'd spotted Mr. Cannetti in a heated argument with two men in a coffeehouse late this afternoon. Of course all the rumors on the street are about the long-running feud between the Cannettis and the Delmonico brothers. . ."

"Turn it off," Barry said.

"What do you mean, turn it off?"

The two anchors weighed in with their opinions while old file footage flashed on the screen behind them—Big Joey Cannetti in handcuffs being led down the courthouse steps, bullet-ridden bodies scattered across a warehouse floor.

Barry snatched the blab-off out of my hands. The television screen blinked, flashed, and went dark.

"Just calm down," Barry said. "I know what you're thinking, but this has nothing to do with us."

"You think so?"

"I know so." He wiped the last of the toothpaste from the corner of his mouth. "These big-time boys, they need to blast the hell out of one another from time to time. That's what they do. You and me, we're nothing. We're the fleas on the rhino's ass. Don't look at me like that, Mr. Worrywart. Sometimes you piss me off, you really do."

I lay in bed for hours, unable to sleep, but I must have drifted off at some point, because I woke up around four and had to go to the bathroom to pee. Somewhere outside a bottle smashed, and a few seconds later there were drunken voices in the alleyway.

It's funny how sometimes you can see things more clearly at night. What was clear was that I needed to get the fuck out. I'd been around New York way too long the way it was. The only question was whether or not I took Barry with me when I left.

There's this old movie, *The Defiant Ones*, where Sidney Poitier and Tony Curtis escape from a prison road crew and the problem is that they're still chained together, which makes things pretty rough. But imagine if Tony Curtis had been chained to Barry instead of Sidney Poitier. He wouldn't have made it to Swamp One.

As I tiptoed back across the room, the reflected light of passing traffic slid along the wall. Barry had his calendar on the nightstand and as the light moved across it I could see the Word for the Day in block letters: CONUNDRUM. Maybe it was just me being in an ornery mood, but I tore the page out, crumpled it up, and tossed it in the general direction of the wastebasket. I probably should have checked to see what the word was underneath, but I didn't.

I climbed back into bed and pulled up my covers. Across the room from me, Barry lay on his side, his head cradled in the crook of his fat arm. He looked so peaceful, it seemed like a crime to wake him.

Chapter Two

I woke up the next morning to the sound of Barry snoring like a lord. I threw on my blazer and went out to get breakfast—eggs sunny-side up and some hash browns that were about as tasty as fried kidney stones.

I must have sat in that diner for close to an hour, turning over everything I wanted to say—how I wasn't going to soft-soap him, I had too much respect for him for that, but we needed to face up to the fact that things weren't working and maybe it was time for us to go our separate ways. I'd try to convince him that it would be good for both of us. Some such bullshit.

On my way back to the hotel, some homeless guy was shaking a coffee can on the steps of a Lutheran church. Ordinarily I stiff these guys, but I gave him a couple of dollars, just for good luck. Entering the lobby, I saw that the jerk behind the desk was on the phone, getting his rocks off letting somebody know they couldn't have their deposit back.

Stepping out of the elevator, I was surprised to find the door to our room ajar. I was sure I'd closed it when I'd left. I pushed it slowly open with my forefinger.

Barry lay facedown in a pool of blood on the floor. He was still in his pj's, one fleshy arm twisted above his head and entangled in the bedspread. Numbed and disbelieving, I took a step forward, and then another one.

As I bent down to touch his shoulder, I heard a faucet go on and off and then a rattle, like somebody pulling a towel off a towel rack. Before I could make a move, this guy came out of the bathroom, wiping his hands on his trousers. He was huge, a walking advertisement for steroids. His gonads were probably the size of peas, but I hadn't seen muscles like that since the last time I saw the Mr. Universe contest.

Any sane person would have taken off right then, but I didn't. I would like to think that I just wanted to fix it in my mind who it was that had done in my buddy. That would have been the brave and manly thing to do, but bravery has never been my forte; I was just too stupefied to move. He leaned over to grab Barry's wallet off the nightstand and when he straightened up, there we were, eyeballing one another.

He had a meat face. A not very smart face. His mean little eyes glimmered over the top of his cheeks, and he had a buzz cut like he'd just joined the Marines. On his feet he had these Italian crocodile slip-ons, with shitty little tassels. Neither of us breathed for one long moment and then he came at me, stumbling over the corner of the bed.

I slammed the door shut and took off, racing past the ice machine and a maid picking up breakfast trays. I hurdled down the stairs three at a time, down one flight and then another. The jerk at the desk gave a shout as I sprinted past him and threw myself at the revolving doors.

The morning was filled with jackhammers. A mob of kids in red T-shirts piled onto a school bus, their counselors shouting and waving. I ran the half block to Broadway and hopped in the rear of a cab idling in front of a bodega. The young African driver roused himself from a catnap.

"Where to?" he said. It smelled like someone had been holding a marijuana convention in the backseat.

"LaGuardia," I said. "And step on it."

As we pulled away from the curb, I looked through the rear window and caught a glimpse of the defective with the buzz cut, wading through the mob of kids arm over arm, like a swimmer struggling out of heavy surf.

The traffic in Harlem was a mess and my driver was not the sort to run lights. He was amiable enough and more than willing to talk. He was from Senegal, his native language was Wolof, he had two brothers and a sister still living in Dakar, and he was taking computer classes at night. I kept checking the mirrors, half expecting a car to come flying up behind us, guns blazing.

Once we got to the Triborough Bridge, things began to open up. I was still too much in shock to be able to focus. All I knew was I needed to get the hell out of town, and fast. The fact that I'd seen the killer's face and he'd seen mine had definitely complicated matters, and I was in no position to be going to the police. It came back to me, the locker key. Could that have been what they were after? But God knows where that was.

We sailed past miles of cemeteries. Shea Stadium floated past and then the old World's Fair site. We finally swung up the ramp into LaGuardia. "So which airline?" the cabdriver said.

I surveyed the names on the metal poles along the guardrail and picked one.

"Continental."

We eased to the curb. I handed him two twenties, told him to keep the change, and hustled off to the terminal. The airport was still undergoing renovation and echoed with the whine of saws and the shouts of workmen. According to the overhead monitors, the first flight out was to Austin, Texas, departing in twenty minutes. The whole idea of

Texas has always scared the hell out of me, but I was in no position to be choosy.

There are moments when having five cards with five different names comes in handy. I charged the ticket on one of my phony Visas and sprinted through the airport, dodging beeping golf carts.

At the gate they were nearly finished boarding. I got in line behind about a dozen people and did a quick check of my ticket. It looked as if I would be in Austin by midafternoon. Not that it mattered. I didn't have anywhere to go for the rest of my life.

I scrutinized my fellow passengers. God knows what I thought Texans were supposed to look like, but these people all seemed civilized enough. About half of them were businessmen, and there were some students and a mother with a pair of bratty kids.

The only one in line to catch my eye was this character a few places ahead of me. The first thing I noticed was how much he looked like me. We weren't exactly spitting images of one another, but it was close—dark-haired, fiftyish, sharp-featured, a little on the shifty side. He was better dressed than I was—he had a certain trust-fund kayaker aura about him, which was not my style at all.

The other thing I noticed about him was how jumpy he was. He was almost worse than me. He kept fidgeting, crossing his arms, uncrossing them, making little sighs, poking at the bridge of his dark glasses, leaning to one side to see what the hang-up was.

The line was definitely not moving as fast as it should have been. I tried to stay cool, but I wasn't doing so great. It kept coming back to me, Barry lying facedown in a pool of blood, the gorilla coming out of the bathroom, wiping his hands on his trousers. For a second I thought I was going to faint. I said a little prayer. Please, Lord, just let me get on that plane, just let that door close behind me, I'll never ask for anything again. Incomprehensible announcements echoed over the PA system.

A middle-aged woman in a yellow jacket came up to the man who looked like me. She had a big smile on her face like she recognized him. When she spoke to him, he acted like he hadn't heard her, but she didn't give up. The guy started shaking his head no, trying to ignore her.

I strained to hear what they were saying, but I was a little too far back. I wasn't the only one who was curious. Some of the others were trying to listen in too, pretending to read their newspapers. One of the students leaned over and whispered something to his buddy. The man who looked like me was getting more and more agitated.

An airline clerk waved us on, trying to hurry us up, and the line started shuffling forward. The woman in the yellow jacket rummaged in her purse and pulled out a pen. When she offered it to the man who looked like me, he gave it a whack, sending it clattering across the floor, and strode off. The woman stared, openmouthed, but the man was not coming back. He tore up his boarding pass, dropped it in a trash can, and headed up the ramp toward the main terminal.

By the time I got on the plane, my nerves were shot. My hands were shaking so bad it took a half dozen stabs to get my seat belt buckled. All around me people were settling in, businessmen powering up laptops, the young mother pulling out coloring books for the two brats, the stewardesses slamming shut the overhead compartments.

I pulled a copy of the *SkyMall* catalog out of the seat pocket in front of me. I flipped through it, staring at the pictures of golf bags, business card cases, orthopedic couches for dogs.

When the magazine slipped from my fingers, I bent to retrieve it. A half dozen dark spots speckled my trousers leg. It wasn't until I tried to flick them off with my thumb that I realized they were dried spatters of Barry's blood.

Getting off the plane in Texas was like landing on the moon. Heat rose off the tarmac in rippled sheets and the grass looked deader than the

Sudan; according to the pilot it was a hundred and five degrees on the ground.

In the terminal businessmen with good haircuts strode past me, flipping through their appointment books. A stuffed longhorn stared balefully from a bookstore window and a couple toothless old codgers with big silver belt buckles gummed their brisket at a barbeque stand.

At the bottom of the escalator was the usual crowd of dumpy guys in shiny blazers, holding cardboard signs, scrutinizing us as we descended, looking for their fares.

There were only three or four people at the Avis desk. I took out my wallet and was flipping through my various credit cards when there was a tap on my shoulder.

I turned. A sultry twenty-something with masses of tangled black hair cocked her head and smiled as if I was supposed to know who she was.

"Mr. Mole?" she said.

"Excuse me?" I said.

"It's okay," she said, lowering her voice almost to a whisper. "It's just us."

I looked past her, trying to figure out who *us* was. Standing by the glass door were two other girls, looking just as breathless and excited as she was. One was this tall, gangly Shelley Duvall type in a miniskirt no bigger than a postage stamp. The other was a cute little African-American number, holding her hands to her cheeks like some awestruck Beatles fan.

"So do you have bags?" the one with the tangled hair asked.

"Bags?" I said. I'd seen a lot of scams in my life, but this was a new one. What were they going to do, take me out in woods, sexually assault me, and leave me for dead? "No, I'm fine, thanks. Now, if you'll excuse me, sweetheart, I need to go pick up my car."

"But we already have a car." I gave her a second look. The other two were moving in, cutting off my escape routes. "We're all part of the program," she said. "I'm Dominique." A stack of bracelets jangled on her arm as she reached out to shake my hand. "And this is Bryn." The girl in the miniskirt gave me a little wave. "And LaTasha." The black girl nodded, shy as a mouse.

I scratched the back of my neck. Program? What was this, some sort of cult? Some foxy spin-off of the Scientologists?

"And what do you do in the program?" I asked.

"Short stories, mostly," Dominique said. "But I'd really like to try my hand at something longer."

I stared at her, dumbfounded.

"She just had a piece in *Tin House*," Bryn said.

"Really?" I said. "And how about you two?"

"Pretty much the same thing. Some creative nonfiction."

"I'm working on a novel," LaTasha said.

A older woman strode by, glaring at me, roller bags in tow. God knows what she thought we were up to.

The whole thing was clearly one of those crazy mix-ups. I should have just walked away, told them they had the wrong guy, but their eyes were shining with such excitement. I hated to disappoint them.

"So what's the plan exactly?" I said.

"We thought we'd take you by the institute," Dominique said. "Mildred's got a couple of papers for you to sign and then I think she's going to take you up to your house."

"Oh, Mr. Mole," LaTasha said, "the house is just wonderful."

"And very private," Bryn said. "It may not be as private as an island in Maine, but it's pretty good."

"And we're not going to bother you, we promise," Dominique said. "We've all been vowed to secrecy."

The other two nodded their heads solemnly. Maine island? Ordinarily I'm pretty quick on the uptake, but this was taking a while to piece together.

It was getting annoying the way they kept referring to me as Mr. Mole, as if I was some friend of Mr. Toad's, but then it occurred to me that I was spelling it wrong. Maybe it was M-O-H-L-E, not M-O-L-E. And the only M-O-H-L-E I'd ever heard of was V. S. Mohle, the guy who wrote *Eat Your Wheaties*, who'd been hiding away on some island somewhere, maybe it was Maine, I don't remember exactly, and no one had even laid eyes on the guy for the past twenty-five years.

"So how did you all recognize me?" I asked.

They looked at one another and giggled. "From your jacket photo."

"Really? You telling me I haven't changed?"

"Not that much. You look a little older," Bryn said, and then put her fingers to her lips, afraid she'd said something wrong.

"We were just afraid, when we didn't see you at first, that maybe you'd changed your mind about coming," Dominique said.

"I understand," I said. It all came back to me, the ruckus at the gate in New York, the man who looked like me tearing up his boarding pass and fleeing.

"So should we go, then?" Dominique said. Her bracelets chimed as she adjusted the strap of her sundress. They were all waiting for me. We must have looked like something out of *Charlie's Angels*.

I glanced through the glass doors at the people loading up their vans, hustling toward the taxi stand. How far did I really want to take this? These girls were total idiots. Did they really think I was a famous writer? Did nobody notice the bloodstains on my trousers?

But then I saw this old guy lurching across the crosswalk on a cane, trying to catch up with his wife. She was way out in front of him, hauling two suitcases, but she wasn't waiting for him. Why he reminded me of Barry, I don't know. He had white hair and honestly didn't look like him at all. Maybe it was just the limp. Just twenty-four hours before,

Barry and I had been walking in Riverside Park, trying to figure out how to get out of the jam he'd gotten us in. He'd been sore at me and I'd been sore at him, so I just walked him and walked him on his bad leg like it was some sort of payback. My eyes began to fill with tears.

"Are you okay?" LaTasha said.

"I'm fine. Or maybe I'm not so fine. I'm sort of at the end of my rope, to tell you the truth."

Dominique put a hand on my arm and the other two moved in a little closer. The fucking shah going into exile couldn't have gotten any better treatment than this. Maybe it was that they heard something like a note of true grief in my voice, but it was as if they were trying to hold me up, trying to protect me from the world.

The car must have been 140 degrees inside when we opened the door, but we piled in anyway, cranking down the windows and turning the AC all the way up. Dominique and I took the front and Bryn and LaTasha got in back. It was a ten-year-old Toyota with hail damage and no more leg room than a broom closet.

I can't tell you how strange all this was. I felt like I'd been dropped down a rabbit hole. The three of them chattered away about their program while all I could think about was how I was now a marked man. If I knew the Cannettis, there would be guys looking for me in every city in America. They either knew who I was or they would find out soon enough. These guys were very good at finding people. I didn't need a program; what I needed was to vanish off the face of the earth.

As we drove into town, I pumped the girls for information, trying to get the lay of the land. This institute they were talking about was called the Fiction Institute of Texas. It was made up of eight writers like themselves, all on these humongous fellowships (twenty-five Gs per year), and my job was to workshop them once a week for a couple of hours.

The only workshop I'd ever heard of was Santa's, and from the girls' tone it sounded like they were doing a lot more than carving pull-toys. They tried to explain to me how it worked, how they brought in their stories or sections of novels and I led the discussion, gave them a few pointers, and generally tried to keep a lid on things.

"So when we get to the institute, who'll be there?" I asked.

"It should just be Mildred," LaTasha said. The two girls in the back hovered over my shoulder, eager as puppies.

"Uh-huh. And who is she exactly?"

"She's the program coordinator," Dominique said.

"And anyone else?"

"Wayne may be there. But he's usually in just in the mornings."

"Wayne?"

"The director. The one you've been talking to."

"Oh, *Wayne*. Of course. My old buddy."

Off in the distance I could see the dome of the state capitol. In my whole life, I don't think I'd ever seen so much sky. We passed a battered truck. A trio of Mexican workers squatted among lawn mowers in the back, their mouths covered by bandannas.

"So from Austin, what's the nearest city?" I asked.

"San Antonio," Dominique said. "It's an hour and a half away. Then there's Dallas and Houston."

"And how far are they?"

"Houston's two and a half. Dallas a little more than three."

"Uh-huh."

I needed a plan. The girls had said there was a house waiting for me, but I was dubious. I'd pushed my luck about as far as I dared. But what choices did I have? I supposed I could rent a car and just start driving. There was a guy I knew once who ran a dog track outside of Denver, but I hadn't talked to him for years. In the movies guys like me usually stop in some shitty little town and get a job working in a grain silo, but to tell you the truth, the whole world west of Trenton terrified me.

"So you were saying that you've all signed these vows of secrecy. Now, what is that about?"

Dominique shot me an odd look. "Well, I think you know what that's about."

"How do you mean?"

"It was your idea, right?"

"Right, but I was just wondering—"

LaTasha piped up from the back. "They gave us these confidentiality agreements we had to sign. It was like we were in the CIA or something."

"No kidding?" I said. "And what did they say?"

"Basically that if any of us spill the beans about your being here, you're gone on the next flight," Dominique said.

"Plus Mildred said they might even yank our fellowships," Bryn said.

As we got closer to town we began to pass taco stands and a series of small garages. "Wow," I said. "That's pretty hard, isn't it?"

"Not to mention pretty insulting," Dominique said. "We're not children. We all know this is the opportunity of a lifetime. If the only way we can get you here is by promising to keep it all under wraps, we're all on board."

"As far as we're concerned," LaTasha said, "you're the invisible man."

"I appreciate it," I said. "I can't tell you how much that means to me right now."

The Institute was a two-story white house on the north side of campus with a wide yard that led down to a creek. As we pulled around to the parking lot, an old woman in a faded print dress stooped over the flower bed, gingerly coaxing dog turds into a dustpan with a stick.

She looked up as the Toyota rumbled across the gravel, her glasses a wonderland of lenses. We all got out of the car and Dominique waved. "Hey, Mildred!" she shouted. "I've got somebody here I'd like you to meet!"

Mildred put down her dustpan and hobbled over, with the sweetest smile on her face I'd ever seen. "My goodness," she said. "I never thought I'd see the day."

I gave her a hug. "This is a great pleasure, Mildred."

She squinted up at me through a cataract haze and patted me on the chest. "We better get you inside before you melt. Girls, thank you so much."

The girls seemed reluctant to give me up, and who could blame them? This was probably the greatest day of their lives, meeting me.

"See you later, guys," I said. "I appreciate the lift."

Dominique tossed her keys in the air, caught them, and gave me a pouty look from behind her mane of tangled hair.

Mildred and I stood side by side, watching as the car pulled out of the lot. I was happy to see them go. It's always great to be fawned over by a bevy of young women, but I wasn't sure how easy it would have been to get out of their clutches. Mildred seemed like she would be easier to outmaneuver.

We went inside and she gave me a tour of the house. The place was like a museum, the walls plastered with framed posters of bearded men with their chins on their fists, and the air-conditioning was state-of-the-art.

She took me upstairs to see my office. I'd never had an office before and this was a nice homey one, with old-fashioned wallpaper and big windows that made you feel like you were sitting right up there with the squirrels and the robins. She showed me how my computer worked, how to retrieve the messages off the phone, and how to adjust the thermostat. I didn't pay her much mind, but it was nice to be inside and out of the line of fire.

We went back downstairs and she took me through the kitchen and showed me where I could keep things. Dozens of little magnets dotted the refrigerator door. They all had words or parts of words on them and someone had been arranging them in short, wacko lines.

> A thousand raw
>
> summer sausages
>
> fall together
> and spring through winter

We proceeded at a snail's pace—her hands were knotted up with arthritis and it was painful for her to reach under the lampshades to turn the switches. She reminded me a lot of a foster mom I'd had once, this sweet old lady from Brooklyn who had terrible tremors and yet somehow managed to take care of four birds, four cats, four dogs, and four of us foster kids, or at least she did until the day we tried to play baseball with one of her parakeets and she had Child Protective Services come get us out of there.

She got a map of the university out of her desk to give me. There was also a thick stack of papers for me to sign. She went into a long-winded explanation about withholding and pension and insurance, and I finally had to cut her off.

"Mildred," I said. "I don't mean to interrupt, but the girls were saying that you had a house for me?"

"That's right," she said, pushing up on the bridge of her trifocals. "It's just ten blocks from here."

"I was wondering if maybe I could take another look at all this stuff tomorrow. It's been a long day . . ."

"Of course," she said. "Just let me run in here for a second and we can go."

She went into the bathroom and I heard the rattle of the lock. I took a deep breath and did a quick look around. A bronze bust of some surly character sat on a table in the hallway and there were several tall cabinets filled with cowboy gear—lariats and spurs, branding irons and old boots.

Squinting at the framed photographs on the wall, I saw that there were names under the pictures—J. M. Coetzee, Margaret Atwood, Michael somebody, Peter Carey, Adrienne Rich. Maybe it was just my imagination, but it felt as if they were glaring down at me.

A three-by-five card was taped up above the door of the office next to Mildred's desk. I stood on tiptoe to read it:

We work in the dark. We do what we can. We give what we have. Our doubt is our passion. Our passion is our task. The rest is the madness of art.

Now, what that meant, I had no clue. The only people I knew who worked in the dark were cat burglars and heating duct repairmen, but what they had to do with the madness of art was beyond me.

I could have walked right out of there. I could have been rid of all this horseshit. God knows what kept me there. Maybe it was just the reassuring hum of the air-conditioning. If I took off on foot, I wouldn't have lasted five minutes in that killer heat.

They kept talking about this house and how private it was. If I could get a good night's sleep, I could be gone before morning. It wasn't as if I needed to keep up this charade forever.

When the phone rang in the office, I nearly jumped out of my skin. I let it ring a second time, a third, and then the answering machine picked up. A man's voice came on, shaky and apologetic.

"Wayne, this is V.S. I'm sorry, but I can't go through with this. I tried. I really did. I made it as far as the New York airport. I'd rather not go into it all now, but there was an unfortunate incident. I'm on my way back to Maine. I feel horrible about letting you down like this, letting Rex down. But I'm sure you'll find someone who can step in and do a much better job than I ever could. I beg you, please, don't try to call. This is all too humiliating. Maybe we could talk in a couple of months, but right now I'm just not capable of it. Forgive me . . ."

There was a soft click when the call ended. I heard a toilet flush. I glanced back quickly at the bathroom door.

I took a step inside the office. It was a hell of a mess—a desk piled high with manuscripts, cardboard boxes stacked in the corners, kids' drawings on the wall. The answering machine blinked red. It was one of those big old clunkers with buttons marked PLAY, REPEAT, SKIP, and DELETE. I leaned over and hit DELETE. There was a slither of tape and another click. I was safe, at least for the time being.

Chapter Three

This being mistaken for a famous writer had its upsides. Not only was the house great, but even greater was the hedge out front, so tall and thick and thorny you would have thought some horticulturist from Witness Protection had planted it.

It wasn't much more than a cottage, really, but done up real classy, with white shutters and a Hansel-and-Gretel thatched roof. Ten blocks north of the Fiction Institute, it was just beyond the student slums in a quiet, tree-lined neighborhood. Inside, it looked like something you'd see written up in a fashion magazine, with gleaming oak floors, professionally scuffed chairs, frilly pillows tossed on leather couches, and, on the walls, oil paintings of cacti and sorrowful horses. A bowl of fresh fruit and a bottle of champagne, gussied up with a blue ribbon, sat in the breakfast nook; all my life I'd wanted a breakfast nook, and now I had one. I was smack-dab in the middle of *I Love Lucy* Land. The gardener came on Wednesday, the maid on Thursday, and if I wanted bottled water delivered, the truck came on Friday. The landlady lived next door and Mildred was sure I'd like her. A founder of the local book festival, she was apparently dying to meet me, and who could blame her?

Mildred showed me the little room I could use as my study, where the linens were kept, how to operate the washer and dryer. I suppose it was sweet, but the last thing I needed to know at the moment was how someone's waffle iron worked. A nice set of silver looked as if it would bring five, six hundred dollars at any hockshop.

"So what time would you like us to pick you up in the morning?" she said.

"The morning?" I said.

"I know Wayne's going to want to take you to breakfast and show you around a little."

What did it matter what I said? By morning I would be long gone. "How about nine?"

"Nine it is," she said. "You're sure you're going to be all right by yourself tonight?"

"Absolutely," I said.

I walked her to the front door and opened it to a fresh blast of heat. "I don't think you're going to regret being here," she said.

"I don't either."

I watched her hobble across the wilted lawn and gave her a wave as she got into her tiny red Miata. The car crept down the street, drifted to the left, narrowly missing two parked SUVs, and disappeared.

I closed the door and locked it. Moving through the house, I peered out the windows. There was a garden in the back and a narrow alley. In the bedroom, a green bedspread matched the green walls. Skinny volumes of poetry lined the bookshelves. Lit up by the late afternoon sun, a Houston Astros baseball cap perched on a windowsill like a dozing cat.

I took off my trousers, threw them in the washer with a cupful of detergent, and punched the start button. I lay down on the bed to take a nap, and when I awoke, dusk had fallen. The lights had gone on in my landlady's windows and I could see the shadows of people moving around inside. In a tree in the front yard a flock of the ugliest birds I'd ever seen were settling in for the night, screeching and whistling like something out of a Hitchcock movie.

I pulled my trousers out of the washing machine and checked the pant leg. The spattering of blood was fainter, but not gone. I tossed the trousers in the dryer and padded into the kitchen to inspect the refrigerator. It was stocked with spicy tofu, seaweed salad, and bean sprouts, with not a scrap of meat anywhere. I stood there in my underwear and tried a little of each, forking the stuff straight out of the plastic containers, but I was too roiled up to eat much.

So what was my next move? It was still early. I could have called a cab, gone back out to the airport, gotten another flight. But a flight to where? I knew enough to know that running around like a scared rabbit was the worst thing I could do. Like Barry used to say, willy-nilly tends to get old Willy killed.

What I wanted to do was call New York, find out from my old buddies if they'd heard anything, if anything had hit the papers, but for the moment I wasn't willing to trust anybody.

So what about staying put? The situation was goofy as hell, but I looked like Mohle, everybody had signed these confidentiality agreements, and now I knew he wasn't going to be showing up anytime soon. Where was I ever going to find a sweeter deal than that?

This required further thought. I fished my trousers out of the dryer, put them on, and sat down at the computer. I hacked away for a half hour or so before I miraculously came up with a couple of articles about Mohle.

He had been born in Newark and raised on the Upper West Side of Manhattan by schoolteacher parents. *Eat Your Wheaties* was the only book he'd ever written, but it was such an overwhelming success he went a little bonkers and retreated to this island off the Maine coast where no one had laid eyes on him in twenty-five years. The rumors were that he did nothing but eat vegetables and practice martial arts.

The more I read, the more Mohle's book came back to me. The main character is this teenager named Hartley, who goes to some private school in New York and, with his buddy Jones, is always getting in trouble. Everyone gives him grief—his mother, his pompous stepfather, his teacher, his little sister—and when he can't take it anymore, he and Jones run away, setting off across the country and having all these adventures.

I remember it as being a pretty good book, but I'd only been a kid when I'd read it. All I'd been interested in was the story. But the brainiacs quoted in the articles seemed to think there was a lot more to it than that.

The guy from the *New York Times* called it a spiritual quest and the editor in chief at some magazine called *Harper's* said it was a devastating critique of American society. A jerk from a podunk college in Idaho had written a whole book about Mohle's literary influences and how you couldn't understand Hartley without understanding Prince Myshkin and Hans Castorp, whoever the fuck they were.

I didn't have a snowball's chance in hell of pulling this off. I would have had to have memorized all the names of his ex-wives and girlfriends, his kung fu instructors, all his colleagues at the *New Yorker*. I would have had to read all the million or so books he'd read, including, apparently, the Bhagavad Gita.

I turned off the computer, went into the bedroom, and pulled on the Houston Astros cap. It was past eleven. I figured the car rental places were closed and that there would be no more flights till morning. But there was more than one way to get out of town.

I found a screwdriver in a red toolbox in the pantry. I put it in my pocket, went to the front door, and eased it open. Insects chanted in the trees and the night was as steamy as a sauna. Letting the door close softly behind me, I made my way up the walk.

I peered around the dense hedge. Cars lined the block in both directions, roofs gleaming under the streetlights. Across the road was a small park half a football field wide.

I strolled down the sidewalk, Mr. Nonchalant, checking out all the vehicles. Now that most of the neighborhood had retired for the evening, my hope was that if I boosted a car the theft wouldn't be discovered for a few hours—more than enough time to drive to Houston or Dallas, catch a morning flight, and get myself seriously lost, one way or the other.

Air conditioners shuddered like jetliners in the darkness. An old man dragged a hose down his driveway, paying me no mind, and through a living room window I could see a ponytailed young woman bouncing up and down to the strains of "Bad Girl" and swinging hand weights.

The heat was sapping. Two blocks down I found what I was looking for: an unlocked '91 Dodge Caravan. Stealing cars was not my specialty, but I still knew enough to know that with some of the older-model vans, all you needed to do was break the casing on the steering column and flip a switch.

I moseyed down an extra block, just to be sure the coast was clear, then turned and came back. I strayed to the curb, went down on one knee as if to tie my shoe, and gave the nearby houses a final once-over. There was nothing moving anywhere, not a sound. I stood up, took a deep breath, and pressed the door handle of the Dodge Caravan.

A howl erupted from the bowels of the park. It sounded like the Hound of the Baskervilles. I jumped back from the car. A snarling Doberman emerged from the trees, yanking a man in flip-flops and cutoffs behind him. For a moment I was sure my goose was cooked, that this was the van's owner, but as they passed under the streetlights I saw the man's goofy, half-crocked smile.

"Sorry about that," he said. The dog wasn't sorry about anything, straining at his leash. The man gave a hard jerk, which only made the animal crazier. In his free hand, the man held aloft his beer in a foam-rubber holder, trying not to spill it.

"Don't worry about it," I said. My heart pounded a mile a minute and I could see drool oozing from the corners of the Doberman's mouth.

"He doesn't bite," the knucklehead said. "He's nothing but a big puppy."

"I see that," I said. I felt for the screwdriver in my pocket; nothing would have given me greater pleasure than putting out the dog's eye.

"So how the 'Stros do tonight?" The man took a swig of his beer.

"The what?" The dog followed my every move with those little hate-filled eyes.

"The 'Stros." He pointed to my cap.

"I don't know. I didn't see."

"Bagwell, I'm telling you, the guy's been on fire." The dog lunged forward again, and again was pulled up short. Beer splashed on the street and the man leapt back, wiping at his shorts. "Goddamn it, Ollie, what the hell's the matter with you? That's it, I'm taking you home! Listen, you have a good night, now, you hear?"

"You too," I said.

He dragged the Doberman down the block, the animal's toenails scraping along the cement. This resulted in a new barking fit, which in turn set off every dog in the neighborhood. It sounded as if I was surrounded by a pack of coyotes. One light went on in an upstairs window, a second on a porch on the far side of the park. A third on the lamppost in someone's yard. I pulled my cap a little lower and slunk off down the sidewalk.

When I got back to the house, I found a bottle of vodka in the liquor cabinet, filled a glass with ice, and plopped down in front of the TV. I flipped from channel to channel before finally settling in with *The Wizard of Oz*.

My idea was that I would wait an hour or so until the coast cleared and take another shot at boosting a car. But after a second vodka—or maybe it was a third, I wasn't keeping count—I found myself getting more and more involved in the movie. I felt for old Dorothy, trying to get back to Kansas, trying to figure out this topsy-turvy world she'd just been dropped into.

I drained my glass and set it down on the floor next to the sofa. My eyelids were drooping. Was I in any shape to drive anywhere? It had been a hell of a day. I found myself thinking how Barry would have loved this story of me passing myself off as a famous writer, but then I remembered that Barry was dead.

I woke to the sound of pounding on the front door. Sitting bolt upright on the sofa, I blinked at the clock in the kitchen. Five minutes to nine. Morning light streamed though the window above the sink.

"Oh, my God . . . Oh, my God . . ."

A bell ding-donged twice, followed by more pounding. The TV was still on, a couple of local anchors horsing around with the weatherman. I pushed off the sofa and moved swiftly through the house. I undid the latch on the kitchen door and slipped into the moist morning air.

The trick was going to be to get across the garden and into the back alley without anyone seeing me. Crouching low, I scuttled from rosebush to trellis to magnolia tree. I had one leg over the picket fence when a voice called out behind me, "Hook 'em!"

I peered over my shoulder. A fleshy man with glasses and prematurely white hair and beard waved from the corner of the house. He pumped one arm in the air, forefinger and pinkie raised, middle two fingers folded under. A gesture like that could get you killed in New Jersey, but this was another country.

"Hook 'em!" he shouted again. "Welcome to Texas!" He let himself in through the gate and strode across the garden, shielding his eyes from the morning sun. "Wayne Furlough here. I'm the director over at the institute." He extended his hand. My head throbbed and my tongue felt like a Brillo pad.

"Oh, that's right," I said. His Hawaiian shirt looked freshly pressed. We shook as I swung down from the fence, careful not to deball myself.

"I'm sorry if I'm a little early," he said.

"Don't worry about it," I said. The man kept beaming at me. I couldn't believe I'd slept nine hours straight.

"How about a little huevos?" he said.

"What's that?" I squinted at him: the sun hurt.

"There's this Mexican place down a few blocks. They have great breakfasts."

It sounded like a terrible idea. "Tell you what, Wayne. I had sort of a rough night last night and haven't had a chance to shower or any-thing. Why don't you just go on to your office and I'll give you a call?"

"I can wait."

"No, no, you're a busy man."

"Not that busy. If you want, I'll just sit out in the car."

A tiny bell went off in my head. "The car?"

"Yeah. It's parked right across the street."

The answer to my problems was staring me in the face. I needed a car and he had one. I rubbed my hand across my mouth.

"Maybe you're right," I said. "A little huevos may be just what the doctor ordered."

He took me to a little hole-in-the-wall Mexican café with murals everywhere and we were the only ones there besides the cook and the waitress. I chose a booth in the back where I could keep my eye on the door—the old Wild Bill Hickok trick. Not that I thought that the Can-nettis would be looking for me here, but you can't be too careful.

The man was beside himself with happiness. I think the only other time I've seen a grin that wide was on the sports page when they ran one of those pictures of some sunburned fisherman standing next to his record tuna.

It was as if he was in the grip of some kind of madness. He unwrapped my silverware for me before I could touch it, waved to the waitress to refill my coffee cup before it was half empty. The names of the writers he knew (all of which were lost on me) were dropping like crabapples in a windstorm. He explained the difference between adobado and tomatillo sauce, the quarterback controversy on the Texas football team, and the workings of the institute. He got a tiny shred of tortilla on his chin and I found myself watching it jiggle up and down like a frantic moth at a lantern.

I was seriously under the weather. I kept drinking water and my head throbbed. Every sound seemed to be ten times as loud as it should have been, from the clanging of pots and pans in the kitchen to the horns of passing cars.

He went on about how I'd been the reason he'd stuck at his writing for as long as he had. Even though he was scarcely in the same league as I was—no one had ever heard of his work, really—he got up every morning at five-thirty to labor away at it in the hope that one day he might actually produce something he could be proud of. The car keys sat on the table between us; it was all I could do not to snatch them and make a dash for it. He began to tell me the plot of his new novel. It seemed to be about growing up in North Dakota and discovering a sack of drowned kittens. Maybe I was still under the spell of *The Wizard of Oz*, but I couldn't help wondering what he would look like in a lion suit.

"So how many people know I'm around?"

"Mildred. Me. Your landlady. The president of the university. Our eight fellows. And Rex, of course."

"Rex?"

James Magnuson

"Now, don't worry. You and Rex are going to be fine. As far as he's concerned, he's ready to let bygones be bygones. I can't tell you how honored he is that you're willing to go along with this."

I gave him a long stare. He shoveled in another forkful of eggs and washed it down with coffee. The tortilla shred miraculously disappeared. He wiped his mouth with a napkin. "Now, that was good, wasn't it?"

"Wayne, can I ask you something?"

"Shoot."

"I don't know if Mildred said anything to you or not, but the airlines misplaced my bags. I was wondering if I could borrow your car for a couple of hours. I'd sort of like to go buy myself some new clothes."

"Not a problem." His brow was beaded with sweat from all the hot sauce. "But before we go, let me give you something." He took a large manila envelope out of his briefcase and handed it to me.

"What's this?" I said. Outside the window, a sooty bum with a sea captain's beard and black army boots pedaled his bicycle slowly by. He was wearing a skirt.

"Just something to make everything official."

I undid the clasp and pulled out a sheaf of documents. It looked like the stuff I'd seen on Mildred's desk, but at the back there was a letter, detailing my duties and compensation. They were going to pay me (or V. S. Mohle) seventy-five thousand dollars to lead a three-hour seminar once a week for fifteen weeks. Plus I had to give a reading, whatever the hell that was.

My eyes started to twitch. "Is everything all right?" Wayne asked.

"Oh, everything's fine," I said. I did the math in my head. They were going to pay Mohle sixteen hundred bucks an hour. Were these people insane?

I set the sheaf of papers down on the table and looked up at him. He seemed suddenly serene. Maybe he wasn't as stupid as he looked.

50

"So we should probably go," he said. "You can just drop me at my office on your way."

When we arrived at the institute we parked on the street and he wrote out directions to the mall on the back of the manila envelope. We both heaved ourselves out of the car and I walked around to the driver's side to give him a clap on his fleshy back. At ten-thirty in the morning, the roof of the Acura was already hot to the touch. Maybe Mohle had the right idea. It sounded pretty good, being up there in Maine, with a cool fog rolling in off the ocean.

I told Wayne I'd probably be back in a couple of hours and he told me to take all the time I needed; he had enough work to last him all day.

"If you've been up since five-thirty," I said, "you probably need a nap."

"No, I'll be fine," he said. That shirt of his was something. I made a mental note never to wear anything with hula dancers on it.

I watched him walk into the institute, waiting until the door had swung shut behind him. He was sort of a sweet guy. I just hoped he had good insurance, because he'd just had his car stolen. I adjusted the seat, shifted into drive, and edged into traffic. I might not have known where I was going, but at least I wouldn't have to listen to any more about his goddamned novel.

There were all kinds of end-of-summer sales out at the mall and I loaded up with two pairs of pants, six short-sleeved shirts, socks, underwear, and a cool pair of sunglasses. I changed in one of the changing rooms and dumped my old clothes in a trash can.

I wandered through the corridors in my new clothes, past the jewelry kiosks and the honey cashew stands. A security guard jawed with a cute clerk from Foot Locker, paying me no mind.

I knew it was time for me to hit the road, but I found myself dragging my feet, I didn't quite know why. Maybe it was that walking away from seventy-five thousand dollars felt like a sin, maybe it was starting to sink in just how hard it was going to be, out there on my own with no one to talk to, no one to help. Barry wasn't always the smartest guy in the world, but I'd counted on him. Without Barry, I had no idea who I was.

As I passed a bookstore, my eye was caught by a bright white cover in the window and then by its title: *Eat Your Wheaties*. I backpedaled a couple of steps to take a closer look. It was Mohle's book, all right, in a snazzy new edition.

How could I resist? I bought a copy, got myself a latte at the Starbucks next door, and settled down at a table in the far corner.

I read for almost two hours. It had been years since I'd looked at the book, but once I got into it, it all came flooding back. There weren't any big words in it at all. It amazed me, how simply written it was.

More amazing was that even though Hartley and his buddy Jones were private school kids and me and Barry had been nothing but young toughs, we'd all gotten in trouble for almost exactly the same stuff—jumping turnstiles, throwing rocks at the traffic on the West Side Highway, smoking dope at Grant's tomb, swiping apples from the Korean fruit stand at 110th. How could I have forgotten all this? I swear that the guy who made Hartley egg creams at the Mill Luncheonette, the one with the numbers stenciled on his arm, was a guy I knew.

It was like reading my own life. This went way past a couple of happy coincidences. This was starting to feel like fucking destiny. My headache had mysteriously disappeared. The two lattes may have had something to do with it, but it was more than that.

Not only did I look like Mohle, I now knew I could sound like him. Some of the things Hartley had thought were exactly the kinds of things I had thought at that age. I had never been on a spiritual quest and Prince Myshkin and Hans Castorp could have been spacemen for all I knew, but I knew I could tell these young writers stories about Korean fruit stands and Grant's Tomb and run-ins with the transit police. Could I last a whole semester without someone seeing through me? It didn't seem likely, but for seventy-five grand, I could at least give it a try.

Chapter Four

When I walked into the Fiction Institute around one o'clock, you would have thought I was a returning war hero. Mildred rushed to get me lemonade and Wayne offered to take me on a tour of campus; they'd even talked to a computer guy about coming over that afternoon for some free instruction. I begged off all of it, as graciously as I could. I said I might just go home, take a nap, do a little reading. This Texas heat, I said, took some getting used to.

For the next week I lay low. I had my meals delivered from a Chinese restaurant and Wayne came over every afternoon for a couple of hours, which gave me a chance to pump him for information.

The first thing I wanted to know was just who this Rex was who was willing to let bygones be bygones. When he told me it was Rex Schoeninger, my jaw nearly hit the floor. I may not have known many writers, but you'd have to have been living in a cave not to know who Rex Schoeninger was. The man was big time. According to Wayne, he'd written more than sixty books (compared with Mohle's measly one) and they were all huge motherfuckers too, thousand-pagers, thick enough to stop a speeding bullet. My ex-mother-in-law had had the complete set in her living room—*The Sands of Vanuatu, The Roman Empire, Byzantium, New Spain, Continental Divide.* She was always telling me that there wasn't a place in the world he hadn't written about.

I'd read an article about him once in *Parade* magazine. If I remembered right, he'd made a shitload of money. Schoeninger was out there, having his junk turned into musicals and movies and TV miniseries, as opposed to V. S. Mohle, who, according to what I'd read on the computer, would hide in his closet to avoid running into his meter man.

"And, as you know, Rex is the source of all these monster fellowships we're giving these kids," Wayne said.

"Of course," I said.

We were sitting in my breakfast nook, sipping lemonade. Wayne had a big round face and was sensitive as a girl; everything showed.

"I know the two of you have had your differences . . . But maybe you'd rather not talk about this."

"No, no, I'm fine. Seriously."

"It takes a big man to come down here and bury the hatchet like this. It's been a long time."

Frowning, I rattled the ice in my glass. Schoeninger and Mohle were old enemies? I was totally fucked.

"I hope I'm not upsetting you."

"No, I'm cool," I said.

"I'm sure it must have been very wounding. For both of you."

"Wounding?" I said. It wasn't a word I used much.

"You know. Just very painful to think about."

"Well, maybe so," I said. "The hell of it is, once you let the genie out of the bottle, it can be kind of hard to get him back in again." One of the great skills you learn making your living on the streets of New York is how to keep talking even when you don't know what in blue blazes you're talking about.

"Isn't that the truth," Wayne said. "But the point is that you came. It was a brave thing to do."

"I don't know how brave it was. I really had no other choice."

"Well, you say that," Wayne said. He hunched forward, smiling, soft-spoken as a school nurse. "You two haven't seen one another in an awfully long time."

"I guess so," I said. "So how long has it been?"

"Rex and I were just talking about that. He says it's been over twenty-five years. According to him, the only time you actually ever met was on the Cavett show."

"I guess we all know how that turned out, don't we?" I said.

"I can't imagine. It sounds like a complete nightmare."

"You got that right."

He leaned across and patted me on the arm. "And that's why what you're doing is so great. It's going to be fine, I promise. He's anxious to see you."

Wayne lined me up with something called an RA. That's short for research assistant, and it's a pretty cushy deal for the old professors. According to Wayne, they use these students to run errands, pick up their laundry, babysit their kids, you name it. For me, it ended up being a lifesaver.

The RA's name was Chester, and Wayne brought him over on Wednesday afternoon. He was a tall, likable kid with a Harpo Marx hairdo and a big grin. His full name was Chester Arthur Fillmore, his great-great-grandfather was Millard Fillmore, and he seemed to be a total stoner.

I sent him off to the library with a list of books I needed, and by seven that evening he was back with a half dozen Mohle biographies. If it struck him as odd that a man would need to read that many biographies of himself, he was kind enough not to say anything, though the boy was so high, I doubt that there was much that struck him as odd.

I spent a couple of days reading about old Mohle. It turned out that the articles I'd read on the computer had barely scratched the surface. There was juicy stuff here, and juiciest of all was the story about his famous pissing contest with Rex Schoeninger.

It all started when they were both nominated for the Pulitzer Prize—Mohle for *Eat Your Wheaties* and Schoeninger for *Continental Divide*. All the literary muckety-mucks figured Mohle was a shoo-in, but in the end, the committee gave the prize to Schoeninger. When Mohle was asked if he was surprised, he said not really. "The Pulitzer Prize is essentially a journalism award and that's pretty much what Schoeninger's book is. The writing is largely cut-and-paste sludge, but it is not as naïve as you'd think. Schoeninger may try to pass himself off as the Grandma Moses of American literature, but behind all that there is something profoundly calculating."

Schoeninger didn't waste any time shooting back at him. His response appeared in the *New York Times* the next day. "It saddens me deeply that Mr. Mohle would be hurt by this. He is obviously a sensitive man, as we know from his work. I have great respect for his writing. At one hundred and forty pages, I don't think anyone is going to mistake *Eat Your Wheaties* for *War and Peace*, but it has been a great balm to the troubled youth of our nation. For that we can only thank him."

Things got worse three months later when the two of them appeared on *The Dick Cavett Show*. If the idea was for the two of them to shake hands and apologize, it didn't work out that way. The descriptions in the books of what happened were bad enough, but what was really hair-raising was a five-minute video clip Chester had found at the A/V library.

On the tape you could see how uncomfortable the two of them were with one another. Mohle looked drunk. Cavett tried to make nice, but wasn't getting anywhere with it. You had to give Rex credit. He at least made a halfhearted attempt at an apology.

"If what I said about Mr. Mohle came across as disparaging, I regret it," he said. "He is an immensely talented writer and deserves our respect." On the video, Rex looked to be in his late fifties, beefy and athletic-looking, the kind of guy you'd want on your city-league softball team. "But I also have to say that I deeply resent the suggestion that there is something dishonest about my work."

Cavett leaned forward in his chair, fiddling with his pencil. "So, Mr. Mohle, what do you have to say to that? I know that all of us sometimes say things in the heat of the moment that we don't quite mean, that might come across as a little harsh . . ."

Slumped down in his chair, Mohle scrutinized his fingernails for several seconds, then finally pulled himself up. "Was I too harsh? It's hard to judge. I'm sorry if I hurt Rex's feelings. The man is clearly a good guy. Look at him. It's just that I don't see the point of all those big books. It's obvious that readers love them, and apparently the Pulitzer critics do too. But what do they really tell us about our souls? They tell us how scrapple is made, how much rainfall it takes to grow a sugar beet, how to tan a buffalo hide. And I guess they tell us exactly what we want to hear about ourselves—that we are noble, hardworking, and ingenious, brave in battle and magnanimous in peacetime. My problem is that I don't think that Rex really believes any of it. I think he's too smart for that. I think it's all a lie."

Cavett nearly leapt out of his chair, waving for Mohle to stop. Rex sat ramrod-straight, mouth as tight as a drill sergeant's.

"Oh, come, now, Mr. Mohle," Cavett said, "don't be preposterous."

"May I say something?" Rex said.

"Of course," Cavett said.

"So what kind of honesty are you looking for, Mr. Mohle?" Rex said. "The kind of thing teenage girls write in their diaries? I have no interest in books where people do nothing but air their dirty laundry."

"Knowing you," Mohle said, "I'm sure you don't have any dirty laundry."

"Would you just shut up for a second?" Rex said. Cavett gnawed hard on the eraser of his pencil. "I have been to war, Mr. Mohle. I have seen good men die. I believe there is such a thing as honor. I believe there is such a thing as heroism. And maybe these things don't matter anymore, or at least as much as a pair of schoolboys playing hooky for a couple of weeks . . ."

There was applause from the audience. Mohle scooted his chair forward. "Rex, Rex, please, there's no reason to take all this so personally. You won the prize, I didn't. Hell, you publish so much, you'll probably win them all, though God knows how you churn those books out so fast, unless you've got a team of catamites down in your cellar typing away twenty-four hours a day."

Now the audience was booing, making garbled shouts. Rex grimaced and pulled at his nose. He raised a finger and shook it at Mohle for three or four seconds before the words came.

"You want me to come over there and smash you in the face? Because if you say one more word, I'll do it. And if I do it, you're hitting the floor and you're not getting up, I swear."

Mohle seemed quite amused by this. He leaned forward and picked up his water glass. "Well, that pretty much ends the conversation, doesn't it? But why don't we see what this will do?"

Mohle threw the glass of water in Rex's face and Rex retaliated by lunging across Cavett's lap and grabbing Mohle by the throat. All three of them went tumbling on the floor. It was a sight to see and was only ended by a stagehand rushing out, waving his arms to shut off the cameras.

As big a mess as that was, it only got worse. Two weeks later, Mohle published a long article in the *Village Voice* giving his version of what had happened, and six months after that Rex responded with a piece in the *Atlantic Monthly* entitled "Getting on the Bad Side of V. S. Mohle."

The damn thing wouldn't die. All the literary hotshots were choosing sides and some famous journalist with a pipe published an open letter to both of them telling them to chill out.

There was no way that was going to happen. Rex ended up filing a four-and-a-half-million dollar lawsuit against Mohle for slander. One of the biographies claimed Rex was out to bankrupt Mohle, and it made some sense. Rex had already made a fortune on his Broadway musical, and while Mohle was earning decent money from royalties, he had just been taken to the cleaner's in a bad divorce.

They finally settled out of court and Mohle disappeared into the woods of Maine. He never showed his face in public again. It sounded rough. At least when they let you out of prison, they give you gate money. By the time Mohle left New York, Rex had pretty much taken him for his last dime.

The place where I was living was almost too quiet. Any sound made me jump—the gardener pushing his wheelbarrow across the lawn, a recycling truck moaning to the curb.

In the evenings, around ten-thirty or eleven, when the temperature dropped into the mid-nineties, I'd go out for a walk to the end of the block and back. After being cooped up all day, it felt good. I could look in the windows of my neighbors, see the old folks laughing in front of their TVs watching the *Late Show*, see some tubby guy working on his teeth, stopping his sawing every now and then to inspect his dental floss.

I worked Wayne for everything I could. I'd gotten him to hire a security guard to check everybody coming into the institute, and he promised to speak to his wife about loaning me her ten-year-old Volvo.

I think it must have been the second week I was there when I woke up, my heart pounding, without quite knowing why. I lay still for a good while, trying to calm down, before I heard a faint rustling from the far corner of the room. A few seconds later, there was a low chuckle and then that rustling sound again.

I sat bolt upright in bed. Barry was hunched over in a chair next to the window, reading *Eat Your Wheaties.*

"Jesus, Barry . . ."

He looked up. Blood streaked his cheeks and forehead. "Pretty funny."

"What's funny?"

"This." He waved the book at me. He was wearing a baggy New Jersey Nets T-shirt and brand-new running shoes. "And you think people are really going to believe you wrote this?"

"Who knows?" The ceiling fan made soft whapping sounds in the darkness.

"When I met you, you could barely write your fucking name." As Barry rose to his feet, I saw a huge wet stain glistening in the middle of his chest. His face shone with sweat. "It's hot in here, isn't it?" He tossed the book on the bed. "I don't know how you stand it."

"What did we do, Barry?"

"What do you mean, what did we do?" He picked up the Houston Astros cap and put it on, tugging at the brim.

"What did we do that they had to kill you?"

"Same old stuff. Same old stuff that we've been doing for years." He went to the window and peered through the slats of the blinds. "You're never going to get away with this, you know that. You think these students are going to be able to keep their mouths shut? No way. It's too good a secret."

"It doesn't need to be for long."

"So how long?"

"Just a month. I pick up a nice check and I'm out of here."

He gave a hearty laugh. "That's good," he said. "That's really good." Taking the bottom of the T-shirt by his fingertips, he pulled it gingerly away from his belly, making a bloody sagging apron of it, and lifted his face to the breezes of the ceiling fan.

That was enough to wake me up for real, whimpering and clutching my pillow. I got out of bed and checked the locks on the doors and turned on most of the lights in the house. I was up until nearly three, flipping from one bad movie to the next, trying to calm my nerves.

Wayne came over on Saturday morning in his wife's Volvo and we took it out for a test drive. It was a clunker—loose clutch, mushy brakes, and whenever it was faced with anything faintly resembling a hill it would start to cough and sputter. It was hard to imagine making a getaway in this lemon.

We drove through some of the neighborhoods and then headed onto the highway. There were not a whole lot of cars out on a weekend morning, but those that were zipped past us. I had the pedal pretty much to the metal and the speedometer never broke fifty. Some of the upholstery on the ceiling had come unglued and sagged down, tickling the tops of our heads.

"It's kind of embarrassing," Wayne said, "giving you a car like this. But it should be able to get you to work and back."

"Don't worry about it," I said. "I didn't figure you'd be giving me the keys to your Ferrari." A sign at the side of the road read WACO 102.

"Ramona called me this morning."

"Ramona?"

"Schoeninger's assistant. She wanted to see if we could find a date for your dinner with Rex."

"Uh-huh." My heart filled with dread. After reading about all the insanity that had gone on between Schoeninger and Mohle, a dinner with the old guy was the last thing I needed. Wayne sat with one hand raised, keeping the drooping fabric from swallowing his head. "So this Ramona, what does she do for him?"

"Pretty much everything. She's the gatekeeper."

"What do you mean?"

"How to put this . . . Rex, as you know, is a major philanthropist. I think he's given away something like a hundred and fifty million dollars. But he still has another twenty million to give away before he dies, and now that it seems as if time may be running short, everybody and their brother has been coming out of the woodwork."

"Did you say twenty million dollars?"

"Yes."

"Wow."

It's amazing the difference a few zeros can make. You could make a case that I would have been a fool to risk my life for twenty grand. But twenty million? That was enough to really get a man's blood going.

Chapter Five

My first class met the last Wednesday in August, and when I came in I was pleased to see that the security guard was in place. He was sitting by the front door doing a book of crossword puzzles, and on the table next to him was a typed list of everyone who was allowed access to the building. He was up in years, with a bit of a belly—he looked almost old enough to have served in World War Two with Schoeninger. His name was Anton Woolley and he seemed genial enough, though I don't think he would have fit anyone's definition of muscle.

When I walked into the conference room, everybody was so quiet you would have thought Elvis Presley had just risen from the dead. I could feel them following my every move. I slid into my chair at the head of the table and counted to ten to calm myself, eyeing all the young geniuses. They were a handsome group and they seemed good-natured, which they should have been, given the cushy fellowships they were pulling down.

I introduced myself and passed out copies of what we were going to do for the semester (syllabus, I think Wayne had called it). I said a few words, pretty much just parroting back all the junk Wayne had told me about how the workshop was a place of perfect freedom, where writers could experiment and fail far from the prying eyes of editors and agents, a place where honesty was the rule, where the gloves were off, yet at the same time a place where they would feel nurtured and supported. It was a real "ask not what your country can do for you, but what you can do for your country" kind of speech and I could see from the glow in their little genius eyes when I finished that they were fairly inspired.

Down at the far end of the table, Dominique was giving me significant looks. She was magnificent in a shimmering rust-colored blouse with a couple of the top buttons undone, exposing her long, lovely neck and a bit of breastbone. I wouldn't call it slutty exactly, but it suggested a certain feast-your-eyes-all-you-want-you-lousy-schmuck kind of attitude.

I asked each of them to tell me a few things about what they were reading and writing. One by one they had their say: Mercedes, a former grade school teacher from El Paso who loved some writer named Sandy Cisneros and had spent the summer tending her parents' dog kennel; Nick, an intense young guy who was the spitting image of this racetrack tout I once knew called Louie the Lip and was working on a series of postmodern fables—whatever the hell they were—based on the Book of Revelation; and LaTasha, who'd been transcribing interviews she'd done with her uncle, a tractor driver in Mississippi.

None of this exactly floated my boat, but after each of them finished, I tried to say something encouraging. "Sounds interesting," I would say, or, "It'll be fascinating to see where you're going to go with that." When Nick tried to lay all that bullshit about the Book of Revelation on us, all I could do was point a finger at the boy and go, "Now, that's an idea!"

I'm sure someone else could have come up with better ways to handle it, but you've got to remember that I'd never been in a college classroom before. All I knew about universities I'd learned from watching Fred MacMurray in *Son of Flubber*, so it was kind of a kick to have everything I said scribbled down in notebooks. It was a little like those stories you read about nutballs who show up in small towns, announce that they're doctors, and start taking out appendixes without having had day one of medical training. One of the nice things about what I was doing, I could be pretty sure no one would die from it.

Whatever I was doing, it seemed to be working. They were loosening up and I was too.

I hadn't thought that much about it, but they were probably a little intimidated by me, so it was a big relief for them to see what a regular guy I was. Before you knew it, I was telling them how much reading Cervantes when I was twelve had changed my life and how the little Indian boy in *Eat Your Wheaties* was based on a real Indian boy I'd met while he was selling baskets alongside the highway with his grandmother, and how I still had the piñon nut he'd given me.

They were eating this stuff up. But just as I was starting to think I had a real talent for this, things got complicated.

Thirty minutes into class, this kid named Mel slunk in, sweating like a hog, bicycle helmet under his arm, red bandanna tied around his forehead. He clomped to the far end of the library and found a place, not at the table with the rest of us, but in front of the window, in a green recliner.

As we continued around, letting everyone have a turn, Mel took out a sketch pad and began to doodle, unimpressed with anything anybody had to say. He was unimpressed with the laid-back Chester, unimpressed with rosy-cheeked Brett, who had gone to Williams and worshipped some Cheever guy, unimpressed with Bryn and her description of her collection of linked stories set in the Upper Peninsula.

Frankly, I sort of agreed with him on that last one. I would have given a stuffed bear to the first person who could tell me what a linked story was.

But what really got my goat was just how unimpressed the little putz was with me. I could feel him sizing me up, raising an eyebrow over the top of his sketch pad at some of the more blandly reassuring things I had to say. When I asked for comments, he chose to pass. He had a foot up on a chair in front of him, one hairy knee raised so he could use it as an easel.

The last person in the room to speak was Dominique, and I could tell from the way the others came to attention that she already had a certain standing among her classmates. She was reading Susan Minot, she said, and finishing a novel based on the story she'd published in *Tin House.* It was about a teenage girl who goes on a cruise with her pill-popping mother and her new stepfather and ends up having a hot affair with a Jamaican cabin boy. She described it in serious detail, pushing back her mass of black hair, running her fingers along the open collar of that eye-catching rust blouse, her silver bracelets jangling.

By the time she finished, Brett's cheeks were glowing like Christmas ornaments. Everybody, in fact, was pretty knocked out by her performance, with the exception of Douche Bag, who was still absorbed in his sketch pad. I was not sure how I was supposed to handle a situation like this, but my instincts told me I couldn't just let it ride.

"So, Mel, what do you think?"

He glanced up from his doodling and rubbed his nose with a knuckle. "That kind of work doesn't interest me."

"What do you mean?" I asked.

He took his foot down from the chair in front of him and lurched forward. Dominique reached for her water bottle. "You know. A divorce. A lousy stepfather. An affair. No offense, but how many stories like that are there?"

"And you don't think they can be well done?" Brett said, a little too loudly.

"Maybe they can be," Mel said. "But it's still just realism."

"And you have a problem with realism?" Brett said.

"My only problem with it is that it bores me."

I stared down at my hand. I had no idea what they were talking about. "So is it realism that bores you, or is it a particular subject matter?" Bryn said.

"Such as?"

"Such as stories about women."

He screwed up his face as if he'd just caught a whiff of gym socks. "I like women's stories. I love Angela Carter. I'm just more interested in stories that take chances. Stories about rich people getting their feelings hurt doesn't exactly do it for me."

It was as if he'd just dropped a lit match on a gasoline slick. In an instant the rest of the class was talking over one another.

"How can you possibly dismiss someone's work before you've even read it? It's idiotic to say you can't write about rich people. What about *The Great Gatsby*? What about Updike? Edith Wharton? Henry James? Tolstoy, for God's sakes," Bryn said.

"When you say you're interested in stories that take chances, what does that mean?" Chester said.

"And how can you just write off realism like that?" Mercedes said.

"The real," Brett shouted, "is the atlas of fiction!"

I tried to keep everything under control. "Guys, guys, one at a time," I would say, or, "I think LaTasha had her hand up here!" But every time I thought I had them calmed down, old Douche Bag would say something else outrageous and off they'd go to the races.

The names of writers I'd never heard of flew like daggers in a martial arts movie—Joyce, Zola, Flaubert, Beckett, Coover. LaTasha kept shooting dismayed glances in my direction as if I was expected to do something.

You can't imagine how pissed I was. We'd been doing great and then this little dickhead shows up and wants to have a literary debate. I knew I had to stop it or I was dead meat.

I slammed my hand on the table. All their heads came up, like a herd of frightened deer. "Okay, guys, enough!" I gave them my Mohleian molar-suck. "This is making me crazy. What do you say we stop blowing smoke? We're here to talk about your stuff, not to bullshit about all this other junk. Everybody talks about what a great writer this Gatsby is. What makes him so great, huh? And why should we care? What does it have to do with this discussion?"

Everything became very quiet, the only sound the whirring of the overhead fan. Bryn looked down at her lap. Mel curled his lip. The others had the stunned look the passengers on the *Titanic* must have had when they heard the first soft thud of the iceberg.

A hand went up. It was Mercedes. "Mr. Mohle?"

"Yes?"

"The Great Gatsby isn't really a writer. He's a character in a novel."

They were all waiting. It felt like a bad day in front of the parole board. "Good Lord, doesn't anybody recognize a joke when they hear one?" I pushed up from the table. "You all want to go on arguing about all this, go ahead, suit yourself, but I'm out of here. I'll see you all next week."

They were agog. I'll grant you, it was a bit of a grandstand move, stomping off like that, but it was effective. It would have been more effective if I hadn't snagged my toe on Mercedes's backpack and stumbled on my way out, but I still made my point.

When I got downstairs, there was a note in my box from Wayne. He said he'd called Schoeninger, who'd said he would like to have me over for dinner on Saturday. His assistant would come by to pick me up at my house at six.

I can't tell you how the idea of Rex's twenty million dollars had burned itself on my brain. It was like waking up one morning, looking out your window, and seeing the Taj Mahal over the back fence.

Even more unbelievable, there were reasons to believe I might even have a shot at it. First of all, he had to give it away before he croaked, which, from the look of it, probably wasn't going to be long. But Number Two, he thought I was V. S. Mohle, his lifelong enemy, the one he'd just about destroyed way back when. What was obvious was that he must have been feeling bad about the whole business for years, and if he wanted to die with a clear conscience, I was more than happy to oblige.

But was I up for the task? Twenty million dollars. I just couldn't get my head around it. It must have been the size of the annual budget of Greenland. When it came to lifting fifty or a hundred clams off a guy, I was your man, but this was something else. This was not going to be like a stroll up the hill with Jack and Jill, this was going to be a climb up Mount Everest. This was going to take preparation.

Night after night I was up late, racking my brain, trying to come up with a scheme to bilk Schoeninger out of his millions. It was tough. I'm at my best with the greed and avarice crowd. What was going to work for an eighty-five-year-old Boy Scout, I wasn't quite sure.

Using the Web, I checked out what he'd already coughed up major cheese for besides the Fiction Institute—a western art exhibition, an annual folklore conference, a fund to help Russian emigre authors.

It was all pretty uplifting stuff, not exactly my specialty, but I did my best, balling up one sheet of yellow paper after the other and tossing them in the general direction of the wastebasket. Was he really going to go for a center for Polynesian dance? A Nobel Prize Winners Wax Museum? An up-from-your-bootstraps choral group? A condensed version of *Moby-Dick* to be distributed free to all the Motel 6's throughout the country?

Schoeninger was no fool. He was going to see through this junk in a second. I needed to come up with something I could pull off fast. The last thing I needed was a proposal he would want to mull over, call in his lawyers to discuss. I was looking for the ultimate wham-bam-thank-you-ma'am kind of scheme.

I missed Barry so much. Even though I was the brains of the outfit, I needed him to bounce things off of. Without him, I was struggling. But it is always amazing and humbling how often, when you're in a real corner, God provides. At one in the morning on Friday, the answer came to me in a blinding flash: a Wampanoag Indian Museum.

At first glance it might seem as crazed as all the other ideas I'd come up with, but the more I thought about it, the more it had going for it. There were the connections to the Pilgrims and early American history, which was right up Schoeninger's alley, and there was the plight of an oppressed and once-noble race, always a crowd-pleaser. The fact that Mohle had been living on an island in Maine for twenty years made it plausible that he might have developed a certain interest in the local lore. The other thing I really liked about it was that this was an area where I had some background. For one of our more elaborate, though ultimately doomed, scams, Barry had me pose as a Mohegan chief so we could apply for a casino license.

I woke up Chester at nine the next morning to tell him I had a little more library work for him.

Saturday night I stood on Schoeninger's doorstep, leaning forward to give the bell a long second ring. At seven in the evening it was still fiercely hot—the thermometer on the bank said 103—and I felt like I was about to expire. Under my arm I had a forty-dollar bottle of Beaujolais that I'd swiped from my landlady's wine rack.

Rubbing the back of my neck, I listened for some sign of life inside, and when I didn't hear anything, I took a couple of steps back to check the windows. The house, if it was Schoeninger's, was a disappointment. It was the kind of place where you might expect a disgraced accountant to live—a flat-roofed number with green shutters in need of paint, a shiny-leaved magnolia tree and a lawn turning to straw in the August heat.

The knot in my stomach was tight enough to double over a weaker man. How was he not going to spot me as a fraud? The only time he and Mohle had ever met face-to-face was that night on the Cavett show, and that had been twenty-five years ago. That was an awfully long while, but was it long enough to save me?

I was about ready to turn and walk back to my car when the door opened. A tall, hippy woman with a Wilma Flintstone beehive hairdo fixed me with an icy stare.

"Yes?" she said, sounding as if she had law enforcement somewhere in her background.

"Excuse me," I said. "Is this Rex Schoeninger's?"

"It is," she said.

"Oh, good," I said. "I'm V. S. Mohle."

"I'm Ramona," she said. "Please, come in. We were expecting you a little earlier."

"I'm sorry," I said. "Finding my way across town was more of a trick than I thought it would be."

"Mmm," she said. I could see she was not the sort of person apologies really worked on. "Follow me."

We made our way down a narrow hall lined with dozens of framed awards that Schoeninger had collected over the years, plus a lot of old best-seller lists, laminated and preserved in redwood frames. Schoeninger sat on the edge of a couch in the living room, leaning on a silver-headed cane. Over the mantel was a huge poster for his newest book, *Dakota*.

I'd expected Schoeninger to be old, but not this old. He was skin and bones, with sunken cheeks and glittery eyes. It was hard to believe this was the same beefy guy I'd seen on the Cavett show tape. His outfit was pretty bozo: a freshly pressed short-sleeved shirt, bolo tie, red running shoes with Velcro straps. His plaid trousers, cinched tight, were a couple inches short, riding up on shiny shins.

"Evening," I said. He stared at me for several seconds without saying anything. He cocked his head to one side, like a robin listening for a worm. I could see he was confused.

"So it's really you?" he said.

"Oh, it's me, all right," I said. "For better or worse." In the kitchen, the hawk-faced cook dropped English muffins into a pop-up toaster. "I apologize for keeping you waiting, but I kind of got turned around out there. But I brought you something." I handed Schoeninger the bottle of Beaujolais.

"I don't drink," he said, "but I'm sure Ramona would be happy to join you. Ramona, why don't you open this for the man?"

Ramona took the bottle without a word and headed for the kitchen. I sat down in an overstuffed blue chair opposite him. A mingy bowl of peanuts was on the table between us. Twenty million dollars, you would have thought the man could have afforded a few cashews.

"So I understand you had a pretty lively first class."

"They kept me on my toes."

"You need to be careful not to let them run over you. They're not quite the geniuses they think they are. But at least they've all read your work."

"I'm sure they've all read your work too."

"Oh, no. Let's not kid ourselves. I write the kind of books their parents read." He took a sip of his iced tea. "I can't tell you how much this means to me. I've dreamt of this day for years. I know it took a lot of guts for you to do it. Most people wouldn't have had the nerve."

"I didn't feel as if I had a choice," I said.

"Neither of us did, did we?" He glanced toward the kitchen. "So are we about ready to eat?"

The food was a disaster. I suppose for Ramona and Schoeninger it might have been passable—some dried-out chicken, burned English muffins, mashed potatoes and gravy—but since Mohle had the reputation of being a big-time vegetarian, the cook had specially prepared for me watery yellow squash, some dented peas, and a pile of Brussels sprouts.

I got the idea that food wasn't that important to Rex. It was me he was excited about. Wayne had been excited too, but this was different. Schoeninger was too proud to fall all over himself, too old at eighty-five to play the sycophant, but I could tell from the keenness of his gaze, the expansiveness of his stories, the way he would lean forward on his elbows to be sure he heard every word, that this was a major deal.

Ramona was still wary as hell. What was she thinking? That I was going to leap across the table and stab him with a fork? But she loosened up once she got some wine in her.

"So, V.S., do you read any of these younger writers?" Rex said. I pointed to my cheek to let him know I was still chewing. "I can't keep up with it all. The kids all rave about this *Jesus' Son*. You know that book?"

I nodded, swallowing hard. I hate Brussels sprouts. They remind me of mutant cabbages.

"Pretty strong stuff," Schoeninger said.

Ramona refilled her glass to the brim. "If I'm not mistaken, this is a very fine wine," she said.

"I figured it was a special night," I said.

"Mailer was down here last year. Walking on canes, couldn't hear, could barely see, but still feisty as hell. And Capote . . . now, that was a sad end. The thing about Updike, he keeps battling, I admire that, but those last books really have fallen off, don't you think, V.S.?"

"Mmm," I said. "Ramona, could I bother you for the salt?"

"That South African fellow . . . you know who I'm talking about . . . the name will come to me in a minute . . . first-rate." Schoeninger used a charred scrap of English muffin to mop up his gravy. "But I'm worried, V.S."

"And what is it you're worried about?"

"The future of publishing. The world has changed so much since you and I got in the business. You know what I think the turning point was? I think it was the Cosby advance. Remember that?"

"Remember it?" I said. "How could I forget it?"

"Everything went to hell after that. The big celebrity books, the chains came in . . . Sales were down, what, thirty percent last year?"

"I don't keep track of that stuff," I said.

That stopped him for a second, as if he thought I might be copping an attitude. "Huh," he said. "I guess that's because you're a wiser man than I am."

"Not wiser," I said. "I just don't like to make myself crazy."

After some half-frozen strawberries and cheap ice cream, Ramona brought out this humongous present for me. Judging from the size, it could have been a TV set, a footstool, a desktop computer, and even after I tore off the wrapping I still couldn't tell what it was. I lifted what looked like an oddly shaped piece of carry-on luggage onto the table (it was light as a feather), and undid the latches.

Inside was a cream-colored cowboy hat.

"Oh, my God," I said. "It's beautiful."

"We hope it fits," Ramona said. "If it doesn't, we can take it back."

"Try it on," Rex said.

I lifted it carefully out of its traveling case and set it gingerly on my head. They both smiled.

"What do you think?" I asked.

"Go take a look," Rex said.

I rose from my chair and peered into the mirror on the kitchen wall. My first thought was that it made me look like a squirrel being swallowed by a pancake.

"It's wonderful," Ramona said, but she was about half drunk and not to be trusted.

I tilted the front brim back and took another glance in the mirror. I still didn't quite look like Gene Autry joshing with the boys down at the corral, but it was an improvement.

"Pretty good," I said. "Pretty doggone good." All my life I'd wanted a cowboy hat and nobody had ever given me one. It sounds stupid, but of all the things people had done for me since I'd landed in Austin, this was the one that got to me.

"You don't think it's too big?" Rex said.

"I think it's perfect," I said. When I shook his hand, his grip was almost more heartfelt than my own.

"Okay, you two," Ramona said. "Hold it right there."

Just like that she was gone. I stood by Rex's chair, bewildered, but in seconds she was back, fiddling with a camera.

My eyes went wide. I opened my mouth to protest, but I was too rattled for any words to come. Rex leapt to the rescue.

"Whoa, now, whoa," he said. "Ramona, I think you can just put that camera away. Our friend here isn't a big one for pictures. Am I right, V.S.? Come on, I want to show you where I work."

Rex took me on a tour of his study. The books went floor to ceiling, and about half of them seemed to be ones that he'd written, thick as bricks, in English as well as in translation. He pointed out all the different editions—Spanish, French, Italian, German, Japanese, Hindi, Hebrew, Farsi, Tagalog.

He led me through a canyon of teetering encyclopedias, yellowing papers drooping over the edges of shelves. A long table was piled high with ring notebooks, mailing envelopes, dictionaries, and atlases.

The novel he was finishing was about Texas, and on his desk was a play set of the Alamo. It was the kind of thing I'd been nuts about when I was a kid—the ranks of two-inch-tall Mexican soldiers in their blue coats, Santa Anna mounted on a plastic horse, Davy Crockett and his doomed pals hunkered down behind crumbling adobe walls, their muskets raised to their shoulders.

He showed me the library he'd been putting together for his Texas book, pulling out old photo albums of cowpunchers and Comanche warriors, muddy oil fields and migrant workers picking grapefruit on the banks of the Rio Grande.

It was amazing. I'd been expecting the worst, but Schoeninger wasn't nearly as nasty a piece of work as I'd thought he'd be, and it didn't look as if I was in any danger of being punched out. There was even something like charm to him, beneath all that crustiness. Hell, I thought, this could end up being a cakewalk. I checked out the mirror on the closet door and adjusted the brim of my hat. I was one cool dude.

"So how far along are you?" I asked.

"About seven hundred pages. Ramona and I still have some research to do, but we're getting close."

"That knocks me out. Congratulations. You work every day?"

"Seven-thirty until twelve-thirty," he said.

"Wow."

Stacks of paper were everywhere. After I reached across to straighten a pile that was tilting like the Leaning Tower of Pisa, I idly picked a page off the top and glanced at it.

The room became very still. I looked back at Rex. His gaze was so level and unflinching I was glad he didn't have a weapon in his hand. He let a photo album fall shut. I felt like one of those tourists who forget to take off their shoes before entering a mosque.

"This is it?" I said.

"Yes," he said. "But it's just a draft."

I glanced at the quivering page again, but it was impossible to concentrate with those crocodile eyes glaring at me. "It looks terrific," I said.

"You didn't actually read it, did you?"

"Not really."

"You glanced at it."

"Right." I set the page back where it belonged. Rex had something more to say, I could tell, but he wasn't saying it. "What?" I said.

"Cut-and-paste sludge. Wasn't that the term?" I felt my mouth go dry. "I'm not trying to start a fight," he said. "But that is the quote, I believe." He took one of the tin soldiers off the table and shook it in his hand like a man about to roll dice. "We said some terrible things to one another."

I pushed my cowboy hat a bit farther up on my forehead. "But here we are," I said.

"Here we are," he said. "And I think there's some important things we have to teach these kids."

I couldn't imagine what those things could be, but I wasn't going to argue. "You mean you and me together?"

"You and me together," he said.

I went in to the institute on Sunday afternoon when no one was around to work on a letter to V. S. Mohle. I must have done five or six drafts, making sure I got everything just right, printed it out on official letterhead, and forged Wayne's signature at the bottom. I said I'd gotten his phone call and was sorry that there had been difficulties, but that I understood. While everyone was disappointed, we'd been lucky enough to hire a top-notch teacher at the last minute. "No apologies necessary," I wrote. "We're up to our ears with work right now. Why don't we just talk next spring?"

Sealing the envelope made me feel a little queasy. Any kind of letter was a risk, particularly when you were dealing with a lunatic like Mohle. There was no telling what he might do. I was just playing the odds. I walked two blocks and slipped the letter in the mailbox in front of the chemistry building.

Living the way I do, you learn to cover all the angles. I had already taken my credit cards with the different names, the phony driver's licenses, and bogus Social Security numbers out of my wallet, sealed them up in a manila packet, and taped the packet to the underside of my desk at the institute. I was afraid of leaving them at my house where my landlady or the maid might stumble across them, and I sure as hell didn't want them on me in case I got pulled over by some traffic cop.

For my second meeting with the fellows I had them do an in-class exercise, which, Wayne had assured me, was a great way to kill an hour. It was one of his favorites: "Describe a field as seen by a cow. Do not mention the cow."

The students went at it, heads down, noses inches from the paper, knees jiggling a mile a minute. Now and then there would be a groan, a sigh, a quick sip of a water bottle, an angry yank of the hair. Every couple of minutes Dominique would look up at me, a faraway look in her eye, sucking at the tip of her pen, and then back to work she would go. The only one who seemed to be having a good time was Mel, who wrote furiously, dashing off page after page, smiling the whole time.

Not wanting to make them more nervous than they already were, I went out of the room for a bit. I strolled into my office, watered my plants, and when I came back I stood in the doorway. I just watched the students for a minute or two, one hand resting on the tall bookcase filled with all the Schoeninger books. I had never seen people working so hard! As I pushed away from the bookcase, I felt it rock forward, and made a mental note to say something to Mildred. The last thing we needed was for it to collapse and snuff out all these promising literary careers under a ton of Schoeninger best sellers.

I went back to my chair and told them to finish up. When they were through, I asked them to go around and read what they'd written. If I'd thought listening to them talk about their work was tough, that was nothing in comparison to having to listen to them read it. What a bunch of goop! I couldn't make heads or tails of it. There were lots of descriptions of ryegrass and fire-ant nests and sun glistening off of rusted barbed wire, which they all seemed to take deadly seriously. When Nick used the term "herbivorean ease" in one of his sentences, I cracked up, thinking he had to be joking, but judging from the way he looked at me, he wasn't.

When we went around the room for comments, they just covered one another's asses. They'd start off with "I love the voice" or "I was intrigued by the egret motif" or "I want to congratulate you on the level of the writing." Then, just to prove how honest they were, they'd toss in a little mild criticism. "It might be interesting if you introduced the dead calf by the muddy stream earlier in the piece."

As for me, I was no fool. There are times when it's best to just go with the flow. "Excellent point," I'd say. "I agree about the voice. Once you get the voice, you're off and running." Or: "I think Brett really put his finger on it. He took the words right out of my mouth, I swear to God."

It would have been a total love-fest if it hadn't been for old Mel. He wasn't quite the son of a bitch he'd been in the first class, but everyone could tell from the tone of his voice just how bored he was. "It's okay," he'd say, "I've got no problem with that," or "Cool, I think it's cool," or "I don't know that I could say anything everybody else hasn't already said." Every time he opened his mouth, the tension in the room cranked up a little higher. Plus, the way he kept rubbing his nose made me suspicious.

It was finally his turn to read. The opening line got the whole class sitting up straight in their chairs. "Each morning before dawn, I felt the tiny cold green fingers massaging my teats." Talk about a whacko story: it was about this alien who comes down in a spaceship to milk this Holstein and then flies off into the clouds to feed his starving family on a dying star. I was pretty sure I'd told them all to limit what they wrote to a page or two, but this sucker went on forever.

The class sat there, stunned. Some of the details were seriously weird. There was the soft gurgling sound the little frog man makes as he pulls and squeezes, the sloshing of the milk in the bucket as the little alien struggles up the metal steps into his spaceship, the Holstein sneaking around, trying to keep the rest of the herd from knowing what she's up to each morning, secretly proud that she's found a purpose to her life that went beyond her species and even her own planet.

I kept checking the clock. Five minutes passed, and then ten. Was the boy mentally ill? Was he going to pull out a rifle and gun us all down when he finished? How could Wayne have let him into this program? Everyone in class was looking over at me, waiting for me to do something.

"Hey, Mel?"

"Yeah?"

"I think that's probably enough."

"I've only got a couple more pages."

"No, no, that's good. We've only got a few minutes and I want to get people's reactions."

The class was steaming, particularly the women. "I really didn't connect to it," Bryn said. Dominique passed, with a disgusted wave of the hand. "I think I'd have to hear it again," was all that Nick would say. Mel sat stone-faced at the back of the room, scratching his elbow.

"So what did you think about it?" he said.

"You talking to me?" I said.

"Yeah."

A sound from the hallway made me look up. Ramona and a Buddhist priest in a saffron robe had just come up the stairs. She opened the door to her office and the two of them disappeared inside.

"It was kind of over my head, to tell you the truth," I said.

"Seriously?"

"Seriously."

He gave his nose another vigorous rub. "So what do you think of magic realism?"

"Magic what?" I said.

"Magic realism," he said.

I couldn't believe it. The little bastard was setting me up. They may have fooled me once with that Great Gatsby crap, but they weren't going to fool me again.

"I have a question for you," I said. "What do you think about Magic Markers?"

"Magic Markers?" Mel screwed up his face.

"Yeah, Magic Markers."

"I don't know. I've never really thought about them."

"You ever notice that if you leave the cap off for a couple of hours they get all dried out and you can never use them again? Think about it."

After class I snuck into Ramona's office and shut the door behind me, lifting the knob gingerly so it would close without a click. A bronze casting of Schoeninger's hands at a typewriter sat on a small table in the corner. The hollow arms were whacked off just short of the elbows, giving the sculpture a *Texas Chain Saw Massacre* kind of feel. On one of the bookshelves there was a picture of her as a girl, sitting on a horse. She was a little chubby, wore glasses, and even though she was trying to smile, she looked absolutely terrified.

I leafed through the correspondence on her desk. It seemed to be mostly fan mail, and I swear seventy percent of it was requests for money.

It was unbelievable, the things people wanted funding for: a photographic expedition to Antarctica, a Japanese art museum in Butte, Montana, a colon cancer research center, a one-man show based on the life of Woodrow Wilson that would travel to all the high schools throughout the land. Best of all was a handwritten note from Tonga.

Dear Sir,

FINANCIAL ASSISTANCE

I am writing you to see financial assistance from you. Due to the ethnic tension, which has been went on for the last three years until now, we have been suffered a lot from the militia groups. Our gardens have been destroyed by militia groups. Our houses have been burnt down.

Therefore I am decided to seek for financial assistance. So that we may start to rebuild our house, schools and hospitals. I hope that you understand very much and hope to hear from you soon.

Yours sincerely,
Robert M. Kotiama

NB—Grateful if you could send me a copy of a book called *Millionaire Next Door.*

I folded the letter and slipped it back into its envelope. As I set it on the desk, a piece of paper floated to the floor. I picked it up. It was an invoice from the Taliaferro Detective Agency on Wabash Avenue in Chicago. The bill was forty-five hundred dollars for the months of June, July, and August.

Chapter Six

You wouldn't believe how many books there are about the Wampanoags—stuff on hut-building, arrow-chipping, and at least a half dozen volumes on the tragic story of King Philip's War.

I must have been reading for three hours a day, trying to turn myself into an expert. It was heavy slogging, but I knew that if I was going to pull the wool over Schoeninger's eyes, I needed to know my stuff.

Thursday night I was sitting on my couch, honing up on the clam-shell jewelry of the coastal tribes, when I heard a banging on the front door.

I slammed my book shut, slid the bucket of KFC onto the kitchen counter, and went to see who it was. I pushed the curtain back in the front hall with a finger, and then let it drop. Rex and Ramona were standing on the front step.

My heart went into overdrive, but it was too late to pretend I wasn't there. I took a couple of deep breaths to calm myself, flung open the door, and gave them the big hello.

"Hey!" I said. "Hey, hey, hey! Look who we've got here!"

"Rex and I were out running errands," Ramona said, "and we wondered if you'd like some ice cream." She lifted a plastic sack to show me.

"Ice cream?" I said.

"It's the best there is. We've got two kinds, chocolate and vanilla."

"Unless you don't like ice cream," Rex said. He was wilting, two huge sweat spots staining his khaki shirt. I didn't like the idea of inviting them in, but on the other hand, it's never a good idea to leave an octogenarian broiling in ninety-five-degree heat.

"No, I like ice cream," I said. "Why don't you guys come in for a minute?"

"Are you sure?" Ramona said.

"Absolutely."

I took Rex by the elbow, led him in, and got him settled on the couch. When Ramona handed me the sack, I took a peek inside at the two bulging cartons. "This looks terrific!" I said. "What do you say I get bowls for all of us?"

"That would be nice," Ramona said.

Ramona took a seat next to Rex while I went into the kitchen. I grabbed the bucket of KFC and pitched it in the trash. Luckily, neither of them seemed to have spied it. I could ill afford being outed as a meat-eater.

I got three bowls down from the cabinet. "So what would you like?" I said. "Chocolate? Vanilla?"

"A little of both would be good," Ramona said. Rex had discovered a copy of the *National Enquirer* under the stack of my Wampanoag books and was leafing through it, too absorbed to answer (it was something I'd picked up at the corner grocery because of the story of the two-headed calf on the cover).

I found my big serving spoon and started to carve away at the rock-solid ice cream. It was a good thing the cleaning lady had been there that morning, because Ramona was giving the place the eagle-eye. I was starting to get pissed. Wasn't it a little rude, dropping in on people unannounced like this? Just when I was settling in for a nice quiet evening boning up on wampum?

I sprinkled a few crushed nuts on the ice cream before carrying the bowls into the living room. Rex set the *National Enquirer* down, took his bowl with both hands, and dug in without waiting for anyone else. I pulled up a chair and snapped on one of the lamps (for safety's sake, I usually kept the curtains closed).

Ramona took a bite and I took a bite. Rex spilled a little vanilla on his khaki shirt and Ramona got a tissue to wipe it off. I took a second spoonful and rolled it around in my mouth, letting it melt.

"So how's everyone doing?" I asked.

"I think we're doing fine," Ramona said.

"And you?" Rex said. He plucked at the wet spot on his collar.

"Good. Real good."

Rex chipped at the block of ice cream with the side of his spoon. "And classes?"

"We're getting along."

"I understand you have them doing exercises," Rex said.

"That's right."

" 'Describe a field as seen by a cow. Do not mention the cow.' "

My face burned. I couldn't believe the little jerks had ratted me out. "Mmm," I said.

Rex was looking very grave. "This was something you came up with?" Ramona asked.

"No, it was Wayne's idea, actually," I said.

Rex licked chocolate off his knuckle. "Sounds like it got a little out of hand."

"So who told you that?" I asked.

"It doesn't really matter," Rex said.

"No, I think it does matter," I said. "A lot."

It got very silent. The grackles were going crazy in the trees outside.

"We were just thinking," Ramona said, her voice as soft and soothing as a nun's. "It must be very disorienting. Being down here all alone, so far from home, teaching for the first time."

"Anyone want any Reddi-Wip?" I said.

They both shook their heads no. Ramona wore huge earrings that looked as if they could have been used as gongs by Buddhist priests. "Wayne tells me that you almost never leave the house," Rex said.

"We were thinking it might be nice if we could take you somewhere," Ramona said. Sunlight glowed dully through the curtains.

"Like where?" I said.

"We could drive you out to the lake to see the eagles."

I slid my bowl onto the table and locked my fingers behind my head. "Uh-huh," I said.

"Something else I really enjoy," Rex said. "There's a pioneer farm just north of town. They have all these wonderful agricultural implements."

I tried to dislodge a piece of nut from between my teeth with my tongue. It was hard to imagine anything worse than an afternoon looking at old plows, but in my business, you learn to play with the hand that's dealt you.

"So what are you doing this weekend?" I asked.

"This weekend?" she said. They glanced at one another. "I'm not sure we could do anything this weekend. We're going to a ranch."

"A ranch?" I said. "With cattle and horses and all that?"

"The whole shebang," Rex said. "It's an amazing place. It belongs to a guy named J. R. Hudspeth. It's been in his family for generations. One of the biggest cattle operations in Texas."

"Wow," I said. "You think I could come along?"

"Come along?" Ramona said. "I don't think we could do that."

"Why not?" The smell of extra-crispy chicken lingered in the air.

"How would we introduce you?" she said.

Sometimes the things my brain comes up with truly amaze me. "You could just say that I'm Rex's assistant. He's already got one. Why couldn't he have two?"

Ramona seemed dumbfounded. Rex stirred his bowl. "You wouldn't be insulted?" he asked. "Pretending to be working for me?"

"I wouldn't be pretending. I do work for you." The house was slowly darkening around us. With the three of us sitting under a single lamp, it felt as if we were huddled in a cave.

"Sounds a little tricky," Rex said.

Ramona's huge earrings swayed as she turned to him. "But it might be fun."

"Fun?" Rex said. "I've never been big on fun."

He went back to scraping up the last of his ice cream. Did he suspect I was trying to pull a fast one? Probably. And probably I was, even though I didn't know quite what that fast one was yet.

"Well, hey, it was just an idea," I said. "I've got plenty to do here. It's just that I've never seen a ranch. It's always been one of my childhood dreams. I've been a big Roy Rogers fan ever since I got a cap pistol for my sixth birthday."

Rex gave me that sideways look of his, as if he couldn't decide if I was dicking him around or if I was just deranged. "You two think we could pull this off?" We both nodded yes. Rex stood and tugged at the legs of his high-water pants. "It's just that I hate lying to people."

"Oh, God, me too," I said. "But I'm not sure this would really count as lying."

"I imagine you would take a more liberal view on that than I would," Rex said. "But what the hell, let's give it a try."

They were forty minutes late picking me up on Saturday morning, and as soon as I climbed into the front seat of the maroon van I could tell something was off. Ramona sat stone-faced behind the wheel and Schoeninger, propped up in the back and engulfed in pillows like a Turkish pasha, looked so grim you would have thought the Russkies had just dropped the big one. I peered over the headrest.

"Everybody doing all right?"

"We're here," Schoeninger said. His Velcro-strapped tennis shoes rested on a red cooler. I glanced over at Ramona. She raised an eyebrow, but said nothing. It seemed wise not to press.

It took us a while to get out of town. There was a lot of new road construction and a junky sprawl that seemed to go on forever: car lots, taxidermy warehouses, Christian academies and real estate developments that weren't much more than gaudy wrought-iron gates, fluttering plastic flags, and freshly bulldozed trails snaking through the cedar.

The silence in the van was unnerving. It was clear that they'd been fighting, which I had no problem with, but what if it was about me?

"You two have been awfully quiet this morning," I said. More silence. "I hope it's nothing I've done."

"She won't let me have a dog," Rex said.

"What's that?" I said.

"Rex, that's not true," Ramona said. "All I said was, we need to sit down and have a serious discussion about this. The cook says she's going to quit if you get a dog."

"Man sells a hundred million books and they won't let him have a puppy," Rex said.

"And who's going to take care of it? Who's going to walk it? And if he gets under your chair and you trip and break your hip—"

"Man climbs the Pyrenees and they think he can't keep from stumbling over a pet . . ."

"Rex, that's not the issue."

We ascended a long hill and all of a sudden we could see for miles in every direction. White goats scampered in the brush and small rock farmhouses baked in the August heat.

"So tell me about this guy we're going to see," I said.

"You mean Hudspeth?"

"I guess that's right."

"The warden here didn't fill you in?"

"Not really," I said.

Rex gave me the rundown. Hudpseth had fought in the Pacific, was a great history buff, and was a fervent believer in cryogenics. The great sorrow of his life was that none of his children had chosen to follow him into ranching. He loved Herodotus, hated Lyndon Johnson, the Sierra Club, and people who built too near the road. He sounded like quite the character.

"So does this guy know I'm coming?" I asked.

"I called him last night," Ramona said.

"And what did you tell him about me?" I asked.

"The bare minimum," she said.

"Ahh," I said. "So how exactly are we going to handle this?"

"Have at it," Rex said. "I'm going to leave it all up to the two of you."

His mood made it hard to have a normal conversation, at least at first, but Ramona and I did our best. She had a million questions. Not only did she want to know who I was going to pass myself off as—her suggestions included a disgraced rabbinical student, a failed journalist, an ex-jockey, someone with a private income trying to find himself—she wanted to pin down every detail. Who had my parents been? Where had I grown up? What schools had I gone to? Was I a good student or a bad one? What were my favorite books?

I found it annoying. What Ramona didn't understand was that I was an old pro at this stuff. All I required was a little artistic freedom.

What I needed from her was a description of the typical

Schoeninger assistant (leaving her out of it, of course). Smart but inse-
cure was my bet. But were they broken people or did they have some
sass to them? And what was Rex looking for when he hired them? A
cheerful personality? Off-the-charts IQ? Someone who knew how to
keep his mouth shut? Or the can-do type?

When I asked her what an average day was like, she reeled off
a list of duties—answering fan mail, taking Rex to the doctor, doing
research, proofreading, shopping for clothes, making travel arrange-
ments, fending off unwanted visitors—but she was still fixated by the
idea of coming up with a credible biography for me.

"I've got it!" she said. "You can be a former yoga instructor! Isn't it
perfect? It's something you already know everything about."

"No way I'm going to go out to a ranch posing as a yoga instructor,"
I said. "Please, Ramona, I can take care of this."

"But we all need to be on the same page here . . ."

"And you need to trust me," I said.

"I've got it." Rex had been silent in the backseat for so long, I'd
almost forgotten he was there.

"What's that, Rex?"

"Your name is F. Horton Caldwell. You've got a Ph.D. from Harvard. You wrote your dissertation on boat-building in the New England colonies and Henry Steele Commager was your thesis advisor.
You taught at Haverford for five years, but when your wife ran away
with a colleague, your life pretty much fell apart, and when I found
you, you were a textbook salesman in Saskatchewan."

I was impressed. I wasn't the only one with a knack for deceit. For
several seconds no one said a word. I took a peek in the mirror. He
stared back at me, his bony old head resting against the pillows. He
looked about as kindly as a parking meter.

"Pretty good," I said.

As we came out of a long curve, I spotted a tin-roofed country store fifty yards ahead of us. A bunch of middle-aged bikers sat on the porch eating PowerBars.

"Let me pull over here," Ramona said. "I promised the Hudspeths I'd call if we were going to be late."

We drove for another couple of hours, the scenery getting wilder and wilder, with the kind of high ridges where you'd expect Tonto to be poking his head over any minute. Up and down we went, through a series of valleys fifty miles across. At the bottoms, the rivers that had cut them were just trickles of water winding through sandbars.

The towns were few and far between. Some were abandoned and those that weren't were dirt-poor. On the open highway there was nothing to see except flocks of buzzards that would wait until the last second before abandoning their splattered armadillo innards and flapping to the safety of nearby fence posts. Rex dozed off in the back, snoring softly. I racked my brain for anything anybody had ever told me about Saskatchewan. Was that the place where they had the totem poles?

Ramona finally pulled over to a high iron gate. She fished a scrap of paper from her pocket, rolled down the window, and punched a series of numbers into a gray metal box. The gate creaked open on rusted joints.

We coasted through and rumbled down a rutted road, clouds of dust billowing behind us. Schoeninger woke up with a start as we rattled over a cattle gap.

"Are we there yet?"

"Almost, Rex, almost," Ramona said.

We bounced down through some boulders and finally we could see the river. Lined with cypress, it was a hundred yards wide above the dam, the size of a small lake. On the far bank, several buildings were set back among pecan trees and huge oaks. Swans glided farther up, near a small island, and a breeze ruffled the surface of the water.

We bounced across a plank bridge and pulled up to the largest of the three cabins. A longhorn skull, eye sockets the size of softballs, glowered from a wooden bench. I got out, opened the rear door, and offered Schoeninger a hand.

"About time, stranger!"

I turned at the sound of the booming voice. A white-haired man in a neatly pressed J. C. Penney short-sleeved shirt hobbled around the corner of the house. He was barrel-chested and energetic, like an old drill sergeant, not exactly the kind of guy you think would want his head frozen after his death.

He helped me pry Schoeninger out of the car, clapped him on the back a little too heartily, and gave Ramona a bear hug. Turning, he raised one corkscrewy eyebrow, giving me a quick once-over.

"So this is the Harvard guy?"

"F. Horton Caldwell," I said. "I'm honored to meet you."

"I'll bet you are." He grabbed Schoeninger by the elbow. "I was thinking we'd throw your bags in the cabin and then I'd take you boys for a little ride around the place."

I got Ramona's camera out of the van, figuring it would be nice to have a few pictures of the old geezers together, and climbed into Hudspeth's pickup next to Rex, leaving Ramona behind to help Mrs. Hudspeth get dinner.

As far as I could tell, the ranch seemed to be about the size of Africa. We kept crossing and recrossing the boulder-filled river and stopped every once in a while to inspect an old Mexican graveyard or check out Hudspeth's new lick tubs.

I could still feel Rex's discomfort with the whole situation and it didn't help to have Hudspeth tease him about it. "So Ramona tells me you've got yourself a vegetarian assistant, Rex. Exactly how many of these characters you got working for you? You've almost got more people running around than I do, and I've got forty thousand acres to take care of."

But once we got out to the farther reaches of the ranch, Hudspeth was too busy auditioning for a role in Rex's next book to pay much attention to me.

Because I was sitting on the outside, it was my job to open all the gates. "Harvard," Hudspeth would say, "get that for me, will you?" I'd hop out, run over, unwrap the chain, and hold the gate open so he could drive through.

I played my part as best I could. When we came to a 150-year-old Comanche campsite, I got out the camera and took some nice photos of the two of them with the river and the cliffs in the background. When we found a perfectly intact cow skull that Hudspeth wanted Rex to take home with him, I was the one who got to carry it back and toss it in the rear of the truck.

When we were standing on a high ridge and Hudspeth spied a family of feral pigs trotting along the bottom of a draw, I was the one who got to run to the pickup, yank the rifle from the gun rack and come running back on the double. Hudspeth grabbed it from me without so much as a thank-you, wheeled, and fired a half dozen wild shots into the brush below us, while Rex and I stood with our fingers in our ears.

The whole thing was hilarious, really, Hudspeth bossing me around without a clue to the fact that I was one of the world's greatest authors. Rex began to relax when he saw that I wasn't taking offense.

It wasn't long before he got into the spirit of it himself. "Horton," he'd say, "would you get a picture of those buzzards over there for us?" Or: "Horton, would you mind holding the canteen?" Or: "Horton, make a mental note. It might be good for you to spend a few days reading up on Black Angus."

And then I'd go, "Yes, sir, Mr. Schoeninger," or "Mr. Schoeninger, I think that's a great idea." Maybe we were laying it on a bit thick, but Hudspeth was too self-absorbed to notice, proudly pointing out six dead coyotes hanging from a tree or explaining about tick fever.

When Hudspeth wasn't looking, Rex would give me a wink in the mirror, or glance up from scribbling in his notebook to throw me a quick, wicked smile. He was having a good time.

We ended up at a big barn where these Mexican cowboys were working cattle. A half dozen pickups were parked next to the corrals, and a couple of horses were tied to horse trailers, their coats dark with sweat. All sorts of cattle-bawling was going on inside the barn—it sounded a little like Times Square on New Year's Eve.

Hudspeth found Rex and me a place to perch on one of the fences and went to check on his foreman. It was a scene, cowboys climbing from pen to pen with long-handled plastic paddles, whistling and hollering. Some of the cattle were getting shots, some were getting tags clipped in their ears, and some were getting their horns wrenched off by a big metal contraption that looked like it had been invented by Hannibal Lecter. There was a lot of dust and the smell of cow shit, panicked animals charging from one pen to the next, cowboys jumping up on the rails, trying not to get trampled as the cattle came through.

Rex waved a fly away and glanced over at me. "You hanging in there?"

"Yes, sir, Mr. Schoeninger, I sure am."

It took him a second to get the joke, but when he did, he burst out laughing. He reached across to give me a slap on the shoulder. "All I know is, you're a hell of a lot better sport about this than I'd ever be."

When Hudspeth came back to join us, he was fit to be tied. One of the cowboys had left a gate open and nearly a third of the cattle they were supposed to be working were off wandering God knows where.

"But nothing we can do about it now," he said. He took off his cowboy hat, wiped the sweat off the band with a finger, and put the hat back on. He looked as if he was ready to murder somebody. "Come on, let me show you around."

He took us for a tour of the barn, leading us through the maze of pens, explaining the various breeds, introducing Rex to some of the cowboys. I was being basically ignored, which was fine with me. I drifted along behind, snapping pictures of trembling animals peering out between planks.

My shirt was soaked through and I was starting to feel a little sick from all the heat and the deafening noise and the smell. I must have been daydreaming about being back at my air-conditioned place, watching a golf tournament on TV, and drinking black cherry soda, because when I glanced up, Rex and Hudspeth were staring back at me with these odd looks.

"I'm sorry," I said. "Were you speaking to me?"

"I was just asking," Hudspeth hollered, trying to make himself heard above the din, "what exactly does a Rex Schoeninger assistant do?"

"What do we do?" I said, raising my voice to match his. I shoved the camera in my wet shirt pocket. "Sometimes we're in the library. Sometimes we run errands."

"What kind of errands?" he shouted. The man was still steamed about those missing cattle.

"Oh, I don't know. Could be anything." In the chute next to me, a Brahma bull bucked and kicked while two cowboys, clinging to the rails above him, took swipes at him with plastic paddles. "We might buy shoes for him."

"You buy Jews for him?"

"No, shoes!" I said. "Shoes!"

"Ahh!" he said. Rex hitched up his belt. I could tell he didn't like this line of questioning any more than I did.

"And we help with the mail," I said. "The amount of mail Rex gets is incredible. From all kinds of people."

"I had an assistant once," Hudspeth said. "All we ever did was get on one another's nerves."

Hudspeth led us out of the barn to one of the smaller corrals, where a circle of cowboys was gathered. "Miguel?" he shouted. One of the cowboys looked up and he and Hudspeth went back and forth in Spanish. It was clear that Hudspeth was not happy.

I could see now that the cowboys had a bull calf pinned in the dirt. A couple of them held the legs, another sat on the neck, and a wiry, gold-toothed man was down on his knees with a pocketknife.

There was no doubt in my mind that this was a setup, that Hudspeth wanted to see if Harvard vegetarians could stand the sight of blood. If Hudspeth could only have known—it was running from the sight of blood that had brought me here. Barry's blood.

One flick of the knife and it was done. The calf gave a pathetic little bleat and the gold-toothed cowboy tossed the testicles into a plastic bucket as if they were no more than a handful of blueberries. The other cowboys let the animal up and he wobbled off into the sunshine.

"So, Harvard, how much of the writing do you do?" Hudspeth asked.

I was looking right at Rex when Hudspeth asked his question. Rex didn't seem to react at all at first, but then I saw those crocodile eyes of his blink once, and then twice. Hudspeth had crossed the line.

"Writing?" I said. "Are you kidding? I wouldn't go near that stuff with a ten-foot pole." I fumbled with my camera, pulled it out of my shirt pocket, and wagged a hand at them. "Hey, you two, stand together for a minute. The light's perfect. This should be a good one."

That night at dinner I was seated next to Hudspeth's wife, Constance, a tall, elegant woman with great manners and a turkey feather stuck in her hair. She'd grown up in Connecticut and was delighted to have another Easterner to talk to. She'd met Hudspeth at a dance at Newport and made it sound as if he'd swept her off her feet, whisked her away to Texas, where he'd been holding her prisoner for the past forty years (except, of course, for the month of October, which they spent at their pied-à-terre in New York so she could see the opera and all the new art shows). She had many, many dear friends from Cambridge—as a young girl she'd been Arthur Schlesinger's mixed doubles partner. She was determined to find someone at Harvard we knew in common.

The meal wasn't bad, a big salad for me (Hudspeth had been kind enough to limit himself to three or four cracks about it) and steaks for everyone else. Best of all was the batch of frozen margaritas that his wife whipped up, thick as Slushies and packing a real punch.

Hudspeth was giving Rex the rundown of his entire family tree, going over everyone from his great-great-grandmother who'd been kidnapped by the Comanches to the distant relative who'd been killed at the Alamo and his uncle who'd disgraced the family by working in the Johnson administration.

From the way his wife kept looking over at him, I could tell this had been a problem before, Hudspeth's monopolizing dinner conversations, and she finally couldn't hold herself back any longer.

"So Rex," she said, "tell us about your parents. Where are they from?"

"I don't have any parents."

The table was struck dumb. Ramona, who'd been sucking the marrow out of a bone, set it down on her plate. Even the row of glass-eyed antelope mounted above the fireplace seemed a little sad.

"Oh, I'm so sorry," Constance said.

"There's nothing to be sorry about," Rex said. "It's not all bad, being an orphan. When you don't know who you are, you kind of get to make it up as you go along."

Eyes down, I chased a chickpea around my plate with my fork.

"But you must have wondered . . ." Constance said.

"Of course I wondered," Rex said. "That's what kids do. But at some point you've got to grow up and put all that stuff behind you. Horton, when you finish with your salad, I think we should probably call it a night."

Rex, Ramona, and I were spending the night in Hudspeth's guest cabin, which was rustic but comfortable, with a stone fireplace, cowhides tacked to the wall, and pine floors that creaked.

When I went to my room, I just lay on my bed, scratching my fire-ant bites and staring up at the stained wallpaper. I was exhausted from the heat and all the hopping in and out to get the gates, but my mind still buzzed.

My pretending to be Rex's assistant had come up aces. Whatever suspicions Rex may still have had about V. S. Mohle, he had been totally won over by F. Horton Caldwell. It's a little confusing, pretending to be one guy pretending to be another, but if it was working, I was game.

The big shocker had been Rex announcing that he was an orphan. In a way, it made perfect sense, tough and wary as he was. But the thing about orphans, they're never as tough as they look. They can be gotten to. Take it from me.

I finally pushed up from the bed and went to the bathroom to brush my teeth. I was dangling my dental floss over the wastebasket when there was a knock at the door.

"Yes?" I said.

"It's me. Rex."

When I opened the door, he was standing a few yards off, rubbing his elbow. His old man face looked spooky in the dim light.

"You going to sleep?" he said.

"Not quite yet," I said.

"I was thinking of taking a walk down to the dam. Want to go with me?"

"Sure," I said. "Why not?"

It wasn't much of a walk, just a couple hundred yards, but under the trees it was hard to see more than a few feet in front of us. As we scuffled down the gravel road, Rex took my arm to steady himself. It felt as if the temperature must have dropped a good twenty degrees.

"After what I saw today," Rex said, "I swear you could have yourself quite a career in acting."

"Oh, I don't think so, Rex," I said.

"I appreciate your putting up with all this."

"I enjoyed myself."

"Really?" Something rustled in the brush off to our left. "When he started waving his gun around, I could have sworn we both were going to die."

The road curved around and we came out of the trees. A sliver of moon reflected off the water and a pair of swans floated far out, looking like ghosts.

We stopped for a moment, taking it all in, but then Rex took a couple of teetering steps down the bank, trying to get to the river's edge. I don't know if he slipped or if his foot caught on something, but he suddenly lost his balance and reached back to grab my hand.

"Woof!" he said.

"You're okay?"

"I'm fine," he said.

He didn't take his hand away, and neither did I. We stood side by side, hand in hand like a couple of schoolgirls, looking out over the dark water. It was pretty weird, but the last thing I wanted was him pitching into the drink. His hand felt like a claw.

"So I hope you got something you could use," I said.

"Oh, you never know what you're going to use. You just have to keep on gathering and gathering. Can I ask you something?"

There was a soft plop in the water, no more than ten feet away. "Sure," I said.

"Did you really loathe my stuff as much as you said you did?"

The person Rex was talking to wasn't even here, was still thousands of miles away. Somehow it bothered me.

"That was an awful long time ago, Rex," I said.

"I know. But best as you can remember."

"Mostly what I remember is that we both lost our minds."

"I still regret getting those damn lawyers involved," he said.

The swans had disappeared behind a small island of cypress. From far off, I could hear the cows still bawling, looking for their calves.

"We don't need to talk about this now," I said, giving his hand a squeeze.

"But one day."

"Right. One day," I said. "But not tonight, Rex. Not tonight."

Chapter Seven

After my big ranch weekend, I was in the mood for a celebration. Monday night I took the Volvo for a spin. I must have driven around for at least two hours, the loose upholstery draped around my head, cruising past the football stadium, the capitol, and a big old park. I was sitting at a red light somewhere in South Austin when I glanced over and saw a barbeque place on the corner. It had big windows and I could see flames in the soot-blackened pit and a big side of beef turning on a spit. Some guy in a greasy apron hacked up ribs with a cleaver.

I sat there with my mouth hanging open. I didn't even notice that the light had changed until the car behind me honked. I eased over to the curb to let everyone pass. When I cranked down the window, I could smell the sweet smoke.

Did I dare go in? I cursed V. S. Mohle's vegetarianism under my breath. It was unlikely that any of my students were going to be inside, but if they were and they saw me stuffing my face with pork, my cover would be blown, but good.

But how much can one man take? I was tired of dutifully eating my dented peas and watery squash when I went over to Rex's, clapping my hands like a trained seal when Mildred brought me carrot sticks in the middle of the afternoon. I wanted meat.

I got out of the car, pulled my hat down low, and went inside. It was a rambly barn of a place, with the barbeque pit and a bar up front, and a pool table and knock-hockey in the back. An old drunk was complaining to a waitress about the government putting corn in his gasoline. I ordered the biggest platter they had and the guy made it for me right at the counter—a half dozen ribs, some slices of brisket, and a healthy serving of sausage. Around all this he artfully arranged a scoop of yellow potato salad, coleslaw, a slice of white bread, onions, and pickles. The peach cobbler came in its own dish.

I carried my tray to the back and found a booth under the Rolling Rock sign. Hunkering down, I attacked my food like a returning POW. The ribs were perfect, tender, with lots of meat on them, and a little crispy around the edges. You couldn't beat the brisket, once you got some sauce on it, and the sausage made pleasing little popping sounds when I bit down on it. Grease dripped between my fingers. The weight of the last few weeks slipped from my shoulders like a yoke from an ox. I made a little stack of bones on the side of my plate and sopped up the extra sauce with my bread.

I felt like a million dollars. Not only were Rex and I now thick as thieves, the whole F. Horton Caldwell thing was working like a charm. Sometimes, honestly, I dazzle myself. America is a great country. Just when you're sure you've lost everything, when it looks like there's no hope, what comes hopping down the trail but an opportunity bigger and better than anything you could have dreamed.

But as I was sucking on my fingers and congratulating myself, I glanced out the front window and there was Barry walking down the street with some floozy on his arm. I about had a heart attack. This was not like the dream I'd had of him, or some LSD flashback. This was the real guy, carrying a little more weight than he should have, with the flyaway red hair and that little limp of his.

It took just three or four seconds before they passed out of sight. I sat there staring down at my pork ribs. How could this be? The last time I'd seen Barry he'd been lying facedown in a pool of blood on a hotel room floor. My mind was like chop suey. The thought of going after him terrified me, but what other choice did I have?

I stumbled away from my booth, strode quickly past the rows of tables, and pushed out the front door. There was no one on the sidewalk, not to my right, not to my left. Across Congress Avenue, a few members of the Pepsi Generation were being stupid, laughing and pushing and throwing headlocks on their buddies.

I walked down to the corner to check out the side street, caught a glimpse of Barry and the floozy teetering around the back of the building. I hustled after them, half running, half walking.

There was a good-sized parking lot behind the restaurant and by the time I got to it, Barry was helping the woman into a red Cadillac down at the far end.

"Barry!" I shouted. "Barry!"

Barry turned and of course it wasn't Barry. They definitely looked alike—it wasn't as if I was totally out of my mind—but this guy was slick, with expensive cowboy boots and fancy jeans with sequins on the back pockets, the kind Barry wouldn't have been caught dead in.

"You got a problem?" the guy said, and he wasn't that nice about it. The woman, peering across the front seat, just seemed confused.

"No problem," I said. "I just thought you were someone else."

The guy shot me one last dirty glance, slid in behind the steering wheel, and slammed his door shut. I stood there, watching the guy back around, and then retreated a step as the Cadillac peeled out of the parking lot, spitting gravel. I don't know if the guy was still looking, but I gave the car the finger as it rocketed off down the street.

The smell of barbeque smoke was sweet and you could see it as it drifted off the roof of the restaurant like fog rolling in off the ocean.

I was a little shook up. It's no picnic, let me tell you, when your mind starts playing tricks on you. Barry was dead and gone. I had to get that through my head.

I had never heard such barking in all my life—high-pitched yips, mournful baying, wolflike howls. I walked up and down the aisles of the animal shelter, peering into one cage after the other. Most of the dogs would rouse themselves as soon as they saw me, trot over to the wire, wagging their tails, looking up at me with soft eyes. Some would jump up and flail a paw through the narrow gap between the gate and the fence. Then there were the ones who'd given up, who would just lie curled up motionless in the dirt, giving me the evil eye as I passed.

Dog pounds have always given me the creeps. They've always reminded me a little too much of the orphanages I grew up in—part of it was the smell, part of it was the wire mesh over the windows, part of it the constant yappy din. The shelter was divided into two sections—the adoptables and the strays—and there were lots of nice young volunteers in fluorescent-green vests to help you pick out what you wanted.

It seemed like at least half the dogs were pit bulls and rottweilers, which were way more than Rex could handle, but I finally found this little brown and white mutt not more than a few weeks old, with floppy ears as smooth as satin.

I paid my seventy-five dollars and carried the little sucker out to the car, trying to keep it from licking my face. None of this was much fun, but it wasn't about me anyway. I'm not trying to pass myself off as a Boy Scout, but sometimes it really does feel good, making someone's day a little brighter.

When I pulled up in front of Rex's house, he was sitting in a folding chair on the lawn, going through a stack of mail while Ramona mowed the side yard. Dranka, the hawk-faced cook, watered potted plants on the front porch, her back turned to the street.

I got out of the car. None of them looked up. The sound of the mower must have drowned everything out. I stood for a moment, watching Rex unfold one of his letters. He was wearing his *Hobo Times* hat. It was a couple of sizes too big and came down nearly to his eyes.

He stared at a letter for three or four seconds, looking more and more pissed off. He put it back in the envelope, then tore the envelope, not once or twice, but three times, and the third time it took real effort, his knobby old mitts trembling. When he tossed the shreds over his shoulder, they fluttered off in the general direction of the bushes.

The dog tried to scramble past me and I had to reach down and grab it. I held it to my chest, trudging across the grass. The little mutt fought me all the way and I was sure it was about to pee all over me.

Wheeling the mower around at the far end of the lawn, Ramona was the first to spot me. The lawn mower sputtered off. I raised a hand in greeting.

"Afternoon!"

Rex raised his head, squinting at me. Dranka turned, hose in hand, water splashing on the front steps. The corners of her mouth pulled down in a scowl. The yard felt enormous. The mutt nipped at my fingers and when I slapped it, the little creep yipped. Rex glanced at the two women, as if this had to be some sort of joke, but when he saw how teed off they were, he got the picture. A big grin spread across his face.

I held the dog out at arm's length. "Got a present for you," I said.

As I handed the puppy over, it squirmed free, tumbling onto Rex's lap. Rex made an oohing sound, lurching forward to catch it before it fell to the ground. When he picked the dog up for inspection, the mutt gave him a lick on the nose. Rex was beaming like a twelve-year-old at Christmas.

"So what's his name?" Rex said.

"I guess we'll have to decide that," I said.

Dranka tossed her hose into the shrubbery and strode across the lawn like a woman who meant business. Same with Ramona, pulling off her work gloves, her eyes narrowing like Lee Van Cleef in those Sergio Leone movies.

"When was this decided?" Dranka asked.

"I don't think it was really decided," I said. "It was just a spur-of-the-moment kind of thing. I was driving around and I saw this sign for the animal shelter and I remembered Rex saying how much he wanted a dog."

The mutt tried to scramble up Rex's chest, slobbering all over the old guy's withered neck. Rex had his chin up, letting it. It was nearly enough to make a man gag.

"Is he housebroken?" Ramona asked. Arms folded, she and Dranka stood shoulder to shoulder behind Rex's chair like a couple of bouncers.

"You know, I forgot to ask." I'd only owned a dog once, back when our son was little and my ex-wife thought it would be cute for him to have a puppy. A white scrap of envelope danced across the lawn.

"I was not hired to clean up after animals." Dranka's voice rose. "I told Ramona this, I told you both . . ."

"I'm sure we could take it back," Ramona said, "if it doesn't work out."

"Oh, we're not sending him back," Rex said.

He set the mutt down on the freshly mown grass. The dog seemed stunned at first, tilting its head, looking back at Rex, one ear cocked. It was as cute as hell, but I could tell from the way Dranka was staring at the dog, she would have drowned the little sucker in the lake if she'd had five minutes alone with it.

The dog gave a sharp bark and went tearing across the lawn. We all looked up. A young mother wheeled a little brat in a stroller down the sidewalk. A second kid, poking along behind, had toddled up on Rex's yard.

The mutt was headed right toward him like it'd been shot out of a rocket. When the kid spotted the dog, his face lit up with delight. He clapped his hands together and opened his chubby little arms.

"Mommy, Mommy, look . . ."

Dranka sprinted to the rescue and Ramona was just a step behind. The mother had turned and was shouting something. God knows what the mutt's intentions were—it was just a puppy, after all—but what it did was jump into the kid's face and knock him on his keister.

The kid wailed as the dog scrambled all over him, barking and nipping at the kid's Reading Rainbow T-shirt. All three women converged at once, like All-Pro linebackers zeroing in on a loose football. For several seconds I couldn't make out exactly what was going on, it was just one big melee, but there were a lot of yips and whacks and fresh crying (the brat, abandoned in its stroller, had joined in on the chorus).

Dranka came out of the pile with the dog, holding it by the back of the neck and swatting its muzzle back and forth like a welterweight working out on the light bag. The mother rocked her weeping, red-faced boy in her arms. When Ramona tried to help—brushing off the kid, trying to push one of his shoes back on—the mother jerked the boy away, yelling something at Ramona that I couldn't make out over all the bawling and yelping.

Neither Rex nor I had moved. I rubbed the back of my neck. "I hope I haven't created a problem," I said.

"It wouldn't be the first time," he said.

The kid, sucking on his thumb, stuck his other hand in the direction of the dog, trying to be friends, but the mutt, still struggling in Dranka's arms, snapped at him, triggering a new round of wails. A neighbor pulled up in a car and got out to see if he could offer assistance. I covered my face with my hand, turning away. Water crept down the sidewalk.

"Maybe I should go turn off the hose," I said.

"Suit yourself," Rex said. "Just bring that dog back here!" he shouted at Dranka. "Goddamn it, those women are going to get me sued."

I went to the house and sidestepped through the potted plants, feeling pretty sorry for myself. Here you try to do something nice for somebody, and look what happens. As I bent down to turn off the faucet, I spied a scrap of torn envelope gleaming under some geraniums. I retrieved it. It wasn't much, just a ragged piece of the return address.

TIVE AGENCY
BASH AVENUE
GO, IL

∽

Over the next few weeks I saw a lot of Rex. Tuesday nights I'd go over to his place and we'd play three-handed hearts with Ramona. Sometimes I'd drop by in the afternoons and he'd be sitting in the living room with one of the students, marking up a manuscript, and we'd all have a nice chat. Whenever I was invited, I'd go along on his research jaunts, floating up a bayou where the pirate Lafitte had once stashed his loot, visiting old battle sites, or driving down to NASA, where the astronauts outfitted him in a spacesuit and let him float around in the pool in the neutral buoyancy room.

We were getting along like gangbusters. In the van he entertained us with his tales of being shot down by the Japanese and surviving three days in a lifeboat, taking peyote with some Comanche medicine man, negotiating safe passage through the Khyber Pass with Afghan warlords.

When people were around, we launched into our F. Horton Caldwell song and dance, with me pretending to be his assistant, and Rex got no end of pleasure out of it. I would make a great show of cutting up his meat or running back to the van to get his sun hat. Everything was, "Mr. Schoeninger, let me unwrap that stick of gum for you," or "Hold on, Mr. Schoeninger, I'll get that door."

For Rex to have buried the hatchet after so many years was a triumph, a dream come true, and he was very proud of himself. Not that he was a saint. During our card games, there was no mistaking the deep pleasure he took in laying the queen of spades on me. Out of the blue, he'd come up with these zingers. "So, Mohle, you're the stylist here. Tell me this. What do you think those people mean when they say somebody writes beautifully? As far as I can tell, basically it means that they use words like *swan* and *glass* a lot."

It was weird. Why the hell would Rex be going to all this trouble? When you were at death's door, why would you invite your oldest enemy down, not just for a couple of days, but for nearly four months? And pay him a king's ransom, to boot?

All I could figure was that whatever had happened between them must have cut awfully deep. And my guess was, it wasn't just the terrible things they had said to one another, but the lawsuit and all that came after.

Let's face it. Rex had pretty much busted the guy financially and every other way. Was Rex to blame for Mohle never writing again and hightailing it off to the wilderness? Rex probably thought so. But look on the bright side. Rex was the one who turned the man into a legend.

Good as we were going, pitfalls were everywhere. One evening Wayne had a small reception for me and Rex and the students at the Fiction Institute. He'd gone all-out. He'd put so many flowers around, you would have thought someone was having a funeral, and the food was terrific. The kids were downing the hors d'oeuvres as if they hadn't eaten in weeks, and the wine—even though it was served in plastic glasses—was flowing.

I was having a hell of a time. Maybe I'd had a little too much to drink, but I got on a roll, entertaining the students with stories about my childhood in New York, telling them about the time we got in trouble when a buddy of mine killed one of the peacocks in the garden of Saint John the Divine with his homemade bow and arrow, and demonstrating our techniques for getting quarters out of pay phones.

I had these kids in stitches, spilling cheap Chardonnay all over themselves. They were in such a state I could have said the word "barometer" or "spritzer" and they would have roared. Every now and then I would look over and see Rex sitting in a big chair by the door, all by himself. (I don't remember exactly where Ramona was—off helping Wayne in the kitchen, maybe.) He nibbled grimly on a cracker, his face like stone.

A couple of times it crossed my mind that it would be wise to call him over, make him more a part of things, but then the kids got going, trying to come up with the greatest first line of a novel ever written.

It was obnoxious, really, and it definitely left me out in the cold (try me on the starting lineup of the '69 Mets and I'll show you something), but they seemed to be having a great time with it.

" 'Call me Ishmael!' " Mel shouted. He was wearing a new blue bandanna in honor of the occasion.

"No way!" Nick said. "That's way too easy."

"How about this?" LaTasha said. " 'Happy families are all alike; every unhappy family is unhappy in its own way.' "

"Oh, God," Dominique said. "Of course. But doesn't that sound like something you'd stitch on a doily?"

LaTasha put her hands on her hips, taking offense. "Give me a break. *Anna Karenina*? Leo Tolstoy? How are you going to do better than that?"

We were all crowded around the mailboxes like spectators at a high-stakes crap game. Bryn raised both arms in the air. She looked like she'd had more to drink than I had. "Hold your horses, guys, I've got it . . ." She put her finger to her lips, making sure she had it all right. " 'It is a truth universally acknowledged—' "

Brett coughed into his glass. "No Jane Austen!" Nick shouted, pointing with his proscuitto-wrapped asparagus. "We've got to have a rule."

"You can't make a rule," Bryn said. "What kind of a P-I-G are you, anyway?"

"I'm not a sexist," Nick said. "You're talking *Pride and Prejudice*! I'm sorry."

I glanced out the window. Someone on the dark sidewalk peered in, trying to figure out what was going on. Chester, his long arms draped around at least four people, raised his beer can.

"All right, everybody," he said, "try this one on for size. 'I am an American, Chicago-born—Chicago, that somber city—and go at things as I have taught myself, freestyle . . .' "

"Not bad," Dominique said. "I'd say it's definitely a contender." I nudged Chester and gave him the thumbs-up, just to let him know I thought so too.

They must have gone on like this for five minutes. It was hard for me, I'll admit. About the best I could do was try to stay out of the middle of it and give whoever was next to me a poke and go, "Now, that was a keeper, wasn't it?" or, "Boy, haven't heard that one for a while." Sometimes I'd just shake my head in mute admiration as if I would have given my eyeteeth to have written something that good.

They were all showing off and I knew that I was the one they were showing off for. If they only could have known what a pain in the butt I found the whole business—like being stuck in your living room with a pack of Jehovah's Witnesses quoting Bible verses. It seemed to me that everyone had been having a lot better time when I was telling them stories from my childhood. I finally slipped away and headed to the kitchen to refill my wineglass, but as I did, I spied Rex struggling to get out of his chair.

"Hey, Rex, let me help you there!" I said.

"I'm fine, I'm fine," he said. I caught his elbow and felt him sway as he pulled himself up. "So what's all the ruckus?"

Out of nowhere Mercedes swooped in to take his other arm. "Oh, Mr. Schoeninger, we need you," she said. Mercedes, as opposed to the others, had dressed up for the party, in red high heels and a sexy green dress."We're trying to come up with the greatest first line of a novel. Ever."

"Oh, that's not hard," he said.

Heads turned and the boozy circle of students parted to greet him. A couple of them patted him on the back. Dominique gave him a gentle hug.

"Hey, Mr. Schoeninger!" Bryn wiggled hello with her fingers.

"Okay, finally we get somebody who knows something!" Nick said.

Rex surveyed them all coldly, as if he wasn't sure how bright they were. His fingers dug into my arm. "So the question is," he said, "what is the greatest first line in all of literature?" The row of famous writers, chins resting on fists, stared down from their posters on the wall.

"That's right," Chester said. Ramona and Wayne emerged from the kitchen with two trays of baby quiche.

"Okay, then," Rex said. He lifted a hand like a preacher about to pray over his congregation. " 'Riverrun, past Eve and Adam's, from swerve of shore to bend of bay, brings us by a commodius vicus of recirculation back to Howth Castle and Environs.' "

Talk about sucking the air out of a room! All of a sudden everybody was looking either somber or worried. Mel shrugged and helped himself to a couple of the quiches.

"I'm sure you all know what that's from," Rex said.

Eyes began cutting sideways. It looked like there were a few people who thought they knew the book, but they weren't going to risk making fools of themselves. I smiled at everybody as if the answer should have been obvious. Finally Mel, shifting a mouthful of hot quiche from one cheek to the other, mumbled, "*Finnegans Wake*, right?"

"Exactly," Rex said.

"I didn't figure you for a big James Joyce guy," Mel said. Dominique shot him a dirty look.

"Sometimes us old guys will surprise you," Rex said. "You want to hear my number two?"

Who was going to say no? They knew what side their bread was buttered on. Yes, yes, they all murmured, bobbing their heads. Rex let go of my arm, standing on his own. The circle widened, giving him room. The man still knew how to claim the spotlight. He made that little preacher move again.

" 'Whether I shall turn out to be the hero of my life, or whether that station shall be held by anybody else, these pages must show.'"

I've never seen a more relieved group of people. "*David Copperfield!*" they all shouted.

Rex beamed and gave me a backhanded slap on my chest. "Remember?"

"How could I forget?" I said.

If he'd been ready to go home a half hour before, he was now getting into the spirit of things. "What about you, V.S.? What's your favorite first line?"

"Actually, I was just thinking about checking out some of those lemon squares," I said.

"Lemon squares can wait," Rex said. He took Mercedes's arm to steady himself. "Come on, show us what you got."

Maybe I was the only one who saw it, but it was definitely there, the hard, devilish glint in the eye, the part of Rex that wasn't such a nice guy, that wanted to cause trouble.

The circle had been on the verge of breaking up—tiny quiches were being passed hand to hand, wineglasses refilled—but Rex putting me on the spot had swung everyone's attention back.

"Come on, Mr. Mohle," Mercedes said, teetering in her high heels. "I'll bet you've got the best one of all."

"I don't know that I have any one favorite," I said. "There are so many . . ."

"So pick one," Rex said.

I glanced at him. What was I going to do, quote from the beginning of *Treasure Island*? "Guys, listen, I'm not very good at this kind of thing. I can barely remember the words to the Pledge of Allegiance."

"I've got one!"

It was Bryn. She waved her hand in the air, tall, lanky, boozed-up Bryn, God bless her. The others stared at her as if she was totally clueless.

"So what you got, Bryn?" I said.

She stepped forward into the middle of the circle, face flushed, and clasped her hands in front of her like a singer before a big audition. Wayne, lugging a giant bag of trash out the back door, stopped to listen.

" 'If you're wondering how crappy a best friend can be, you need to start with mine.' "

When she finished, she squinched up her shoulders and gave me a shy little Shelley Duvall smile, as if she'd done the cleverest thing anybody had ever heard of. Everyone else looked as if they were about to gag.

I started clapping, very slowly, just so she didn't feel bad. No one joined me. "Yeah, Bryn, there you go. That's dy-no-mite." Now all the weird stares turned on me. "You guys didn't go for that?" I said. "I know it's not exactly *Finnegans Wake*, but I liked it."

"I guess you should like it," Mel said. "You wrote it."

"I wrote it? No way! You've got to be kidding me. Rex, can you believe it? What's happening to my mind?" The way everyone's mouth was hanging open, you would have thought they were a bunch of dead fish in the bottom of a boat. Wayne, still at the back door with his bag of trash, rubbed his cheek furiously.

I decided to try another approach. I began to chuckle, putting my fist to my nose, shaking my head as if the joke was too rich to share.

"Oh, God, look at you all! If you could only see your faces! I'm sorry . . . I'm sorry . . . I really should stop playing with you all like this, but sometimes I just can't help it."

Dominique stood frozen, a quiche just inches from her parted lips, unable to take a bite. What was so unfair about the whole deal was that I'd actually read *Eat Your Wheaties*, just a month before, but what was I supposed to do, memorize every line? I put my arm around Rex's shoulders.

"Did I write that line?" I said. "Of course I wrote it, if you can call that writing." Rex slipped out from under my arm. "I worked on that first paragraph for a month. Everything I'd come up with was garbage. And then one day it was as if the heavens opened and there it was. 'If you're wondering how crappy a best friend can be . . .' Man, it was like it was just burned on my brain."

I'm telling you, there's an art to blowing smoke. Were they buying it? Most of them had these sheepish smiles on their faces as if they were coming around. Mercedes still looked as if she was in a coma, but Mel let go with a big guffaw as if I was the funniest guy who ever lived. Rex, working over his teeth with his tongue, did not seem happy. He was not a man who enjoyed having his leg pulled, one way or the other.

"Forgive me, please," I said. "Maybe I've been living up in the woods too long. People up there develop strange senses of humor. What do you say we go finish off those lemon squares?"

Chapter Eight

M y check arrived on the last day in September. After withholding and insurance, it came to nearly twenty grand. When I pulled it out of the envelope, all I could do was stare at it, all printed out, my name in capital letters—V. S. MOHLE. It was a real check from a real place. And this wasn't like my usual ill-gotten gains. I'd earned this money.

Great as that felt, I now was faced with the problem of what to do with it. Ordinarily I would have found myself one of those shady limo-service/tattoo-parlor kinds of places and had them fix me up with a phony duplicate of Mohle's Social Security card and driver's license, but this wasn't an ordinary situation. I'm no expert—Barry was always a lot more up on this stuff than I was—but my impression was that there were armies of high-tech geniuses coming up with new ways to nab malefactors like me every month.

But my ace in the hole was Wayne. The night after I got my check, I had dinner over at his place. It was a modest house, the walls decorated with the quilts of oppressed groups from around the world. I liked his wife, a gentle librarian from Manitoba by the name of Faith. Their two daughters had been shipped off to the neighbors for the evening, which

I appreciated. How could you expect an eleven-year-old to keep her mouth shut if she met someone as famous as me?

We stood around in the kitchen, drinking red wine and noshing on baba ghanoush, while I entertained them with tales of New York. After a second glass of wine, Wayne and I excused ourselves and went out back to check on the barbeque. When I saw the smoke rising above the grill, my heart leapt, but as I got closer, I saw there was nothing but portobello mushrooms, limp red peppers, and onions. This vegetarian thing was getting old, but at least I wouldn't be dying of scurvy.

Wincing from the heat, Wayne flipped the slices of peppers with a pair of tongs. "So Wayne, could I ask you something?"

"Of course."

"Ramona and Rex. What's the deal there?"

"The deal?"

"Yeah, you know. I'm still trying to figure it out."

"Rex, you know how generous he can be. Sometimes he gets these crazy ideas. Ramona's the one whose job it is to say no. And God forbid if you try to go around her."

"Where's she from?"

"Oh, she grew up in England. Spent some time bumming around. He met her when he was doing research for *New Spain*. She was working on some cruise ship in the Caribbean, and he hired her on the spot to be his typist. They've been together ever since." Wayne was wearing the same Hawaiian shirt he'd had on the first time we met. I guess it must have been his party shirt. "It sounds as if you and Rex have been getting along."

"I've got no cause to complain."

"Good," he said.

"You haven't heard anything different, have you?"

"No." The way he said it, I wasn't sure I could believe him. "It's just that Rex has his moods."

"How do you mean?"

Wayne picked up a spatula and began to rake the sooty bubbles on the grill. "He has the deans and vice presidents constantly jumping through hoops. He likes to stir things up. I just didn't want you to think it was you."

"No, I understand." I swatted a mosquito that had settled in on my arm. "So Wayne, I wonder if you could do something for me."

"Anything. You name it."

"You know I got paid the other day."

"Right."

"You know what a hopeless flake I am," I said. "The problem is I have this weird thing about banks. I wonder if you could cash it for me."

"You have it with you?"

"I do," I said. I scanned the surrounding yards, just to be sure no one was peeping out their windows, then pulled my warm, bent check out of my back pocket and offered it to him.

He tried not to show it, but I swear he gulped when he saw the amount. "Wow," he said.

"I hope it's not too much," I said.

"No, no," he said, his voice quavering. "I can do this." He turned the check over. "You haven't endorsed it."

"Oh, I'm sorry," I said.

He handed the check to me, patted his trousers, and fished out a blue ballpoint. I took it from him and used the wall of the garage for a hard writing surface. I scrawled *V. S. Mohle* on the back of it, careless and easy as Nolan Ryan signing a baseball.

"Here you go," I said.

He cupped the check in his hand and stared down at the signature for way too long. I could tell there were a lot of things whirring around in his brain. I wiped sweat from around my neck.

"Any problem?" I said.

"No problem," he said. "But I was just thinking. The signature's probably worth more than the check is."

That night I ended up calling my ex-wife in New Jersey, and why I did, I have no fucking idea, unless it was that getting that check had stirred me up in some idiotic way. It was nearly one in the morning and I woke her.

"Hello?" Her voice had not lost its usual note of suspicion.

"Dora?"

"Yes?"

"It's Frankie." There was such a long pause I thought maybe we'd been disconnected. "You still there?"

"Where are you?" she said.

"I can't tell you."

"You can't tell me? You wake me up in the middle of the night to tell me you can't tell me where you are? I thought you were dead!" For a second it sounded as if she was going to cry.

"So you heard."

"Of course I heard!" Over the years, Dora had turned into something of a hysteric, most of that directly attributable to me. "It was in all the papers, about Barry being shot. And then the police came by . . ."

"Huh." I belched softly. I'm telling you, all those seared vegetables can wreck havoc on a person's digestive system. I was sitting on the couch in the living room, the phone on my belly, my feet resting on a stack of Mohle biographies. "So they know I was with Barry?"

"Well, weren't you?"

"What did you tell them?"

"What could I tell them? That I hadn't seen you for how many years? That you haven't sent your son so much as a birthday card?"

I rubbed my hand across my forehead. "Dora, please."

"The police weren't the only ones."

"What do you mean by that?"

"There were two other friends of yours that dropped by."

"Who was that?"

"One of them was Claude something. I don't remember the name of the other one, but he had a scar over one eye and he must have weighed four hundred pounds. He could barely make it through the front door . . ."

"Dora, those guys were not friends of mine."

"They said they were. They said they wanted to talk to you about some business matters. They said if you got in touch with me, I should call them first thing. They said they would make it worth my while."

"So are you going to call them?"

"What sort of person do you think I am? You think I want to see you dead? All I want is for you to stop dragging me back into all your horseshit . . ."

I hate it when she uses foul language; it's something she picked up from her father. "Dora, I didn't have anything to do with Barry being killed. I'm as in the dark about all this as you are, I swear."

"How am I supposed to believe that? Tell me how."

My head throbbed. The cactus painting on the wall had begun to undulate. What could I have been thinking? These old marriages, you think there's going to be solace there, when, really, all there is is grief.

"Oh, and you know what else?" she said.

"What else?"

"They came back. Just last night."

"Jesus Christ. And what did they want?"

"They didn't want anything. They were just checking. I'm going to hang up now."

"Did they leave you a phone number? These guys?"

"I think I threw it out."

"Are you sure? You couldn't go look?"

"It's the middle of the night, Frankie. I've got to get up and go to work in the morning."

"It's important, Dora. I'm trying to get to the bottom of things."

"Are you? We were married for ten years. I don't remember your ever getting to the bottom of anything."

There was a click and then, after several seconds, a dial tone. I sat for a long time, rubbing my chin with a thumbnail. It had been a big mistake, calling. I swung my feet off the pile of biographies. On the cover at the top of the stack was the famous photo of Mohle, but the edges were whited out so he looked like God peering out of the clouds. Mohle had the right idea. Go live on an island, keep to yourself, don't bother people, and don't let them bother you. Everything else was too fucking sad.

When I met Dora she wanted to be a singer. She was good too. She could have been the next Barbra Streisand if it hadn't been for those faltering high notes. She was just twenty-five, the miniskirted daughter of a body-shop owner in East Orange. She looked a little like Annette Funicello on *The Mickey Mouse Club*, only sexier.

We got together at a good time. I was in my mid-thirties and it was the one moment in my life when I was within a hair of legitimacy. Barry and I were selling lots for a development in Arizona Barry had dubbed the Lake Havasu Estates and the money was rolling in.

Dora and I had a classic whirlwind romance. I took her to the best restaurants, bought her candy and flowers, took her out to Belmont for the races, but the real reason she fell for me was my mouth.

She loved to hear me talk. It almost makes me wince, remembering the pictures I painted for her about the life we were going to lead. The apartment on Fifth Avenue, the summers in the south of France. We would hire her the best voice coach in the city and through my exclusive contacts in the music business (a pal of mine had once been Perry Como's wardrobe guy), we would get her launched. It was as if I was blowing glistening soap bubbles and she was a little girl with her hand outstretched.

We made love for the first time in her bedroom on her parents' bowling night. She turned out to be more expert than I imagined. We did things that night that no one in *The Mickey Mouse Club* could have imagined in their wildest dreams. Her orgasms were operatic; I had to put a finger to her lips to keep her from alerting the whole neighborhood. Afterward we lay side by side in what was no more than a child's bed. I had never been surrounded by so much pink.

We were married after six weeks, and six weeks after that I got a letter from the Arizona attorney general, requesting that Barry and I appear for a hearing. There had been a number of complaints that the lots we were selling at the Lake Havasu Estates were nowhere near Lake Havasu, but sixty miles out in the desert.

I tried to keep the bad news from Dora as long as I could. Barry and I lost everything. It was a shock for Dora, but she was more noble about it than I deserved. Though, frankly, one bump on the head, who can't be noble about that? It's when you realize that someone's dragging you by the ankles down a long stairway that it starts to get hard.

Both Dora and I tried our best to make it work, but I think it was too much of a shock for her, once it dawned on her that she was stuck with a run-of-the-mill con artist. The kid coming along didn't make it any easier. From time to time I would try to straighten up and fly right—selling bank vaults, running a driving school. I even worked at Dora's father's body shop for six months, hammering the dents out of bent fenders until I just couldn't take it anymore. These regular jobs, I felt like I was holding my breath underwater. There was no hope in them, no upside, and I've always been a sucker for the upside. When

Barry showed up with his scheme for getting a casino license, I was easy pickings. All I would have to do was pass myself off as a Mohegan chief, drive up to Oswego, and alter a few tribal ledgers.

I'm not proud of what I did. I turned Dora into a harridan. I humiliated her in front of her friends and family, in front of the world, and left her with a boy to raise. But how could I stay? She didn't believe in me anymore.

The next day when I poked my head into Wayne's office, he had his feet propped up on his desk as he read over some application. I rapped on the wall. I hadn't meant to startle him, but I did. He lurched forward, feet slapping the floor.

"Hey," he said. "Just the guy I was looking for. I've got something for you."

He reached into his desk drawer, pulled out five thick envelopes, and handed them to me. They were filled with fifties.

"Wow," I said. I thumbed through the bills in one of the envelopes. There is nothing more comforting in the world than the flutter of greenbacks. "I don't know how to thank you."

"Forget about it," he said. "It was nothing." Just above his head was the row of remaindered copies of his first novel, *Winnowing*.

"They didn't give you any trouble at the bank?"

"Why would they give me trouble? It's a university check and I've known these people forever."

I took a moment to try to suss out his mood. "So how they hanging these days, Wayne? Everybody treating you all right?"

"Everybody's treating me fine," he said. "Why do you ask?"

I stashed the envelopes in my inside jacket pockets, three in one, two in the other. I felt a little bad for the guy. Here he was, thinking he was helping out a famous writer, and all he was really doing was setting himself up for ten to fifteen for bank fraud. "No reason. You just seem a little quieter than usual."

"Oh, I don't know," he said. "Sometimes I just wonder why I even bother."

"Bother? Bother with what?" I asked. He flicked at the application on the desk with the back of his hand. "You're not thinking of giving up, are you?" He shrugged. "You mean giving it *all* up?"

"The writing hasn't been going very well. It's just so hard to get anything done, between the students and my family. I feel like I'm being eaten alive."

"This is crazy," I said. "Maybe it's a little tough, but, Jesus . . . You've got the goods, Wayne. You know you do. And that's all that matters. I've read *Winnowing.*" I pulled one of the copies of his novel off the shelf and flipped to the last page.

"Listen to this. 'But then there was no need to do anything else than wait for the combine to complete its slow circling of the field, to feel the rush of grain beating through my hands, feel the first stirrings of the afternoon wind against my face, the only sound the rattle of the auger when we lagged behind and the hushing of wheat flowing into filling barns during the long, bright day.' You think any of the kids I'm teaching upstairs could come up with something like that? In a million years?"

He leaned back in his chair, eyeing me, fist to his lips. "Who's to say?"

"Christ A-Mighty!" I said. "The book did well, right?"

"Not so well, actually."

I scanned the inside of the back flap. "But it was critically acclaimed."

"Well . . . in a way. It was a finalist for the Abigail Schermerhorn Prize."

"There. You see?" I wriggled the novel back into its place on the bookshelf. Through the slats of the blinds, I could see Anton out on the driveway, eating a doughnut, trying not to get the powdered sugar on his uniform. "Pardon my French here, Wayne, but you've got to stop worrying about all these little shits! Seriously. You've got to learn how to be selfish. Take it from me. If I hadn't been selfish, I would be nothing. Absolutely nothing."

"I appreciate your saying all this," he said. He was still pretty much down in the dumps, but the clouds were beginning to part. I have to admit, I do have a gift.

I slapped him on the arm. "So what you working on there?"

"Just my application to Bellagio."

"Bellagio? You going to Vegas?"

He looked at me blankly for a second, and then laughed as if he'd just gotten the joke. "Oh, no, this is in Italy. Lake Como."

"Oh, that's more like it," I said. "Anyway, if you want to put my name down as somebody who thinks you're a hell of a writer, feel free."

Chapter Nine

Rex and I had been dodging it for weeks, the Big Conversation. It had gotten to the point where I thought it might not even happen, that he'd just decided to let sleeping dogs lie, so when it did happen, he caught me totally off guard.

We were down on Padre Island. He and I were taking a walk out on the pier at sunset. Ramona had gone back to the hotel room to make phone calls.

The place was a far cry from Jones Beach. There were shitty little waves and way out in the Gulf you could see oil derricks sticking up like the tips of witches' hats. There were a lot of Mexican fishermen sitting in folding chairs along the railing with bait buckets and long springy rods, and one of the guys was wrestling his hook out of the mouth of a hardhead catfish with a pair of pliers.

"So V.S.," Rex said. "Can I ask you something?"

"Of course."

"That night on Cavett. Were you drunk?"

"Absolutely," I said. "I was ripped out of my mind." I glanced at him. He tapped his cane along the wet planks of the pier, not looking at me. "Listen, Rex, I don't even know how to say this—"

"You don't have to say anything," he said. "It's over. Ancient history." Gulls screamed, dropping shells. "You know one thing, though? I don't think Cavett did a very good job of refereeing the whole thing."

"I don't think so either," I said. "I think he was egging us on. Remember how he would twirl that little pencil of his? And that smirky little smile?"

"Oh, yeah."

"I'm telling you, the guy was a real little Smurf." Down on the sand below us, an old woman built a sand castle with a couple of grandchildren. "I don't even remember what we were fighting about."

"The Pulitzer Prize," Rex said, as if I were the dumbest man in the world.

"Oh, right. Can you believe that? They give those things to cartoonists!"

I knew that wasn't exactly a brilliant thing to say as soon as it was out of my mouth. The sun was setting blood-red behind the clouds and some of the fishermen were starting to pack up for the day.

"So did you go to the ceremony?" I asked.

"I did."

"And how was it?"

"Nice enough. There was a fancy dinner."

"And did you give a speech?"

"A short one."

"I'll bet you handled it well," I said.

A great shout went up behind us. A teenage boy had caught a stingray that flopped back and forth on the end of his line while his friends ran for cover.

"I should have never filed that lawsuit."

"I will say, you took a pretty big chunk out of my hide."

"But, Jesus, some of the things you said about me . . ."

"I know," I said. "Pretty out of line."

We'd come to the end of the pier. All along the beach bits of plastic glistened like diamonds and a mattress slid back and forth in the surf.

"Hell," Rex said, "when you made that remark about catamites? I didn't even know what they were."

"I'm not sure I did either," I said.

He gave me a quick look and then laughed. It wasn't a big laugh, but it was enough to make me laugh too. Before you knew it, we were both cackling away like what I'd just said was the funniest joke anyone had ever made. Rex roared so hard tears came to his eyes. I honestly thought he might pee in his pants, the way he was stomping around.

We would try to stop, but all we had to do was look at one another and away we'd go again. We might have kept it up forever if a gull hadn't swooped in and nearly taken our heads off.

I wiped a bit of spittle from the corner of my mouth. "You know that thing I said about making scrapple? I want to apologize for that. I'll bet it's damn interesting."

"It is," he said.

"You know when you had me on the floor?"

"Yeah?"

"With your hands on my throat? I thought I was a goner. Right there on national television."

His eyes got all dark. "We made such fools of ourselves."

"I know."

"So was I the reason?" His face glowed in the setting sun and his jacket was zipped up to his chin. With his jaw set the way it was, he looked like the Indian chief you used to see on a nickel.

"The reason for what?"

"The reason you stopped writing."

Through the planks I could see the dirty water rippling in and out. I didn't speak for several seconds, letting him twist in the wind. "God knows, Rex," I said. "A lot of things went into it."

One bit of good news was that my getting Rex the dog turned out to be a stroke of genius. He loved the little mutt. Sometimes Rex would even bring the dog along with us on our trips, and we'd have to pull over at rest stops so it could take a whiz and run around barking at squirrels. Sometimes I'd hear Rex talking to the dog in the backseat and sometimes, when I looked back there, I'd see the dog licking away at his face. According to Ramona, it even slept in the bed with him at night, and in the evenings it would sit in Rex's lap and let him scratch its belly while they watched Jim Lehrer.

To tell you the truth, it was a nasty little animal. It had foul breath, nipped at your ankles when you weren't looking, and raised a horrible ruckus every time anybody came in. It got on both women's nerves, but it really drove the cook crazy. Dranka was the one who had to clean up after it, and when she was around, it would retreat under the table and start growling. God knows what went on between the two of them when the rest of us weren't there.

I tried to make it up to her as best I could. Whenever I went over to Rex's for those lousy dinners, I'd try to slip a twenty-dollar bill in her apron pocket. I told her it was just a little appreciation for all she did. It worked pretty well. In our odd way, we were almost becoming friends. One of the basic rules in my profession is that if you're planning to scam a guy, you don't want to piss off his cook.

This being famous, honestly, everybody should try it. Basically I'd been despised my whole life, sometimes with good reason, so being revered was quite the eye-opener.

Every afternoon Mildred hobbled up the stairs to bring me my hot chocolate. Every time I showed up at the institute, Anton, the security guard, would rouse himself out of his chair, bowing and scraping like I was the King of England. Nick kept me for a half hour one morning, telling me how *Eat Your Wheaties* had been his sister's favorite book. When she was dying of some freaky kidney deal he would go by the hospital and read her a few pages until she went to sleep; they were just three pages from the end when she passed away. By the time Nick finished telling me this, we both had tears in our eyes.

Then, of course, there was Wayne. I'll admit it, he got pretty annoying, poking his head in my office every couple of hours. The man was deceptive. At first he'd look like he was on the verge of bolting, all sheepish and apologetic, half in the door, half out. "I hope I'm not interrupting," he'd say, but if you gave him the slightest bit of encouragement, you were stuck for forty-five minutes.

"Is it a little warm in here?" he'd say. "Maybe we should turn down the thermostat." Or: "We really need to get you a better lamp for that desk." Or: "How's that car running?" The guy was in a constant state of anxiety. All he wanted was for me to like him. And I did like him, but Christ Almighty.

The guy was a bundle of nerves and nothing made him jumpier than the reading I was scheduled to give. We must have gone over the details a half dozen times—how long I should read, whether I wanted to take questions or not, what he should say in his opening remarks.

It sounded as if he'd been slaving away on that damn introduction for months, even though our audience was just going to be Rex and the students. The guy would actually get a little teary-eyed when he talked about it, how this was probably going to be the high point of his life, sharing the podium with a genius like me. Meanwhile, all I was worried about was pronouncing all the words right.

About the only one who wasn't sucking up to me was Ramona. She usually came by the institute just a couple times a week, but when she did, there was a constant parade of people angling for Schoeninger's money. Because my office was right next to hers, I got to see them all—Scottish headmasters in kilts, ex-senators with their four-hundred-dollar haircuts, ruddy marine biologists in knitted sweaters, Ivy League librarians in tiny red-framed reading glasses, African tribesmen, mountain climbers with fancy English accents, survivors of atrocities around the globe.

I only caught bits of conversation when they were in the hallway, but I could tell Ramona had a knack for giving people the heave-ho without ever being rude. This was the big leagues. Some of the people were flatterers, others acted like you were supposed to get down on your knees to kiss their rings. Some treated Ramona as if she was their long-lost daughter, others were mysteriously pissed off. There were cacklers, back-slappers, and those who spoke in breathy whispers. Some tried to make it fun. Others used the old trick of acting as if they already had a deal when they didn't, and became dumbstruck when Ramona had to point it out to them.

I had no idea how many great things there were to be done in the world! And all it took was money! It was a real education for me. Sometimes eavesdropping on all this made me feel like a first-grader who'd never learned his ABCs.

Was I intimidated by the competition? I might have been, except that I had a couple of things going for me that none of them had: not only did I have V. S. Mohle as my sword and shield, but I was the guy who had given Rex his dog.

So how were my classes going? They were pretty dicey, to tell you the truth. With regular coaching from Wayne, I was beginning to pick up some of the creative writing lingo, but there was no way I was going to get it all down in a few short weeks. I was flying by the seat of my pants. The students would be jabbering away about the third person versus the first person and I'd be wondering, where did the second person go? Sometimes when they argued about some literary dispute, my mind would go into a cloud, like it used to when I was in New York and found myself in a subway car where everyone was speaking Cantonese.

I'd been able to coast through September on the exercises Wayne had recommended, plus, of course, my own stories. The kids loved them—all my tales of the Korean grocer chasing us down Broadway with a broom, of our sneaking into movie theaters in Times Square, of how when you'd have a big snow in New York the whole city would shut down and we'd take cookie sheets, cardboard boxes, whatever we could get our hands on, and go sledding in Riverside all day long.

They liked to hear about when I got famous too, about the time Brigitte Bardot showed up unannounced at my island in Maine to plead with me to join her in her crusade to save the world's endangered species, about Marlon Brando sending me the motorcycle jacket he wore in *The Wild Ones* for my fortieth birthday, about the night I spent drinking with Little Richard and Ernest Hemingway.

Did the students know about the feud between Rex and me? Of course they did. No one said anything, but you could feel it in the air. I'm sure they were talking among themselves. Why wouldn't they? Here they were, with ringside seats for the final round of one of the great heavyweight bouts in literary history.

The problem was when their stories came in, because what they turned in weren't stories. Nothing happened in them. A divorced father buys a Christmas tree for his kids and when he tries to decorate it, the lights won't work. A Mississippi tractor driver finds an Indian arrowhead while he's plowing, but it slips out his overalls that night while he's playing the slots at the casino. A girl visits her father's grave in the North woods, gets high, has a flat on her way back to her mom's place, and she doesn't have a jack. It sure wasn't *Swiss Family Robinson.*

The pieces that weren't tearjerkers were so clever they made your teeth hurt. Nick wrote this thing where Elijah's in the desert, being fed by ravens, when Elvis Presley shows up in a pink Cadillac, fresh from Vegas, stoned out of his mind on pills and speaking Aramaic.

If reading these suckers was tough, the class discussions were tougher. The rule seemed to be that when your story was being workshopped, you've got to sit there and not say a word, while everyone in the room goes around and says any damn thing about it that comes into his head.

They had no end of suggestions. More of the mother. Less of the mother. Turn the mother into an aunt. Change to third person. Use more subordinate clauses. Raise the stakes. Cut the backstory. Fill us in on the narrator's history. Where they really went nuts, though, was when they caught somebody using a cliché. Apparently it was considered worse than murdering your children. I wasn't going to mention it, but for my money, these stories could have used a few more clichés. It's always darkest before the dawn, say, or it's not the size of the dog in the fight, it's the size of the fight in the dog. Something for you to hold on to. Mel had turned in four pages that read like the instructions you fish out of a prescription bottle.

As far as my responses went, I had worked up a couple of good genius expressions. The first was to put my fingers to my temples and screw up my face like I was passing a world-record turd and then, without warning, sit bolt-upright in my chair, bang my forehead with my fist, and shout, "I've got it!" The other was to get this faraway look in my eye and let my arm slowly float off the table and start making soft little sounds like a man in touch with the gods.

I had learned a couple of important lessons. I couldn't get away with merely echoing what the students said, and giving my honest opinion wasn't the best idea. When I suggested that it would be interesting if LaTasha made her Mississippi tractor driver a woman instead of a man, she looked as me as if I'd been whacked a few too many times with the Dumb Stick. I learned to keep it cryptic.

One of my favorite bits was to flip through a manuscript and randomly pick out a word. "Take a look at page seven," I would say. "Three lines down. You see the word 'ploddingly'? You need to go home tonight and spend an hour meditating on exactly what that means and I think the whole story will open up for you."

They'd made it pretty clear to me from the start that they expected written comments. The idea scared me to death. What I decided to do was to mark up the stories with different-colored pens. I drew arrows and circled paragraphs, slashed Zorro-like Z's through long passages of dialogue. I added stars and checks of various sizes, tossing in a few question marks when there was room. By the time I finished, some of the pages looked like the freeway maps to downtown L.A.

Nick and Bryn were the first to get the marked-up manuscripts turned back to them. Their eyes got big as pie tins. As they leafed their way through the Technicolored pages, their faces got paler and paler. Bryn quietly slipped her story into her backpack, but Nick finally got up his nerve to say something.

"I'm just curious," he said, his voice shaking, "about these marks."

"Oh, you don't need to worry about that," I said. "Those are just my reading notes to myself."

My ace in the hole was just how in awe of me they were, despite my various screwups. It was nice that they would leave little gifts outside my office—a bottle of fine scotch, a handpicked bouquet, a couple of peyote buttons in a hand-carved Mexican box, a slender volume of short stories by some glum-looking loser you've never heard of—but what really made it great was the hush when I walked into the room.

I turned out to be so much wittier than I thought I was. My most casual remarks turned out to have hidden depths. I had a dog once when I was a kid and he didn't look at me with half the admiration these kids did, plus I had to feed the dog. I had an aura and somehow it felt as if I was just getting my due.

The kids were shy around me. It was a couple weeks after Rex and Ramona and I had gotten back from our trip to the coast that Nick finally got up enough nerve to ask the question they were all dying to ask.

"So why did you quit writing?"

The room got quiet real fast. Dominique glared at him and LaTasha looked like she wanted to crawl under the table. Everyone knew what he was asking. He wanted to know about my feud with Schoeninger, but damned if I was going near that one.

"No, no, that's all right." I pressed my palms together in front of my lips, considering what to do. I could have just refused to answer. But there's one thing that most people don't understand about con artists. The key to getting people to show confidence in you is for you to show confidence in them.

I got up from the table and went to close the door. They all stared at me like a nest of young owls. "So why did I quit writing? I can trust you to never repeat this to anyone?"

Around the table they were all nodding and mumbling. I scrutinized them for three or four seconds, then went to the window and gazed out at the parking lot, brooding. I rubbed my hair and finally turned back to face them.

"I suppose, my friends, I quit writing because I got tired of feeling as if I was a fraud. After *Eat Your Wheaties* came out, my life turned into a three-ring circus. Everyone wanted a piece of me. I was getting invitations to the Easter Egg Roll on the White House lawn, Sinatra called to see if he could get me to cut an album with him . . . I didn't tell you about that? I thought I did. Then I got myself caught up in some real messes. It was madness. I started drinking. I started doing a little drugs."

How were they taking all this? It was hard to tell. Except for LaTasha, who was sneaking me little sympathetic smiles, no one would look at me. They seemed a little stricken and embarrassed. Mercedes had her head bowed as if she might be praying. Mel kept gritting his teeth and every so often he'd surreptitiously thumb through the copies of his story, checking on the comments the others had made on his manuscript.

"There was no time to write, and even when there was time, I couldn't focus. I'd work on a single page for hours, and at the end of the day I'd look at it and realize that it was nothing but an imitation of something I'd done five years before. I was turning into a caricature of myself. I'd wake up in the morning, look in the mirror, and think, Who is this guy? That's why I moved to Maine and cut myself off from everyone. I was trying to get in touch with that still, inner voice."

Brett shot me this quick, sidelong glance. The bit about the still, inner voice, by the way, is not original with me. I read about it in one of those inspirational creative writing manuals Wayne had lent me.

"God knows I've tried. For years I tortured myself. I must have started a dozen different books and ended up throwing them all in the fireplace." Mercedes looked up for the first time, her eyes brimming with tears. "I suppose I've made my peace with all that. The way I've come to understand it, when it happens like it happened with *Eat Your Wheaties*, you are just the instrument. It's like there's a wind blowing through you."

Again, that's from the manual. I can't recommend it too highly. If I remember right, the author is from some teacher's college in Missouri. The title is *The Wings of Prometheus*.

"But how are we supposed to make ourselves the instrument of something?" Bryn said.

"You can begin by listening to your heart," I said. "There are a few things I do know. Writing is not about cleverness. It's not about proving how smart you are. You're not going to be able to fake your way through this. For openers, I'd say, start telling the truth."

∞

Don't get the idea that I'm illiterate. I've read books all my life. I loved *Swiss Family Robinson.* In my first couple of years of high school, before I dropped out and hit the streets with Barry, I had a couple of great English teachers who made us read all kinds of things—*The Red Pony, Silas Marner, The Call of the Wild.*

But what I was learning was that these were not titles that cut any ice with the hotshots I was running with. I was working like a son of a bitch to catch up. I swiped the tapes of these Lannan Literary Videos from the institute library and watched them at home when I was washing the dishes or brushing my teeth. They had great writers—Seamus Heaney, Carlos Fuentes, Kazuo Ishiguro, Andrei Vozesensky—reading from their work and giving their views on things. I just let it wash over me, picking up the lingo.

But nothing was as valuable as my time with Wayne. We spent hours together. I kept picking his brain, asking about little things I could say in class. He was more than happy to do it.

I guess he figured that after twenty-five years in the woods I was pretty clueless about how much the writing game had changed. Nowadays if you wanted to be an author, you didn't just go out and write a book, you needed to get a whole gang of people to show you how to do it. Apparently there were now hundreds of these programs all over the country, and he filled me in on every one of them.

He took it all damn seriously. He spent a whole afternoon talking to me about why we all need stories and how they have the power to change our lives forever. I couldn't have agreed more. I'd been telling stories all my life, but I guess I'd never realized until now what a noble calling it was.

It never fails. Every time you figure you got it knocked, something comes along to trip you up. This beautiful October afternoon, we were coming back from East Texas, where we'd been visiting an old lady whose grandfather had been one of the original oil tycoons. We stopped off at some 7-Eleven to use the restrooms. We were at the counter, buying Rex a Snickers bar, when Ramona went, "Hey, how about this?"

We all looked down and there in the magazine rack was the newest *Time* magazine. A little banner cut across the upper corner reading TEN GREATEST NOVELS OF THE TWENTIETH CENTURY.

Of course she picked it up and started thumbing through it, looking for the article. The various turkey hunters and young amphetamine addicts in line behind us were getting restless, and Rex didn't seem that happy either.

"Here it is," she said. Rex acted as if he hadn't heard, slapping the Snickers bar on the counter and handing the Indian attendant two dollars. "Wouldn't you know it," Ramona said. I peeked over her shoulder.

The list had been put together by some Bloom guy, with little photographs of the jacket covers. There was *Eat Your Wheaties*, right between *Cancer Ward* and *Ulysses*.

A farmer with attitude bellied past us and slammed his beef jerky and Fanta orange soda down next to the cash register. Ramona turned to show the magazine to Rex. "Isn't this something?" she said.

Rex was trying to tear open the wrapper of his Snickers bar with his teeth and having a hard time of it. He spat out a corner of brown plastic. "Congratulations," he said, sounding like a kid who'd just discovered his turtle had died.

"Ahh," I said, "these magazines, what do they know? Now, if I'd made the Best Dressed List, that would have been something."

Rex did not speak again the rest of the way home.

My inspirational speech to the class may have seemed like a brilliant idea at the time, but it created a couple of problems. First of all, it had obviously been a mistake confessing to them that I felt like a fraud, because Mercedes, Bryn, and LaTasha came in to see me over the next few days to tell me that they felt like frauds too. There were more than a few tears shed, but with a little TLC I was able to get the girls back on their feet.

The second problem was dicier. Mel was such a contrary little son of a bitch, I should have realized that whatever I told the class to do, he was going to do the opposite. If I told them to forget about trying to be clever, it was only going to make him try harder to be a laugh riot. If I told them to write from the heart, the schmuck was sure to write as if he had ice water running in his veins.

The next story he brought in was the journal of an American woman astronaut, stranded in space with a chimpanzee. They've been out there for three months. They're able to survive by cannibalism, gnawing away at the corpses of her three Russian crewmates who died when their capsule was hit by a meteorite.

The woman and the chimp have become lovers and for a fifteen-page story there was an astonishing amount of sexual activity. The two of them have invented their own language and have come up with new names for various body parts. A breast is an Albert and the male organ is a fudge.

The story created an uproar. Mercedes found it repulsive. Bryn thought it was juvenile. Brett hated the ham-handedness of the satire and LaTasha admitted she'd been too embarrassed to finish reading the thing. Nick thought it was too derivative of some Eastern European with a lot of consonants in his name I'd never heard of.

Mel sat still as a lizard on a leaf, the only sign of emotion the tinge of red at the top of his ears. It was hard to imagine that he would have been happy about the reactions he was getting, but who could tell? Everything the kid did seemed calculated to hack people off.

I'd had enough of this mess. I leaned forward and clapped my palms flat on the table. "Well, good," I said. "Sounds like you've got them all going today, huh, Mel? Any last thoughts?"

I had hoped to end the discussion, but when I looked up, what did I see but Dominique's hand in the air. If there was one person I didn't want to call on, it was Dominique, but it didn't seem as if I had much choice.

"Yes?" I said.

"I just wanted to say that that was the most misogynistic story I've ever read." Bryn, LaTasha, and Mercedes nodded in agreement. Brett, sitting next to Dominique, eyes closed as if deep in thought, had his arm on the back of her chair and seemed to be caressing her shoulder with his fingertips. "Not only was it blatantly degrading to women, I had no idea what the writer was going for. Was I supposed to be shocked? Was it supposed to be funny? If it was, the jokes were lost on me."

The others may not have gotten to Mel, but Dominique did. The way his nostrils were twitching, he looked like a horse about to kick down its stall. "How about you?" he said. He glanced over at me. "Were the jokes lost on you?"

"Not lost exactly," I said.

He ran a thumbnail across his front teeth. "I appreciate your honesty," he said.

"Don't get me wrong," I said. "I'm not saying—"

"No, no, you don't need to apologize." His bandanna had gone limp under the barrage of criticism. Resting just an inch above his eyebrows, it made him look like Captain Hook on a very bad day. "But I want to be honest too. When I came here, I had the crazy idea that there'd be this community of serious artists. I thought people would be getting after it, you know what I mean? Maybe I was being naïve. But I don't see how what we're doing in here is worth spit. Doing these stupid exercises and bullshitting each other about how great our work is. I'll level with you. I don't think I've learned one thing in here. As far as I'm concerned, we might as well just give Rex Schoeninger his money back. And I'm not afraid to tell him that."

Alarm raced through the room like an invisible mouse. They may all have been artists, but they were not happy about the idea of anyone messing with their money. Jaw set, Mel shoved his bandanna a little higher up on his forehead, ready to go to war.

"Anything else?" I said.

"No."

I surveyed the faces around the table. Red as a beet, Bryn leaned forward on her elbows. LaTasha sucked at the tip of her pen. Nick looked as if he'd just swallowed a lime. Even the easygoing Chester was teed off and ready to come to my defense, a finger in the air.

I may never have run a classroom before, but I knew enough to know that I couldn't let anyone else do my dirty work. This was all on me. The last thing I needed was this jerk going to Rex Schoeninger.

"I suppose we could sit around and discuss this," I said, "but that doesn't seem like a whole lot of fun. I'll tell you what. How about I let you go home a little early today? But, Mel, I'd like you to stick around for a minute, okay?"

If Mel was fazed by this, he didn't show it. I sat stone-faced while the other students packed up their backpacks. As Dominique pushed up from her chair, she slid her copy of Mel's story the length of the table. Mel did not reach out to stop it and it fluttered to the floor.

The students filed past me. Brett even patted me on the shoulder as if I was some grieving widow. When they were gone, I got up and closed the door. I still wasn't sure how I was going to play this. It wasn't as if I could send snot-face home with a note to his parents.

When I turned to face him, he was retrieving Dominique's copy of his manuscript from the floor. "So that was quite a little show you put on," I said.

"I guess it was."

I leaned forward on a chair, giving him the evil eye. The table was so long it made me feel like I was talking to someone at the other end of a bowling alley. "I can't believe you let those guys get under your skin like that. Really, it's a goddamn shame."

"And why is that?"

"Because you're the most talented guy in the class."

For a second I thought the poor guy was going to choke. "You're shitting me."

"No, I'm not. Whatever the gene is that you need to make it in this crazy racket of ours, you've got it, kid. You haven't put it together yet, not by a long shot. That story you turned in was crap. But when we start talking sentences, when we start talking paragraphs, when we start talking the way a mind works, I don't think I've ever seen anything like it."

I did all this with a straight face. Mel ran his thumb over the corner of his mouth, still skeptical. "Then how come—"

"How could I say something like that in front of the others? It would make them feel like throwing in the towel."

Someone had left an empty water bottle on the table. I picked it up and tossed it in the wastebasket, giving Mel a little time to let everything sink in. I almost felt sorry for the kid. He had no chance, not really. If what I was saying was true, this was the greatest day of his life. How was he going to say no to that?

"But what should I do?" he said.

"You can stop acting like an idiot, for one thing. And forget all that stuff about trying to find a community of artists, whatever the hell that is, and forget about whether or not I can teach you anything, because I probably can't. You've got work to do."

I went to the window and opened it a crack. Brett and Dominique walked arm in arm down the sidewalk in front of the institute, Nick bouncing alongside, gesturing wildly.

"Also, while you're at it," I said, "you might want to give this sex-in-space thing a rest."

"But—"

"Do you ever write other kinds of things?"

"I keep a journal. Or I did this summer."

"What kind of journal?"

"I was working on a road crew up in Oregon. I'd get up every morning and write for an hour or so, just to keep my hand in. But, God, I couldn't bring that stuff into class." He gaze wavered. "You wouldn't be willing to take a look at it, would you?"

"I suppose I could do that," I said.

"It's not like it's polished or anything."

"I understand," I said. Sometimes it would be so great to be a real writer. I would love to be able to describe to you the look in that boy's eyes—the hope, the confusion, the fear. You would have thought I'd just offered him an all-expenses-paid trip to Honolulu.

"Can I say something?" he said.

"Sure."

"I think it's great that Schoeninger gives us these big bucks, but, seriously, his books are pretty much crap. You've got it all over him."

"Hey, get out of here," I said. "I've got work to do."

Chapter Ten

Later that afternoon I drove over to Rex's. He'd called to let me know that he was curious about how the students were doing, and I'd promised to bring a few of their pieces by, even though I wasn't sure how great an idea that was.

Traffic was horrible and it must have been six-thirty by the time I got there. A big Suburban and an Ozarka delivery truck were parked out in front of his house, so I had to park a good thirty yards up the street.

I was about to open my door when I saw Dranka in Rex's driveway, getting out of her car. She dropped down, out of sight behind the front of the maroon Civette. After half a minute, she popped up again, looking totally stricken.

Her hands flew to her hair. She pounded the hood with her fist and then, turning away, covered her mouth with her forearm. The woman was beside herself.

Frantic, she scanned the street, but I guess she missed me, tucked behind the Ozarka truck the way I was. I had no idea what was going on. I hated flat tires as much as the next guy, but it wasn't as if they were the end of the world.

I watched as she went into the garage and came back with a slick black trash bag. She surveyed the street a second time before disappearing behind the front fender. I leaned forward on the steering wheel, trying to figure out what she was up to. Long shadows stretched across parched lawns. The neighborhood might as well have been deserted. It was that time in the evening when everyone was eating supper.

She stood up again and lugged the trash bag around the side of the car, heading back to the garage. Whatever was in the bag wasn't big, but it had a little heft to it. Like a cabbage, say.

When Rex came out of the house it stopped her in her tracks. He didn't see her at first. He cupped his hands to his mouth and called, "Mingo! Mingo!" I could hear him even through the closed windows of my car.

When he did turn and see her, it took him by surprise. They talked back and forth for a couple of minutes. She was a sly one, old Dranka, trying to sneak the bag around behind her hip, bit by bit. I had no clue what they were saying, but I was enjoying it. I liked the idea of Dranka squirming. I liked it a lot.

Rex walked out on the lawn and called down the street. "Mingo! Mingo!"

Once his back was turned, Dranka took a couple of steps toward the trash bin in the garage. But his back wasn't turned for long. He spun around and spoke sharply to her.

Maybe he wanted her help. He clearly wanted something, the way he was getting agitated, the way he was pointing at her with a long bony finger.

She held the bag out at her side and gestured as if to say, *Just give me a second*. But then the bag moved. It wasn't much, just a twitch, a quiver, like a fish rippling the surface of a lake. Thirty yards away, I might have thought I'd just imagined it, but Rex saw it too.

He stared at her dumbly for several seconds and then began striding across the lawn. She backed into the garage, putting the bag all the way behind her. But she tripped over a rake and tried to run for it. Rex lunged for the bag and caught Dranka's wrist.

They pulled and jerked, spun around, both of them hollering. She was so much stronger than he was, it looked as if she was about to sling him into the side of the house. It was a terrible thing to see. I should have jumped out and broken the whole thing up, but I couldn't move.

Rex lost his balance finally and fell on his side. Dranka had no choice but to let go of the bag. She put her hands over her face as he opened it. He didn't have it open for long. He turned his head away, like a man about to be sick.

Dranka stood over him, trying to explain, pointing back at the driveway. I got out of my car just as Ramona came out of the house. Rex, propped up on one arm, chest heaving, stared at the grass. Only when Dranka offered him a hand up did he start to yell at her.

"You're fired, do you understand? I never want to see you in this house again!"

She pleaded with him. She pressed her hands together under her chin like a little girl praying. She grabbed his arm. None of it did any good. He just kept shouting as he pushed to his knees and then careened all the way up.

Dranka finally turned and stumbled off to her car. Rex followed her, still yelling things, until Ramona ran across the lawn to grab him. I stood in the middle of the street, amazed. Dranka yanked open the door of the Civette, shouting back at him.

"You'll be sorry for this, Mr. Schoeninger!"

"Get out of here!" he shouted. "You think you scare me? Don't be stupid!"

Red-faced, she glared at him across the roof of her car. "You think I am stupid? I am not as stupid as you think. Dranka knows things about you, you have no idea what I know. You will pay, I promise, you will pay." She ducked into the Civette, backed out of the driveway, and sped off.

Ramona tried to comfort Rex, tried to pull that wispy-haired head to her chest, but Rex was not a big one for hugs. He flailed, fighting his way out of her embrace. He stalked back into the house with Ramona in pursuit.

I made my way onto the lawn. The open end of the bag rustled and blew in a little breeze. I touched the black plastic, but decided not to look inside. I didn't need to look inside. The dark red stains on the driveway were enough.

After a minute, I went to the house and knocked. I ended up knocking quite a few times, and just as I was about to leave, Ramona came to to the door. She looked like hell.

"I'm sorry," she said. "This is not a good time."

"Is Rex okay?"

She closed her eyes for a second as if it pained her to even hear such a stupid question. "Not really. No, he's not okay at all." Rex bellowed from the other side of the house. "I'll be right there!" she shouted back. She touched my arm. "I need to . . ."

"I understand," I said.

It kind of killed me, seeing Rex having to go through something like that. Nothing's harder than losing a pet that you love, and if you're old and alone, it makes it even worse.

Dranka had hated the dog (I hadn't been that fond of it myself), but from what I had seen, it looked like what happened had just been one of those freaky accidents. Not that anyone was ever going to convince Rex of that. It was a mess all the way around.

But what had really gotten my attention was all that stuff Dranka had shouted at him over the roof of her car. Maybe it was nothing. Maybe it was all idle threats. People will say all kinds of crap when they've just been axed. But this was different. This sounded like she really had the goods on the guy.

I got to the Fiction Institute about noon the next day. A safari guide type with a parrot on his shoulder sat in the foyer, waiting for his appointment with Ramona, but everybody else seemed to be at lunch, which made it easy enough to go through Mildred's desk and find the list of Rex's emergency numbers. Just under a long column of cardiologists, lawyers, agents, and repairmen was penciled in *Dranka Zivanovic, cook*, with both phone number and address.

I tried to call, and when I didn't get an answer I drove to South Austin to see if I could find her.

Dranka lived in a small stucco house in a seriously funky neighborhood. Two doors down, a half-naked man balanced on one leg in his backyard, waving his arms, doing his Asian thing, and across the street, a hundred strings of colored bottle caps rotated from the branches of trees.

Dranka had a chain-link fence and a plastic pink flamingo tilted over a cheesy water feature. I let myself in the gate and made my way warily across the dead lawn. When you're dealing with a woman who's just run over a puppy, you can't be too careful.

I knocked several times on the door of the screen porch, but no one showed up. Her car was parked on the street, so I figured she had to be around. I cupped my hands to my eyes and peered through the screen. There were at least a couple lights on.

I eased around the side of the house. Edging between a couple of recycling bins, I glanced through a window and was startled to see Dranka at her kitchen counter, whacking away at a bloody slab of meat with an enormous knife. She must have sensed my presence, because she turned and glowered at me.

I raised a hand in greeting. She flailed the knife in the air, waving me away. I gave her my most winning smile and put both palms up to show her what a mean-no-harm kind of guy I was. I pointed to her, then to myself, made little yak-yak signs with my fingers to let her know I wanted to talk.

She began shouting something I couldn't make out and went storming off toward the rear of the house. I moved quickly, making it to the back steps just as she came stumbling out onto her deck.

"Go on!" she shouted. "Get out of here! I've had it with whole bunch of you!"

"Dranka, I want to tell you how sorry I am about all this . . ."

"Sorry? How could you be sorry? A big man like you . . ." She still had the knife in her hand and her apron was flecked with blood.

"Just listen to me for a second," I said. "I'm here to help."

"Why you want to help? You're all the same, you famous writers. We little ants to you. You like to set match to us, see us fry. I have no job. Sixty years old. What am I going to do?"

"That's one of the things I wanted to talk to you about."

"Everybody think Rex Schoeninger such a great man. That I should be proud to work for national monument. What do they know? He is hard man. Cold as iceberg. He worse than Tito."

"You think I don't know that?" I said. "That guy destroyed my writing career. Oh, we all know how he likes to act like Mr. Good Guy, but he's got a mean streak a mile wide. He said terrible things about me. Why do you think we didn't speak for twenty-five years?"

That stopped her for a moment. The idea that the two of us might somehow be kindred spirits took a while to digest. "He have no right, firing me."

"Hey, you're preaching to the choir, sweetheart," I said.

She tested the edge of her knife with a thumb, then set it down on a window ledge. She pinched a dead leaf off one of the potted plants, and her face softened with regret.

"It was an accident. That little dog, you know how he could be. He pee everywhere, hop on furniture, when I hang up laundry, he tear it off line. When I try to upbraid him, Rex say, do not upbraid him, he is just puppy, so I do what he say, but he like wilderness dog, run inside, outside, under table, nobody can keep track where he is."

"So what happened exactly?"

For a moment I wasn't sure she was going to answer me. "I cook Rex his supper. It was late. I tired, I want to go home, but he want me to run by the pharmacy first. They have little chocolate mints, his all-time favorites. All I want to do is go home, lift my feet up, watch my show, but what can I do?

"I go out and get in the car. Maybe I in a bad mood, maybe I in a hurry, I don't know. All I thinking is, Chocolate mints, chocolate mints. I squeeze the gas. I hear this yelp, then crunch. It sound like you take a bunch of sticks in your hands and break them all at once."

"Oh, Jesus, Dranka."

"I get out of car. Look underneath. At first I don't see anything. I still hoping I run over cardboard box. But then I see him. He look so small, lying there. I didn't know what to do. I knew Rex never believe it accident. My mind go many miles every hour. All I can think, I can't let him know this. I check up and down the street. No one. I think, if I can get rid of the dog, Rex will think it just run away, it will be better for all of us." She grimaced, rubbing the hell out of her elbow. She was coming to the part she wasn't so proud of. "So I got a garbage bag from the garage."

"I know," I said. "I saw."

"You saw?"

"I was sitting across the street. In my car."

Taken aback, she glared at me as if I was some kind of traitor. "So you saw everything, then."

"I saw the bag move."

"It was dead! It was dead! I swear to you! But sometimes, dead things, they twitch. For a long time."

The sun was directly in my eyes. I squinted up at her, grinding my heel into the dead grass. "I'm sure it must have been horrible," I said.

Something strange was happening to her face. Her eyes went wide with what looked like alarm, her lower lip curled down, and she started to grimace. It took me several seconds to realize that she was crying. She wasn't good at it. She turned away from me.

"I'm sorry, Dranka," I said.

She turned back to face me, full of scorn. "Oh, you say that already. Everybody say they sorry. But nobody as sorry as Dranka." She wiped away her tears angrily. "You want a drink?"

"That might be good," I said.

She showed me into the kitchen and got a couple of shot glasses and a bottle of slivovitz out of the cupboard. It looked as if she was in the middle of some serious cooking—pots and skillets everywhere, a hacked-up shoulder of lamb on the counter, ringed by potatoes, garlic cloves, celery, onions, a bunch of herbs and spices.

We sat down at the table and she poured us each a shot of the plum brandy. Leaning across the table, we toasted God knows what.

"So would you like me to speak to him?" I said.

"What for?" she said. "He never going to hire me back. Why would I want to work for him anyway? He's an old man, he starting to lose his mind. All day, all he does is sit in his room and type, type, type. And yell at me. Dranka, get me this, Dranka, get me that. But he will pay for this. He is going to pay."

I sipped at the slivovitz. "I heard you say that. But, really, Dranka, what could you possibly do?" I said.

"I know things about him."

"I know things about him too. What I know is that he is the most boring man in America. I'll bet you ten dollars he's never jaywalked in his life. Rex is one of those guys who put their hand over their heart when they sing the national anthem."

She stared at me for a second, then polished off her drink, got up, and went back to the counter. I watched her cube the shoulder of lamb with a series of expert strokes.

"Here you go, vegetarian boy, chew on this." She snapped off a stalk of celery and tossed it to me. It was crisp and tasteless. "He not the man you think he is."

"Who is?" I said.

I put my celery stalk down on the table and poured myself another brandy. The house was small and dark. A single parakeet rustled in a birdcage in the hallway. The walls were plastered with cornball paintings on glass of peasants strangling geese and dancing around haystacks. Dranka shook a pile of salt, pepper, and paprika onto a large platter.

"He do some bad, bad things," she said.

"And most of them he did to me," I said. "I'm sorry, Dranka, but if this is the best you've got, I wouldn't get my hopes up."

I was pleased to see that she was getting pissed. Rolling the nuggets of lamb in the spices, she looked back at me like I was a naïve little fuck. "You know he was married before?"

"I guess I knew that."

"Four times."

"So? That's not bad, but it's not exactly a record."

She lopped off a hunk of butter, letting it drop into a frying pan, and bent low to adjust the flame. "His second wife, she big drinker. They have terrible trouble, but all the same, they adopt a little boy. Like idiot, they think it will solve everything. But it only make everything worse. When they get divorce, she get baby." She moved the melting butter around in the pan with a wooden spoon. I nursed my drink, brooding.

"This woman, she have no business raising a baby by herself. She go back to judge, make a big scene, crying, carrying on about how she can't do this. So the judge ask Mr. Schoeninger if he can take boy. He say no. He have too many great books to write."

I glanced at her. She had to be making this up. After what he'd done to her, she was willing to say anything. All the same, she had me going. I'm an orphan, and as far as I'm concerned, throwing an orphan out in the street is something you should burn in hell for. She took the platter of lamb and dropped the tiny cubes into the skillet. They made a low hissing sound, like an aroused snake.

"Where is this boy now?"

"Nobody know. A couple of years ago, Rex start to feel bad about this. He hire a detective to find the boy, but so far, nothing."

I picked up the stalk of celery and took another bite. It tasted like wood. "You have any proof of this?"

"Oh, I have proof, all right."

"What kind of proof?"

She looked back over her shoulder at me, her eyes shining like a sly little girl. "I make copies of everything." She sidestepped back to the stove and began to stir the meat.

"Are you going to show me?" I asked.

She corralled a cube of lamb with the spoon and lifted it to her mouth. She blew on it a couple times and took a careful bite. "You want me to show you?"

"Show me? You bet I would."

She wiped her fingers on her soiled apron. "You stay right there."

After she left the room, I sat for a minute, rolling my shot glass back and forth between my palms. The smell of roasting meat slowly filled the room. If what she'd said was true, it would be huge, just what I'd been looking for. But as funny as it sounds, there was a part of me that didn't want it to be true. I sort of liked Rex, and if Dranka was right, there was a side of him that was way uglier and more fucked up than I'd ever bargained for.

I went to the stove and snuck a plump piece of lamb. It was the best thing I'd ever tasted—the snippets of hot fat, the smoky bite of paprika, the juicy, tender meat. It was so good, I had myself a second.

I scanned Dranka's shelves. She must have had a couple dozen cookbooks, everything from *The Joy of Cooking* to Julia Child. Curious, I pulled one down called *The Taste of Serbia* and a photograph fluttered to the floor.

It was a picture of Rex and Dranka in happier times. He sat at a table with his Medal of Freedom draped around his neck. Dranka leaned over him, presenting him with a chocolate birthday cake. Both faces glowed in the light of the flickering candles.

I stuck the photograph back into the book and wedged the book into its rightful place on the shelf. I was considering snitching a third piece of lamb when Dranka came back into the room with an oversized mailing envelope, stuffed to bursting.

"You see for yourself," she said.

I sat down at the table and shook everything out of the envelope. Dranka returned to her cooking.

She had collected a hodgepodge of stuff, some of it dating way back. There were X-rated letters from his former wife, adoption agency documents, foster care reports, a big bundle of correspondence from the detective office, but the real killer was an exchange between Rex and a Connecticut family court judge.

The judge had written to say that Schoeninger's ex had proven, in the eyes of the court, to be unfit to raise the child. She'd been drinking, dropped the kid in a bathtub of scalding hot water, and ended up taking him to an emergency room. The judge's question was, would Rex, as the adoptive father, be willing to come forward and raise the boy.

Dranka hadn't been lying. There it was in black and white: Rex writing back no, he would not. He had been traveling more and more—he was supposed to spend six months in Japan for *Life* magazine, and after that he would be on the road promoting his new novel. In his opinion, it would be best to find the boy a stable home somewhere else.

"I know how hard this must sound," he wrote, "but sometimes it's necessary to be hard. It's not as if I'm condemning the child to the slums of Calcutta. As you know, I grew up an orphan and have done moderately well for myself. Some people have no ear for music. Others have no knack for parenthood. I fear I am one of those. I will confess to you, I shudder at the thought that if I took this boy, it would be just another way for that psychotic woman to keep her hooks in me. It is time to bring this sad experiment to a close."

I put the letter down and pushed it away from me. Dranka moved the meat back to the platter and began to fry the onions and the garlic in the pan. "So what do you think I should do?"

"What are you planning to do with this?" I asked.

"I sell it to Oprah."

"Jesus Christ, Dranka, you can't do that."

"If she not want it, I sell it to Jerry Springer. Let the whole world see what a fake he is."

Dranka moved the meat back to the platter and began to fry the onions and garlic in the pan. If the woman thought she was getting on Oprah, she was loony. They would throw her out in ten seconds. But that didn't matter. What mattered was that in the right hands, the stuff I'd read was pure gold. I needed it all for myself and I couldn't afford to let her muck it up.

"No offense, Dranka, but you may be in over your head here. These people will eat you alive."

"Let them try," she said.

"Have you ever dealt with these media people before?"

"No."

"Are you going to get yourself a lawyer, then?"

A shadow fell across the hawklike face. "I not sure."

"Don't be a fool. You're not going to be able to pull this off by yourself. You walk in and all these people are going to see is a pissed-off ex-employee with a green card and a bunch of crazy allegations. There could be a movie deal in this, a seven-figure book contract, who knows? But you're going to need a pro on your side."

"Somebody like you?"

"It doesn't have to be me," I said. "But right now I'm the only friend you got."

Her eyes narrowed. "So you looking for a cut of this?"

"Good Lord, you think I'm doing this for the money?"

"Why else you do it? You think Dranka an idiot?"

I sighed and locked my fingers behind my head. I didn't really want to do it, but it looked as if I didn't have any choice but to trot out the heavy artillery. "Okay, I'll level with you," I said. "Yesterday after you drove off, I went up to the house. I was hoping to talk some sense into the old guy, how as far as I could see the whole thing had been nothing but an unfortunate accident. But he was so hot he wouldn't listen to anybody. He was talking about going to the cops."

Her eyebrows arched like caterpillars. "The cops? Why would he go to the cops?"

"Dranka, I'm sorry. Maybe I should have never brought this up."

"He's going to have me arrested because I ran over his dog?"

"It's not just that. He claims you've been taking things."

The wooden spoon went still above the black skillet. I watched the color creep up her neck. "What kind of things?" she said.

"Oh, different stuff," I said. "Money. He claims he actually saw you going into his wallet when you thought he was taking a nap. Food. Stuff out of the freezer."

Furious now, she pointed the spoon at my chest. "Food? He's complaining about food? If I no take it, it rots!"

"Right. But there was some other stuff too. More expensive stuff."

I had the woman back on her heels. She turned to rinse her hands in the sink, to hide her face from me. It might seem as if I was a genius, but, honestly, it's not that hard. What five-hundred-dollar-a-week cook isn't going to be stealing from her eighty-five-year-old employer?

"I think he said something about some of the gifts from his trips . . ."

Even though she was turned away from me, I could see her flinch as if someone had poked her in the ribs with a stick. She wheeled around, her face pale.

"You mean those Japanese boxes?"

"I think, yeah, I think that's what he said."

"I never touch those things! I promise you. He loses things all the time. He accuses me of stealing his socks."

"I'm not saying that any of this is true, but I just thought I should warn you. And in case they get a search warrant, I don't think you want any of this stuff lying around the house." I patted the stack of letters and documents.

"So what am I going to do?"

"First of all, I think we need to have another drink," I said.

We sat and drank for a couple of hours. I'd put the fear of God in her. For the moment at least, any thoughts of selling Rex's story to Oprah was out the window. All she was worried about now was how to keep from being thrown out of the country.

She was furious that Rex had been spying on her. "What is this, Russia? Who could live like this, with him watching like an old buzzard from a tree? So maybe I take a twenty-dollar bill out of his wallet once in a while. I supposed to go to prison for that? This is a man who throw a baby to the dogs. Nobody ever do anything to him for that."

From time to time she got up to finish her cooking, transferring everything to a casserole dish, adding potatoes, sliced peppers, and tomatoes, and finally sticking it all in the oven. She was kind of a nice woman, once you got to know her. A little crooked, but so was I. I may have mentioned how hatchet-faced she was, but I could see where she could have almost been pretty when she was young.

It wasn't long before she was pleading with me to take the packet of letters off her hands. She matched me shot for shot, getting more and more worked up. At her age, how was she ever going to get a job after this?

By the time we finished the bottle of plum brandy, she was resting her head in the crook of her arm. "This is the end. There is no hope. What can I do? I have no one to help me."

I patted her hand. "I will help you, Dranka."

"You? You're just a writer, how can you help?"

"I don't know yet," I said. "But we'll come up with something."

I walked her to her room, laid her down on the bed, and closed the door softly as I left. I straightened all the papers on the kitchen table and jammed them back in the mailing envelope. As I was about to leave, I caught the smell of something burning. I turned. The stove light was still on. I got a couple of hot pads and opened the oven door, wincing at the blast of heat.

I was not exactly steady on my feet, but I managed to set the casserole on the counter and take off the glass top. Aromas rose, peppery and succulent. There was some crispiness around the edges, but except for that, it was perfect. Tomatoes still bubbled away. I turned off the stove and tugged a dangly piece of lamb out of the stew. I juggled it from hand to hand for several seconds to let it cool.

I turned my head sideways, took a couple of quick nips, then tore the meat in two with my teeth. The room still swayed like a ship in a storm. I wiped my hands on a towel so I wouldn't get the envelope greasy, picked up the packet of letters and documents, and let myself out the back door.

When I got home, I fixed myself a strong pot of coffee and sat down with my packet of info. There was a bunch of letters, held together by rubber bands and paper clips, between Rex and the detective agency, that I hadn't had time to go over at Dranka's.

It sounded as if everybody was getting pissed at everybody. Rex was making noises about firing the whole lot of them. He'd paid them lavishly for two years and he wanted results. The head of the agency shot back that they were doing the best they could. They had assigned their finest investigators to the case, but they had warned Rex in the beginning that this would not be an easy one to crack. The trail was several decades old, records were destroyed or lost, and many of the people they would have wanted to interview were dead.

Our investigator tells me that the last time the two of you spoke, you mentioned that you once visited the boy in one of his foster homes. That is a piece of information that never came up in any of our previous conversations, and seems so unlikely I assume he's gotten it wrong.

Is it true? And if it is true, would you please give us all the details of that visit? Where it took place and when? Just put down everything you remember, whether it feels relevant or not.

I don't mean to chide you, Mr. Schoeninger, but this is just the sort of thing we should have known from the get-go. We pride ourselves here at the agency on leaving no stone unturned, but we will not be able to succeed without your fullest cooperation.

The letter Rex sent back was three pages long, single-spaced, and huffy.

I must say I don't think there's any reason for anyone to get his nose out of joint. It is true, I did see the boy at one of his foster homes. His first one, in fact, after the judge had removed him from the care of my ex-wife.

The judge and I had come to the painful decision that the child should be once again placed for adoption. I asked if I could see him one last time. It was highly irregular, of course, but things were different in those days, and the judge was able to arrange it.

I imagine that this would be the first week in March, 1953. Daniel was staying in a home on the outskirts of Bridgeport. Unfortunately, I can't remember the woman's name, but it was something Irish. McManus. McMurphy. I believe it was Locust Street. A two-story clapboard house. The woman was one of those anxious types, with big bunny slippers. She had two kids of her own and three foster kids. Plus cats. Place stank of kitty litter. Lots of trikes and dead plants in the yard.

The boy was taking a nap, but the woman said I could go in and see him. There were a couple of bunkbeds and the kid was asleep in one of the bottom ones. I took a little chair and sat next to him. Clothes were scattered on the floor everywhere. Tucked under his arm was this carved wooden buffalo with a broken horn that I'd brought back from my trip to Wyoming. It seemed like a miracle that he still had it, after all the bouncing around he'd been doing.

So much of what I remembered was him crying, so it was quite something to see him sleeping peacefully like that. His neck and arms were still red from where he'd been burned. He'd grown a lot in a year. Lost almost all of his baby fat.

I finally touched his face. I don't know that he even woke all the way up, but he opened his eyes and smiled. "Daddy," he said, "Daddy." I held my hand out to him and he took my thumb. It was something he'd always done when I was putting him to bed. He'd grab my thumb and hold on so I couldn't sneak away. We were like that for a couple of minutes, him looking at me, me looking at him, and then he went back to sleep. After a little while I could feel his grip relaxing and then his hand just fell away. I got up and tiptoed out of the room. Shut the door without making a sound.

The woman was feeding her cats. We may have talked for ten minutes. She knew of my books. She weaseled fifty dollars out of me to get a nice little sailor suit for the kid. She wanted me to know what an exceptional boy he was, so intelligent, you could see it in his eyes. She kept telling me how I didn't need to worry, she treated her foster kids just like her own. She may not have a lot of money, she said, but she knew how to create a happy home.

I remember going out to my car, walking across the yard. It was March and it was miserable. I got all this crap on my shoes. I found a stick and must have sat in my car for five minutes, scraping the mud off.

Other details? She had a heavy Boston accent. Her husband worked for the railroad. I defy you to tell me what use any of this could be to anyone, but there it is.

I got up to wander the house. I was going nuts. Did Rex still think he was going to find a kid after forty years? This was total fairy-tale stuff.

It took a while for it all to sink in, just how outrageous it was. On the one hand, it was just what I'd been looking for. This was good enough to ruin anybody.

At the same time, it struck a little too close to home. How could an orphan turn away an orphan? How could *anyone* turn away an orphan? You adopt a kid, he's adopted. You don't get to take him back to the grocery like he's a rotten chicken.

Crazy shit was going through my head; maybe it was just that combination of slivovitz and strong coffee. What if I was Schoeninger's adopted son and all the money was legitimately mine and I didn't even have to con him out of it? Wouldn't that have been a kicker? Could I possibly have been adopted and given back? I'd bounced in and out of so many foster homes, everything ran together.

Most of the places had been real dumps—the basement apartment where I'd lived with the Cuban building superintendent and his wife, the second-floor walk-up on Delancy Street with the fat woman who sat watching soap operas all day long with a switch in her lap that she would use on any of us kids who got too close, the place in Brooklyn where wild dogs ran up and down the hallway and the water in the kitchen sink would never turned off, just gushed, hour after hour.

There was no way I was Schoeninger's kid, but if I had been, think about how differently everything would have turned out. I would have spent a lot of time with babysitters when he was off researching his books, but when I got older, he most likely would have taken me along sometimes, and I would have met warlords and Catholic cardinals and learned how to shoot elephants. Knowing him, he probably would have been strict. I doubt that he would have given me much of an allowance, but all the same, I would have known all that money was there, waiting. I would have been a popular kid, but I would have never been quite sure whether people liked me for myself or because I had such a famous father. I would have turned out to have been a good citizen, the sort of rich guy people are always trying to get to serve on muckety-muck boards, instead of this selfish little menace to society.

As I was pouring the last of the coffee down the drain, there was a knock at the door. I froze. Could it be Dranka? Her stuff was everywhere, laid out on the table in the living room, on the chairs, strewn on the floor.

The second knock was louder than the first. I set the coffeepot down noiselessly in the sink, praying it was just a magazine salesman, some poor schmuck working his way through college, and not a vengeful Yugoslavian cook armed with a kitchen knife. I still didn't know what I wanted to do with her junk, but I knew I could come up with something a lot better than selling it to Oprah.

I stood there for another minute before I heard a dull thump at the door and the sound of retreating footsteps. I gave it a little more time, just to be sure, then went to the curtains in the hall and peered out. The sidewalk was empty, and in the street no one but a five-year-old wobbling to and fro on his bike, his father trotting along behind, shouting instructions.

I opened the front door. On the stoop was another large manila envelope. Jesus Christ, I thought, the last thing I need right now is more information. But when I opened it and pulled out the sheaf of papers, I saw it was just muddy xeroxes of Mel's summer journal.

I can't tell you how relieved I felt! I stuffed everything back in the envelope and gave it a heave-ho onto the sofa. One of the great things about student work, you can always put it off until later.

Chapter Eleven

I'd never dug a grave before. It's more work than you think. Rex had picked out the spot, under the magnolia tree in the far corner of the backyard. It took Ramona and me a good half hour, taking turns with a shovel and a pickax.

It hadn't rained for a couple of months and the ground was hard, but what made it really tough was the limestone that seemed to be everywhere, just a few inches below the surface.

We hacked and chipped away, digging down a couple of feet, but the question was, how deep was deep enough? The last thing you wanted was some raccoon coming along and clawing everything up.

Rex, a St. Louis Cardinals cap shading his eyes, stood watching as I got down on my knees to pull out some of the snaky tree roots. I yanked and tugged, the roots making little popping sounds as they gave. As dry as it was, once you got down far enough, the earth still had that musky rotten-leaf smell to it. I tossed three or four broken limestone slabs onto the lawn and sat back on my haunches to rest.

"How does that look?" I said.

"That should be fine," Rex said.

I pushed to my feet, wet shirt clinging to my back. Rex nodded to Ramona, who put down the pickax, crossed the yard, head bowed, and ducked into the half basement under the house.

I patted Rex on the elbow. "You doing all right?" I said.

"I'm doing okay."

On the far side of the fence a mockingbird, wings flailing, attacked the side mirror of the neighbor's car. I pinched the corners of my eyes. I was tired, and not exactly in a sweetheart of a mood. I'd been awake half the night, thinking about how Rex had shafted that poor kid. And now we were supposed to feel sorry for him because his dog died, a nasty little mutt that was nothing but trouble? Give me a break.

As Ramona emerged from the basement, Rex raised a hand to his mouth and then let it drop. She had Mingo in her arms, wrapped in a white towel. It was not the moment to ask, but it made me wonder if they'd been keeping him in the freezer. She moved slowly across the lawn, like a bride coming down the aisle. I leaned over to roll the wheelbarrow out of the way.

She stopped in front of Rex and pulled back the towel so he could have a look. Out of the corner of my eye, I caught a glimpse of Rex running a hand over the dog's curly coat, scratching him gently behind the ears.

The body was still stiff with rigor mortis, legs sticking out like the legs of a Thanksgiving turkey. I don't know if it was Ramona or not, but someone had cleaned him up pretty good. The head was turned away from me, so I really couldn't see, but it didn't look mashed, so much as weirdly twisted, jaws frozen open, teeth bared.

Ramona turned to me so I could make my farewells, but I shook my head no. She knelt down and laid the scrawny little body in the bottom of the hole.

She struggled to her feet and brushed off her hands. We just stood there. It must have been for two minutes. Over in the next yard, the mockingbird rat-tat-tatted at the mirror, crapping all over the side of the car. It would have been nice to have had a little prayer, or a song to sing, or even, God help me, a poem. Anything would have been better than just standing there, staring down at that crumpled mess laid out on a white bath towel.

Ramona finally bent to retrieve the shovel. She handed it to Rex. He stabbed it several times into one of the piles of dirt until he had a goodly amount, then hefted it, let the loose soil trickle down into the shallow grave.

Ramona reached out to take the shovel from him, but he wasn't done. He raked together a second spadeful and a third, and rained them down on the body of his dead pet.

He was not a great shoveler. He was old and not strong. He spilled about half of every load before he got it to the grave, and sometimes, swinging the curved blade into the dirt piles, he would miss altogether and nearly fall. His St. Louis Cardinals cap was all cockeyed. I was starting to worry about him pitching into the hole, but he finally flipped the shovel away. As he turned to stride back to the house, I could see tears glistening on his cheeks.

Ramona went after him and caught him by the wrist. She put her arm around him, comforting him as they made their way across the deck and into the back hallway.

I rubbed at my face, trying to figure out what to do. Part of me would have been perfectly happy to walk away and leave it all, but that didn't seem right.

I picked up the shovel and got to work. There's something spooky about burying things, something that makes you feel bad, but I kept lobbing dirt in there and slowly the dog began to disappear. From time to time I'd stop to nurse the twinge in my back. I was not a man used to physical labor.

It had been a hell of a thing, seeing Rex turn on the old water-works. But knowing him, I'll bet he wasn't even crying for the dog. He probably was just crying for himself. He had to know it wasn't long before he was going to be down in a hole like that.

The mockingbird had given up attacking the mirror and was flit-ting from tree to tree. I heaved a heaping spadeful onto Mingo's head, finally obliterating it. Only a paw remained visible. Rex was going to be awfully lonely without that dog. One thing you had to say about Mingo, he never wanted anything from Rex except an occasional scratch on the belly.

I got the wheelbarrow, filled it with the rest of the dirt, and pushed it to the edge of the grave. When I tipped it up, the dirt slid out in one raspy rush. I tamped the soil down with the flat of the shovel and then stomped around a bit, sealing everything tight.

A cat crept across the backyard. When I turned, it stopped to stare at me with huge yellow eyes. All I could think was, if Mingo was alive, he would have had that cat up a tree before you could say spit.

When I got home there was a message from Dranka on my answer-ing machine. "Please call me. I need to get my letters back. I speak to my friend this morning and she give me name of lawyer. I will be here all day."

I set the phone back on the receiver. This did not sound good. My hope had been that I would have been able to put her off for a few days until I came up with a plan, but it looked as if I could bid sayonara to that idea.

I called her right back. I tried to strike an amiable tone, joke around a little, but she was in no mood for small talk. Now that she was sober and had a good night's sleep under her belt, she was loaded for bear. She was over being afraid. If Rex wanted to have her arrested, let him try. He had nothing on her compared to what she had on him. It was time for the world to see just what sort of man he really was.

"I think we need to talk," I said.

"Okay," she said.

"You say where."

There was a Japanese garden where she went sometimes. It was in the big park not far from her house and almost no one was ever there. I said it sounded fine with me.

First thing I did was drive by Kinko's and make copies of everything in Dranka's packet (you never know when these things are going to come in useful), and tossed the duplicates in the trunk of my car. I was fifteen minutes late getting to the Japanese garden and she was stationed outside the ticket office, looking like somebody in those Marine Corps recruiting posters.

It was the first time I'd seen her without her apron on. She was wearing baggy sweatpants, black running shoes, and a T-shirt with a wolf howling at the moon and mountains in the background, the kind of thing you'd buy at a national park souvenir shop when you didn't have a lot of money to spend. Her gray hair was combed out, almost to her shoulders, and I could see the serious muscles in her arms.

Right off she wanted to know if I'd brought her stuff. I said I had. I got it for her and she locked it in her car before we went for a walk down in the garden.

It was nice. There were lots of twisty paths, stone shrines, pools with giant orange fish, little trees pruned like poodles. It seemed a little hoity-toity for someone like Dranka, but women will surprise you.

I let her vent for a while. She told me more terrible stuff about the way Rex treated her, how he'd go over the receipts every time she came back from the grocery store, how he'd fire her one day and hire her back the next.

"You know his problem? Is like that movie *Wizard of Oz*. He is like Tin Man. He has no heart." On the hillside, a portly gardener pulled weeds, staring at us as if we were a pair of adulterers. "All this giving money to people, it nothing but big act. I with him all day. I see how strange he is. People come to the house for dinner, after a while he get bored, leave the table, go into other room. When I go to check, I see him, bending over his globe, spinning it around, looking for his little islands. He is, what do you call it? A frozen fish."

I decided not to mention that I'd just come from burying Mingo. We ducked our heads, making our way through a short rock tunnel. A bamboo teahouse perched on the cliff above us.

"So this friend of yours who told you about the lawyer, who is she?"

"She Albanian woman. She work at IHOP."

"Uh-huh. And the lawyer? Did you call him?"

"I have appointment with him tomorrow."

"So how much do you know about him?"

"He help my friend with her landlord."

"Jesus, Dranka." Traffic hummed in the distance. I'd picked up a pebble in my shoe and was starting to limp. "Now listen, I've been thinking a lot about this. Of course you can pay your guy five hundred dollars an hour if you want, but I've got another idea."

"What idea is that?"

"I'm going over to Rex's this afternoon. What I'm hoping is that he's come to his senses, that he's going to drop the whole business about the cops. But if he hasn't, I'm going to tell him I'm leaving."

Dranka stared at me as I sat down on a bench, took off my shoe, and shook it. A white pebble no bigger than a snowflake fell into my hand. "You would do this for me?" she said.

"I wouldn't be doing this just for you. I'm sure it was rough on the old guy, losing his dog like that, but the way he's behaving, it's disgusting. I can't be around a man like that."

I retied my shoe, stood, and bounced up and down a couple of times. "And what do you think he'll do?" she said.

"I don't think there's any question what he'll do. He can't afford to lose me. I don't think there will be any more talk about the cops."

We walked down the gravel path. She was silent, mulling it all over. I took her elbow as we crossed a humpbacked bridge. Below us, huge fish drifted to the surface and sank into the darkness like orange submarines.

"What about about my job?"

"Forget about the job," I said.

"Forget about the job? I can't forget about the job. What am I supposed to do? I am old woman. All I know is cooking. Nobody want me here. They have all these pretty Mexican girls. They work for shit."

"I think you need to work for me."

"For you?"

High up, a jet left a stuttery trail of white as it sped across the sky. "I'm only going to be here for another month. Then I go back to Maine. You ever been there?"

"No."

"Talk about quiet. I've got this place on an island. In the winter, there's snow up to your waist. Deer and moose coming out of the woods. It's so still sometimes all you can hear is the chickadees flitting around the bird feeder. There's just nobody up there. And in the summer, it's so beautiful. The crashing waves, the gulls screaming, the lobster boats putting around in the bay." For a guy who'd never been to Maine, I was making it sound pretty good. "You ever wake up in the morning and see the sun rising over the ocean?"

"No."

"Something like that, it can change your life. And there are blueberries everywhere. Big suckers. Have you ever made blueberry cobbler?"

"Of course." She sounded offended.

"Of course! What am I thinking? Listen. I'm not the neatest guy in the world. Not to mention, a lousy cook. And there's no way you're going to find anybody any good up there. God knows, I've tried. The way I see it, I've got a problem. So how much was Rex paying you?"

"Five hundred dollars a week."

"How about if I paid you a thousand? Plus a nice little cabin in the back where you can stay for free."

She shot me one of her raptor looks. "Is this some kind of trick?"

"Why would I want to trick you?"

"I don't know. Maybe you just try to save him. Maybe you grateful he bring you down here, treat you like a big shot."

"Hey, people have treated me like a big shot before, and I ran like hell. It's simple. You need a job. I need help. You can say yes, you can say no. But if you say yes, I don't want to hear any more of this Rex stuff. None of that cheese-ball lawyer stuff either. I just want to go back up to Maine and lead a quiet life. How does that sound to you?"

A boy in a red cap teetered on stepping-stones, making his way across one of the pools while his father watched. "I think about it."

"Good."

We schlepped up the long hill to the cars, neither of us saying another word. I could see her turning it all over in her mind. She was not a woman to be trifled with, but I had her going, I could feel it. I hate to take advantage of immigrants, but I confess it gave me some pleasure, imagining her showing up at Mohle's front door in the middle of winter, the astonished looks on both their faces when they saw one another.

Was it cruel of me, getting her hopes up like that? Everybody needs a dream, right? And how many of them last? I say, let people enjoy them while they can.

I saw her to her car. Juvenile offenders careened around the parking lot, hefting fifty-pound bags of mulch. She seemed a little shy around me all of a sudden and I didn't quite get it. It wasn't as if I'd asked her to marry me.

When she opened her door, I saw the mailing envelope jammed between the two front seats. It was all I could do to keep from reaching out and snatching it.

"So we'll talk?" I said.

"We don't need to talk," she said.

"No?"

"I do this. I cook for you."

I would have hugged her, but she didn't seem like the sort of woman you hugged without written permission. "Oh, my God, Dranka, that's so great."

She hitched up her sweatpants. "I will need a month vacation."

"You got it."

"And no pets."

"No pets. Do you ski?"

"When I was a child. In mountains of Yugoslavia. Every day in winter." For one terrible moment, I had a vision of what her relatives from the village might do if they ever caught up with me.

"When we get up to Maine, we're definitely going to have to get you some skis. January, February, it's the only way to get around."

Chapter Twelve

Late the next afternoon, I was wheeling my trash basket out to the street when a beat-up Toyota pulled to the curb. Hands waved wildly through the windshield.

Bryn and Dominique were out of the car in a flash and leapt across the lawn like gazelles. What a pair of knockouts! Dominique was in a shimmery satin blouse, black jacket, and slacks, Bryn in a pink knitted deal that made her look like Joni Mitchell doing "Both Sides Now." This was definitely not the way they dressed for class.

"Oh, Mr. Mohle," Bryn said, "we're so glad we caught you. We were afraid you might have already left."

I pulled the trash container hard against the curb. "So what's happening?" I said.

They exchanged sly looks. "What's happening?" Dominique said. "Oh, we can't tell you that. Not yet."

"It's a big surprise," Bryn said. "But you'll be happy. We promise."

I gave her a dubious look. When people say things like that to me, it's been my experience that it never works out well. They weren't kidnapping me exactly, but Dominique snuggled up to one arm while Bryn slid around behind me, cutting off any chance of escape.

"Great," I said, "sounds great. Well, I should probably let you girls go."

"No," Dominique said. "You have to go with us."

"Go with you? Now, wait a minute."

"You have to, Mr. Mohle," Bryn said. "You have to."

They didn't seem to be drunk. I had every right to be pissed at them. Supposedly the first thing everyone had drilled into them when they arrived was respect for my privacy.

"Listen, I hate to disappoint you," I said.

"You'll regret it if you say no," Dominique said.

"And where is this you're thinking of taking me?"

"We can't tell," Bryn said. "That would ruin everything."

"I'm sorry," Dominique said. "Maybe we were interrupting your work."

I gave her a hard look. Was she being snide with me? If I hadn't written for nearly thirty years, why would I be writing tonight?

"We'll never ask anything of you again," Bryn said. "Truly."

Across the street, a couple of kids sailed down a driveway on their scooters. I sighed. Beautiful young women in high spirits. Who adored me. It's a hard combination to resist. And what was I putting up such a fuss for? My other option was another long night watching John Wayne reruns.

"So how long will this take?" I asked.

"No longer than you want it to," Dominique said.

"Okay, fine," I said. "Just let me get my jacket."

I sat scrunched in the back of the car with a set of jumper cables, a copy of *The Man Without Qualities*, and a couple of bottles of wine wrapped in fancy paper. I was not totally at ease about what we were doing, but the two of them in the front seat were so full of chatter and good cheer, it seemed rude to ask more questions.

We drove over to the East Side and wound through a neighborhood of big trees and tiny vegetable gardens before finally easing up in front of a small yellow house with a tire swing in the side yard.

I leaned forward to peer out the window. "This is it?" I asked. Several cars lined the street and a motorcycle that looked an awful lot like Mel's was chained to a telephone pole.

"This is it," Bryn said.

"You want me to bring the wine?" I said.

"Definitely."

As we made our way up the broken walk, each of them took a firm grip of one of my arms to keep me from bolting. The voices inside the house were loud and beery. When we got to the porch, Bryn bounded up the steps and threw open the door. "We got him!" she shouted.

A cheer went up. Beaming like Vanna White, Dominique led me into the house. All my students rose to their feet, applauding.

I rubbed my forehead with a trembling hand. Whatever the occasion, I didn't see how it could be a good thing. Had I just won another award? Please, God, I prayed, don't let it be the Nobel Prize. Rex was pissed off enough the way it was.

"Well, what the hell is this?" I said.

All eyes went to LaTasha, who stood at the drink table, struggling to open a bottle of wine. "Come on, Tash, tell him!" Chester said.

Mercedes took the bottle of wine out of her hands. "Go on, Tash," Mercedes said. "You need to tell him."

Chester grabbed her by the wrist and pulled her into the center of the circle. She pushed his hand away and raised her eyes to meet mine. I was struck by how tiny she was, not much bigger than those kid gymnasts. She was dressed up too, in a wispy green Tinker Bell outfit and black ballet slippers.

Her voice was so soft I could barely hear her. "I sold my book," she said.

"Sold your book?" I said. "That's fantastic."

Nick leaned against the fireplace, heavy-lidded, a blissful smile on his face. He looked stoned out of his mind. "Tell him the rest," he said.

LaTasha put both hands up, shaking her head. "No, no, the rest of it doesn't matter."

"She sold it for seven hundred thousand dollars!" Brett shouted from the kitchen.

"Holy shit!" I said. I glanced from one face to the next to be sure this wasn't some kind of joke. It didn't look as if it was. Chester gave Nick a high five. Mercedes put a hand to her mouth, tearing up.

"And how did this happen?" I asked.

"I owe it all to you."

"To me?"

Their eyes followed my every move. It was as if they were the White House staff greeting the president after his return from a diplomatic mission.

LaTasha scratched her elbow, shy as a schoolgirl. "Remember in class, the day you told me I needed to change the tractor driver from a man to a woman?"

"Yeah."

"I thought you were crazy. I thought it was the worst idea I'd ever heard." Someone snickered. "Who had ever heard of a woman tractor driver in Mississippi? And even worse, I knew that if I followed your advice, I'd have to change everything."

She fingered a vase of roses on the hall table. It looked as if everyone had brought her flowers. She gave me a sidelong look.

"If it had been anybody besides V. S. Mohle, I would have just blown the whole thing off. But after a week of just being mad, I sat down and started to fiddle. The next day, I fiddled some more.

Things caught fire. It wasn't long before I was working eight, ten hours a day."

Bryn draped an arm over Mercedes's shoulders. Chester sucked soulfully on a beer bottle. They were all hanging on her every word. If they'd heard the story before, they were hungry to hear it again.

"I finally showed it to Rex and he loved it." Her voice became even softer and I had to lean in. "He sent it to his agent, who sold it in three days."

"Wow," I said.

"And what else?" Mercedes said.

For the first time LaTasha broke into a sly smile. "The agent says they're about to get a movie deal too. Halle Berry is interested in playing the lead."

In the kitchen Mel was doing serious damage to the chips and hot sauce. "Rex knows about this?" I asked.

"He does. He said he couldn't be happier."

I surveyed the circle of students. They were all happy for her too, but some of them seemed a little rattled, as if they weren't sure what to make of this.

"Come here," I said.

"Me?" LaTasha said.

"Yeah, you," I said.

I gave her a big hug, half strangling her in the crook of my arm. "I think we all need a drink," I said.

Before you knew it someone had shoved a plastic cup in my hand and someone else was pouring cheap champagne into it. We toasted LaTasha and we toasted me. We toasted Rex and the writing life and God knows what else.

I must have stayed three or four hours. After dead dogs and blackmailing cooks, I needed something to raise my spirits. People had brought food. There were cookies, a chocolate cake, a big salad, a bucket of Popeyes, a couple of pans of lasagna heating in the oven.

It was like we were all back in the Summer of Love. Once they got enough cheap champagne in them, all traces of jealousy disappeared. Some were tender, others so wound up with the news they couldn't stop talking. Nick's dreamy smile never left him and every so often Mel would rear back and howl like a wolf. It was all for one and one for all. If it could happen to LaTasha, it could happen to them.

Even more crucial, I was now an official genius. I sat in a big chair in the kitchen, eating spinach lasagna, twirling long strings of hot cheese on my fork. One by one all the students came by to congratulate me. I could see a new shine of respect in their eyes. I was smart enough to know that some of them had been beginning to have their doubts, but that was all behind us now.

Everyone slapped me on the back and someone even kissed me on the cheek. They were waiting on me, bringing me cake, refilling my champagne glass. Can you blame them? Who's going to pass up a chance to touch the mantle of the king?

Later on in the evening I found myself out in the backyard, sitting at a picnic table, taking a breather. It's funny how, with all that happiness around me, I could find myself starting to feel old and sad. Part of it was the alcohol, part of it was that I couldn't hear that well with all the noise around me. But more than anything, I knew I couldn't match their energy. For them, the night was young. For me, all I was thinking about was a nice soft pillow.

I'd been busting my brain for three days, trying to figure out how to use Rex's secret. It wasn't as easy as it looked. If I'd been out to blackmail the guy, it would have been a cinch, but I couldn't do that. If I hadn't already been passing myself off as V. S. Mohle, I might have taken a shot at announcing myself as the long-lost son, but that was obviously out of the question. I loved the idea of doing something with the carved wooden buffalo with the broken horn, but what? The trick of it was, I had to use Rex's secret without letting him know I knew it. I needed to just brush his cheek with it, not clobber him over the head.

I went through the packet of documents at least four times. What had gone on between Rex and his wife had been brutal. In a letter to his lawyer, Rex described walking in, finding his wife with another man, and pulling him off her. In a letter to her lawyer, she described him as a cold-hearted bastard, a phony, a snob, less than a real man, accused him of making her feel worthless from day one of their marriage, of having no interest in anything except advancing his own career. In an affidavit for the court he testified to coming home, finding her passed out on the floor, the baby wailing in its playpen.

It was hard to believe that this was the same guy who'd entertained us endlessly in the van with stories of outfoxing Afghan warlords and driving dogsleds across the Yukon. This was as down and dirty as it got. As long as there was a child, she had him by the short hairs. In the end he did what he had to do to be the man he wanted to be. He cut them both loose.

Rex was not a man you messed with. He'd obliterated Mohle, and he'd obliterated his ex-wife and kid. He was master of wiping the slate clean, but sometimes it didn't wipe clean enough. Forty years later, he was still suffering. My job was to find a cure and, I promise you, it was not going to come cheap.

When I went back inside, they were singing "Wichita Lineman" and I joined in, swaying back and forth, our arms around one another's shoulders.

As I was pouring myself one last glass of champagne, Mel came up and asked if I'd had a chance to look at his journal yet. I said that I hadn't, but that I hoped to get to it soon. His bandanna was at such an alarming angle it made me think he'd either been partying way too hard or had suffered a serious head injury.

"This is all pretty great, huh?" I said.

"I guess," he said. "I have to admit, it sounded kind of loony to me too, the idea of turning a tractor driver into a woman. So how did you know it was going to work?"

"You never do know," I said. "The thing is, you've got to keep wrestling with the stuff until you get a real headlock on it. Throw it up against the wall and see who salutes it." In the living room, Chester snapped pictures of LaTasha and Bryn, the two of them clowning for the camera in Panama hats and flashing peace signs.

"You ever get the feeling, Mel, that you're really close to something great, but you can't seem to take that last step?"

"Oh, yeah," he said.

"Well, that's when you've got to hang in there. No matter how frustrated or pissed off you are. It's like opening a safe. You've just got to keep spinning that dial until you hit the right combination."

"Huh," he said. He couldn't tell if I was being profound or if I was just drunk. I clapped him on the shoulder.

"But you already know this, don't you, Mel? If you'll excuse me, I should probably go see if I can find someone to give the old man a ride home."

The next morning I turned my house upside down looking for the copy of Mel's journal, and finally found the manila envelope under some old newspapers. I poured myself a strong coffee and settled down at the kitchen table with the stack of xeroxes. I didn't expect it to be a lot of fun, but I figured the sooner I got the pushy little bastard off my back, the better.

It turned out I was in for a big surprise. In a way it was a mess—muddy pages with doodles and song lyrics and coffee-mug rings, but once you got past all that, it was pretty good reading. It was the story of these homeless kids Mel had ended up smoking dope with over the summer. A gang of them lived under a bridge in southern Oregon, about a mile from where Mel had been working. The girls brought in a little money by selling themselves to the truckers who came rolling through on the highway. The guys spent most of their time panhandling at the 7-Eleven and stripping copper tubing out of abandoned buildings.

Mel would drop by a couple of times a week to cop a joint and take his turn on the guitar. He had detailed notes on all of them—the runaway from Oklahoma called Muskrat, who had silver studs in both eyelids, prayed to Jesus every night, and couldn't go to sleep without her teddy bear; the grimy leader of the pack named Brother Wilson, who claimed he was receiving messages from Mars. Mel must have had a knack, because they pretty much told him everything—about the crack-addict mother who had stuck Muskrat's head in the oven, turned on the gas, and nearly killed her, about the alcoholic father who stormed out one Christmas Eve and was found dead in a snow-drift the next morning by a road crew, about Brother Wilson's uncle, a one-legged race-car driver, who locked Brother Wilson in the cellar when he wet his bed.

I couldn't quite figure out just how much Mel was buying into all their bullshit. At times it seemed like he was hip to it, at other times it seemed like he was swallowing it hook, line, and sinker. They were constantly hitting him up for money and, at the end of the summer, Brother Wilson stole the keys to Mel's truck, drove it into a ditch, and cracked the differential.

Here it was, the final piece of the puzzle. If I couldn't do some-thing with what Mel had just given me, I was a disgrace to my profes-sion. I spent the rest of the morning and half the afternoon pacing the floor, scrawling notes, weaving everything together. As they say in *The Wings of Prometheus*, to be a writer, you've got to be a magpie, steal a little from here, borrow a little from there, and that's what I did. If I handled this right, I was going to break Rex's heart and pick his pocket at the same time.

Chapter Thirteen

The week of my reading had arrived. With all that was going on, it had slipped up on me, but when I poked my head in Wayne's office on Monday morning, I was still cool and relaxed, figuring I didn't have much to worry about. But Wayne had a couple of surprises for me.

"So tell me again, Wayne, how many people are going to be there?"

"Pretty much just us. The students. Rex, of course. Ramona. Mildred. I asked Faith. I hope that's okay."

I sucked at my teeth. "No problem," I said.

"And your landlady. She's been asking about it. I really couldn't not invite her."

"I understand," I said. He fiddled with his pen. I could tell from the way he was beaming up at me that he hadn't quite come clean. "Anyone else?"

"Just one," he said.

"And who's that?"

"The president."

I was dumbfounded. "Of the United States?"

"No. Of the university."

"Jesus Christ."

"V.S., it's not going to be a problem, I promise you. He's the nicest guy in the world and he's the one who approved the appointment. He's a huge fan."

"A fan?" I wiped my hand over my mouth. "If there's one thing in the world I don't need, it's more fans." I'd wounded him, his eyes turning soft as a baby seal's. I slapped his desk. "Just joking, Wayne, just joking. I'm sure it's going to turn out fine."

But was it going to be fine? I wasn't so sure. I knew it sounded simple, as if all I had to do was stand up, read what Mohle had already written, and sit down again. But I'd never been to a reading, much less given one, and I knew from my students that readings were not to be taken lightly. This was not like teaching. When I taught, all I had to do was lie back in my chair, and act like the referee while the kids had at it. With this, I was going to be standing up front, all eyes on me, and everybody expecting me to thrill the pants off them.

I'd asked Wayne what section of the book I should read, but he was no help at all. "There are so many wonderful scenes, you really can't go wrong. I'm sure whatever you pick will be terrific."

I finally decided to do the last ten pages. It had a lot of funny stuff in it, plus there weren't that many hard words. I probably spent ten hours in front of my bedroom mirror practicing all my gestures, working up the accents for the different characters. I marked the book up so I knew where to pause, where to make a witty off-the-cuff remark.

Was I overdoing it? Maybe I was. After all, I was going to be playing in front of a home crowd. But then there was Rex and the university president. Rex would be tough enough, but the thought of reading to a guy with advanced degrees up the wazoo had me terrified.

The night of the reading I was nervous as a cat. Wayne and Faith came to pick me up at my house. Wayne was gussied up in his blazer and UNICEF tie and I could see that his wife had made sure he'd gotten a haircut. She looked pretty sharp herself in a Guatemalan shawl and clogs.

Faith couldn't have been more excited, but Wayne was distracted and a little out of sorts. We pulled into the parking lot behind the Fiction Institute just as Ramona was helping Rex out of their van. They had the president of the university with them, a tall, Scandinavian-looking fellow with a hell of a handshake.

The institute was lit up like a cruise ship. All the lights were blazing in the house and there were lights in the yard too, shining up into the trees. Through the windows I could see people bustling around.

At the door Anton checked everybody off a list like he thought he was working security at the White House. The downstairs I could hardly recognize. Whoever had catered the thing had vanished, but it looked as if they must have been working all afternoon. All the desks were pushed into the corners, replaced by tables with fancy linen and fancy food—stuffed mushrooms and crabcakes and artistic chocolate desserts. A dozen wine bottles cooled in ice buckets.

We were the last to arrive. Upstairs the students were crowded around the conference table. My landlady, standing in the back and looking gorgeous, gave me a cheery wave.

It took a while to get settled in. I hid out in the hallway, going over what I'd marked to read while Wayne introduced the president to everybody. All the kids were coming up to Rex to offer condolences about his dog. It was clear how much they loved the guy. Of course they didn't know the things I knew.

I had a lot more on my mind than any goddamned literary reading. There was no telling how many hours I'd put in refining my trap for Rex, but if I do say so myself, it was a masterpiece. This was no penny-ante pigeon drop in Grand Central, this was high art. All I needed now was the right moment to spring it.

When you have so much riding on something, you can't be too careful. You've got to tend to the smallest detail. It was like those old Tarzan movies when they're digging those elephant pits. Not only do you need to spend a week with shovels and picks making this big old hole and planting bamboo spikes in there, but then you've got to cover it all with branches and palm fronds and moss and stuff so it doesn't look any different than the regular jungle floor.

Wayne's introduction was a hell of a thing. I swear he went on for a half hour. He must have worked on it for a month. He had quotes from Mohle's fifth-grade teachers and fancy Yale professors. He compared me to Mark Twain and Walt Whitman and a whole slew of other people I'd never heard of. He went on about how generations of young people around the world had been changed by the reading of my book. Down at the other end of the table Rex looked like a wolverine chewing on his intestines.

Wayne got more and more worked up. This whole time, I had to just sit in a chair next to him, staring at the back of his freshly shaven neck. He told a story about the lowest moment of his life, when Faith was pregnant with their second child and they were living in his in-laws' basement. Every agent in New York had rejected his work and he had three hundred dollars in the bank.

Then one afternoon he wandered into a used bookstore and found an old copy of *Eat Your Wheaties* marked down to ninety-nine cents. The pages had turned yellow and half of them were falling out, but he sat down at a table by the window and began to read. He hadn't looked at the book since he was a teenager and now it spoke to him in an entirely new way.

"What was it exactly?" Wayne asked. "The clarity of the voice? The beauty of the language? Whatever it was, all my self-loathing and doubt just fell away and I knew that I couldn't give it up, couldn't give up writing, whatever the cost. I knew that a life devoted to creating one thing as extraordinary as those crumbling pages was not a life wasted . . ."

Wayne's lips started to tremble. He stopped to gather himself. "Let us make no mistake about it. Tonight we are present at one of the great moments in the history of American literature. Tonight it is our privilege to hear V. S. Mohle read from his work for the first time in his entire career."

He put a hand on my shoulder. His nostrils quivered. It was a terrible thing to witness. "Please welcome . . ." His voice broke and he had to lower his head before he could continue. "V. S. Mohle!"

The place went wild with applause. Everybody rose from their seats. I got up out of my chair and gave Wayne a big hug, patting him on the back a few times to console him for not being me.

People kept clapping, even though I raised my hands a couple of times to calm them. In the end, all I could do was stand at the lectern, smiling and nodding, until they finally sat back down.

I cracked my book open and peered out over the audience. Faces shone with adoration. The president looked like he was about to pop, he was so proud. You would have thought I was Charles Lindbergh landing in Paris.

I began by thanking Wayne for his wonderful introduction. I thanked Rex and the president for bringing me here, and talked a little about my talented students.

"As I'm sure most of you are aware by now, there was a party the other night to celebrate one of these remarkable young people getting her book accepted. But let me assure you, there are going to be many, many more parties like it, for all of these kids . . ."

I adjusted the light on the lectern. Out of the corner of my eye, I saw Ramona whispering something in Rex's ear. "Wayne's asked me to read a little to you tonight, so I thought I'd take a shot at the final scene, where Hartley ends up in the ghost town in New Mexico. Some of you may remember it . . ."

Three or four of the students smiled as if I'd made the best joke. Of course they knew it. They'd probably memorized it word for word.

I figured I could scarcely go wrong with the ending, there was so much great stuff in it. Hartley and his buddy Alex have run away from high school and have been knocking around in the West for a month or so, but they've started to get on one another's nerves. Their big dreams of working on a ranch haven't panned out and the on-again, off-again search for Hartley's father has been a complete bust.

But then in Denver they run into Hartley's aunt, a tall goofy woman who collects glass giraffes. She hadn't seen Hartley's father for over a year, but she got a postcard from him just a few months before, saying that he was going off to live in a ghost town in New Mexico.

Before you know it the boys are on a Trailways bus, headed south. This was where I started reading, right at the part where they're meeting all these wacky characters, including a garlic farmer who claims to be a former English lord, and some hippie girl who lives with Geronimo's grandson on a mountain outside of Taos.

After a long drive through the night they arrive at this ghost town south of Santa Fe. Collapsing mine shafts dot the hillside and there are row after row of abandoned shacks. It's Sunday afternoon and the only places showing any signs of life are a general store and a biker bar playing bluegrass music.

This is way too freaky for Alex, who just wants to get the hell out of there, but Hartley's come too far to turn back now. The first place he tries is the bar, but nobody will give him so much as the time of day. For an hour they wander through the town, stopping everyone they meet but getting absolutely nowhere, until they run into a chatty little six-year-old sucking on a Popsicle on the steps of the general store.

Her name is Eleanor and she's one of those cute kids who have a lot of cute things to say. She asks if they know what's the fastest animal in the world, and when Hartley says it's the cheetah, she's impressed. Hartley asks her if she knows a man named Walker Dixon. She shakes her head no.

Hartley doesn't let it drop. "How about a tall skinny man with a little mustache? From New York?" She keeps shaking her head. "With kind of big ears? Like mine?"

Eleanor gets a puzzled look on her face. "Does he swallow spoons?"

"Yeah, he does," Hartley says. It was his father's one trick, his surefire way to entertain any kid under the age of eight.

"He lived here for a while," Eleanor says. "But I don't think he does anymore." She's a funny-looking little girl, this Eleanor. She's got freckles and braids, droopy black socks, and a gingham dress out of *Little House on the Prairie.*

"Could you show us which house he lived in?" Hartley said.

"Oh, geez," Alex says, but Hartley gives him a hard look to shut him up.

Eleanor tosses her Popsicle stick away and leads them back into the rows of miners' shacks. Most of them are abandoned, but through some of the windows Hartley can see the shadows of people moving around.

A couple of mangy dogs start to follow them. Eleanor jabbers away. Did they know that llamas spit? Did they have a TV? She didn't. Her mother didn't believe in it. She went to New York with her mother once and they went to a museum where a giant whale hung from the ceiling. A lot of kids might have been afraid, but she wasn't, because she knew it wasn't real.

Alex limps along the coal streets. All he wants is a pay phone where he can call his parents and have them send him a plane ticket home. He's sure the place is full of escaped felons and deranged drug dealers and that they're about to be murdered. He has on the Haverford sweatshirt he's worn the whole trip, hoping it would help him get laid if the girls they met on the buses thought he was old enough to be in college.

When they come to the shack where the man who swallowed spoons once lived, Alex decides he'll just wait outside. Eleanor takes Hartley by the hand and leads him through the gate.

Inside, the shack is stripped of everything except a stained mattress, a three-legged table, and an icebox with a few pieces of petrified fruit. Animal droppings speckle the floors.

But when Hartley checks the closet, he sees this tan jacket crumpled in the corner, the same jacket his father always wore when they played baseball in the park. Hartley picks it up. Going through the pockets, he finds an old strip of pictures taken in a photo booth in Grand Central when Hartley was ten, snapshots of him and his father mugging for the camera.

When I started reading all this, I did pretty good. I was using my pauses, doing all the accents, etc. I was getting a few laughs, maybe not as many as I expected, but enough to keep me encouraged.

Then, when I was about halfway through, something weird happened. You know the scene in *The Exorcist* where the devil's voice starts coming out of Linda Blair? It was sort of like that. Eerie as hell. It was as if the words just took over. All my pauses, all the cool bits I'd planned to act out, all the marks in the margins to remind me to make meaningful eye contact? I went sailing past them like an Eskimo on a runaway dogsled. I was lost in the story.

When I looked up at the faces around the table, I saw they were lost in it too. Wayne was squeezing his wife's hand, Bryn had her eyes closed like she thought she was at some sort of séance, and Rex was as still as a sphinx, chin resting on his knuckles. You had to figure it must have been pretty rough on the guy, realizing that he could write another fifty books and he'd never be able to write anything half as good as what he was listening to.

But something even weirder happened when I got to the part where Hartley is looking at the strip of pictures of him and his dad. He's feeling sadder than he's ever felt in his life, but he's pissed off too, pissed off that he's come all the way across the country for nothing, pissed off that his mother might have been right when she kept telling him he needed to forget his father, that he wasn't the man either of them knew anymore. Something had happened to him, his mother keeps saying, and all the best doctors in New York couldn't tell them what it was.

Hartley still can't understand it. How could a person turn into another person? How could his father, who had once loved him, who'd shown him how to throw a curveball, who'd spent hours helping him with his science projects, who had made up stupid songs to make him laugh, turn into this big fat zero, this tumbling tumbleweed?

Eleanor's still saying all these cute things, like did fish ever sleep, and through the window Hartley can see Alex leaning against a fence with one shoe off, checking his blisters.

Eleanor wants to see the pictures and Hartley finally hands them over. "Is that you?" she wants to know.

"No," he says. "That's someone else."

"But he looks like you."

"Maybe so."

She offers him the pictures. "You want them back?"

"No, you can keep them."

He hangs the tan jacket up in the closet. But before he shuts the door, he grabs the sleeve and covers his nose and mouth with it, hoping to catch at least a whiff of his old man, but all he gets is a snotful of coal dust.

So when I came to the part about the jacket, I started to cry.

When I looked up at everybody, they were all crying too, some of them biting their lips, the president of the university pinching the corners of his eyes.

God knows why I broke down like that. Probably it was all Wayne's fault, getting us all worked up the way he did. Maybe it was just my allergies. Or maybe reading it all out loud just brought it all back, me walking out on my son, my father walking out on me.

One thing I know for sure. Rex was totally wrecked. I swear, V. S. Mohle was right there in the room with us. And if he'd driven a shiv into my heart, he had to have driven one into Rex's heart too.

Chapter Fourteen

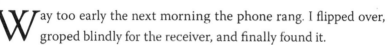

Way too early the next morning the phone rang. I flipped over, groped blindly for the receiver, and finally found it.

"Hello?"

"V.S.?"

"Yeah?"

"It's Rex."

"Rex! How you doing?" I rubbed the sand out of my eyes. The clock on my bedside table said seven A.M.

"I'm doing fine," he said. "I have a proposal for you."

"What's that?"

"How would you like to go to Waco?"

"I'm sorry?"

"There's a mammoth museum up there I want to take a look at."

"You mean woolly mammoths?" I said.

There was a long pause like he thought I was an idiot. "No, Columbian mammoths. Ramona was going to drive me, but there's no reason you and I can't handle it. Make it a boys' day out."

I glanced out the window. It was barely light. "What time were you thinking?"

"Why don't you show up here at nine?" he said.

I hung up the phone and staggered off to the bathroom to splash some water on my face. What the hell could this be about? The man might have said something about what a triumph my reading had been, or how moved he was, just as a matter of courtesy, but he was such a strange bird, you never knew what was going on in his head.

When I drove up to the house two hours later, Rex and Ramona were on the front lawn waiting for me. Ramona didn't seem happy. A small cooler had been packed with treats and drinks, and the decision had already been made that we were taking the van rather than my wreck of a Volvo.

Ramona had all sorts of instructions for me, a map, and a list of numbers to call in case of trouble. As we pulled away from the curb, Rex gave her a wave through the window, like a little kid going off to camp, but she was already walking back toward the house.

Rush-hour traffic on the interstate was a mess. It took an hour to get past all the Dennys and the El Chicos, the Taco Bells and the Wendys, but after that we were out in the open country where it was mostly farmland and abandoned fireworks stands.

If we'd been traveling with Ramona, Rex would have been in the back with his pillows and blankets, but because it was just the two of us, he got to be up front. He fiddled with the radio for a while, but it was hard to find much except sports talk shows, sermons, bad choirs, and right-wing survivalists selling canned peaches that would last a hundred years. It wasn't long before he snapped it off. We hit some road construction around Jarrell and everything narrowed down to one lane. I bent over the steering wheel, stifling a yawn.

"That was quite a night last night," he said.

"Thanks," I said. "It's a great little program you've put together here."

"Can I ask you a question?"

"Not a problem," I said.

"What exactly do you do up there in Maine all day? Just sit and stare at the ocean?"

"Not as much as you'd think. Not these days."

"How do you mean?"

"It's a bit of a story."

"Please, go ahead."

On uneven pavement, the steering wheel vibrated in my hands. It looked as if the moment I'd been waiting for had arrived. "You know I live on this island," I said.

"Right."

"Once a week I ferry across to get my mail. I usually go by the 7-Eleven to buy groceries. For years I've seen the kids sitting outside with their bedrolls and mangy dogs. Sometimes they'll hit me up for cigarettes or a few dollars. You know how poor that part of Maine is. I'm not sure it's ever made it out of the Depression."

A big-roofed church sat in the middle of a pasture. A couple of men in cheap suits and cowboy hats got out of their pickups, Bibles under their arms. I felt my stomach fluttering. Was I really ready to do this? But if I just let it go, when was I ever going to have another chance?

"One day I asked a couple of them to help me load firewood in the back of my truck. I paid them a little something for it and we got to talking. Turned out there was a gang of them living under this bridge. Over the next few weeks I would ask them to do a little work for me from time to time. The stories they would tell, good God, you couldn't make them up . . ."

Frowning, Rex massaged his knee. "What kind of stories?"

"The girls were selling themselves to the truckers coming down from Canada. They guys were stripping copper wire out of abandoned buildings to sell for scrap." If it wasn't bad enough that I was an imposter, I was now a plagiarist as well. "These kids really had been through something. One of them had a crack-addicted father who stuck the poor girl's head in the oven and turned on the gas . . . It was a miracle she survived . . ."

I spotted a cop car camped back in a grove of trees. When I tapped my brakes, Rex put a hand on the dash to brace himself.

"But there was one of these characters that kind of got to me. This little wet rat of a kid, maybe twelve or thirteen. He was a funny guy, always went around with this beat-up teddy bear his mother had given him before she died.

"He'd been in a dozen different foster homes and busted out of all of them. He took to me. I don't know what it was, maybe just that I'd put a couple bucks in his pocket, fed him lunch a few times. His name was Freddie. The kid really cracked me up. I swear he could have been a stand-up comic. I remember giving him an old winter jacket of mine. He thought it was the best damn thing in the world, even if it about swallowed him up."

Out of the corner of my eye I kept track of the old geezer. He cleaned his fingernails, flicking the dirty bits away with his thumb.

"Maybe that's where I went wrong," I said. "Maybe it was like feeding seagulls. Once you start, you know you're going to have a problem on your hands. It wasn't very long before I could barely get rid of him. This was right when I was trying to get back to my writing. I'd look up from my desk and there he'd be, right outside my window, raking up pine cones. Or eight o'clock in the morning, there would be a knock on the door and there he was again, bringing my mail up from the ferry."

"Hah." Rex's laugh was not a good one, dry and unfunny.

"I must have lectured him three or four times about how I needed my privacy, how I couldn't have him hanging around all the time. But he was such a needy kid. He wouldn't show up for a week or two and then he'd be back again, like one of those bad pennies."

I was walking a fine line. I wasn't trying to suggest that the kid was actually Rex's son. That would have been loony. Hell, after all these years Rex's kid would have been close to my age. All I wanted was for it to seem like one of those amazing coincidences. All I wanted was to delicately remind the old guy of what a shit he'd once been.

"The whole thing came off the rails when I had to go down to Boston for a few days to take these tests. When I got back, I pulled into the 7-Eleven to get some groceries and there was this cop. He told me that one of the sheds behind my house had burned down.

"Apparently some of Freddie's older buddies had talked him into taking them on a tour of my place. Things got a little out of hand. They'd gone in, gotten into my liquor cabinet. They didn't have enough nerve to party in the house, so they went out back to the shed where I kept my tools. But it wasn't just tools. I had a lot of boxes stored in the rafters, filled with manuscripts I'd never finished, notes for all those books I'd never gotten around to writing . . ."

"Jesus," Rex said.

"Sometime during the night, one of the kids tipped over a candle, and when the fire caught they were all too crocked to do anything but run. The cops said if it hadn't been raining the house and half the island would probably have gone up as well."

"So did they catch these kids?"

"It didn't take them long. It sounded like Freddie sang like a canary. At first everybody was making noises about sending them off to reform school, but I went in to see the county judge and talked him out of it as best I could."

"Are you telling me you just walked away from it all?"

"I didn't walk away at all. When I got hold of Freddie I gave him the dressing down of his life. I let him know just how disappointed I was in him. I told him that for him to do something like that, after all I'd done for him, was like a dagger to the heart. I said a lot of things I shouldn't have. I called him a punk. I called him spineless. A loser. I told him I never wanted to see him again. Tears were streaming down his face and he was hugging that teddy bear to his chest, begging me to give him another chance."

Rex fumbled through the glove compartment and finally came up with a packet of Nabs. I could tell I had him agitated. The only question now was how far did I want to push it.

"And where was this?" he said.

"Right out in front of the 7-Eleven. All his buddies were watching. He kept grabbing at me, but I finally just swatted his hand away and walked off."

In the field to my left, a monster piece of farm machinery I didn't know the name of spewed great clouds of chaff.

"I didn't see him all that winter. A couple of times I asked some of the other kids if they knew where he was, but they didn't. The guy at the hardware store said he'd heard a bunch of them had caught the bus down to New York City. I thought about the boy a lot. I regretted being so hard on him. Regretted saying some of the things I'd said. But what was I going to do? He was gone.

"There was a record snowfall that winter. Spring took a long time coming, but finally the eaves started dripping, a few of the birds came back, and the snow started falling out of the trees. One April morning I'm out with my shovel, trying to clear a path down to the shore, when I see something brown in one of the snowbanks. At first I think it's just a dead woodchuck or a squirrel, maybe. Up in that part of the world, all kinds of things die in the winter. They'll be buried and you won't find them until spring—deer, porcupines, all kinds of small animals. But when I go to check it out, I see it's the teddy bear . . ."

The glance Rex shot me was a killer, as if he thought he'd been accused. But I'd gone too far—I had no choice but to go on.

"I pick it up. It was solid ice. I swear it must have weighed five pounds. One of the button eyes was missing. I had no idea what to do. I look around like someone was supposed to help me. But then I see this frozen sleeve."

"What do you mean, frozen sleeve?"

"It was there. In the snowbank. The frozen sleeve of the coat I'd given him." A sound came out of Rex and he raised a hand in protest. "I'm sorry, Rex," I said. "You don't need to know this."

"No, go on. Tell me."

"I got down on my knees. I was like a dog digging for a bone . . ."

"So was he there?"

"He was."

Rex tore at the cellophane wrapper of the Nabs with his teeth and then, when he couldn't get it open, tossed the packet into the backseat.

"When I finally brushed all the ice and snow off him, he looked so peaceful, as if he was just taking a nap. One of his boots was missing and he had an arm in the air as if he was waiting to be called on. I don't know how long I sat there, just staring at him. My fingers were burning from digging in the snow. I remember the gulls crying and once in a while the booming of the ice breaking up in the bay. Why am I even telling you this, Rex? I've never told anybody."

Head bowed, Rex stared down at his veiny hands.

"You know what really got to me? That he was just a hundred yards from my house. The coroner said he'd probably been there for a couple of months. They found an old sleeping bag and some food in one of the other sheds. I kept imagining him standing out in the pines, too afraid to come in, watching me at my desk. That's when I made a vow."

"What vow was that?"

"That I was never going to turn my back on those kids again."

"Uh-huh." He wiped a bit of cellophane from his tongue. "So what have you done about it?"

"Well, over the years I've been buying up these little parcels of the island. Right now I've got myself a sizable piece of real estate. I've decided to donate it all to create a place for these kids."

"What kind of a place?" His voice was low and distracted.

"It's sort of a school, sort of a shelter. I've been talking to a lot of people."

"What kind of people?"

"Experts," I said. "People who know a whole lot more than me. Harvard Education School types."

"Right," he said. We passed a closed fireworks stand. "Is there anybody going in on this with you?"

"Going in on it with me?"

"On the money."

"Well, there was a guy." This was always the tricky part. The road opened up to four lanes. I stepped on it, zipping around a long line of Army trucks with their lights on, soldiers huddled in the back. "I probably shouldn't mention names, but he's from this lah-di-da Massachusetts family and he's going through this messy divorce. It looks as if it's put the kibosh on the whole deal."

"How much was he going to pony up?"

"Five million."

The number made him sit up straight. You would have thought someone had just given him a whiff of the smelling salts. "Five million?"

"Yeah."

"That's a lot of money."

"It is."

"You really think it's going to solve anything?"

"I'm sorry?"

"What you've been through . . . Good Lord . . . but I don't know that throwing money at it makes it any better."

Stone-faced, he stared out the window and didn't talk for a long time. So many things raced around in my head. I cursed myself. I'd had the man on the ropes, but the talk of money had brought him back to the land of the living, to the world where everyone was sure to hit him up, sooner or later.

A hint of a smile on his lips, he looked back at me. "V. S. Mohle as Florence Nightingale. It's quite an idea."

"I guess it is."

He leaned back to retrieve an orange from the cooler. "Is there any way you're going to be able to get out of it?"

"Get out of it? I don't want to get out of it."

"I don't want to pry, but you must have already sunk a fortune into this."

"I don't know if I'd say that, but I've spent a few bucks."

"It's a shame we weren't in touch earlier. We might have been able to do something. Right now, I'm pretty tapped out." Rex dug into the rind of the orange with his fingernails, making a real mess. "You still got that teddy bear?"

"I keep it in my window."

"Listen, V.S., you did the best you could. You've got to stop beating yourself up over this. We've all done things we're not so proud of, but we can't always fix them. And at our age, we're getting a little old to play hero." He opened his window a crack and let the bits of orange peel sail on down the road behind us.

"Would you mind if I ask you a question?" he said.

"Of course not."

"So is this why you came down here? To ask me for money?"

"Ask *you*? Are you kidding me? No way."

"I didn't think so. I was just curious," Rex said. Birds rose and fell over a field of stubble. In the distance I could see the gray water tower of some two-bit town. When Rex leaned in to give me a punch on the shoulder, his eyes seemed almost merry. "So what do you say we go check on your woolly mammoths?"

When we got to the museum there was a four-man delegation there to greet us. Rex was in the grandest mood, shaking hands with everybody, asking about their families. Walter Cronkite couldn't have done it better.

They took us on a VIP tour of something called the dig shelter. We made our way along a catwalk above the remains of a dozen or so of these monsters. There were huge curved tusks, shattered skulls, vertebrae, toe bones the size of salt shakers. According to our guide, these mammoths had been bigger than elephants, fourteen feet high. Enormous herds of them had roamed the plains of Texas some fifty thousand years ago, along with camels and saber-toothed tigers and giant sloths.

Rex ate this stuff up with a spoon. In a way he looked like a fossil himself, with his bony old head. He scribbled notes and asked a million questions. Me, I shuffled along behind like a doomed man. What had I thought would happen? I'm ashamed to admit it, but I honestly thought Rex and I were going to end up on our knees, two old foes praying for the forgiveness of our sins together. It would have been a beautiful thing. If everything had gone the way I'd planned, the man would have been begging to give me his money.

But Rex was no sap. I'd offered him a chance to redeem himself and he'd slapped it away like a hockey puck. The story I'd cooked up for him had been perfect. All these years later, I'm still moved when I think about it. And wasn't it always the surefire way to get close to somebody, confessing to something you know the other guy is guilty of?

But when you've got somebody like Rex reeling, you've got to close, and I hadn't closed. He'd held, he'd covered up, he'd danced out of range like the pro he was. And if he'd sussed me out, if he sensed I knew his secret and was using it, he had to have total contempt for me, even if he hadn't let on. I wasn't a fool. I knew there could be hell to pay for this.

For the next few days I was in bad shape. The state I was in, I couldn't have beaten a chicken at tic-tac-toe. I had that horrible four-in-the-morning-in-Atlantic-City feeling you get when you've put every cent you've got on the roulette table and lost and you're going to have to borrow twenty bucks from the hat check girl to take the Chinese bus back to Manhattan.

I couldn't believe that Rex had turned me down. Part of me still was hoping that he would change his mind, that I would get a phone call saying he'd had a chance to think things over and he'd realized that if he didn't go in with me on this damn deal he'd never be able to live with himself. The call never came.

Maybe I shouldn't have been feeling so sorry for myself. Wayne had just cashed my November check, which meant I had another eighteen grand tucked under my bed. I had enough stashed away now to give me a good start anywhere.

So why was I taking it all so personal? I was really starting to dislike Rex. There was something crass and cold about him. Mohle had been the first to spot it and Rex had tried to break him for it, just like he was trying to break me. This was just round two.

When I walked into the conference room on Wednesday, I found half the class seriously sunburned. Dominique, Nick, Bryn, and Chester were lined up in a row on the left side of the table, faces red as lobsters. All four of them wore dark glasses, as if they were backup singers for the Blues Brothers. Across the table, the pasty-faced Brett pretended to ignore them, making last-minute notes on the back of a manuscript.

The first story up for discussion was Mercedes's. It was about an old Mexican woman living on the border who late one afternoon walks down to a family cemetery. When she falls, she can't get up, and ends up spending the night on the ground. The moon rises. She hears owls calling in the cottonwoods, varmints rustling in the brush. She is visited by the ghosts of her husband, the daughter who was killed in an auto accident after her senior prom, her sister who was shot to death by a jealous lover.

It was depressing as hell, but at least it wasn't boring, and it seemed to me that there should have been a lot to talk about, so I was surprised when the discussion fell flat. Mel, who had somehow turned himself into Mr. Goody-Goody Two-Shoes, was the only one who kept it from being a total disaster. He must have had three pages of notes, plus a lot of encouraging things to say. Brett, on the other hand, was too morose to do much more than point out a couple of grammatical slips.

But the real problem was that the four Blues Brothers obviously hadn't read the story. Bryn and Dominique at least had the courtesy to try and fake it, parroting Mel's comments, but every time I looked Chester's way, I caught him nodding off. It made me pissed, but I held my tongue until the break, when I pulled him into my office and demanded to know what was going on.

He scratched at one of his crusty ears. "We drove to Las Vegas for the weekend."

"Las Vegas? Nevada? Are you kidding me?" I was still so pissed off about Rex stiffing me, I was in no mood to cut anybody any slack. He hung his head like an eight-year-old. "How far is that?"

"Eleven hundred miles."

"You mean each way."

"Each way."

"So you weren't able to get to the stories."

"We meant to, and we would have, but the car broke down in the desert on the way back." All that ultraviolet damage seemed to have knocked off a few of the boy's brain cells.

"Jesus Christ," I said.

It was clear enough how miserable he felt about letting me down, but what wasn't clear was exactly what they'd been up to. Two boys, two girls—who was sleeping with who? That was the million-dollar question. I could hear the voices of the other students drifting past the door. "We better get in there," I said.

The other manuscript we were scheduled to talk about was Brett's, but Brett had a surprise in store for us. We settled down around the table and everyone was pulling out their copies of the stories when Brett raised his hand.

"Mr. Mohle?"

"Yes?"

"I hope this isn't too irregular . . . but that story I handed out last week . . . I had a chance to look at it . . . and it's a piece of crap, honestly . . . I'd really rather we didn't discuss it."

I leaned forward, resting my chin in the palm of my hand, trying to control my irritation. Brett was right about one thing. It had been a piece of crap, and I'd spent two hours reading it. "So what do you suggest we do?"

"I wrote another one. Over the weekend. And I've brought copies for everyone. I was thinking I could read it aloud and everyone could just follow along." He took a quick glance at the clock. "We've got time, right?"

I scanned the faces around the room. What a bunch of louts. I remember Wayne telling me that the first rule of teaching is to maintain control of one's classroom, but what was I going to do? Half of them hadn't read Brett's other manuscript anyway. "That would be fine," I said.

Whatever else you want to say about it, Brett's story woke everybody up. It was about three young artists living in New York—Desiree, a tall, beautiful painter with wild hair and silver bracelets, her lover Bronson, a WASPy and athletic muralist (I hadn't even known there was such a word as *muralist*, but you learn something every day) from a wealthy Connecticut family, and Nils, Bronson's best friend—a brainy nutball, a bit of a fanook—who created wacko sculptures out of vacuum-cleaner hoses and bicycle frames, fingernail clippings and artificial limbs.

The three of them are together pretty much 24/7. Bronson and Desiree have these knock-down, drag-out fights. A lot of them are about her early success, which, according to Bronson, is due more to her being a hot number than to the quality of her work. Jealous as a tick, Bronson is convinced she's been having an affair with a big-shot gallery owner, but he's never been able to prove it.

They both tell their troubles to Nils, who has plenty of troubles of his own. On the way home after a night at a SoHo bar, Nils makes a drunken pass at Bronson. Bronson gets weirded out, says something nasty, and Nils slinks off like a whipped dog. When Bronson calls the next day, hoping to soothe any hard feelings, all he gets is a machine and Nils never calls him back.

That weekend, while Desiree is in Boston for the opening of a new show, Bronson digs through her things and finds a diary tucked away in the back of a drawer. Reading it, he discovers that Desiree's been sleeping with Nils off and on for the past month.

On Sunday night, rather than wait for her at his apartment, Bronson takes the subway to Grand Central to meet her. I'm no literary guy, but the last paragraph was a doozy.

"They got off the train together, Nils swinging his backpack onto his shoulder, Desiree maneuvering her rolling suitcase around a pair of conductors. There was such a crush of people that they passed within four or five feet of Bronson without seeing him. She put a hand on Nils's arm to steady herself as they got on the escalator, and as they ascended, Nils looked back and said something that made her laugh, the sound musical and faithless and free, echoing in the cavernous space."

I was amazed Brett could even read it! His voice did waver a couple of times, but he made it all the way through, the red faces on the left side of the table growing redder by the minute. Dominique rested her hands on her books in front of her, chin up, Miss Stoneface, while Nick twitched and took guilty peeks at the others, like an accused man checking out the jury. Mel seemed mildly amused; but Mercedes looked pretty glum. She knew she'd been trumped. Let's face it, ghosts in graveyards may have their charms, but they can't hold a candle to a rich boy losing his girlfriend.

I suppose you had to admire Brett's nerve, but, honestly, what had he been thinking? If he thought this was going to get him another date, I'm afraid he was sadly mistaken. It wasn't as if he'd tried to disguise anything. Not only did the names of the characters start with the same letters as the names of the people they were based on, but the details were lifted directly from life—Dominique/Desiree's habit of running a finger down a man's sleeve when she was being ingratiating, the way she fiddled with her bracelets; Nick/Nils's knock-kneed run, the way he splattered food on himself when he was trying to eat and talk about big ideas at the same time.

When Brett finished reading, you could have heard a pin drop. Bryn rubbed a knuckle across blistered lips. Chester pressed both hands to the sides of his Harpo Marx hairdo. For a moment I considered letting them all go early, but I'd pulled that one too many times already.

"Comments?" I asked. My question just hung there.

"It seems like a real departure from your other work," Chester said.

"Good," I said. "Anyone else?"

"I thought it was pretty sniggery," Mercedes said.

"I did too," LaTasha said. "I thought it was awfully self-pitying."

"I thought it was a mess," Bryn said.

"I didn't," Mel said. "I liked it. I thought it had a lot of edge. But I've got some notes."

Good old Mel. He must have taken five minutes, going through what he thought worked and what he thought didn't, pointing out where a scene might be expanded, a sentence tightened, a chunk of exposition tossed. Now that I'd called him a genius, he'd turned into my right-hand man.

Dominique finally took off her dark glasses and fixed Brett with a lidded stare. Nick, elbows on the table, jiggled his knee a mile a minute. Neither of them had said a word, and who could blame them? She'd been accused of being a slut and he'd been accused of being a pansy. Pale as a ghost, Brett tried manfully to write down everything Mel had to say.

"Other thoughts?" I said when Mel finished his spiel.

"And what do you think of it?" Dominique said. It was me she was talking to.

"What do I think of it?" I said.

"Yes."

I took a quick glance at Brett. He was looking at me with the soft, pleading eyes of a lamb being led to slaughter. The boy was dying to be rescued, but as far as I was concerned, it was every man for himself.

"As a story? As a piece of writing?" I said.

"As anything."

I scowled. These sunburned jerks needed aloe vera more than they needed my comments, but I wasn't going to say that. I rolled a pen between my palms. I racked my brain, trying to remember if there had been any advice in *The Wings of Prometheus* about how to handle situations like this.

"I thought it was promising," I said. "There were some vivid details. I particularly like the way you describe escalators in the story. My big question is, who are we supposed to like? Isn't that always the question? Or maybe we're not supposed to like anyone. Which would be fine too, but we would just need to know that. I think you could do more with the rich family in Connecticut. How rich are they? Where does the money come from? What part of Connecticut are you talking about? That stuff is always interesting. Now, the bit about finding the diary . . . how many times have we seen that? I hate to say it, Brett, but that's kind of taking the easy way out."

I took a quick survey of the table. Did they know that I was blowing smoke? I suspect they did, but I didn't care. I was just trying to get us all out of there alive.

"I think it would be a big help if you went back to read some early de Maupassant." I was sort of proud of that, the de Maupassant remark. Wayne had just been telling me about him, and I think I may have even pronounced it right. "And that scene in Grand Central . . . how late is it? Maybe our hero gets pickpocketed. Every other goddamned thing happens to him, why not? He's emotionally upset, he's probably not paying attention. I'm not trying to rewrite your story for you, but late at night at Grand Central, there are some real sleazeballs out there . . ."

Mel hung around after class to ask me if I'd had a chance to look at his journal. I told him to close the door. Bewildered, he did as I said.

"Well, well, well," I said.

"Yeah?" he said.

I shoved him hard in the chest. He staggered back, looking alarmed. "You are really something."

"So you read it?"

"Yes, I read it. I don't know how to say this exactly, but every once in a very great while you read something that you feel could really change your life." I wasn't going to tell him that I'd been hoping it was going to change mine, until Rex shot that puppy down in about ten seconds.

"You liked it?"

"I was knocked out by it. Now, don't get me wrong. It's rough. But if you put a couple of years into polishing this thing, you could have yourself a gem. But you have to promise me something."

"What's that?"

"I don't want you to whisper a word about this to anyone. And I don't want you showing it to anybody. This is just between you and me. All right?"

His eyes went wide. "Right."

"This is the problem with young writers, I've seen it a million times, they end up talking their books to death. There's no quicker way I know to lose the magic. Silence and cunning, my friend, silence and cunning." A couple of acorns rattled down the roof. "Could I ask a question?" I said.

"Sure."

"Those kids that you met last summer, under the bridge . . . You keep in touch with them at all?"

"No. I don't know how I would."

"They didn't disgust you at all?"

"What do you mean?"

"It must have been a little foul."

"You get used to it."

"Mmm. And you probably never told them you were taking notes on them."

"No."

"Well, good. I guess it's better not to let people know you're a writer."

Chapter Fifteen

Friday night I had an awful time sleeping. Maybe it was something I ate, but every time I managed to doze off for a few minutes, I found myself in a terrifying dream about my son. In it I was supposed to pick him up after school, but traffic was insane. When I finally got there, he was gone. I ran around the parking lot, asking people if they'd seen him, but they just stared at me as if I was an idiot. Everything was jumbled up, but in one of those bits I saw him in the back of a station wagon that was driving away. He had his face to the rear window and when he saw me he was crying and I was running and running and there was no way I would ever catch up.

As upsetting as the dream was, when I woke up Saturday morning, what I needed to do next was crystal clear. There was no more time for moping or feeling sorry for myself. So Rex had turned me down. Did that mean the game was over? No way.

What I needed to do was give it another shot. I needed a fresh approach. Maybe I could tell him I'd just had some wonderful news. I could tell him some old friend had called out of the blue to say they were donating three million to the cause, which meant that if I came up with just a couple of million more, a drop in the bucket for a high-roller like him, I was home free. With a little thought I was sure I could come up with an even better story than that. Hell, wasn't I a professional at this?

The key was not to drag my feet. I gulped down a cup of coffee, got into my car, and drove right over. It was barely nine, but I figured Rex had been up writing at the crack of dawn.

When I pulled up to the house, I noticed a blue Lexus convertible parked behind Ramona's pickup, but didn't think much about it. I angled across the dead grass. Canadian geese honked high up, somewhere over the clouds. I guess fall had to arrive everywhere sooner or later, even in Texas.

The front door was ajar. I rang the bell a couple of times, but when no one came to greet me, I let myself in.

"Hello?" I called.

No one answered but I could hear voices at the back of the house. I hesitated for a couple of seconds, not sure what to do, but finally made my way down the hallway. I never figured there was any point in being shy.

Peering around the corner into the living room, I saw Rex, huddled on the couch with two people I'd never laid eyes on before. They were leafing through some sort of coffee-table book. The woman was a knockout—tall, with killer cheekbones and huge almond eyes. The guy could have stepped right of of *GQ*. Middle-aged and natty, with a brush mustache and red suspenders, he looked like David Niven in one of those movies where he went around hitting on the wives of clodhopper Midwesterners. They were all so absorbed by whatever they were looking at no one noticed me at first.

"Morning, Rex," I said.

Rex's head came up so fast you would have thought someone had fired a rifle. He stared at me, his face ashy-white.

"What are you doing here?" he demanded. The man and the woman looked up, smiling amicably.

"I was just in the neighborhood. I thought I'd drop by and say hello," I said. From the way he was glaring at me, I could tell he had no intention of making introductions. I stepped forward and extended my hand to the woman. "Hi," I said. "I'm Horton Caldwell. Rex's assistant." She lifted her fingers to me almost as if she expected me to kiss them. I was tempted. "I'm Francesca," she said. "It's a delight to meet you." Her accent was vaguely European.

The guy with the suspenders rose from the couch and gave me a manly handshake. "Dudley. Dudley Stainforth," he said.

"So where you from, Dudley?" I said.

"Florence."

"You mean North Jersey?"

"No, Italy, actually."

Out of the corner of my eye, I saw Rex quietly close the coffee-table book and slip it in between his knees. You would have thought I'd just walked in on a major drug deal.

"So you two here on vacation?" I asked. Ramona came out of the back hall with a stack of Rex's freshly ironed shirts.

Stainforth glanced over at Rex, not sure how much he was supposed to say. "A mix of business and pleasure," he said.

Ramona set the shirts on the kitchen counter. "They're offering Rex this wonderful prize," she said.

I glanced from Stainforth to Rex and back again. Stainforth had an awkward smile on his face, and Rex just looked cross.

"Rex, is this true?" I asked.

"I suppose it is," he said, not meeting my eyes. "But I haven't decided whether to take it or not."

"And what prize is this?" I asked.

"It's called the Vita Nuova Prize," Stainforth said. "We give it each year to the writer who best exemplifies the Dantean spirit."

"Wow," I said. I had no clue what "the Dantean spirit" meant, and I wasn't all that sure about "exemplifies." Rex squinted up at me. "This is fantastic," I said.

"We'll see," he said.

"I've been having a terrible time getting him to say yes," Stainforth said. "So I decided to fly over for a few days to see if I could talk some sense into him."

"Good luck with that," I said.

"And Horton," Ramona said, "the place where they hold the ceremony? Oh my goodness."

"Here, let him see," Francesca said. She wrestled the coffee-table book out of Rex's hands and gave it to Stainforth. I caught just a glimpse of the title: *Dante's Florence*, with an introduction by none other than Stainforth himself.

Stainforth riffled through the pages until he found what he was after, then held it out for me to look. "Here's a couple of shots of the villa where we conduct our festivities."

I stared down at a full-color spread of a garden perched high above the city. With pools and fountains, the rows of pruned cypress trees, the garden looked as if it was sitting up in heaven. The overlook was lined with busts, and Stainforth made a point of identifying them one by one.

"Da Vinci here . . . Michelangelo . . . Dante . . . Petrarch . . . Horace, missing his nose, I'm afraid." I leaned in to get a closer look. They all seemed pretty much the same to me, with Beatles haircuts and togas draped over their shoulders. Ramona came to join us, peering in.

"And here's Boccaccio," Stainforth said, "right down on the end. If the weather is good we like to have our little ceremony out here. Unfortunately, the day that Rushdie came, it rained like the dickens and we had to move everything indoors."

"So where do the writers stay?" Ramona asked.

"You can't see it in the picture here," Stainforth said, "but the main part of the villa is back a hundred yards or so. It's got great views of the Arno, and on a clear day you should be able to see the Ponte Vecchio from your bedroom windows."

"Well, I'm happy to hear that," I said. Oh, if you could only have heard the way he said "Ponte Vecchio"! It must have taken years to get that one right.

Rex watched me as I flipped through the stiff pages. He thought he knew what I was thinking and he was dead wrong. I was irritated, sure. But it had nothing to do with prizes. What it had to do with was the fact that I'd come over here to have a real conversation about helping out some homeless kids in Maine. But was there any way I was going to convince him of that? Not in a million years.

"Cool," I said. I handed the book back to Rex. His eyes had not left me once.

"You think I should take it?" he asked.

"The place looks beautiful," I said.

"That wasn't my question."

"Rex, I'm the last one you should be asking about this. Seriously."

He didn't find my answer satisfying. His look was close to murderous.

"Horton doesn't believe in prizes," he said. "He's a purist. He was a very promising historian when he was young. People expected great things of him, but he's such a perfectionist, he made it awfully hard on himself." He cracked the book open and tilted his head to have another look at the pictures. "But I need Horton. Horton keeps me honest. But I do believe he thinks I'm a bit of a glory hound."

"Rex, if you want to take this prize, you should take it."

He clapped the book shut. "I'll need a day or two to think about this."

I patted Stainforth on the back. "Very nice to meet you," I said.

"And very nice to meet you!" he said. He seemed a little rattled by all the strange goings-on in the room, but at least he had his good manners to see him through. "Listen, I don't know what you're doing tomorrow, but Francesca and I are planning on taking Rex and Ramona to brunch. I'd be honored if you could join us."

"Horton hates brunch," Rex said.

"But, hey," I said, "with a group like this, who could say no? I'd love to come."

The next morning at eleven they came by to pick me up and we drove to this fancy Mexican restaurant on the north side of town. It was quite a place, one of those joints where you'd want your daughter to have her wedding reception if you had a couple million bucks to burn. The lobby was a jungle of ferns and palm trees and, best of all, there was a beady-eyed parrot in a cage that looked as if it would bite off your finger if you came anywhere close.

The hostess showed us to a far room and seated us in chairs that must have been carved by Aztec slaves. Over orange juice, Stainforth tried to regale us with his adventures entertaining the various winners of the Vita Nuova Prize. He told us about truffle hunting in the Apennines with his good friend Wisława, about driving all over Florence late one night, trying to find a cassette of *48 Hours* for Kenzaburō Ōe, who was a huge Eddie Murphy fan. He told us about the uproar some Finnish author had created when he sent his pasta back, and about the brilliant lecture Kundera had given on the European novel.

The only problem was that Rex was in one of his moods. Part of it, I'm sure, was that he was not happy about my having horned in on their party, but it felt as if it was more than that. Restless and irritated, he was only half-listening. Ramona seemed out of sorts too, which I'd always taken to be an early warning signal.

Rex sprinkled salt on a chip, then looked over his shoulder, trying to get the waiter's attention. When he finally slid the salt shaker to the middle of the table, Stainforth stopped talking.

"It sounds remarkable," Rex said, "absolutely remarkable. But I did a lot of thinking last night." Francesca straightened in her chair, her beautiful almond eyes widening. She had on this red dress she could have worn to the Oscars.

"Dudley, I can't tell you how moved I am by you and Francesca offering me this prize. I am deeply honored. But I have no illusions about how I am viewed by the literary world. I know my place. And I don't want to make a fool of myself. Or of you. Regretfully, I'm afraid I have to say no."

Francesca gave a small cry. Stainforth looked as if he'd just heard that his mother had died. Head down, I stirred my margarita with a straw. I have to say, I was impressed with old Rex.

It took Stainforth several seconds to recover, and when he did, his voice was still shaky. "May I say something?" he said.

"Of course," Rex said.

"I don't want to disagree with you, but I think it's impossible for any writer to know how he is viewed by the literary world. But I do know that our selection committee approached their task with the utmost rigor. They all agreed that what you've accomplished is monumental, and they're some of the most distinguished writers and critics in Europe. I'd give you their names if I could, but I'm afraid I can't."

Rex toyed with his silverware. He was wearing his favorite bolo tie, the one with the Texas star, and cinched up tight it made him look a little like a child.

"But please," Rex said, "I hope you're not telling me that they consider what I do high art."

"High art?" Francesca said, as if she'd never heard the term before.

"The truth is," Stainforth said, "we've struggled with this issue for years."

"What issue is that?"

"What constitutes serious literature. I've always felt . . . and the majority of our committee has slowly come around to my side on this . . . that we've been hampered by too rarified a definition." I began to down my margarita with long, steady sucks. The guy was starting to get on my nerves. "Look at the history of the novel. Look at Balzac, Dickens."

"Exactly," Francesca said. "If you're looking for a contemporary writer with that sort of ambition and scope and engagement with the world, I think Schoeninger is the first name you come up with."

"Let's not overdo this now," Rex said.

"Probably half the people in this room have read a book of yours," Stainforth said. "Every summer cabin in America has a shelf of your novels. That counts for something."

"I'm not saying it doesn't count for something . . ." Rex said.

"Every year we get dozens of letters from lawyers and housewives, high school teachers and GIs, asking how it can be that we've overlooked you for so long," Francesca said.

"They're not writing us about Djuna Barnes," Stainforth said.

Ramona took a chip. She had been silent for a long time, which wasn't like her. All I could figure was that she was a little intimidated by these two being so damn good-looking.

"I understand that you might be wary," Stainforth said. "We know you've taken your hits."

Rex shot me a sidelong glance. "'The Grandma Moses of American literature'?"

"Oh, that!" Francesca said. "That was just silly!"

Stainforth seemed astonished. "That's it? V. S. Mohle?"

"I'm not just talking about Mohle," Rex said. "But the fact is that I was offered one other prize in my life . . ."

"That's not true, Rex!" Ramona said. "What about all your presidential medals?"

He waved her away. "They don't count. I'm talking about serious literary prizes. And that one turned into holy hell."

I licked the salt off the rim of my glass while Stainforth scratched his neck. "But Rex," he said, "how can you still be fretting about that? The man was clearly disturbed. That was just small-minded jealousy."

"Not entirely."

"What a vile human being!" Francesca said. "And that book of his! Am I mistaken, or isn't it totally dated?" Rex, to his credit, seemed skeptical. Francesca turned to me. "Horton, have you tried to read it lately?"

"I have, actually . . ." A sharp kick to the shin made me jump. When I glanced up, Ramona was shooting me threatening looks, eying me the way a secret service agent might eye a potential presidential assassin.

Rex had had enough. "What do you say we get something to eat?" he said. He put his hands on the arms of his chair as if he was about to get up. The rest of us sat there, feeling bad.

The old guy was aching for the prize. Anyone could see it. But how could he accept it with V. S. Mohle sitting across the table from him?

I needed to do something. They may have been great-looking, but I didn't trust Stainforth and Francesca any farther than I could throw them. I may not have sussed out exactly what their game was yet, but, honestly, did it matter? The problem was that if Rex turned the prize down, he was going to blame me. I knew the way the man's mind worked.

All I wanted was another shot at the man's money. That wasn't going to happen until I got back into his good graces. It was time for a little magnanimity of spirit.

"You know what I think?" I said.

They all swung around to look at me. "What?" Rex said.

"I think you should take it," I said. "I think these two are absolutely right. You deserve this. What have you written? Sixty books?" In a small alcove, a trio of Mexican women in native dress rolled out tortillas, pounded them flat, flipped them onto huge black skillets. "You've got two million readers and you're still brooding over what some idiot said about you twenty-five years ago?"

"I wouldn't exactly call it brooding," Rex said.

"What are you afraid of? Do you really think he's going to come out of the woods to denounce you? Do you really think he doesn't regret acting like such an asshole?"

I wasn't sure Ramona was buying my act. She'd already formed some pretty strong opinions of me, whoever the hell she thought I was. She rose from her chair, ready to head to the buffet tables.

"Rex," I said, "I'll bet you dollars to doughnuts, if he heard about your getting this prize, he'd be the first to congratulate you."

"You think so?" he said.

"I know so," I said. I reached across and put my hand on his. Francesca and Stainforth exchanged glances.

"Okay, then," Rex said.

"Okay?" Stainforth said.

"And what does that mean, Rex?" Francesca put the question softly.

"It means that Ramona and I are coming to Italy."

Stainforth gave a short, swift jab, like a tennis player who's just served an ace on set point. Francesca was so excited she barely knew what to do with herself. She gave Rex a hug and me a kiss on the cheek. Ramona was grinning like a banshee. If the three of them had had confetti, they would have thrown it.

Stainforth got up to shake Rex's hand. He squeezed my elbow and mouthed a silent thank you. Everybody was congratulating everybody. It was hard to keep track. Rex sat smiling quietly through all the commotion, but he'd been moved by what I'd said, I could tell. We all retrieved our glasses. When we raised them to give a toast, it was my eyes he sought, and when he found them he gave me a two-fingered salute.

The food was great. There were enchiladas smothered in a thick smoky green sauce, shredded pork wrapped in banana leaves, peppers stuffed with raisins and nuts and ground tapir. A mariachi band came through with trumpets and guitars, their black outfits glistening with silver studs, enormous hats tilted back like Steve Martin and Chevy Chase in *Three Amigos.*

My second margarita was better than my first. It's a beautiful thing, how well people can get along, once they stop getting in one another's way.

My shin was hurting like hell, but everyone was having the best time. Ramona and Francesca chatted away like long-lost sisters—it turned out that one of Francesca's cousins had gone to riding school in England with Ramona's brother, so they had stories to tell. But the best part of it was seeing Rex laugh, loose and easy, like a man who's just been told by the doctor that he doesn't have cancer. It was a great thing I'd done.

I was sure Stainforth and Francesca had something up their sleeves, but what did it matter? They would be flying off to Italy in a day or two and then I'd have the old guy to myself. And right where I wanted him.

Stainforth paid the bill while Rex spoke to a couple of the diners who'd come up for autographs. As we were walking out Rex got the bright idea of taking Stainforth and Francesca for a tour of Austin. We piled into the van, drove through the university, and took a spin around the capital.

We ended up at Barton Springs, where we all got out and strolled to the chain-link fence to have a look. It was a cool, sunny November afternoon and the pool sparkled, a couple hundred yards of clear water, set down in pale limestone cliffs. A half dozen swimmers were out doing laps, and people dotted the sloping lawns like seals, sleeping, catching a few rays, rubbing one another with suntan lotion, while a pair of tattooed kids did cannonballs off the diving board.

Ramona launched into a history of the place and was doing a good job, but after a couple of minutes Rex lost interest and plopped down at a picnic table. Francesca was quick to join him.

"So Rex," she said, "I hear one of your students sold her novel for a lot of money."

Rex gave a tired smile. "Isn't that something?"

"Oh, it is," she said. "It's very exciting."

Pigeons strutted across the gravel, looking for food. Nasty, pigeons. Barry always used to tell me that the most vicious animals in the world were the rabbit and the pigeon, and I believe him. I rubbed at my eyes. Tequila, I tell you, it's the devil's drink.

"It looks as if she's on her way," Rex said. "Now all we need to do is figure out what to do with the rest of them."

"It's a problem, isn't it?" she said.

"Oh, it is," Rex said.

"Dudley and I were just talking about this."

"Really?" Rex said.

"Please, Francesca," Stainforth said. He helped Ramona pull her shawl over her shoulders. "This is not the time."

"No, go ahead," Rex said. "I want to hear."

Francesca looked up at Stainforth with those big almond eyes of hers. "Is it all right?"

"Whatever Rex wants, that's fine," Stainforth said, his fingers still resting lightly on Ramona's back. I could tell from the glow on her face that she liked it.

"Well, anyway," Francesca said, "for some time now we've been talking about how to make ourselves more relevant, how to open ourselves up to the modern world a bit." She tossed back her wonderful mane of hair. "And one of the ideas we've been playing with is offering talented young writers like your students six-month residencies."

My ears perked up, and not in a good way. "Residencies?" I said.

"You have some opinion about residencies?" Rex said.

"Not really," I said. I should have stopped right there, but I'd had a couple of margaritas. "I'm no expert, of course, but I've gotten to know Rex's students fairly well. I'm not sure another residency is what they need. You don't want them to get too pampered."

Rex's face clouded over. "Pampered?" he said.

"You know what I mean? You don't want to hand them everything on a silver platter. Isn't it about time for them to go out and get a dose of the real world?"

"Oh, they'll be getting a dose of that soon enough." He chewed on his upper lip for a couple of seconds. The thing about Rex was, when he got his dander up you could usually see it coming. "The point is that we need to help them however we can. Those young people over there are going to be the great writers of the next generation." I was sure he had to be kidding, but it didn't look as if he was. I couldn't help but roll my eyes. He caught me at it. "You don't agree?"

"Rex, there's no way you can know that. They're just kids."

His jaw tightened, set like an old sturgeon. "I've read their work. Have you?"

"Some of it, yeah."

"I promise you, they're going to leave us in the dust. Not to mention, they're not going to be wasting half their lives in petty feuds."

I would have laughed out loud if I'd dared. What did Rex know? Maybe they wouldn't get involved in feuds, but they certainly weren't above running off to Las Vegas with their buddy's girlfriend. I looked over my shoulder. A bunch of parents and toddlers loaded onto a kiddie train.

"I'm sorry, Francesca," Rex said. "You were saying . . ."

"Oh, yes," she said. "Anyway, we've just started a building campaign to put up these nice little bungalows."

"Good for you," Rex said.

"We see it as a kind of refuge," she said. "Sort of a modern-day version of the monastic retreat."

"A little like Yaddo then?" Rex said.

"But different. Think Yaddo with Etruscan tombs," Stainforth said.

"And a Roman aqueduct just up the road."

They were good, these two. Real pros. And where was Ramona, now that she was needed? Totally smitten. The defenses had been breached.

From far off I heard the rattle of a diving board, a whoop, a splash. I spied a greasy packet of abandoned french fries on the far bench of the picnic table. I retrieved it and began to toss bits of the soggy fries to the pigeons and squirrels.

"We know there are a lot of residencies," Francesca said. "But we think this could be something special." She recrossed those long beautiful legs of hers and put her hand on Rex's sleeve, talking only to him.

"The location alone . . . just to be surrounded by the examples of the great classical authors . . . to walk the same hills that Dante walked, to breathe the same air that Petrarch breathed. I think it could force these young writers to set their sights a little higher."

"I'm sure you're right," Rex said. Pigeons soared in from everywhere, nearly taking Ramona's head off.

"And I've also had this idea," Francesca said.

"Please, tell me," Rex said.

"Now I know this will sound *really* crazy, but I've even thought of inviting opera singers."

My head came up. Could she be serious? I've never been to an opera, but I've seen a little of it on TV when nothing else was on, barrel-chested characters wandering around the stage in wigs and buckle shoes.

"Rex loves the opera," Ramona said.

"Ramona, how perfect!" Francesca slapped her hands and turned back to Rex. "Don't you think your students could get a lot out of that? It would be wonderful for them to attend a master class and see how hard these singers work."

"Christ A-mighty!"

Everyone turned to stare as if that had come from me. And I guess it must have.

"You have a problem with that?" Rex said.

I tossed the last couple of limp fries into the mob of thrashing birds. "I don't know if it's a problem, but I just don't think your students would be all that excited by the idea of hanging out with a bunch of opera singers."

"So who would they be excited by?"

"Oh, I don't know. Barry White, maybe."

Not a flicker of recognition from any of them. "Barry White?" Rex said.

"You know. The Walrus of Love. 'Can't Get Enough of Your Love, Babe.'"

The way they gaped at me, you would have thought I was speaking Chinese. "I'm afraid I don't understand," Rex said.

"It's not going to work, Rex! You can't make somebody a great writer, no matter how much you give them. They're going to do it or they're not. You had to make sacrifices to be a writer. Why shouldn't they?"

His eyes narrowed, as if he suspected that I knew more than I was supposed to have known. "Maybe because I wouldn't want anybody to have to go through what I went through," he said. He kicked at one of the pigeons, sent it fluttering away, and looked up at Stainforth. "So I take it you're looking for partners?"

"We are," Stainforth said. "But please, let's be clear about this. We're not asking you for money."

"Absolutely not," Francesca said.

"And why not?" Rex leaned forward, the cuffs of his plaid trousers riding up on his gleaming shins.

"It wouldn't be right," Stainforth said. "Here we are, giving you this big prize. It would look terrible."

"I don't care how it would look," Rex said. A lifeguard's whistle sounded in the distance. "If it would make you more comfortable, I could give it anonymously. No one needs to know." Francesca and Stainforth glanced at each other. Nothing was supposed to come this easy. "So how much is it going to cost you?"

"What did we say, Francesca?" Stainforth said. "We were looking at those figures the other day."

"Let's see now. We were thinking fifteen to twenty bungalows." She brushed a leaf from Rex's lapel. "And then there's this extraordinary sixteenth-century church we were hoping to restore for readings and concerts . . . I'd say five million."

Black disks spun before my eyes like the wheels of Roman chariots. I was about to pass out. Ramona raised a finger to lodge an objection, but Rex put a hand up to stop her.

"Consider it done," he said. He rocked forward several times, trying to get up. Stainforth took his elbow and eased him to his feet. "And now, if you don't mind, I need to go home and take a nap."

Walking back to the van, I limped along behind the others. I felt as if I'd been pole-axed. Five million dollars? Rex was giving them my five million dollars? Whatever our differences, I'd always considered Rex to be a man of his word. But just the week before he'd told me he was tapped out. Now apparently he wasn't. What was I supposed to do? Put on a spectacular red dress and start batting my big almond eyes?

Maybe it was my own fault. I was the one who'd given my blessing to this unholy alliance, and now I was paying the price. But it was a killer.

Waiting as everybody wrestled Rex into the van, I glanced up at the hill above the parking lot. A boy stood in the trees, staring down at us. He was ten or eleven, shivering in his bathing suit. He had something pressed to his chest, a towel, probably, but given the state I was in, it was hard not to imagine that it was a teddy bear, held close, and that it was snow, not light, flickering through the branches, a snow that was only going to keep falling harder and harder.

Chapter Sixteen

When I got back to my house, I kicked into high gear. I phoned Chester and told him I had a task for him. I asked him to go to the library, collect anything he could find by Dudley Stainforth, and bring it to me, the earlier the better. As soon as I hung up, I sat down at the computer and began to do some serious checking on my own.

On the surface, everything looked legit. The man had credentials up the wazoo. Princeton undergraduate, All-Ivy squash player, Rhodes Scholar, Harvard Ph.D., winner of the Prix de Rome and a Guggenheim, some big-deal translation of *The Divine Comedy*, seven years on the Yale faculty, before putting together the Vita Nuova Prize.

I found a list of all the previous winners, which wasn't that useful, since I didn't recognize any of them—Günter Grass, Nadine Gordimer, Milan Kundera, Kenzaburō Ōe, Maguib Mahfouz, Wisława Szymborska.

The pictures were more helpful, a lot of them of Stainforth placing a chunky gold medal around the neck of some white-haired old geezer or strolling with a group of tuxedoed donors through a courtyard where water rushed from the eroded mouths of lions. Maybe I was just making it up, but it seemed to me that in nearly every photograph, Stainforth had just a trace of a smirk, the look of a man who was used to being the cock of the walk.

Around six, I went for a walk to clear my head, and when I got home there was a stack of books on my front stoop, three volumes of Stainforth's translation of *The Divine Comedy* and a skinny collection of essays on the Borgias.

I spent all of Monday morning stewing over what my next move was going to be. I thumbed through Stainforth's version of *The Divine Comedy* (what a nasty piece of work that is!) and then got back on the computer to see what else I could dig up. There had to be a pissed-off ex-girlfriend out there somewhere, a whiff of a scandal, some old enemy willing to talk, but I'll be damned if I could find anything.

I did come up with a few articles about the Vita Nuova Prize. Most of them were in Italian and the half dozen I found in English were at least ten years old. I read statements from the judges and excerpts from the writers' acceptance speeches, which were mostly about agony and sweat, sorrow and beauty, whether or not we could survive as a species. Your basic climb-every-mountain stuff.

You ever see a dog when he knows there's a rat under the porch and he can't get at it? It drives him out of his mind. That's how I was. Stainforth was a phony. It oozed out of him like oil out of a smoked chub. The problem was I couldn't prove it.

Early that afternoon I called Rex's, hoping to have a candid conversation with him, but Ramona was there to intercept. She said he was having a nap, but she let me know that they'd had the most wonderful lunch with Stainforth and Francesca. They'd ended up at the office of the president of the university and he'd gotten so excited about their idea he'd called in the provost and the director of development to join them.

"He went for the bit about the opera singers?" I asked.

"He thought it was fantastic. I think that's probably what sold him on the whole idea."

"Isn't that something?" I said. "Listen, Ramona, I was wondering if Rex would have any time in the next few days. I'd love to sit down, catch up a bit."

Her voice went cool as a doorman's. "Of course. One of the things Rex mentioned to me this morning . . . we're flying to Big Bend on Thursday. He's got some research to finish up. He wanted to know if you'd like to go with us."

"I'd love to," I said. "And what about Stainforth and Francesca?"

"They're leaving tomorrow," she said. "But they'll be back soon enough. It's amazing how this has all taken on a life of its own."

There was no more time for shilly-shallying. Tuesday morning, after a cup of coffee and some toast, I sat down at the phone with a list of every name I'd been able to find that had anything to do with the Vita Nuova Prize—donors, judges, staff, interns, the works.

You ever try to make an international phone call? Do you have any idea how many numbers you have to punch in? You get one wrong, you have to start all over again, and even if you get it right, you're probably going to get somebody who doesn't speak English.

I must have been on the phone for eight hours straight. It was mind-numbing work. For most of the names on the list, I was never able to track down a number. A lot of the time, even if I had a number, nobody would answer or I'd get a machine, in which case I'd just hang up. When I got somebody who only spoke Italian, I'd get off as quick as I could.

I was able to reach maybe twenty people who spoke passable English. Most of those were pretty much what you'd expect. They went on and on about how wonderful it was, and a couple of the ex-interns remembered working for Stainforth as being the most glorious summer of their lives.

But then there was this other handful. The line I was using was that I was writing an article for *Harper's* on the Vita Nuova Prize, and as soon as I said that, several of them hung up on me. One woman burst into tears. A former donor who built heavy machinery in St. Louis kept repeating, "I'm not at liberty to say."

A professor from Manchester, England, who'd served as a judge during the early days of the prize, lit into me. He wanted to know who I was and why I would be writing such a thing. He bombarded me with questions. Did Stainforth know I was doing this? And what was the name of my editor at *Harper's*?

"I want you to know that I haven't spoken to any of these people for years," he said. "I've washed my hands of the whole affair."

"But why would you need to wash your hands?" I said.

"It's none of your damn business," he said. "It was a grand idea. And in some ways he did a grand job."

"And in other ways he didn't?"

"Young man, I do not need you putting words in my mouth! I wasn't born yesterday. I know perfectly well what you're after, but you're not going to get it from me. Good day!"

When he slammed down the phone, it sounded as if it echoed halfway across the Atlantic.

It was getting discouraging. I pressed my fingers to my eyes and then glanced at the clock. It was four and I hadn't had anything to eat since breakfast.

I walked over to Guadalupe and had myself some soggy sweet-and-sour pork, which helped settle my nerves. Eight hours on the phone, and what did I have to show for it besides a crick in the neck? Oh, I suppose you could say that I'd made progress. I now knew that somebody was hiding something, but as Barry used to say, that and a token will get you a ride on the IRT.

My next move came to me in a dream, or something close to it. I woke up before dawn on Wednesday, listening to the thud of newspapers in driveways, the cooing of doves. I must have been lying there for an hour, letting little wisps of things float in and out of my brain like leaves on a slow-moving stream.

It was so obvious. The only people I hadn't contacted were the actual winners of the Vita Nuova Prize. I suppose there were good reasons why I hadn't. Not only were world-famous writers going to be a bitch to track down, but they were going to be surrounded by a wall of people like Ramona whose job it was to keep people like me as far away as possible.

But on the other hand, I knew about famous writers, being one myself. There wasn't anything special about them. It wasn't as if they were rock stars or Wall Street bankers or Jerry Seinfeld. They were just ordinary Joes who'd been sitting at their desks for years moving little men around their little toy towns. And if anybody was going to be able to tell me about Stainforth, they could.

But what could I offer them that would coax them out of their holes? Another prize? These guys had enough prizes to choke a horse. A teaching gig? Pathetic. A cover story with a big-time magazine? Fat chance. No, I was going to have to offer them something they were all hungry for, no matter how much they denied it: a major movie deal.

After a quick breakfast, I went out to the screen porch in back with my phone and started punching in numbers for Paris, London, Tokyo, Warsaw.

I was too careful at first. Afraid of setting off a firestorm of calls to Hollywood, all I said to the various lackeys was that a very prominent director was interested in adapting their boss's work to the screen.

When they asked for the name, I said I could not divulge that at this time. That didn't cut much ice with anyone, though Kenzaburō Ōe's assistant promised to pass on the information.

It wasn't until I threw caution to the winds and told Günter Grass's secretary that I was Steven Spielberg, and that I wanted to make a movie out of *Cat and Mouse*, that I finally got through to a live author.

Günter couldn't have been nicer. The first thing out of his mouth was how *E.T.* had always been one of his favorite films.

"But *Cat and Mouse*, it would be a hard movie to make." The man's accent made him sound like a bouncer in a really tough bar. "Who were you thinking of casting?"

"The actors I've been talking to are Leonardo DiCaprio and Tobey Maguire."

"Ja?"

"Leo loves the book. And after *Titanic*, it will be a great change of pace. How would it be if I had Leo call you?"

"I would be honored."

A sound like the pattering of rain made me turn. My glamorous landlady, thumb over the end of her hose, sent a soft spray over the flowers in her backyard. I felt bad about sticking her with a couple thousand dollars in international calls, but what can you do?

"Good," I said. "He's a thoughtful young man. Oh, and Günter, while we're on the phone here, can I ask you one other thing?"

"Of course."

"Do you know a man named Dudley Stainforth?" The silence was so long I though the line had gone dead. "Günter, are you still there?"

"Ja, ja."

"I was asking you about Dudley Stainforth. I believe he gave you the Vita Nuova Prize."

"Ja, he did."

"V.S.!" My landlady's voice cut through the morning air like a scythe. I looked back over my shoulder. She waved gaily, one arm stretched high, like the queen on a homecoming float. "How are you this morning?" she shouted.

I gave her the A-okay sign. "You met him, then? Our friend Stainforth?" Günter said.

"Yes, just recently," I said. "I found him quite a charming guy."

"That's one word for it," Günter said. "And how did you meet?"

"He's offered me the prize, actually," I said.

"Really?" he said. "I thought he only gave it to writers."

My landlady tossed her hose aside and walked toward the gate between the two yards as if intending to come over and have a neighborly chat. I put a hand up to stop her and it did stop her, but it didn't put her in a good mood. Think about the way Girl Scouts look when you tell them you're not going to buy their cookies.

"I guess he's making an exception!" Silence on the other end of the line.

"You don't approve?" I said.

My landlady, downcast, ran her fingers along the top of the picket fence. I held up the phone and pointed to it to let her see that I was on a call. We gestured back and forth like a couple of baggage handlers on the runway until she finally got the picture and retreated with a mock-curtsy.

"May I speak frankly?" Günter said.

"Of course."

"If I were you, I wouldn't go near it with a ten-foot pole."

"And why is that?"

"Has he asked you for money yet?"

"Well, in a way . . ."

"And he still has that little vixen working for him?"

"Francesca? Oh, absolutely. But it's a real prize, isn't it? The list of people he's given it to is remarkable."

"That's true. I give him credit. His taste is impeccable. And in the beginning, it was a very reputable operation. The problem was, he liked to throw the money around. There was a big financial scandal. Most of his major donors left him. Steven, maybe you don't want to hear all this."

"No, please, go on."

"It was hard to say what happened to him exactly, but he got desperate and everything took a turn. He started putting on more and more events, trying to raise money. At first many of the writers tried to help him, but after a while it felt as if he was parading us around like animals in a petting zoo. You see what I'm saying, Steven?"

"Of course."

"One summer he asked me to come back to present the prize to a great Russian writer I've admired all my life. He was very old and very ill. He had spent years in a prison camp, wrote his most important books there, without pen or paper, been poisoned by the KGB.

"I'd never met him, and so when I got there I asked Stainforth to introduce me. He takes me to the table. There he sits, this great Russian writer, his beard down to his waist, looking like the unhappiest man I'd ever seen.

"In the chair next to him was the mistress of some hedge fund manager from Miami. She had amazing breasts. I could barely take my eyes off them. Later I heard that the hedge fund manager had paid twenty thousand euros to sit next to the great man for dinner."

"It sounds like a circus," I said.

"It was a circus," Günter said. "Maybe these things are always circuses, but most people have the sense to disguise them as something else. Stainforth was too blatant about it. The final straw was when he was caught forging some of the writers' signatures on his fund-raising letters. I suppose it's a shame. He really had something and in the end managed to turn it into the laughingstock of the literary world."

"So people know about this?"

"The people in the know, know about it. The last thing I heard, he's been trying to peddle the prize to all these rich American novelists . . . Stephen King . . . Dean Koontz . . . All those guys turned him down, but some old English mystery writer would have lost all her money if her brother hadn't stepped in. So did he show you the book?"

"What book is that?"

"The one with all the pictures. With the beautiful gardens and the fountains and the busts of the great writers lined up on the wall . . ."

"He did."

Günter roared again, even louder than before. "He's very good, isn't he? You have to hand it to him. But, Mr. Spielberg, if I were you, I'd stick to my Oscars. This man is a jackal."

After Günter hung up, I went to the kitchen and set the phone on the receiver. I headed to the front door, hoping to intercept my landlady and soothe any ruffled feathers, but as I checked for my keys, the phone rang. Sure that it was Günter calling me back with one more juicy morsel, I leapt across the living room and picked up on the fourth ring.

It was LaTasha, wanting to know what stories we were supposed to be discussing in class. For a second I was struck dumb. Class? What class? Then I remembered it was Wednesday. I told her not to worry. There weren't any stories, but I was cooking up something good, I said.

I went to the office and spent an hour flipping through *The Wings of Prometheus* looking for exercises, but it was hopeless. I was agitated. I suppose I should have been happy. I now had proof that Stainforth was as big a snake as I'd suspected he was. The Vita Nuova deal was a total fraud. A prize that even Dean Koontz had said no to? That tells you something.

My next step was going to be the hard one. I knew I was already way out on thin ice. You make a hundred international phone calls, you're bound to stir things up. God knows all I'd set in motion. One thing I knew for sure. In a couple of days, Günter was going to be calling Spielberg's office about his movie deal. Would they be able to trace it back to me? And how long would that take?

I lay down on the floor of my office, buried my head in my arms, and took a twenty-minute nap. When I woke up, I was better.

I got out a yellow pad and tried to come up with an exercise on my own. My first half dozen ideas were terrible. Describe the worst picnic you've ever been on. Describe the death of your favorite pet. Describe how the parents of your favorite cartoon character met. Describe a thawing refrigerator from the point of view of a frozen chicken. But then I hit on something that seemed a perfect fit, given the morning I'd had. Write a single page that begins with these four words. *I wish I'd never.*

When I gave the students their exercise that afternoon, they settled down to work without complaint. I went to the window and stared out at the shadows of clouds moving across the burnt-up grass.

After the morning I'd had, I was still steaming. What had me most upset was the idea of Rex being played for a fool. I know, I'd been playing him for a fool for months, but that was different. Rex and I had a relationship.

I hate it when people think they can take advantage of us writers. They think we're naïve, that we have our heads in the clouds, that we're so hungry for any crumb of praise they can treat us like children.

I'd thought some terrible things about Rex, I'll admit it, but look at all the good he'd done for people. He'd given these kids the biggest shot they'd ever have, and they knew it. He read their stuff, spent his afternoons talking to them about it, treated them like his own sons and daughters. He was an old man, flickering in and out, and now Stainforth came waltzing in and was going to turn him into the laughingstock of the world. What was I going to do about it? It wasn't clear.

I had the kids go until half past two and then I had them read what they'd come up with. The first three or four were terrific. The one thing Chester would never do again was go hang-gliding on acid. The one thing LaTasha would never do again was call her junior high school principal a honky. Mel would never again scrawl DECEASED across his alumni bulletin before mailing it back, and Brett would never again try to tickle the football coach's bare foot under the door of the bathroom stall.

I felt like a genius. We were cruising. Everyone was having a great time, laughing, bursting into a round of applause when each reader finished. So why did I call on Dominique? Didn't I know it could only mean trouble? There were a couple others who still hadn't read. But Dominique had a way of letting you know when she was ready and she was definitely letting me know, leaning forward on her elbows, staring at me from under those lowered Cleopatra eyebrows of hers.

"Dominique?" I said. "You got something for us?"

She picked up her pad, bracelets jangling, and took a long look at it. "This is a little different," she said.

"That's fine," I said. "Let's hear it."

"It's a poem."

"All the better," I said.

She pushed back a mass of black curls. She didn't look at anyone while she read.

I wish I'd given X a kiss on the cheek
Rather than that flicker of tongue
While Y waited outside in the car.
I wish I'd never gone out for margaritas with X
After Y had cried for two hours about his father's death.

I wish I'd never tried to sleep with two men at the same time
And I really wish they hadn't been writers.
I wish I'd kept my diary under lock and key
I wish I hadn't tried to lie my way out of it
Or that I'd been better at it.
But if wishes were horses
Even beggars would ride.

She folded the paper in two and stared at Brett, who stared back, nostrils twitching. Nick slumped in his chair as if he wanted to slither under the table. Chester had his pen clenched in his teeth like a pirate, and LaTasha, for no reason I could understand, seemed to be grinning.

"Can I see it?" I said.

She handed me the piece of paper and I reread it silently. All I could think was, these were the characters Stainforth and Francesca wanted to send off to Italy to see what they could learn from opera singers. These were not people you wanted to put in a bunch of bungalows together.

This crap that Dominique had written, what was the point of it? Was this all there was in the world to write about? How many versions of this story was I going to have to read? Why couldn't these kids be more like Schoeninger and write about people founding leper colonies and inventing barbed wire? Schoeninger's characters may have talked to one another like they were giving commencement addresses, but at least they were doing something with their lives besides screwing each other's girlfriends.

When I finished reading, I looked up at Dominique. She stared back at me, almost as if she was daring me to say something. If she'd meant to shock her classmates, she'd succeeded. Me, I wasn't that impressed. I'd just spent the morning on the phone with Günter Grass. Compared to Stainforth, Dominique looked like Little Bo Peep.

People lie. People cheat. People read one another's diaries. Welcome to the Fun House. I handed the paper back to her and gave her a pat on the shoulder.

"You guys knock me out, you really do," I said. "How about for next time you all bring in a page from your favorite author? And be prepared to talk about what's so all-fired great about it."

After the students left, I went to my office, turned off the computer, and headed downstairs. The place was quiet as a tomb. It was after five and Mildred was gone for the day. The lights were out and on the bulletin board the flyers advertising summer residencies fluttered like moths under a slow-moving fan.

I peered through the slats in the blinds. Chester, LaTasha, and Mercedes argued madly with one another, strolling down the sidewalk.

I went to the kitchen and checked the refrigerator. After the day I'd had, I was starving. Things did not look promising. There were a couple of cartons of yogurt, some celery sticks, and, way in the back, a Ziploc bag.

I retrieved the bag and was delighted to see that it contained three chicken wings. God knows whose they were. One of the students'? Probably not Mildred's. Maybe they were left over from the reception after my reading, but that had been a while ago. I didn't want to get ptomaine poisoning, but those wings did look good.

I opened the bag, lifted one of the wings out with thumb and forefinger, bent over the sink, and took a bite. What a happy moment! There was more meat there than I'd expected, and the cayenne pepper gave it some fire.

I nibbled and gnawed, swaying back and forth like a harmonica player. To do justice to a chicken wing, you need to be a real artist with your tongue, but fried skin and spice and a touch of grease, you can't do a whole lot better. The only thing you needed to make it perfect was a little blue cheese dipping sauce.

I tossed the first wing in the garbage and was going to town on number two when I heard a sound. It was almost like a moan, but I wasn't sure what it was. Was it near? Had it come from outside? Was someone having sex up in the conference room? I couldn't tell.

I stood very still for half a minute, just listening, a mangled chicken wing in my right hand. Then I heard the sound again. This time it sounded more like a grunt, like someone being hit in the belly. It was not coming from outside or from upstairs. It was down here on the first floor with me.

I dropped the second wing in the trash, sealed the Ziploc bag, and put it back in the refrigerator, stealthy as a spy.

I eased the refrigerator door shut and made my way silently to the front hall. Except for a few rays of late afternoon sun glaring through the blinds, the place had the gloomy feel of an abandoned subway station.

I was freaking out. Could it be the cleaning crew? The campus police? Maybe one of those fund-raiser guys who'd had an appointment and somehow gotten locked in.

There was a pair of offices on the east side of the building. One door was shut and the other, Wayne's, was open, but there was no light on inside. I took another three or four quiet steps and tilted my head so I could peer inside from a safe distance.

Wayne stood at the window in a shiny blazer, his back to me, bouncing from foot to foot. His fists were clenched. Every few seconds he would punch at the air, short jabs, and make these little sounds.

"Wayne?" I said.

I pretty much scared the wits out of him. He spun around so fast he nearly fell. "V.S.?"

He was wearing an artistic tie. I didn't think I'd ever seen him so dressed up, but he looked like a kid, a really embarrassed kid.

"You okay?" I said.

"I'm fine. Just fine. Please, come in. Let me turn on a light."

He snapped on the lamp next to his desk. I came in and warily took a seat on his couch. His face was pale and splotchy as an under-cooked salmon.

"So what's going on?" I said.

"A lot, I guess," he said, rubbing the back of his neck.

"Okay."

"I didn't think anyone else was here," he said.

"I didn't either," I said. I licked my peppery lips.

"But I'm glad you're here. I guess it's only right to tell you first."

"Tell you what?"

He leaned against his desk. "I'm not quite sure how to say this . . . I don't know if you're aware of it or not . . . there's no reason that you should be . . . but your presence here has probably had a bigger effect on me than on anyone else."

"Now, Wayne, you don't have to flatter me," I said.

"I'm not flattering you. You know that poem by Rilke?"

"Which one?"

"The one where he's looking at the statue of Apollo? And the trick of it is that the headless torso is somehow scrutinizing him . . . And the last line is, 'You must change your life.'" I stared at him, speech-less. That didn't sound like much of a poem to me. "I didn't become a writer so I could end up directing a writing program. I did it because

I thought that one day I would create something great, something that would endure." Brooding, he fingered the brass buttons on his sleeve. "But I had a family, kids to raise. I always thought this was going to be temporary, this teaching thing. I figured that sooner or later I would write a novel that would knock everyone's socks off and I'd be able to go back to writing full-time, but that never happened." He loosened his tie, grimacing. "So I suppose you could say that in the past few years I've settled in. I've resigned myself to being a good citizen, a good teacher, a passable father . . . writing when I can catch an hour here and there. But then you showed up." Covering my mouth with my hand, I worked a bit of chicken loose from between my teeth with my tongue. "It's funny, when you first got here, I was suspicious."

"How do you mean?"

"I don't know. You didn't seem that interested in talking about books. You seemed a little too bewildered. I could tell that your head wasn't in it. You were perfectly polite, but it was as if all you really wanted to do was hide. But then I figured it out. Of course you were bewildered. Of course you wanted to hide. You were a real writer and what we were doing had nothing to do with real writing, with all our exercises and workshops . . . It was as if you were from some other planet. You made me realize what a fraud I was . . ."

"You're being too hard on yourself."

"I don't think so."

"So what exactly—"

"I'm going to quit."

"What?"

"I've already spoken to the head of graduate studies. I haven't said anything to Rex about it yet, but I will."

"But how will you live?"

"We've got a little savings and Faith will go back to work full-time.

If I'm ever going to write anything worthwhile, I've got to give it a real shot. I have a friend who has a cabin in Montana . . . he's offered to let me use it for as long as I'd like."

"But what about your kids?"

"They'll stay here, but I think they'll be all right for a few months. I really need to get away and isolate myself and pour everything into this for once in my life."

"And Faith is taking it okay?"

"There have been some hard nights. And a few tears. But she's a trouper, she really is."

I put my fingers to my temples. It felt as if the roof was falling down around my head. Was I living in a madhouse? These people were nuts, all of them—Wayne, Rex, the students, the Russian guy with the long beard writing his books in prison camp without pen or paper.

"Maybe I'm a fool," Wayne said, "but I've devoted my life to this."

"So Wayne, what was all that punching about?"

"You mean when you came in?"

"Yeah."

His face reddened. "I'm sorry, that was a little . . ."

"I know, but what was it? Were you celebrating? Were you trying to psyche yourself up? Or were you just scared?"

"I don't know. Maybe it was because I'd finally done a big thing."

"Uh-huh," I said. "You don't think this is a bit rash?"

"I'm just doing what you did."

"Yeah, but I didn't have all the responsibilities that you have."

"You don't think I should do it, then," he said.

"I don't know what you should do. I'm not God," I said. What I was, was a guy who stole people's chicken wings out of refrigerators, but I wasn't going to tell him that. He wasn't happy with what I had to say. He turned away, pushed aside the blinds, and stared out.

I'd about had it with being an inspiring presence. I sucked at an orange spicy knuckle of my right hand. All I could think of was Wayne's poor family, living on rice and beans, the kids turning into sullen juvenile delinquents while he pounded away at some third-rate novel up in the wilds of Montana. Really, this whole writing thing was worse than heroin.

"I think it's brave of you," I said. "I admire your guts."

He pivoted to face me. On the shelf above his head was the row of his remaindered books. "But if you thought I was making a mistake, you'd tell me, right? You wouldn't lie to me?"

What a question. All of a sudden I was supposed to be everybody's social worker? I liked Wayne. He'd been a huge help to me. He'd cashed my checks, done everything he could to make my life comfortable, taught me everything I knew about the writing game. So did I owe him? Maybe I did. But there was no way I was delivering the bad news, not at a moment like this.

"Wayne, come on," I said. "I think we've gone through too much together for me to start lying now."

Chapter Seventeen

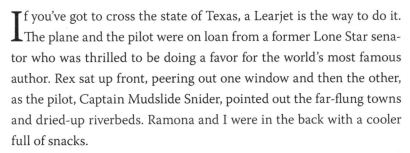

If you've got to cross the state of Texas, a Learjet is the way to do it. The plane and the pilot were on loan from a former Lone Star senator who was thrilled to be doing a favor for the world's most famous author. Rex sat up front, peering out one window and then the other, as the pilot, Captain Mudslide Snider, pointed out the far-flung towns and dried-up riverbeds. Ramona and I were in the back with a cooler full of snacks.

Captain Snider turned out to be a total Schoeninger fan. He'd grown up in Abilene, had collected Comanche arrowheads all his life, and his great-grandfather had punched cattle for Charlie Goodnight. Our flight was five hundred miles and he peppered Rex with questions the whole way.

As the first rumple of mountains appeared and the Learjet tilted to the south, Mudslide asked me what it was like, working for Rex. Speaking loud to make myself heard over the jet engines, I said it was the experience of a lifetime.

"I learn something new from him every day," I shouted. "He's got a heart as big as all outdoors, even though he doesn't always like to let you know that. He's made a difference in more people's lives than you can imagine." In the mirror, I saw Rex fix me with a long stare. Really, sometimes the guy was as hard to read as the expiration date on your credit card.

We began our descent. Light glinted off the Rio Grande. From a certain height, the raw landscape looked like a skin disease, but as we got closer I could make out abandoned homesteads and thick stands of reeds along the river.

Captain Snider brought us down on a landing strip at the edge of a half-built luxury hotel just a stone's throw from Mexico. A van waited for us at the hangar. Schoeninger signed a couple of dog-eared paperbacks for Mudslide while Ramona and I loaded our bags in the car, and then we were off, rumbling past an eighteen-hole golf course, a restaurant straight out of *Gourmet* magazine, and some tin-roofed shacks where brown-skinned workers stared at us from the shade of their narrow porches.

We had an hour-and-a-half drive ahead of us, and the country got wilder and wilder, full of weird rock formations and played-out quicksilver mines. We zipped through a hippie ghost town. The mountains ahead of us kept rising.

I stared out the window at the endless, cactus-riddled expanse. The national park had been pieced together out of what had once been ranches, but I couldn't imagine how a cow could survive out here, much less a human being. We flashed past a pair of German tourists in short leather pants hopping around in a field of purple sage, snapping pictures.

Ramona was chipper as a chipmunk, pointing out the sights, reading from her guidebook, asking me about my students. She had the glow of victory about her and she was trying to be sensitive about my feelings. Rex, on the other hand, was in one of his foul moods. I ignored it for as long as I could, but I finally had to say something.

"So, Rex, you looking forward to this today?" I asked.

"Not particularly."

"Something wrong?"

"Yes, something's wrong. Wayne called me last night."

"Ahh," I said.

"He told me that he resigned from the university. He said that you encouraged him."

"I wouldn't say I encouraged him exactly . . ."

"He said that you were his inspiration. It wasn't him that I brought you down here to inspire."

"I understand," I said. Far out, I spied what may have been a couple of antelope.

"This is going to be a total train wreck," Rex said.

"I'm sure you'll miss him," I said. "But a man's got to do what a man's got to do, right?"

"The man has no talent. Have you ever read anything he's written?"

"I've read a bit."

"He's a lovely guy, an excellent teacher, and he does a hell of a job running the institute. But nothing's going to happen with this book he wants to write."

"Did you tell him that?"

"I did."

"Wow. And what did he say?"

"It was hard. But I figured everybody deserves the truth. Right?"

"Right," I said.

Not that I believed that. I'd been thinking long and hard about what I was going to say today, and in the end I'd decided I wasn't going to say anything.

What good was it going to do me to blast Stainforth out of the water? It sure wasn't going to help me get any more money out of Rex. All it was going to do was piss him off and create a big ruckus.

No, I needed to keep my mouth shut and let it happen. Let Stainforth take Rex to the cleaner's. Rex seemed happy as a clam about it. What did it matter? I only had three classess left and one more check to collect. Then I was out of here. I'd gotten away with murder, let's face it, and I'd be leaving with a nice chunk of change in my pocket. I needed to ride this one out.

We wended our way up into the Chisos Basin and drove to the motel. Schoeninger and I waited in the van while Ramona went inside to get the keys. There were mountains all around us and at five in the afternoon shadows were already beginning to creep up the red rock walls. A man in an A&M hat and fancy cowboy boots lugged a cooler up the steps to his room.

When Ramona came back with the keys, her idea was that Schoeninger should take a nice nap and then we could meet for dinner. Rex wasn't having any part of it. There was plenty of daylight. We would go splash a little water on our faces and then go exploring.

Thirty minutes later we were poking our way up the Lost Mine Trail. Rex stopped at each of the trail markers, scribbling notes in his red notebook. On the path ahead of us were giant fornicating grasshoppers, brown goo oozing from their mandibles.

We were in shadow, even though the spiny peaks above us were still in light. Rex stopped at the switchbacks to catch his breath, sucking air like an asthma victim, but after a minute or two he would wave his cane at us and we'd be off again.

When we finally came to an overlook, Schoeninger collapsed on a stone bench and beamed at us. He gestured to the view. There were canyons on either side of us, one filled with sunshine, the other with mist.

"Ramona, how about a picture of the two authors here?"

When she didn't answer, I glanced over my shoulder at her and saw her face go blank with horror. "Rex, I'm sorry. I didn't bring the camera."

He cocked his head to one side, disbelieving. "I thought we agreed that you were always to bring a camera."

"We did," she said. "I just forgot. I guess in all the rush . . ."

"So where is it?" The ground around us was littered with squashed prickly pear blossoms that looked like purple tulips.

"In the van. I think."

"Uh-huh."

"If you want, I can run and get it."

"And how long would that take?"

"Fifteen minutes," she said.

Not a chance in the world, I thought. It would take her at least a half hour, and it would be totally dark by then. I couldn't believe he was going to make her go back, but I was wrong.

"We'll wait here," he said.

She disappeared quickly down the trail. Schoeninger lifted his binoculars to his eyes and stared out across the hazy plains of Mexico, looking as forlorn as Robinson Crusoe. I squatted on my haunches. Mountain ranges glowed around us. I'd read in a pamphlet that there were mountain lions up here. It would be just my luck to give the slip to the mob, only to be eaten by a puma.

After a minute he lowered the field glasses. "You want a look?"

"Sure."

I lurched to my feet and took the binoculars from him. Fiddling with the focus, I squinted through the lenses. It was hard to tell exactly what I was looking at, mountains and desert and sky all swimming together.

"So Ramona said you wanted to talk to me," he said.

I glanced back at him, letting the glasses fall to my side. He was wearing a white windbreaker with red, white, and blue cuffs and U.S. OLYMPIC TRACK emblazoned across the chest. It looked three sizes too big.

"Yeah, but that's all right," I said. "Everything's fine."

"Seriously?"

"Seriously," I said.

"So what did you think of Stainforth?" he said.

"He seemed like a nice guy."

"I thought you didn't take to him." The hazy air smelled of something burning.

"Take to him? What do you mean, take to him?" Rex was starting to get under my skin. "He may have been a little full of himself, but the man's entitled. He's accomplished a lot." A breeze rattled through the shiny-barked trees.

He took the binoculars back from me, ducked under the strap, and hobbled to the edge of the cliff. A bird shrieked somewhere below us. He raised his field glasses, scouting out stuff over in Mexico.

"Mingo would have had a hell of a time up here, wouldn't he?" Rex said.

"I think he would have," I said.

All these years later, I still think about that moment. I don't know what it was that got to me. Maybe it was just him standing so near to the edge. Maybe I was worried about him falling. He looked so little. I swear, one stiff wind would have taken him right over into the canyon. Maybe I was thinking about us burying his dog together, or about us both being orphans, but I just didn't want anything more bad to happen to him.

"Before you give the guy any money, though, you might want to check the guy out," I said softly.

"What's that?" He was still squinting through the binoculars.

"You might want to check the guy out!" I said, raising my voice.

He rested the glasses against his stomach, looking back at me. "And why is that?"

"Just to be sure," I said.

Another breeze riffled his wispy hair. "So I take it you've done some snooping around."

"I made a couple of calls."

"Jesus Christ, I thought we were finally beyond all that."

Darkness welled out of the canyons. I wanted to stop what was happening, but I didn't know how. The first truly kind thing I'd ever tried to do for Rex, and it was turning into a disaster.

"Rex, there is a problem here."

"Problem? What kind of a problem? Aren't there always problems?"

"The man is a fraud." Rex was stunned by what I'd said and I guess I was too. A chipmunk scurried out of the trees, rose up on its hind legs, saw us, and scurried back. "For years he's been going around trying to sell that prize to anybody with enough money to make it worth his while. Stephen King. Dean Koontz."

As he pivoted, his cane skidded in the loose rock and he nearly fell. "Dean Koontz? Who told you that?"

"Günter Grass."

"Günter Grass?"

"And a lot of other people. I've been making calls for two days. This prize is a joke. There's not a serious writer in the world who would go near it."

Rex teetered to the left and the right. "But you were the one who told me to take it!"

"I didn't know what I know now, Rex! I'm just trying to protect you."

"Protect me? What do you think I am, a child?" Scrubby trees surrounded us, spooky as monks. "So where the hell is Ramona?"

"I'm sure she'll be along."

"Look how dark it is. We're never going to be able to get any pictures in light like this."

He sucked on his teeth, making a disgusted little whistle, then spun away from me and set off down the slope. He wasn't on the regular trail, but on one of the steep shortcuts carved out by hikers over the years.

"Rex, watch it! Let me give you a hand!"

"Ramona?" he bellowed. "Ramona, where are you?"

Appalled, I hesitated longer than I should have, but finally headed after him, skidding sideways through the loose red dirt.

"You think I need any of their awards? I've got drawers full of them. I've got medals from five presidents! I don't need Stainforth! I don't need any of you! You're a bunch of vultures, all of you, picking over my bones! Ramona! Goddamn it, where is she?"

He zigzagged down the incline, poking his cane this way and that like an out-of-control skier trying to stay upright with only one pole. For an eighty-five-year-old, he was moving at an amazing clip, but I could have caught him if I hadn't snagged my foot in a tangle of weeds. By the time I pulled free, Schoeninger had put another twenty yards between us.

"Rex! Wait up!"

He was back on the main trail, but something was wrong; he listed to the left like a car with a flat.

"Rex, do you hear me?"

I began to run. When the path cut back sharply, Schoeninger barely managed the turn, careening through some rabbitbrush before staggering back on the trail. Without warning, his cane gave way under him and he fell. I rushed to his side, knelt down, and put a hand on his shoulder.

"Get away from me! Get away!" He struggled to push himself up, but couldn't do it. Panting, he rested his cheek on the ground. I took his hand.

"Rex? Rex, are you all right?"

He didn't move his head. His eyes rolled toward me, wide with fear. He tried to form words, but couldn't. It was almost as if his tongue was too big for his mouth. "I can't feel my arm," he whispered finally. "I can't feel anything."

I knew there was no time to waste, but Schoeninger had a grip on my sweater with his good hand and wasn't about to let go. I tried to calm him, tried to explain that I needed to go get help, but he just stared at me with the dumb, needy eyes of a dog. He had no color at all in his face and there were little twigs and bits of dirt embedded in his cheek. I was finally able to pry his fingers loose one by one, sweet-talking him the whole time. As I rose from my knees, I saw a flicker of light on the trail above us. The light wavered, disappeared, and then reappeared again, one switchback down from where it had been before.

"Who is it?" I shouted. "Is anybody there? We need help over here!"

There was no answer, but the light kept moving closer. A young woman ranger finally emerged out of the darkness. She couldn't have been more than twenty-five, and a black plastic garbage bag was slung over her shoulder. She had that college softball player look—healthy, a little stocky, blond hair clipped close and combed back into a ducktail. The wavering beam of her flashlight slid from Schoeninger to me to Schoeninger again.

"So what happened?" Her voice was flat, as if Rex was no more than a fallen limb blocking the path.

"I think he may have had a stroke," I said. "He says he doesn't have any feeling in his arm."

She leaned forward, peering down at Rex. "So how you doing?" She spoke a little too loudly, as if she thought he might be deaf.

"Not too good."

"Are you breathing okay?" His answer was too garbled to understand. "I'm sorry?"

"I need a doctor."

She patted him on the shoulder. "Well, sir, if you can just hold your horses a bit, we'll see if we can get you one." I saw that I'd been wrong; she wasn't so much heartless as scared.

She looked over at me. "If you'll stay with him, I'll see if I can get someone up here."

"That would be great," I said.

The ranger unhitched her walkie-talkie from her belt, turned her back on us, and walked off a few paces. Schoeninger tugged at my hand. "What's going on?"

"She's making a call."

"You think she knows what she's doing?"

"She's fine, Rex, she's fine." I could smell sumac out in the darkness.

"She seems like a bit of a blockhead to me."

"She's just young," I told him. He said something so slurred I couldn't make heads nor tails out of it. "What's that?" He tried again, but it was no clearer. I could see that one side of his face was frozen, as if he'd just gotten out of the dentist's. I went to one knee so I could hear. "I'm sorry, Rex . . ."

His eyes were full of tears. He took the words one at a time. "I . . . don't . . . want . . . to . . . die . . . here."

"No," I said. "And you're not going to."

The ranger wandered to and fro, talking to the air, or that's what it looked like. I was able to pick up bits and pieces of what she was saying. I took off my sweater and balled it up for Schoeninger to use as a pillow. As I wedged it under his head, I heard something in the woods below us. A moment later Ramona appeared, laboring up the trail, the camera strapped to her wrist.

When she saw us, she stopped in her tracks thirty yards away. The whole thing must have looked like a catastrophe—Rex on his back, bony knees raised, me crouched over him, the ranger on her walkie-talkie, the beam of the flashlight shining off the mesquite. It was impossible to see Ramona's face clearly at that distance, but she gave a low cry. Rex lifted his head.

Starting to run, she stumbled for a step or two, the camera clattering along the stones. The ranger whirled at the sound. Ramona rushed to his side.

"Oh, my God, oh, my God," she said, taking his hand. "Did you fall?"

His jaws worked as he tried to form the words. "I'm . . . not . . . well."

"The ranger's calling someone," I said. Ramona stared across at me. She'd already made up her mind about whose fault this was.

"You . . . brought . . . the . . ." Schoeninger said.

"Yes," she said. "I brought the camera." Tender and woeful, she brushed a couple of twigs from the side of his face.

"I guess we wouldn't want to get a picture of this, would we?" he said. It sounded as if his mouth were full of eggs.

"No, I guess we wouldn't."

The ranger came down the slope, stiff-legged in her sturdy boots, snapping off her walkie-talkie. "There should be a helicopter here in ten minutes," she said.

"And will there be a doctor?" I asked.

"There should be a medic and a nurse," the ranger said. She slipped the walkie-talkie back on her belt. "So what exactly were the three of you doing up here?" She did not seem happy with us.

"This is Rex Schoeninger," Ramona said. "The writer." The ranger stared blankly. It was just our luck; we'd apparently found the only person in the Western world who didn't know who he was. "He's researching a book."

The ranger raised an eyebrow, but held her peace for four or five seconds. "It's an awfully long way up here," she said. "Especially for a man his age."

She had said it would be ten minutes; it felt like an hour. The ranger went to the overlook to wait for the helicopter, and after a bit I joined her. The last traces of the sunset streaked the bellies of the clouds. The stillness was overwhelming. I found myself wondering how many millions of years old the mountains around us were and thought of asking Rex, but then I remembered that even if he knew, he wouldn't be able to tell us, given the shape he was in.

I quizzed the ranger about what hospital they would be flying Schoeninger to, how long it would take to get there, and what kind of medical attention they might be able to give him here on the ground. She didn't seem to know much.

Every now and then I took a peek over my shoulder. Ramona knelt, her head bowed, stroking Rex's hair. I was nervous about what he was telling her, or at least trying to tell her. I was to blame; what was new about that? I suppose I could have argued that the hike up the mountain had been more than his system could handle or that with an old guy, you never knew, the arteries can pop anytime. But I knew better. What the hell had I been thinking? It's never a good idea to level with anybody, but especially not with somebody Schoeninger's age. Truth is a killer.

At the first sound of the helicopter, the ranger moved to the edge of the overlook and I followed her. The whirring grew to a roar. Lights shooting everywhere, the helicopter rose out of the canyon like a monster in a Japanese horror movie. The ranger motioned me away, and then began waving her hands above her head. Looking back, I saw Rex craning his neck and Ramona trying to restrain him.

The helicopter hung above us as its searchlight swept across the bouldered slope and the scrubby trees, and then began its descent. I had no idea what a racket those things could make. Dust blew hard as a windstorm, tattering the bushes. I covered my face with an elbow, protecting my eyes.

The helicopter settled on the scarred expanse at the cliff's edge. A medic and a nurse climbed out, both in jumpsuits and helmets, lugging gear. They spoke briefly with the ranger—I couldn't hear what they were saying with all the noise—and then we all trooped down the slope.

Ramona, the ranger, and I stood back as the medic and the nurse bent over Schoeninger, asking him questions. Where was he hurting? Could he lift his arm at all? Did he have allergic reactions to anything? What kinds of medications was he on? When Rex had trouble making himself understood, Ramona answered for him. The medic was making wisecracks like he thought he was Alan Alda. They checked Schoeninger's pulse, put an oxygen mask on him, and started him on an IV drip. Ramona stood mutely by, watching with fingertips pressed to her lips. I stared at Rex's shiny white tennis shoes with the Velcro straps, splayed out in the dust.

The pilot was still in the helicopter, the searchlight shining on us as if we were at some movie premiere. Rex was being very good, very still, but I could see his eyes darting this way and that above the oxygen mask. Ramona spoke with the nurse, filling her in on Schoeninger's medical history while the medic and the ranger trotted back up the slope. I squatted at Rex's side, watching his chest rise and fall. It had gotten cold, and without my sweater I was starting to shiver in my thin blue cotton shirt.

As I shifted my weight from one leg to the other, I spied Rex's little red notebook under a cactus, just a few feet from his head. I retrieved it and flipped through the first few pages. His writing was such a mess, all I could make out were a few words—*ocotillo, catclaw mimosa, peregrine falcon nest, redberry juniper.*

"So what's that?" he asked.

"It's your notebook," I said. "I'll keep it for you."

"I knew it couldn't be for real," he said.

"What's that?" I asked.

"That award. I knew it all along . . ."

The ranger and the medic returned with a stretcher. They moved Schoeninger onto it one leg at a time, and then lay the IV bag on his stomach. Ramona reached into her pocket, found the keys to the van, and handed them to me.

"I'm going to go with them," she said.

"I'd like to go too," I said.

"There's only room for one."

"Mmm." From her tone, it didn't seem like a good idea to argue. I watched the medic pull a strap across Schoeninger's chest. "So is it a stroke?" I asked.

"Probably. They won't say." Crickets yakked it up out in the piñons.

"Where are they flying him?"

"To Austin. We'll call his doctors on the way."

It took all of us to carry him back to the helicopter, two on each end of the stretcher and Ramona walking alongside with the portable oxygen tank. The distant peaks loomed in the darkness.

As soon as Schoeninger was on board, the medic went to work, tearing open his shirt, shaving his chest, getting him hooked up to a heart monitor. The pilot gave Ramona a hand up.

The ranger and I retreated, the beating of the rotors pulsing in my ears. I knew everyone was just trying to help, but seeing the medic and the nurse working furiously over him really got to me; it looked as if they were trying to rip him apart. But just before the door closed, I saw, through the tangle of bodies, tubes, and wires, Schoeninger raise two fingers in a V, as if he were Churchill, rallying the nation.

Chapter Eighteen

It took me nine hours to drive back to Austin, rolling into all-night truck stops every so often to stoke myself on coffee. I was pretty much flipping out. I would have given anything to have been able to blame someone else for what had happened, but it was hard. Stainforth was a snake, but in the end what it came down to was, if I'd been able to keep my mouth shut, Rex would have been sleeping like a baby in that motel up on that mountain.

The landscape rose and fell, like pages turning in a book. It was a hundred miles between towns and I flipped from radio station to radio station, trying to find something to keep me awake. I had to pull over once for one of those immigration roadblocks. Fierce lights made me shield my eyes as one of the agents strolled to my car, but after a word or two he waved me through.

As it got later, there was almost no one else on the road. At one in the morning I passed two semis loaded with cattle heading off to slaughter. Edging alongside, I could see the wet noses pressed to the perforated metal, the eyes glowing in my headlights.

Now was the perfect time to bolt. What was I going back for? To defend my honor? It didn't make any sense. I was a man who'd run out on a wife and child, run out on my best buddy as he lay murdered on the floor of a hotel room. Why not go for the trifecta?

I got in about four A.M. and went directly to the hospital. All the little old lady behind the desk would tell me was that Schoeninger was in the intensive care unit and that no one was allowed to see him until official visiting hours. I drove back to my place and fell into bed. As exhausted as I was, it took forever to go to sleep, the white lines of the highway scrolling down the insides of my eyelids.

It was after eleven by the time I got up. My head was stuffed. I didn't know if I was coming down with a cold or if one of those famous Austin allergies had just blown in. I jammed a handkerchief in my pocket, ate a stale English muffin and a glass of juice at a diner, and headed back to the hospital.

Riding up in the visitors' elevator, I braced myself for the worst, expecting to run into Ramona, but when I got to the room, the only other person there, besides Schoeninger, was Maria, the new cook, reading the funnies. Asleep, Rex was surrounded by a forest of poles, tubes coming out of him everywhere. Maria folded her paper and stared up at me, seriously frightened. I wondered how much she'd been told.

"How's he doing?" I said.

"No one will say," she said. "They've been giving him lots of drugs. He's been sleeping the whole time." She was a small round bird of a woman with gentle eyes and a shawl pulled tight around her shoulders.

"So what have they . . ."

"Tests. All night. All kinds of tests."

"Uh-huh. And where's Ramona?"

"She went home for a couple of hours to get some rest."

I glanced at the tube in his nose, at the shiny plastic bag of liquid hanging from one of the poles. It was two-thirds empty. Schoeninger's arms looked so thin, his skin hanging in folds.

"If you want to take a break, I could watch him for a while."

Big panic came up in her eyes. "No, no, it's okay. I'm fine."

"I know you're fine," I said. "But I'll bet a cup of coffee would do you a lot of good, wouldn't it?" The woman was in a state of total confusion. "If there's a problem, I'll ring for the nurse. So where's the button?"

"Right there on the wall."

"Great, now you go on. And take your time. It sounds like you've had a rough night."

Compared to Dranka, the woman was a pushover. She struggled out of the recliner and approached the bed. She leaned over and patted his hand. As she left the room, she gave me one last glance, big-eyed as a rabbit.

I took her chair and sat there looking at the old guy. I'd been too squeamish to ask exactly what they'd done to him, but it looked as if there had been a lot of poking and prodding. I wondered if they'd snaked one of those little tubes in through the thigh, worked it all the way up to the heart. Maybe it was just my imagination, but it seemed as if one side of his face was off-kilter, like something you'd see in a second-rate wax museum. Rex moaned.

I took the red notebook from my shirt pocket and laid it on the side table. My eye lit on the briefcase on the windowsill. It had Schoeninger's initials on it—RLS—same as Robert Louis Stevenson's.

A food tray rattled past the door. I stretched out, hands behind my head, crossing my feet in front of me. I waited another minute to be sure Rex was thoroughly asleep. One long step and a lean, and I had it. Back in my chair, I undid the zipper, tooth by tooth, glancing up every couple of seconds. Rex had started to snore.

I opened the briefcase. There was no will, no sheath of legal documents. It was mostly junk: a bottle of Zantac, a tattered Texas road map, a New York hotel bill, the annual report of some Boston mutual fund, a million pens, some yellow legal pads, a box of dental floss. It wasn't until I started digging down in the side pockets that I finally found something worth paying attention to.

His checkbook had his initials embossed in gold on the cover, same as the briefcase. There were six checks left. I flipped to the back. Schoeninger was one of those people who really keep records. It was all down there—the eighty dollars paid to the plumber, the hundred and ninety to the dentist, sixty-five for the phone bill, five hundred each week to Dranka. He'd even entered every ATM withdrawal.

The balance was a little over fourteen thousand dollars. I sat there staring at it for a good long time. You can't go much lower than stealing a dying man's checkbook, but could it really be considered stealing? After all I'd done for the guy?

I was slipping the checkbook into my trousers when I heard Schoeninger start to sputter and cough. I glanced up. Rex blinked at me, heavy-lidded as a turtle.

"I'm so glad to see you," he croaked.

"I'm glad to see you too," I said.

"I'm sorry . . . just so sorry . . ."

"I don't know what you've got to feel sorry for," I said.

"Did they treat you all right?" His voice was slurry with drugs.

"Who's that?"

"Those people."

He seemed to fall asleep for a moment. The blare of a doctor being paged over the PA system jerked him awake again. "I brought something for you," I said. His eyes were crusted slits. I took his red notebook from my shirt pocket and held it up so he could see. He had no clue what it was. I set it on the side table. "I'll just leave it here for you."

"You cried so much," he said.

"I beg your pardon?"

"Sometimes you would cry all night. We would have to get up three or four times. I just didn't know . . ."

"Didn't know what?"

"Didn't know how to be a father . . ." His voice trailed off and after a few seconds he was snoring again.

I stared at him. What was he trying to pull? Did he think I was a total sap? People think they can get away with anything, once they're on their deathbeds. Checkbook in my trousers pocket, I eased out of the room.

A mother in a wheelchair waited at the elevator, holding her newborn baby in her lap, wrapped in a pink blanket. She was letting her two other brats have a peek at their monkey-faced little sister. The pony-tailed father held the strings to three helium-filled balloons shaped like chubby hearts. He looked goofy from lack of sleep. I gave him a congratulatory nod and he grinned in return.

The elevator doors opened. Standing at the rear, wedged in behind a red-nosed man on crutches and his doughy wife, was Ramona, shooting me daggers. For a second I thought about running, but how stupid would that have been? I needed to tough this one out. I held the door for the man on crutches and his wife, then grabbed Ramona by the elbow as she tried to slip by me.

"God, I'm so happy to see you. I've been looking for you everywhere."

She brushed my hand away. If she'd had a nap, it hadn't been a long one. She looked mean as a rattler. "So no one's gotten around to locking you up yet?" she said.

"Locking *me* up? Stainforth's the one they should be locking up. Do you have any idea what that guy's been trying to pull off?"

"Rex told me. In the helicopter."

"It's incredible. The guy turns out to be a total scam artist."

She closed her eyes for a second, as if it was physically painful to listen to me. She wore a splotchy SMU sweatshirt and a pair of hip-huggers that looked as if their hugging days were over.

"I talked to him on the phone last night," she said.

"You talked to him? When?"

"After we got to the hospital and they took Rex into intensive care. I called him in New York."

"So what did he say?"

"He was stunned. He said he couldn't believe Rex and I would take the word of some embittered graduate student."

"Graduate student? Who's he talking about?"

"He was talking about you. F. Horton Caldwell. I told him that it was just a ruse."

"Uh-huh." I was starting to get a very bad feeling about this. "And who did you say I was?"

"V. S. Mohle." We moved back down the hallway toward the nurses' station.

"That must have been a bit of a shock to him."

"It was."

"And what did he say?"

"He said that can't be V. S. Mohle. And I said, but it is. Rex hired him to come down and teach for a semester. I explained about how it was all so hush-hush and how the students had to sign those confidentiality agreements. Please, he said. Enough. I know V. S. Mohle. I've met V. S. Mohle."

"He claimed he met me? Ho-boy. Now, that really takes the cake."

"He said he flew up to Maine a few summers ago to try to talk you into taking the Vita Nuova Prize."

"Ramona, my God, what a liar the man is!"

She shot me her best Perry Mason stare. "We called him."

"Called who?"

"V. S. Mohle. Last night. Stainforth had his number in his address book and somehow he was able to set up a three-way conference call. I spoke to him."

I rubbed at the corners of my eyes. The hall smelled vaguely of whatever it is they pickle frogs in. "Ramona, do you think there's someplace we could go to talk about this? A coffee shop, maybe?"

"It must have been after midnight there. You can imagine how upset he was. He said he'd called and left a message for Wayne at the institute at the end of August, explaining that he'd been having some health problems and wouldn't be able to come."

You ever wonder what an onion feels like being peeled? That was me.

"But that doesn't make a bit of sense," I said. "This guy knows about Wayne? I have no idea who this character is, but it wasn't me. This is getting way too deep."

An orderly strode past us, giving me the fish-eye. "It was him," Ramona said.

"I'm sorry?" I said.

"It was V. S. Mohle that I spoke to. So the question is, who are you? And where did you come from?"

"Ramona, listen to me. I know this must be very confusing and we're both very tired. What do you want to do? Check on me? Go ahead, go check on me. Meanwhile, Stainforth is playing Rex like a violin and I can prove it. You want someone to call? Call Günter Grass. I'll give you his number."

Ramona cupped her hands over her nose and mouth as if she were about to weep. I reached out to comfort her, but she jerked away. A surgeon checking his charts glared at me over the top of his ultra-cool reading glasses. Everybody at the nurses' station was alert as deer.

"Please, don't," she said. "I need to see about Rex."

"Of course you do," I said. "But I just need to say one more thing.

You're the one who's supposed to protect Rex from people like Stainforth. That's why he hired you."

She pivoted away from me and began to sob, her shoulders rising and falling. "Here," I said. I tugged my handkerchief from my trousers pocket and, as I did, heard something slap softly at my feet. Ramona and I both stared down at the checkbook with the monogram etched in gold.

"What's that?" she said.

"Nothing," I said. I bent down, snatched the checkbook, and stuffed it back in my pocket.

"Excuse me, but I think that's Rex's checkbook."

"Rex's checkbook? Ramona, that's ridiculous."

"Let's see it, then."

"I can't believe it's come to this, I really can't."

She grabbed at my trousers pocket, but I fended her off, clutching her wrist. "Would you let go of me? Please, let me go."

I did as she asked. She was humiliated, flushed, out of breath. For a moment neither of us was sure what to do, or what the other would do. Then she turned and raised a hand to the nurses' station. "Miss? Miss! Would you please call security? This man is a thief!"

It seemed as if we had the attention of half the staff of the hospital, not to mention some fat kid sitting on the radiator with his finger up his nose. One of the nurses reached for the phone. I sprinted for the stairs.

Chapter Nineteen

⁓

I raced up the ramps of the parking garage, screeches of birds echoing all around me. They were recorded on some sort of tape loop to
frighten off grackles and keep them from crapping all over the doctors'
BMWs, but to me they sounded like the hyenas in those freaky nature
documentaries.

I didn't have a minute to waste. I fired up my car, backed out, and
spiraled down, level after level, tires screaming on the turns, throwing the fear of God into a thick-legged woman suffering from varicose
veins and sending her clumping for the safety of the stairwell. At the
tollgate I handed the attendant three dollars with trembling hand, half
expecting a squadron of security police to come hustling out of the
hospital any second.

I gunned across Thirty-fifth Street, running a red light at Guadalupe. If Ramona really had talked to Mohle, there was no telling who
Mohle must have called by now—good old Wayne for sure, and maybe
even the police.

What I was dying to do was zip by my house and grab the thirty
grand in cash tucked under my mattress, but I didn't dare. The house

would be the first place the cops would go. But what I couldn't do without was the manila envelope full of false credit cards, drivers' licenses and bogus Social Security numbers I'd taped to the bottom of my desk at the Fiction Institute.

When I got to the institute I circled the block, just to be on the safe side, and then parked out in front of the building so I could make a quick getaway. Striding down the walk, I fished my keys out of my pocket, but it turned out I didn't need them. I was astonished to find the front door unlocked and the alarm making low, annoying beeps. I pushed the door open about a foot and stared inside. The house was dark, all the shades drawn, and across the room, on Mildred's screensaver, big google-eyed fish swam back and forth, going nowhere.

I tried to tell myself it was probably nothing. Mildred was always complaining about the cleaning crews not locking properly when they left and Wayne had given a couple of the students keys so they could come in on the weekends to watch Lannan Foundation tapes in the library. It seemed stupid to let myself be scared away so easily. I probably could have survived without my stash of credit cards, but if I had it, life was going to be an awful lot easier.

I slid my keys back in my pocket, stepped inside, and closed the door quickly behind me. I was all the way to the stairs before I heard the rustling, like rats in an attic. I stopped and stared up at the landing above me. There was no sign of a light.

The voices in my head telling me to get the hell out of there kept getting louder. The problem was, nothing made any sense. Wayne had his own key; he had no reason to break in. Ditto the campus police. Who could it be, then? Some student fiddling with the VCR up there in the dark? Maybe one of those homeless guys who lived along the creek had busted in, looking for the petty cash box. But what would they be doing upstairs?

I crept noiselessly up the stairs and paused on the landing. I heard the hollow thump of the wastebasket in my office. My heart was racing now, but I had come too far to turn back. I inched forward, sliding my back along the wall, and peered around the edge of my door.

The office looked as if it had been run through a Cuisinart. Books and manuscripts were heaped on the floor, the couch was pulled away from the wall and stripped of its cushions. The fabric of one of the overturned chairs had been ripped away, exposing metal springs.

The man was so still I didn't see him at first. He stood motionless on the far side of my desk, like a plaster saint tucked away in the alcove of some gloomy church. For one crazed moment I thought I was staring at my reflection in the dusty window behind him, but it wasn't a reflection. The last time I'd seen this guy was at Kennedy Airport. We were the same height and roughly the same age, with the same narrow shoulders and gaunt, hangdog faces. The only big difference was that, in flannel shirt and black turtleneck, he was dressed way too warmly for Texas in November.

He didn't seem to be aware that I was there. Head slightly bowed, he gazed down at what looked like my grade book. After several long seconds, he began to thumb through it, breaking the spell.

"How'd you get in here?"

Startled, he jerked to attention. As he closed the grade book, I saw that he had all my credit cards lined up on the desk in rows, like a dummy's hand in bridge. The manila envelope lay crumpled and torn next to the wastebasket.

"I mean, goddamn it," I said. "Look at my office."

"Your office? Your office? Who the fuck do you think you are?" It really was amazing how much he looked like me.

"And who the fuck do you think *you* are?" I said.

"You asshole! You stupid, stupid asshole!"

I put up a hand. "Hey," I said. "Watch your language, okay? Seriously. We're not going to get anywhere standing around and calling each other names. I'll tell you what. You give me my cards back and I'm out of here. I'll never bother you again. Scout's honor."

"Give you your cards back? You've got a hell of a nerve. After what you've done to me, you think I'm going to let you waltz out of here?"

I pressed my fingertips to my forehead. I could feel a migraine coming on. He came around the corner of the desk.

"You have harmed me!" he shouted. "You have harmed me deeply! You think this is a joke? You come down here, you cash my checks, you tell these students God knows what about what it takes to be a writer, you make a travesty out of everything I've ever stood for—"

"Everything you've ever stood for? And what is that exactly? You promised Rex Schoeninger you were coming to teach and you copped out on him. So I borrowed your name for a few months. Big fucking deal. The way I see it, I covered your ass. Maybe I can't write for shit, but I know how to handle people. I gave them hope. I brought light into their eyes. And what have you been doing, up on that island of yours, resting on your laurels and shucking clams? No offense, but I was a better you than you've ever been."

I could see him trying to figure out just how unbalanced I was. For all he knew, he was dealing with the same kind of psycho that killed John Lennon.

"You know where I just came from?" I said. "The hospital. Rex Schoeninger is on his deathbed. It was a hell of a wonderful thing he wanted to do, bringing you here. Imagine that, a great writer like him, doing something like that—"

"A great writer? Have you ever tried to read one of those things?" He tossed the grade book on the desk, his lips twitching with contempt. I could see why Rex had once been tempted to strangle the guy.

"So what do you say you let me have the cards back and we'll call it even?" I said.

"No."

"No?"

I surveyed the room, feeling a little dizzy. There was no time to waste. Under the legs of the side table was a CD of country songs Chester had burned for me. My coffee mug, handle freshly broken off, nestled in the strewn pages of student stories.

"Maybe I haven't made myself clear enough," I said. "I understand how you might be upset. I'm sorry about that. But let me assure you, there was nothing personal in what I did. I was just in a bit of a fix. I have the utmost respect . . . I've been over all your stuff. Everything you've ever written. Not that there's a whole lot of it. I even gave a little reading for the students. They were blown away. The way I see it, we're both in a jam here. If we get the cops involved and it ends up in the press, you're never going to hear the end of it. Now, if you want me to write you a check for what I owe you, I'll do that. But I would like my cards back."

Mohle scooped a half dozen of the cards off the desk and began to flip through them. "So which one of these guys is you? Hugh O'Neill? Rick Archbold? Ricardo Rodriguez? Hard to imagine you passing yourself off as a Hispanic guy—"

I lunged for the cards. My mistake was forgetting Mohle's reputation as a practitioner of the martial arts. Before you could say Jack Armstrong I was sailing headfirst across the desk. I did an ungainly half somersault to the floor, landing hard on my shoulder. I grabbed for the chair to use as a shield, but Mohle was on me like a panther. He yanked me to my feet and pinned my arm behind my back. Running me across the room, he slammed me into the edge of the door.

I crumpled to my knees and then, after a moment, bent down and rested my forehead against the metal grating covering the air duct. I clawed at the rug with my fingers, trying to get my wind back. My ears were ringing and the room rocked to and fro like a fishing boat in the swells. I could taste something salty in my mouth, and it felt as if he'd knocked a few of my teeth loose.

When I was finally able to raise my head, I could see Mohle standing in front of the window, looking like Jackie Chan—arms spread, palms open, ready to do battle. "Jesus Christ," I said. I wiped some blood from my split lip. Mohle didn't move. I staggered to my feet, slipping and sliding on the scattered books, and put a hand against the wall to steady myself.

"Okay, you win," I said. "You want the cards? Take 'em. They're yours."

As he stepped away from the window, a flash of reflected light caught my eye. A black Escalade was pulling up in front of the building. Two goons got out. One of them was the guy who'd killed Barry, wearing a knit navy-blue cap that made him look like a longshoreman in *On the Waterfront*. The other was a skinny character buttoning up his vinyl coat. The skinny one just stood there, surveying the street.

"So just answer me this," I said. "If you hated him so much, why did you ever agree to come down here? You just want to spit in his eye one more time before he died?"

"None of your damn business."

"That's a lot of help." I glanced down at the man in the vinyl coat, who was staring up at our window.

"What are you looking at?" Mohle said. One of my ears still buzzed.

"Nothing," I said.

He backed off, hands still cocked, and then bent to scoop the scattered credit cards off the rug. "I'm going to go outside now and wait for Wayne," he said. "You can go or stay, whatever you want. But I'm going to take these with me."

I could have warned him, but I wasn't exactly in a charitable mood. I watched him gather the rest of the cards, drivers' licenses, and Social

Security cards and stuff them in his trousers pockets; he was daring me to stop him. I stood silently, nursing my swollen lip, as he strode past me and moved quickly down the stairs. Once I heard the front door slam, I returned to the window and peered out the curtains.

The man in the vinyl jacket shielded his eyes as he scrutinized the backseat of my car. His buddy had gone around to check out the driveway. When Mohle walked out the front door, the head of the man in the blue knit cap came around like the head of one of those bobble dolls. Mohle stepped off the curb and looked down the street. The man in the vinyl jacket rose slowly, like a snake rising to the sound of a flute.

His partner must have said something, because Mohle turned back to him, smiling, but as they talked a little more and the man in the knit blue cap began to move toward him, the smile went away. The killer gestured to my car. Mohle shook his head no. The killer gestured to the house. Again Mohle shook his head no. The thug in the vinyl jacket circled behind the cars so they would have him penned in. In my mind I was thinking, Do I make my break now, or do I wait?

When the guy in the vinyl jacket put a hand on Mohle's arm, Mohle took care of it with a nifty whirling motion like something out of a samurai movie, but the guy in the vinyl jacket didn't seem to get the message. He grabbed Mohle around the neck, trying to throttle him; in a second he was doubled over, coughing and holding his stomach, and in a second after that, he was facedown on the asphalt, felled by a karate chop.

The problem was that in all this commotion, the killer in the blue knit cap had come up with a snub-nosed revolver, and by the time Mohle had spun around, the killer had it trained on him and was hollering and waving him toward the house.

At first Mohle just stood there as if he couldn't believe what was happening, but he was no idiot. Raising both hands, he backed over the curb and across the lawn. The guy in the vinyl jacket was on his feet again, but wobbly; his partner gestured furiously for him to come on.

I heard one door slam and then another as everybody rumbled into the house. There was all this shouting going on, but I couldn't make out any words.

I scanned the room wildly, looking for a place to hide. There was a low closet behind my desk, but it was chock-full of the files of rejected applicants. There was the window, but it was a good twenty-foot drop to the sidewalk. The last thing I needed now was a broken leg. There were other windows in the library that opened onto the roof, but the floor was creaky. I was afraid that if I moved at all, I would be sure to alert them.

I jumped at the sound of a gunshot. I heard glass shattering and then there was utter silence. I stood stock-still, blinking. I was already responsible for the death of one great American writer; was I now going to be responsible for the deaths of two?

It felt as if the silence went on forever, but finally I heard a low murmuring coming through the metal grating in the floor. I got down on my knees and put my ear to the checkerboard of metal bars, but I still couldn't hear clearly enough.

The grating was held in place by three tiny screws—the fourth was missing. I undid them carefully with my thumbnail, put them in my pocket, and then lifted the grating with the kind of caution a father might use to lift a sleeping child. I set it on the rug next to me.

At the bottom of the air duct was a second grating, but the voices were clearer now. I could even see, through the crosshatch of bars, the three men directly below me. Mohle was curled in a fetal position in a chair, covering his head with his arms. The glass in the framed poster above him had been smashed by the bullet; jagged shards glistened everywhere on the carpet.

The thug in the knit blue cap hovered above Mohle. He held the revolver in both hands, and the way he was resting the barrel alongside his mouth, you might have thought he was a painter considering his next brushstroke. His pal cowered a few steps off, at the very edge of what I could see.

"Just how stupid do you think we are?" the man in the blue knit cap said. "What do you mean, you're not the man we're looking for? We've been on your trail for four fucking months, buddy boy."

"He's . . . upstairs . . ." Mohle's words were barely audible.

"What's that?"

"The guy you're after . . . he's upstairs . . ."

The man in the blue knit cap hit him across the face with the barrel of the gun. Mohle toppled from the chair like a sack of grain. The two thugs loomed over him. Lying on his side, Mohle cupped his hands to his nose.

On my belly, I stared down through the air duct like an ice fisherman peering through the ice. Once, a long time ago, I had been trapped in the stairwell at the Children's Center by two of the older boys who thought I'd stolen money from their lockers. Maybe I had stolen the money, maybe I hadn't, but what I remember is how I pleaded with them, how I kept talking and talking, saying anything that came into my head. I remember how they stared at me, stupid as cattle, not listening to any of it. Words weren't going to stop them. Words never stop anybody, really. It was a lesson I learned early: there are people in this world who, if they've made up their minds to beat you, they're going to beat you.

"Check his wallet," the man in the vinyl coat said.

The thug in the cap straddled Mohle and dug down in one of his pockets. It looked a little like he was groping him, but Mohle was in no shape to resist. A half dozen loose cards slithered to the floor. Checking the other pocket, the thug in the cap came up with a handful more.

"So what's that?" his partner said.

The thug offered what he had and retrieved the rest. His partner looked through them and laughed.

"Nice try, buddy boy. You really had me going for a minute there." He went to one knee. The thug in the blue knit cap stepped back. Viewed through the tiny squares of the grating, all of their movements were jerky, like a movie being run at the wrong speed.

"I'm going to be very straight with you, okay?" the man in the blue knit cap said. "And I want you to be straight with me. You and your pal Barry ran off with the key to a locker that matters a great deal to us. If you don't know where that key is, we have ourselves a big problem . . ."

"I don't know anybody named Barry. I don't know about any key. I'm just a writer—"

The man in the navy-blue cap kicked Mohle in the wedding tackle. Mohle writhed on the carpet, making terrible sounds.

"Jesus Christ, mister!" the man in the vinyl coat said. "We're so sick of this! You're a writer? So what did you ever write?"

"*Eat . . . Your . . . Wheaties . . .*" Mohle gasped.

"*Eat Your Wheaties?* Sure. And I played center field for the Yankees. Now listen to us. These buddies of ours have talked to your wife and kid. They both basically agree that you're a lying, worthless bag of shit, but if you hope to ever see them again, you're going to have to come up with that key for us . . ."

"I don't have a wife . . . I don't have a kid . . ."

The man in the blue knit cap put the revolver to Mohle's head. I pushed away from the grating, bracing myself for what came next. As I did, I must have dislodged some of the gunk from the edge of the vent. I heard a *ting*, and as I stared down, horrified, I could see the faintest plume of dust drifting into the foyer below.

The thug in the navy-blue cap barely noticed, swatting at his ear, but his partner flinched as if he'd been stung by a wasp. He looked up instantly, squinting one eye at the grating and the softly descending trickle of grit. We were face-to-face, no more than a dozen feet apart, and though I could see him, I was praying he couldn't see me.

"I think we need to go have a look around," he said.

I pushed to my feet and picked my way silently across the minefield of books and scattered manuscripts. Tiptoeing through the library, I went first to the windows that opened onto the roof of the back porch. If I could just get out there, I would be able to climb onto the main roof and to safety.

The first window I tried was totally jammed. The second I was able to open six or seven inches. I bent down and tried to lift it from below, but the frame was warped. One side came up two inches and then the other side came up three and then the window stuck altogether, no matter how hard I tugged.

I could hear thumping on the stairs; it sounded like a team of Clydesdales. Frantically I surveyed the room. The other two offices were locked. There was a bathroom, door ajar, but that would be the first place anyone would look. For a second I considered smashing one of the windows with my forearm and leaping onto the roof of the porch, but it didn't take long to see how suicidal that would be.

Next to the door was a portable blackboard, set up on a tripod, and the bookcase with all the Schoeninger books. I squeezed my way past the blackboard and pressed myself behind the bookcase. It wasn't much of a hiding place—the shelves couldn't have been more than a foot wide—but it was all I had.

The light on the landing snapped on. A floorboard creaked. The first voice I heard was Mohle's, no more than ten feet away.

"This is what I've been trying to tell you. We're all in the same boat here. You've been ripped off, I've been ripped off—"

"Just shut up."

The voices moved away. It sounded as if they'd gone into my office.

I thought I heard a clank on metal; they must have discovered the loose grating. All the talking stopped. I leaned my head against the bookcase and felt it teeter.

Without warning, there was a voice, alarmingly close. "Okay, buddy boy, we're tired of playing. You can come out now."

I turned my head sideways, not daring to breathe. Mohle, the weasel, was the first one to enter the room. Stooped, with his hands cupped over his bleeding nose, he looked like a medieval monk. The man in the blue knit cap was at his heels, prodding him forward with the barrel of his gun. They took one cautious step into the room, and then another.

I had no idea why they didn't see me right away, except that I was tucked in between the blackboard and the bookcase and they both seemed focused on the half-opened bathroom door.

The thug in the vinyl jacket was another story. Being slammed into the asphalt by Mohle had shaken all the bravado out of him. His eyes darted this way and that. When he spied me, he jumped like a six-year-old in his first fun house. For a moment he was too overcome to even speak. He tugged at his partner's elbow. I reached for the corner of the bookcase with both hands.

The killer in the blue knit cap turned. A slow smile spread across his face; I don't think I've ever seen a look of such pure pleasure. "Well, what do you know."

The bookcase ran from floor to ceiling, nearly ten feet high. It was nothing but Schoeninger books. All his novels were there, in English and in their many translations—Spanish, Italian, French, German, Dutch, Japanese, Urdu, and Hindi. There were large-print editions for the elderly and buffalo-hide-bound editions for the well-heeled. The novels must have averaged eight hundred pages; you had to figure two pounds apiece. Multiply that times fifty books, multiply that by eight for all the translations, throw in a few heavy bronze plaques and a lethal-looking paperweight made up of a piece of the Berlin Wall encased in glass, and you were looking at something over half a ton.

As unstable as the bookcase was, it did not tip as easily as I thought it would, but when it came, it sounded like the Hoover Dam collapsing.

The thug in the cap was buried instantly. His partner tried to dodge out of the way, but got his legs tangled with Mohle's, and that fraction of a second doomed them both. Books thundered down on them, knocking them to the floor.

I stood for a moment, staring at the three of them as they moaned and coughed under two million years of history, but there wasn't time to gloat. I leapt like a gazelle over the fallen bookshelf and ran down the stairs.

As I came out the front door, a police car was pulling to the curb forty yards to my left. I sprinted to the Volvo and threw myself in behind the steering wheel. Starting the engine, I glanced in the rear-view mirror. Wayne was running toward me, red-faced and hollering, arms waving. Walking fast up the sidewalk behind him was a big old cop.

I yanked the transmission into drive and squealed away from the curb. As I did, the rear window exploded in a shower of glass. I looked over my shoulder. Wayne was spread-eagled on the lawn, covering his head. The cop had his revolver drawn as he scurried for cover behind a row of parked cars.

The last thing I saw before the line of trees blotted everything out was the cop firing up at the second floor of the Fiction Institute. As I sped off, I was still able to hear the erratic exchange of gunfire, but after a couple of blocks, the sound became less distinct. If you hadn't known better, you would have thought the pops were nothing more serious than something you'd hear in a penny arcade.

Chapter Twenty

I'm not sure there's any reason to go into all the details of my escape, as hair-raising as they were—ditching the Volvo behind a Shamrock station in Round Rock, hitching a ride with a simpleton truck driver, catching a Trailways bus in Dallas. The point is that twenty-four hours later I was standing on Michigan Avenue in Chicago with a hundred dollars in my pocket, not a friend in the world, and a whole new life to piece together.

By Tuesday the story was in all the papers. It stayed there all week. There were pictures of the two thugs being led, handcuffed, into the Travis County Jail. (They were identified in the caption as low-level functionaries of the Delmonico crime family.) There were interviews with Ramona and Wayne and the president of the university, who was appointing a panel to explore how such a hoax could have gone undetected for as long as it did. The old mug shot of me they ran made me look like a deranged serial killer.

Waiting for the storm to pass, I spent most of my time in a fleabag hotel near Wrigley Field. Television and the newspapers I picked up in the lobby were my only connection to the outside world. It seemed as if there was something on every other channel I turned to—footage of Mildred, fighting her way through a crowd of reporters on the back steps of the Fiction Institute, an interview with several of the students talking about how shocked and betrayed they felt, a clip of some old coot who claimed I'd swindled him out of his retirement money fifteen years before. God knows where they'd dug him up, but the geezer was still irate, shaking his cane at the camera.

The media had a field day. There was a skit on *Saturday Night Live* and Dave Letterman made wisecracks about me a regular feature of his opening monologue: "You read about this con artist down in Texas who passed himself off as V. S. Mohle? He taught a semester and nobody figured it out. You could never fool a New Yorker with something like that. Mayor Giuliani shows up at a press conference dressed as Marilyn Monroe, we're on to him in a minute."

I read a piece by some guy named Rich in the *New York Times*. I'm not sure I understood much of it—what the term *bricolage* means, I have no idea—but the general drift was that I was a symptom of everything wrong with society. We were living, he said, in a time of virtual reality, computer-driven images, spin doctors, and the death of the author, not to mention the blurring of the line between high and low culture. It was the Age of Postmodernism and the Big Lie. It was a historical moment when we couldn't tell the difference between the original and the copy. He compared me to Milli Vanilli, Andy Warhol's Brillo boxes, Bill Clinton. Here I was, thinking I was just a poor schlub, trying to get by, and it turns out I was what was happening.

But I had more important things to do than sit around reading press clippings. Once I was finally able to get up enough nerve to venture out on the street, I started working a few short cons in some of the bars and bus stations around town to put a few dollars in my pocket. It took a little scuffling around, but by the end of the month I was a new man, with yet another driver's license and Social Security number. The snug little beard I'd grown made me look like the marine biologist in *Jaws*, but it wasn't the worst disguise. I never did have the heart to use Schoeninger's checkbook.

As comfortable as I was being back on the streets, I knew that it was only a matter of time before the cops or the replacement troops for the Delmonico family showed up looking for me. What I needed was to drop off the face of the earth for a while.

One Sunday afternoon I struck up a conversation in a sports bar with this fellow from Wisconsin. He was down from Neenah-Menasha, visiting his sister. When I mentioned to him that I was thinking of relocating, he suggested that if I didn't mind a little cold weather, I might try their Division of Motor Vehicles. In just the last year, three people had retired in his office alone; if I wanted to apply, this was the time.

A month later I was living in Appleton, Wisconsin, Harry Houdini's hometown, working as a license examiner. It was the middle of January and in the mornings when I scurried out to scrape the windshield on my car, ice crystals would bead up in my beard like glistening Christmas decorations. When the wind chased snow across the playground of the parochial school next door, it felt as if I was exiled in Siberia, which, come to think of it, was probably what I deserved.

The people I worked with were nice as pie. They were always inviting me to some Friday night fish fry or trying to fix me up with the youth director at their church. More often than not, I said no. I developed a reputation as a loner and a bit of an odd duck.

During the week I gave driving tests, bracing my knees against the dashboard as pimply sixteen-year-olds spun their fathers' cars into snowbanks and palsied senior citizens mistook the gas pedal for the brake as we careened back into the DMV parking lot.

The winter nights were long and in the mornings I'd have to drive to work with my lights on, crawling through sleet and rain. There wasn't a day I didn't think about Rex and wonder if he was still alive. I wondered if Ramona had ever told him what a fake I was. I kept going back over all my screwups, like a dog coming back to inspect its vomit.

Sometime in March the snow began to melt and just when everybody started to get their hopes up, a storm would drop another four inches. Three days later it would warm again, water would run in the gutters, and finally one Sunday morning I saw my first robin in a muddy yard.

A week later I was having lunch at Wendy's when I picked up a discarded copy of *USA Today* from the table next to me and saw that Schoeninger had died. The obituary went on for half a page, detailing his rags-to-riches career, his world travels, his blockbuster best sellers, and his extraordinary philanthropy. It talked about him being an orphan and how all his life he'd been haunted by the mystery of his origins. It mentioned how he'd been dismissed by the critics—one reviewer had compared his prose to the lone and level sands of Ozymandias. In the end it hadn't mattered what the critics said—he'd kept generations of readers reading.

There was a picture of him—it must have been at least forty years old—dog-paddling in some jungle pool. The lei around his neck floated on the surface of the water. What made the photo so strange was that he was swimming with his glasses on, the kind with the old-fashioned clear frames. It made him look a little like a midwestern banker. He was a little hefty and grinning like he was having the time of his life. If the picture hadn't had a caption under it there was no way I would have believed this was the same man as the scrap of a human being I'd left in a hospital bed four months before.

The article said there would be a funeral in Austin on Saturday and a memorial service in New York on Tuesday.

I sat there unable to finish my double cheeseburger. Contrary to what you may believe, phony guys have feelings too. I remember Barry once, he'd just lifted the life savings off this poor sucker, but as the guy was getting out of the car, he slammed his finger in the door. Barry felt just terrible for him, insisted on taking him to the hospital, and even paid for his bill. Barry was a big softie. Or what about Mark McGwire, the guy who broke Roger Maris's home-run record? The man was totally pumped on steroids, he knew he was a fraud and half the country suspected it, but when he hit number sixty-two, the stadium went crazy. He picked up his kid and ran over to the stands where all the Maris family were sitting. He gave the sons big hugs and when he turned and took off his hat to acknowledge the cheers, the tears streamed down his face. The man was as fake as a two-dollar bill, but what he was feeling was real. He didn't deserve it, but he felt it, all the same.

That Sunday I put on my white shirt and tie, dragged my blazer out of the closet, and went off to church. I don't know exactly why I went. Maybe I was trying to cover my bets. I probably hadn't been inside a church in twenty-five years and it was a lot different than I remembered. There was no organ, just this bearded guy in a woolly sweater with a guitar, and right in the middle of the service you had to give everybody around you these hugs.

All the regulars were smiling at me, I guess because I was a newcomer, but I did nothing to encourage them. There were some hymns, a little reading from the New Testament, a few announcements, and then we all got down on our knees for a moment to recite the Lord's Prayer.

I closed my eyes and leaned my forehead against my clasped hands. I've never been a big fan of the Lord's Prayer, to tell you the truth. Give us this day our daily bread—who's going to argue with that? But having to forgive *all* the sins of *all* your enemies before you get forgiven for yours? Anybody but a sap should be able to cut a better deal than that.

But this time it kind of hit home. Don't get me wrong. It wasn't as if I was totally blaming myself for everything that had happened. Maybe

I'd been a snake, but Stainforth had been a nastier one. Besides, Rex pretty much had one foot in the grave when I met him. What did I have to feel guilty for? Hadn't I given him what he'd paid for?

Still, I missed him. I missed our trips knocking around Texas. I missed listening to his stories about crossing the Khyber Pass. I even missed our hearts games, seeing how happy it made him when he laid the queen of spades on me.

When I sat down in the pew again, I felt something jab me in the rump. I tilted to one side and reached around. Something was stuck inside the hem of my blazer, something hard and the size of an arrowhead.

The youth choir rose to sing "Faith of Our Fathers." I undid one of my brass buttons of my coat. Some of the lining had come unstitched and, slob that I was, I'd fastened it in a couple of places with safety pins. I shook the hem of my jacket, working whatever it was around to the front.

Some old granny farther down the pew shot me disapproving looks. I slipped my hand inside the lining, groped around, and finally found it—something egg-shaped, an inch or two long.

The youth choir looked like angels in their white smocks. I eased my hand out of my coat, put it between my knees so no one else could see. I opened my palm. For a moment I had no idea what I was staring at. It was oblong, snarled in thread, and fuzzy with lint. Once I picked at it with a fingernail, the threads unraveled easily. My heart lurched sideways in my chest. I closed my hand tight around Cannetti's locker key with its red plastic top.

Sometimes God answers our prayers in mysterious ways. Somehow I made it through the rest of the service. I shared my hymnal with the dork next to me, I listened to the sermon, greeted the minister afterward, and politely refused his invitation to stay for the hour of fellowship.

I staggered out into the snow. A wiser man would have flushed that key down the toilet. One man had already been killed for it. Goons had been crisscrossing the country to get their hands on it. V. S. Mohle had gotten the crap beaten out of him when he couldn't come up with it. Didn't I have any sense at all?

That afternoon I sat in front of the TV, watching infomercials and a golf tournament from Hawaii, but all I could think about was how many lockers there had to be in New York. Five thousand? Ten? And who was to say that the locker I was looking for was even in Manhattan? It could be in the Bronx or New Jersey, and even if I did finally find it, there was no guarantee that whatever Cannetti had put in there was still around.

Slumped in my chair, I just kept turning the key over and over in my hand. What I was considering doing was, let's face it, incredibly stupid. At the same time, I felt as if I'd just downed four espressos. Maybe some guys aren't cut out to be virtuous. Here I'd been an ordinary Joe, going to work every day, paying my taxes, keeping my nose clean, and all it had done was make me feel like a big faker.

I called my supervisor that night and told him I had to take a couple of days off for personal reasons. He was a real prince about it. I spent the next two hours trying to book a flight. I finally found one for the next day and it cost me an arm and a leg, but I wasn't worried about the money. What mattered was that I was back in the game. I felt more alive than I'd felt in months.

I flew into LaGuardia Monday night. On the plane someone had left an old paperback copy of Schoeninger's *Continental Divide*. I read a hundred pages or so, which took me from the cooling of the earth's crust to the origin of the beaver.

As my cab rattled across the Triborough Bridge, I found myself leaning forward, holding on to the frayed strap, staring at the lights of the city like some country bumpkin. The East River swirled below, dark as oil. My stomach was bad. I felt like I was in one of those old western movies where John Wayne creeps into the Comanche camp to cut loose the horses while all the braves are still sleeping.

Once I checked into my hotel, I was in for the night. I had no reason to believe that anyone was actively looking for me, but there was no point in testing fate; when you're on the streets of New York, there's no telling who you're going to run into. I ordered room service, read another hundred pages or so of *Continental Divide*, and watched a poker tournament on ESPN2. It took me a while to go to sleep; after the perfect stillness of Appleton, the horns and clatter of the city kept jarring me awake.

The next morning I was up at the crack of dawn, scouring Port Authority, Grand Central, and Penn Station. It was worse than looking for a needle in a haystack, my search for Locker 324, and it came to nothing. In Port Authority the numbers only went up to 199. At Grand Central there was a 324, but my key didn't fit. There was a 324 in Penn Station too, unlocked, with nothing inside.

It was a little past ten by the time I finished, and I felt like a sap. How could I have overlooked the most obvious thing? In public train and bus stations, they cleared all the lockers at least once a month.

The escalator carried me up out of Penn Station and spit me onto the street. What now? It was hard to believe I'd blown five hundred dollars on an airline ticket for this. Feet aching, I hobbled through the crowds, heading uptown. Fire trucks blared and I was getting that familiar rawness at the back of my throat. How far I had fallen. It had just been a few months before that I'd been sitting at a table, surrounded by adoring young women, discussing point of view.

A sharp rap buckled the back of my knee. I spun quickly, ready to give somebody a piece of my mind, but it was just a pair of actresses coming out of a dance studio, swinging their gym bags.

Funny how the mind works. Sometimes it's like slogging through mud, and other times it's like riding on lightning. Cannetti had had a gym bag too, just like those actresses, and one thing about gyms, they had lockers, and not the kind that get cleaned out every month.

I found a hotel on Thirty-seventh Street and ducked into a phone booth. I went through the Yellow Pages and wrote down the names of all the gyms within a ten-block radius of Penn Station. There were fifteen of them. Not the smallest number, but I wasn't about to lose heart now. It was time for a little shoe leather.

The first three turned out to be total busts. One was like a eighties disco joint with mirrors everywhere, the Bee Gees playing on the intercom, and these swinger types in sweaty leotards and cycling pants scoping each other out. The second was nothing but old Chinese people doing slow-motion karate moves. And the third was like an old-fashioned Y, with a bunch of juvenile delinquents mugging one another on the basketball court.

At each of them, I presented myself as a prospective new member, and asked if they would mind if I looked around. I checked out all three changing rooms. In two of them, the lockers used combinations, not keys, and in the Chinese gym, they didn't have lockers at all, just big wire baskets.

It was noon by the time I got to gym number four, the Ninth Avenue Sports Club, and I was wearing down. The place wasn't much. Stuck between a Puerto Rican market and a Greek souvlaki stand, it looked more like a typewriter repair shop than a gym. In the front window were an array of bodybuilding magazines, a pair of barbells, and a scattering of dead flies. A bell tinkled as I pushed through the front door. A squat old guy who could have been one of the sparring partners in *Raging Bull* sat behind the main desk reading something in the *New York Post* to a black security guard. The sound of the bell made him drop the paper to his lap.

"Can I help you?"

"Yeah. Yeah, maybe you can. I live right around the corner and wondered if maybe you'd be interested in any new members."

"We're pretty full up here."

"So when do you think you might have some openings?"

"No telling. A month or two."

"Huh," I said. I picked one of the brochures off the desk and glanced through it. All the photos had to be at least forty years old. I could feel the two of them watching me. "Looks great," I said. "It would just be so convenient, you know? A gym in the neighborhood. Would you mind if I looked around?"

He took a minute to mull over his answer. "That's fine," he said. He motioned with one of his busted-up hands. "Down there on your right."

I edged down a narrow, rickety staircase and made my way past a couple of handball courts where scrawny young toughs with boils on their necks careened from wall to wall. Beyond the handball courts was a weight room that had seen better days. In the far corner a pail sat on a treadmill to catch a slow drip from a bulge in the ceiling. Over the stationary bicycles was a poster for a Carmen Basilio middleweight bout in 1961. I had the place nearly to myself. A couple of huge guys who looked as if they'd just returned from a hard night of hijacking semis tossed a medicine ball back and forth between them, making *oof*ing sounds every time they took it in the belly.

I wove my way through the rowing machines and pushed through the door marked MENS. A couple of old geezers in their underwear sat on a bench, pulling on their socks and talking about their prostate operations. When I murmured hello, they barely nodded back.

Clouds of steam hung in the air and I could hear showers running. There was no turning back now. I moseyed down the main aisle, sidestepping a patch of busted tile. The place smelled of rotten jockstraps.

I scanned the lockers on both sides of me. Most of them had built-in combinations, but in the far corner of the farthest row were five that were coin-operated. Three were in use. Two were empty, with the keys still in them—keys with tops of red plastic.

I glanced over my shoulder. The two old guys were out of my line of sight now, though I could still hear them muttering about how many times they had to get up at night.

I ducked into the row to take a closer look. The number on the three lockers in use were 320, 321, and 324. I squatted, hand to my eyes, and tried to peer through the ventilated slats of 324. It was hard to make out much, but what I could see was enough. A curved section of a stitched leather handle pressed against the slats.

I stood up and felt my trousers pocket for my key. As I did, pipes groaned and then I didn't hear the sound of water anymore. I turned. An old man the size of a sea lion stepped cautiously out of the shower, one hand on the wall for balance. He didn't see me at first and for five or six seconds I stood there watching him retrieve his towel and begin to scrub at his elbows.

When he finally looked up he wasn't so much startled to see me as offended. You would have thought I was some kind of pervert. He lifted one foot, teetering, and wiped his toes, glowering at me. The man had to weigh at least three hundred and fifty pounds, a planet of pink flesh. I couldn't imagine him using that stairway; they must have lowered him down here with a crane.

I patted my trousers pockets again, front and back. "Seem to have lost my car keys." I said. "You haven't seen an extra set anywhere around here, have you?"

"Uh-uh." For all I knew, the man could be Cannetti's uncle.

"Well, I guess all I can do is hope I somehow left 'em at the office."

The man made a sound in his throat like he was clearing phlegm. I gave him a one-finger salute and sauntered out of there as coolly as I could. Upstairs, the desk clerk and the guard took turns banging the sides of an old TV.

"Nice place you've got here," I said. "I'll come back later and see if I can get myself on a list, okay?"

The desk clerk was in no mood for conversation. He gave me a glance and then went back to whacking the balky television.

I wandered the streets in a daze. It was unbelievable. How could Cannetti possibly store whatever it was in a day locker for six months and no one touches it? On second thought, maybe it wasn't so hard to believe. What better place to stash something than a mob gym? It was like walking in Little Italy—safest place in New York because no one dares mess with anybody else.

The locker must have been some kind of drop. Cannetti must have left the bag in there, with the arrangement being that he would meet the sellers later, give them the key in exchange for whatever they were selling. When it turned out he didn't have it (because I had it), things probably turned ugly. Trust me, I know these people.

I suppose it should have made me feel guilty, but I wasn't in the mood for shedding any tears over Cannetti. I had plenty of problems of my own. The last thing I wanted was to end up like him. The trick was going to be how to get back into that gym and out again, without arousing suspicion. The good news was that the place had not been that busy, even at noon. My guess was that by midafternoon it would be pretty dead. What I needed was to give it a rest and come back later to check things out.

I blew an hour nosing around midtown. It was sort of like old times. The figurines of the Statue of Liberty were still for sale in the souvenir shops and a man in a clown suit passed out flyers in front of the Peep-O-Rama.

I bought a *New York Post* and found a bench in Bryant Park.

Leafing through all the editorials about Rudy Giuliani's wars on the squeegee men, I stumbled onto a piece about Rex's memorial. There was a long quote from Rex's literary agent. "For all the terrible things V. S. Mohle said about him, in the end Rex won hands down. He was a better person and a more dominating presence. Mohle will certainly occupy a very particular, if perhaps precious, place in the literary firmament, but Rex Schoeninger conquered the world." According to the article, the service was to take place at two o'clock at the Founders Club.

A guy with a bad haircut and thick-soled shoes sat on a bench directly across from me. I asked him if he had the time. He looked annoyed, but fished into his pocket for his watch. Ten past one, he said.

I took a moment, rubbing the ink off my fingers, trying to decide what to do. The Founders Club, if I remembered correctly, was in the low Sixties, just off Fifth. No more than twenty blocks away. I wasn't crazy enough to think I could actually attend the service, but how great it would be to be a fly on the wall. Maybe there was a way, if I was careful enough. There was no telling who was going to be there. Ramona, maybe, and maybe even good old Wayne.

I headed up Fifth Avenue, zigzagging through the crush of grim-faced shoppers. It didn't take me long to get there. By a quarter to two I was stationed across the street from the Founders Club, munching on a Sabrett hot dog. Office workers sat on the low walls of a huge plaza, eating lunch and soaking up the sun.

One by one the limousines began to arrive. Under the cover of the Sabrett stand umbrella, I watched the great and the near-great emerge, elderly men in thousand-dollar suits and razor-thin women who looked like they ran things. Two groups of stylish young women, all dressed in black, converged on foot. They twittered and swirled on the sidewalk like a flock of starlings before disappearing inside. A couple of shady-looking characters in badly fitting trousers and scuffed shoes—writers, I figured—snubbed their cigarettes out in the gutter before trudging up the steps.

My stomach churned. The hot dog had been a mistake and the sauerkraut an even bigger one. Wiping mustard off my chin, I watched the last stragglers disappear inside the club. Two doormen stood talking, hands clasped behind their backs. Fuming, I crossed the street. As I passed the club, I took a sidelong glance. Shadows flitted behind frosted glass. One of the doormen, a hard-eyed man who I suspect must have been charged with war crimes in one country or another, gave me the kind of glare you'd give to a stray dog looking for scraps.

I kept walking, playing it casual, and didn't stop until I was halfway down the block. When I looked back, both doormen had disappeared. Don't be a fool, I told myself. This is not the time to be doing anything rash. I had business to tend to, important business. All the same, what harm could it do to poke my head in? This was not the kind of opportunity that comes along every day.

I retraced my steps. When I came to the club entrance, I peered in through the decorated glass. Everyone seemed to have vanished. Cracking the door open, I took another look. The two doormen, backs turned, were helping a pair of white-jacketed black waiters set up tables at the far end of the lobby.

I slipped inside, using my hand to keep the door from closing too abruptly. Up the stairs I went, head down, trying to look as if I knew where I was going. To my left, beyond a wide marble staircase and some faded tapestries, was a larger room where people sat dutifully in rows of straight-backed chairs.

Three or four men lounged in the doorway. I joined them, peeking over their shoulders. The room was decorated with portraits of various nineteenth century robber barons, stout as walruses in their dark suits. A mirror that must have been swiped from the court of a French king loomed overhead.

The guy at the podium was a slender fellow in his mid-fifties with a colored handkerchief in his breast pocket and the offhanded ease of a talk show host. Leaning forward on his elbows, he went through a list of Schoeninger's accomplishments—best-selling author of all time, philanthropist, champion of education, racial tolerance, and international understanding.

No one seemed to be paying any particular attention. I could see three or four reporters in the crowd, writing pads on their laps, but one of them was studying the fancy molding above the high windows and another was checking messages on his cell phone. An older man with a gleaming bald head was already snoozing, his wingtips firmly anchored in the legs of the chair in front of him. All the young women in black passed notes like junior high school girls. I figured they had to be secretaries from various publishing houses, given an hour off to make sure there was a respectable turnout.

The MC took a seat while two videotapes were played, one sent by Tom Brokaw, the other by Jimmy Carter. Brokaw apologized for not being able to attend—he was in Milan reporting on the World Trade Organization meetings—but he said what a great friend Schoeninger had been and told a story about how they'd met on a dogsled during the filming of an NBC special in Alaska. Jimmy Carter was also sorry not to be there—he was visiting North Korea, trying to talk the dictator out of nuclear testing—but he too remembered Schoeninger with fondest regard and had always appreciated everything Rex had done for Habitat for Humanity.

One by one, other speakers trooped to the podium—the director of a museum of western art in Missoula, a decrepit old actress who'd starred in *The Sands of Vanuatu* some forty years before, New York's most powerful real estate mogul in a suit so shimmery it seemed to be made of sharkskin. The museum director talked about the size of his endowment, the tiny actress sang a few bars of "Good-bye Yankee-Boy" in a crackly voice, and the real estate magnate let us know what a great guy he was, flying Schoeninger here and there, putting him up in his big hotels in the Caribbean, lining him up with the top cardiologists in Manhattan.

It was all hogwash. Everybody kept talking about how the world had been Schoeninger's home, when, really, he had never been at home anywhere. Everybody said what great times they'd had with him, but the truth was, the times you had with him weren't always so great, not when I knew him. He wouldn't let you. One of his greatest pleasures in life was making people jump.

I could have given quite a sermon. I could have given those bored reporters a hell of a lot to write about and I was half tempted to do it, but then I spied my landlady, looking as elegant as ever, on the far side of the room. I'm not saying I'm a coward, but the thought of facing her after racking up that humongous phone bill was more than I was up to.

I slipped quietly away, spun through the revolving doors, and headed toward Fifth Avenue. I crossed over into Central Park and strode toward the lake. Somehow it had turned into one of those perfect spring days. Japanese tourists were getting their caricatures done by alcoholic sketch artists, and the benches were full of businessmen playing hooky, ties loosened, faces tilted to the sun. Jamaican nannies chatted while their young charges wrestled over plastic shovels in the grass.

It had been a terrible mistake, coming up here, walking into that fucking building. What was I doing, turning into some kind of sap? Let them say whatever they wanted about Rex Schoeninger. As far as I was concerned it was over. And all that V. S. Mohle stuff? It was hasta la vista, baby. My name was Frankie Abandonato, I was back on the streets of New York, and I had a job to do.

I caught a cab at Columbus Circle and took it to the sports club on Ninth Avenue. A blind beggar rattled his cup out front, his seeing-eye dog sleeping beside him. I walked past the window a couple of times to scope the place out. There wasn't anybody at the front desk, which seemed almost too good to be true. It wasn't until I got my nerve up to poke my head in that I saw the note taped to the phone: PLEASE RING FOR SERVICE.

I wasn't going to get a better opportunity than this. I took a deep breath, crossed the lobby, and headed down the rickety stairs. The handball courts were empty, but I could hear some sort of commotion beyond the hallway. I approached the weight room warily and peered in. At the far end, the desk clerk and the security guard were absorbed trying to get a sparrow down from the rafters.

The desk clerk took huge wobbly swings at the bird with a long-handled strainer, the kind you'd use to clean your swimming pool. The strainer may have been long, but it wasn't long enough. All the desk clerk had managed to accomplish was to keep the sparrow flying back and forth, perching for a moment on a pull-up bar or a stationary bike, and then taking off again for the safety of a ledge near the ceiling.

The security guard tiptoed around, whistling, a blue blanket stretched between his arms—what he hoped to do with it, I had no idea. I stood watching as the two men crept through the rowing machines, pointing and arguing strategy, while the bird tilted its head from side to side, keeping a beady eye on them.

The good news was that no one had noticed me. I moved quickly to the locker room, pushed through the door, and made sure it didn't make a sound as it closed behind me. The place was deserted. I made my way down the center aisle, stepping over a couple of wet towels. Kneeling in front of Locker 324, I retrieved the key from my pocket. When I slipped it into the lock, there was a satisfying click. The door squeaked when I opened it. Stuffed inside was a brown leather brief-case. It took me a couple of hard yanks to pull it free.

"There you go! You got 'em! Don't let him get away!" The shouts from the weight room grew louder and then faded away.

The briefcase weighed a ton and was stuffed tighter than a Thanksgiving turkey. My guess was, it wasn't filled with manuscripts. I picked it up and stuck it under my arm like a halfback toting a football. I went to the door, opened it five or six inches, and peered out. At the far end of the weight room, the desk clerk lay on his stomach, the long-handled strainer stuck out in front of him. Head raised, he had both hands clenched tight on the near end of it, like a man about to fire a high-caliber gun. At the other end, the sparrow thrashed in the green mesh, chirping. The security guard hovered above the bird with his blanket. The desk clerk cursed him as a fool and a coward, and finally the security guard dropped to his knees, smothering the sparrow in a cloud of blue cotton.

I stood there waiting as the two men disentangled the bird, first from the blanket and then from the netting. They huddled together, rubbing the sparrow's head with a finger, trying to calm it.

I made my move, striding swiftly across the floor, trying not to rush it, trying to look as if I belonged. I nearly made it.

I was ten feet from the hallway when a corner of the briefcase banged against the handle of an exercise bike. "Hey! Hey, you!" It was the desk clerk. I kept going as if I hadn't heard. "What are you doing?"

I took a glance over my shoulder. The security guard stood clueless, cradling the bird to his chest, but the desk clerk was on his way, marching briskly across the room.

I sprinted down the hallway, past the handball courts, and charged up the stairs. I jostled past a couple of guys with gym bags.

"Hey, buddy boy, watch it!"

I took the stairs three at a time, never looking back. I could hear the desk clerk shouting somewhere below me. All I had to do was drop the briefcase and I could have outrun him easily, but there was no way

I was going to give it up, not now. The case was made of that cheap vinylized phony leather stuff, slick and awkward to hold.

I sucked air, using the handrail. I reeled across the lobby and out the front door. I had no idea what tripped me. All I know is that I went flying. I put my hands out to break my fall. I hit the sidewalk hard, with open palms, whacking my chin on the sidewalk.

It took several seconds for my head to clear, but when it did, I became aware that there was some sort of hubbub going on around me. I squinted to my right. The briefcase lay seven or eight feet away, limp as a deflated balloon. Packets of fifty- and hundred-dollar bills were scattered everywhere on the sidewalk.

Ninth Avenue is a busy street, night or day. There were lots of people out, and lots of them just kept walking, nothing was going to faze them. This was New York, after all. But a lot of them were fazed, seriously fazed, staring down at the money at their feet like the Three Magi staring down at the Christ child. One or two were looking around, trying to spot the hidden camera.

My chin was wet. When I reached up to touch it, I realized there was blood. A dog barked furiously at close range. I glanced over my shoulder. The blind beggar sat cross-legged on his mat, tugging at the leash of his seeing-eye dog. You don't see that many self-satisfied beggars, but this guy was grinning ear to ear, Mr. Crime-Stopper. His cane lay across his knees.

The desk clerk stood in the shadow of the sports club doorway, winded, pissed, and temporarily stymied. The security guard peered over his shoulder, cradling the sparrow.

The spell was broken by a clatter at the curb. A tattooed bike messenger darted through the crowd, slid to his knees, and went right to work, scooping up packets of money and jamming them in his backpack.

"Hey, you!" I shouted. "What the hell you doin'? That's mine!"

He paid me no mind, and that encouraged the others. A Con Ed worker abandoned his jackhammer and started pitching packets back to his buddy. A Mexican dishwasher shoveled money into his apron. A big-faced woman who looked like Julia Child made polite little dips, snatching stacks of hundreds and dropping them into her Macy's bag. A shoving match broke out between two high school kids. This was it, philanthropy for the masses.

"Goddamn it!" I shouted. I grabbed two or three packets, scrambled to my feet, and retrieved my sorry-looking briefcase. I could taste blood in my mouth. "You!" I pointed at a pencil pusher in a cheap suit stuffing money inside his jacket. "Give me that!" He did as he was told.

Horns sounded. The crowd had grown, spilling out into the street and backing up traffic. The blind beggar, his sight miraculously restored, crawled under people's legs, gathering in stacks of cash like a winner at poker gathering in chips.

I needed to hightail it. I pushed my way through the crowd and was nearly free of it when I spied Julia Child delicately rescuing a packet out of the gutter. I grabbed her wrist before she could drop it in the Macy's bag. For a woman who'd spent her life whipping up soufflés, she was one tough cookie. She wouldn't let go and I wouldn't either. We tugged back and forth. She finally tripped over the curb and fell into me. I fell too, landing hard on the sidewalk with her on top of me. Elbow to my eye, she screamed.

I pushed her off me and lurched to my feet. I grabbed my briefcase and her Macy's bag and was about to make a dash for it when I saw three human-growth-hormone specimens in cop uniforms headed right toward me.

I pivoted, thinking I would somehow escape back into the crowd, but the crowd had retreated, leaving me stranded on my own little island. If I was a real writer, I could probably break your heart right now, letting you know how alone it felt, what was going on in my mind and everybody else's mind, and all the little details of it too, Julia Child weeping and pointing and a sparrow flying low, just over people's heads, before winging its way to freedom. But I'm not a writer. Not much of one, anyway, and all I can tell you is, it really sucked.

Chapter Twenty-one

I can't tell you how happy I am to be finally writing the last chapter of this book. I thought I'd be able to finish it in a year and here I am, halfway through an eight-year sentence. The writers' group here at the prison is almost all new faces. The former Secretary of the Treasury's been out for eighteen months, making big bucks on the evangelical lecture circuit, and the mutual-fund manager is living happily in the Bahamas with his twenty-five-year-old bride. Even Dr. Pajerski's split. Last June she quit to take over as the director of the Walter Van Tilburg Clark Writers' Colony in Reno, Nevada. I find it amazing that she never did ask me to send her the manuscript when I was done.

Not that I'm complaining. The guards don't carry guns and the food's not half bad—the coq au vin is as good as anything you'll find in those midtown bistros. We sleep six to a cell, in bunk beds, but there is no concertina wire and no high walls, just boundary signs posted all over the grounds. I try to think of this as my own Stegner Fellowship.

Though it was rough in the beginning, I'll admit. I got several furious letters from my former students. They were all difficult to read, but one from Dominique was a killer.

Did it give you a lot of pleasure, playing us for fools? I'm sure a lot of it must have been a real laugh-riot, given how young and naïve and starry-eyed we were. Oh, but we worshipped you! We wrote down everything you said. We spent hours trying to puzzle out all the arrows and loops you scrawled across our manuscripts.

It stung. It stung a lot. All the same, we'll get over it. None of us ever want to see your face again, but we'll be fine. But the way you took advantage of Mr. Schoeninger was unforgivable. He was old and you used him. He was a great man and you mocked him. He believed in us, invested everything he had in us, and what did you believe in? Your own cleverness? And where has that gotten you? About where you deserve. May you rot in hell.

Dora came to see me a few weeks after I was incarcerated, supposedly to discuss our son, but I suspect her real reason was to let me know just how well she was doing. She's remarried, to an assistant principal at a junior high school, and, honest to God, he sounds like Ned Flanders, Homer Simpson's wimpy next-door neighbor. Dora says he's a great listener, whatever the hell that means. As far as my son goes, I talk to him on the phone every couple of weeks. Our conversations are what you would call guarded, but they're progressing. He's turned into this fanatical baseball fan. It makes me wonder if maybe way back in his mind he does remember me pitching Wiffle balls to him in the park.

I only had one other visitor that first fall. The guard came to get me midafternoon one Sunday, visiting day, to say that there was a man named Victor Miller there to see me. I said I'd never heard of the guy.

"So what does he look like?" I said.

"He looks a little like you," he said. "Not exactly a stud."

So when I go down to the reception area, there's old V. S. Mohle sitting on a bench next to a bunch of wives and girlfriends. Before I had a chance to beat a retreat, he was up on his feet with a big shit-eating grin on his face.

What could I do? I stood there scratching my neck as he crossed the floor. He'd put on some weight since I'd seen him last and he looked happier. In his down vest and stone-washed jeans you would have thought he was heading off on some ski vacation.

We shook hands. "It's been a while," he said.

"A while."

"You doing okay?"

"Well enough."

Some of the women were giving us the double-take and one of them, a blonde in leopard-skin pants, leaned over to whisper something in her friend's ear.

"So what brings you by?" I said. "Just driving through?"

"No, I came to see you," he said.

"Ahh," I said. "Well, maybe I should give you a little tour."

I took him through the exhibition of my fellow inmates' artwork and then we strolled through the grounds. It was awkward at first (for all I knew, the man was going to pull a gun and shoot me), but it eased up when we started swapping stories about our boyhoods on the Upper West Side, jumping turnstiles, smoking dope at Grant's Tomb, stealing apples from the fruit stands.

It was a beautiful day. The Henry Moore sculpture glistened like a glazed doughnut in the afternoon sun. An embezzler from Houston was giving his wife a bear hug, his face buried in her hair. She stood on tiptoes, making little whimpering sounds.

"I just want to apologize," Mohle said.

"Apologize? For what?"

"For the last time we met. I said some things I'm not very proud of."

"Well, I did too," I said. "But we were both a little stressed, you know what I mean?"

One of the small-time dope dealers looked up from feeding the swans in the duck pond and stared at us, crossing himself as if he'd just seen a pair of ghosts.

"You know he'd been sending me letters," he said.

"For how long?"

"For years. Never out-and-out apologizing. Just putting out feelers."

"And what did you do with them?"

"Tore them up and threw them in the trash." At the front gate, a guard listened to the Patriots game on the radio.

"Then why did you ever agree to come down here?" I asked.

"It was the money, really. Seventy-five grand for three months? Who could say no? I guess it mattered a lot to him, not to go out feeling like he'd made a fool of himself."

"And then you ended up bailing anyway."

"It just seemed too weird to me. I didn't see any point."

"He thought he'd destroyed you. He wanted to make it right."

"So did you make it right?"

"Not really," I said. I could hear the shouts coming from the volleyball court. It sounded like everyone was having a good time. "Tell you what," I said. "There's a pretty spot up here. Let me show you."

I took him up to the Nob, the giant hill that's the highest point on the prison grounds. You can see everything from up there, from the rows of dormitories and the guard station to the distant farmers' fields and the roadside stands selling pumpkins and apple cider.

It was a serious climb. By the time we got to the top, I was so winded I had to sit down on one of the rotting benches to recover. Mohle, the picture of cardiovascular fitness, wasn't even breathing hard.

"I need to tell you something," Mohle said.

"Sure," I said. "Go ahead. Shoot."

"Last February, just before Rex died, this crazy Yugoslavian woman came to my door."

"Oh, Jesus."

"Exactly." A chipmunk poked its head out from between boulders, sniffing for food. "She said she'd come to work for me."

"So what did you do?" The sun had begun to set behind the hills.

"What could I do? The woman was terrifying. And she didn't have a penny on her. Apparently she'd been looking for me for a couple of months."

I bent down, picked up a small rock, and juggled it in my palm. If I'd been fourteen, I would have thought it was the perfect rock for throwing at cop cars. "So?" I said.

"So she's been working for me. She's a wonderful cook. She makes this lamb stew that's remarkable."

"Yeah, I know."

"And her stories . . . my God . . . Sometimes it's nice to have a little company in the evening."

I gave him a sharp look. Had Mohle really come all this way to tell me that he and Dranka were getting it on? Try to get that image out of your head.

"There's just one thing. She's got this envelope of old letters."

"Ahh," I said. "I've read them."

"Sometimes she swears she's going to do something about them."

"Like what?"

"Go to somebody. Create a ruckus."

"And that's why you came to see me?"

"That's why I came to see you. So was he really the bastard she says he was?"

"No," I said. I rose from the bench and hurled the stone as far as I could, heard it ricochet through the trees. "I'd say he was pretty much like the rest of us."

I wiped my hands on my trousers. Below us, I could see some of the inmates saying goodbye to their wives and girlfriends. There was a lot of hugging and kissing going on. A mother tried to pull a wailing child from his father's neck.

"What do you think about his walking away from his kid like that?"

"He's not the only one who's ever done that," I said. A horn sounded, signaling the end of visiting hours.

"So what should I do?" he said.

"I say burn 'em. Burn the whole lot of them. And pay her an extra twenty bucks a week. That should shut her up," I said.

"That's what I was thinking."

"You should probably be going."

"I guess. You walking down?"

"No. I think I'll stay up here for a while."

We shook hands. I watched him pick his way down through the rocks and disappear into the dark pines. It was another couple of minutes before I spotted him again, a tiny dark figure scuttling across the parking lot. Someone stopped him for a moment (my guess was it was just another of those autograph hounds), but Mohle put his hands up, waving him off.

Mohle got into his car. The horn sounded a second time. I zipped up my jacket. It was getting cold, now that the sun was almost gone.

I watched Mohle's car slip around a Trailways bus and pull slowly past the guard station. Mohle turned on his headlights and I could see them flickering through a row of trees as he sped north. I raised my hand but I'm pretty sure he never saw me.

Rex turned out to be quite the prophet. Our ex-students have been tearing up the pea patch. Six of the eight have already published books, which makes them the most successful class in the history of the Fiction Institute. Now when people ask me about the famous writers I have known, they're as likely to be asking about the young ones as the old.

Dominique joined a convent in Nebraska, and after the account of her spiritual journey appeared in the *Atlantic Monthly* she was interviewed by Bill Moyers for PBS. Mel published a piece in the *New Yorker* about what it was like to be taught fiction writing by a fraud. I thought he took a few cheap shots, particularly when he described my "rodentlike furtiveness," but the article created quite a furor and landed him a six-figure book contract. LaTasha's novel won the PEN/ Faulkner Award and one of Mercedes's stories won a Pushcart. Bryn was picked up by Farrar, Straus just last month. Chester has joined the staff of McSweeney's and his memoir of taking hallucinogenic drugs with Amazonian Indians was the subject of a *National Geographic* special.

Brett somehow managed to finagle the research for Rex's half-written epic out of Ramona and came up with a hell of an advance to finish the book. The last I heard he was somewhere out in West Texas hunting buffalo with bow and arrow. The only one who hasn't made his way into print is Nick, but in just the last year I've started to hear from him. He sends me his manuscripts, which I read and send back with comments. I'd like to do more, but I'm afraid at this point in my career, a blurb from me wouldn't do him much good.

Writing all this may have been a terrible mistake. If I ever publish this, there could be two million Schoeninger fans howling for my head on a plate. All I need is some parole officer whose favorite book is *The Sands of Vanuatu* and I'm dead meat.

The problem is, if I don't tell you about him, Rex will vanish, I swear to God. He'll become just another one of those names chiseled into the sides of public buildings. So here he is. I have no illusions about being a great stylist—not like Fielding and Flaubert and Nabokov and whoever the fuck those other guys were—but if the book you hold in your hand has allowed him to draw a few more breaths, I'll be a happy man.

Though, come to think of it, it would also be nice to make a few bucks with the damn manuscript. Maybe I could even sell it to the movies and end up playing myself. If it doesn't work out, I'm warning you now: if you're in a pizzeria in New York and some guy with a Golden Gopher tie, a Ronald Reagan haircut, and a lottery ticket wants a little favor, just put your hand over your wallet and walk away.

Acknowledgments

The list of writers who have helped me with this book is long. Rather than name names, let me say how crucial they have been to this novel seeing the light of day. I will forever remember their support, their thoughtful suggestions, and their invaluable readings of early drafts. Frankie Abandonato, the narrator of *Famous Writers I Have Known*, takes a jaundiced view of literary friendships, but I do not. They are one of the joys of my life.

I would also like to thank Star Lawrence, whose patience, wisdom, and generosity still seem miraculous to me. Ryan Harrington has been terrific and Melody Baxter's fierce championing of the book came at the perfect time.

Thank you too to Emily Forland, who picked up the baton from Wendy with such grace; to Kathleen Orillion, who has an unparalleled ability to spot the problem; and to my son, Billy Magnuson, whose eagle eye saved me a dozen times.